"*GOD IS A BULLET* IS A TRIUMPH FOR BOSTON TERAN . . . IT'S SO GOOD THAT IT TAKES MY BREATH AWAY."
—*San Jose Mercury News*

"A stunning debut . . . *God Is a Bullet* features one of the more demonic fictional villains you are likely to encounter. . . . It is that rare first novel you truly do not want to put down."
—*Minneapolis Star Tribune*

"[An] astonishing literary thriller . . . Teran's sparse, riveting, third-person style is perfect for his dark and philosophically mesmerizing story. . . . [Readers] will be drawn in by the pure poetry and clarity of Mr. Teran's vision and the brilliance of characters and plot."
—*The Dallas Morning News*

"*God Is a Bullet* is a stunner of a suspense novel, body-slamming its way down an uncharted rocky terrain of pain, fear, horror, bravery, and redemption. . . . Teran's voice is fresh, unique, and explosive. He has delivered a work that is too good, too important, and too painful to be ignored."
—LORENZO CARCATERRA
Bestselling author of *Sleepers* and *Apaches*

Please turn the page for more reviews. . . .

Also by Boston Teran

NEVER COUNT OUT THE DEAD

Books published by The Ballantine Publishing Group
are available at quantity discounts on bulk purchases
for premium, educational, fund-raising, and special
sales use. For details, please call 1-800-733-3000.

GOD
IS A
BULLET

Boston Teran

BALLANTINE BOOKS • NEW YORK

A Ballantine Book
Published by The Ballantine Publishing Group
Copyright © 1999 by Brutus Productions, Inc.

This is a work of fiction. Names, characters, places, and incidents are the product of the author's imagination or are used fictitiously. Any resemblance to actual people, living or dead, or to actual events or locales is entirely coincidental.

www.ballantinebooks.com

ISBN 0-345-43988-0

This edition published by arrangement with Alfred A. Knopf, a division of Random House, Inc.

Manufactured in the United States of America

First Ballantine Books Edition: April 2002

10 9 8 7 6 5 4 3 2 1

— TO MY MOTHER AND FATHER —
One died before the beginning.
One fell along the way.
I am always us.

According to Aztec myth, the sun god Huitzilopochtli was responsible for driving back the darkness—the moon and the stars—at the start of each day. He required strength for the struggle and he needed to be nourished with human blood.

Archeology Today

Blood and Family
Darkness and Death
Absolute Depravity
.44

Written on the back of
an envelope containing a
letter sent by the Son of
Sam to Jimmy Breslin

God and Satan, why they're no different than the government or McDonald's. Just franchises to keep the money coming in by giving the locals something they can depend on.

Edward Constanza,
"Letter to the Editor,"
Los Angeles Herald Examiner,
1984

THE PEARL

I

FALL 1970

It is 7:23 on a Sunday morning when the Sheriff's Department in Clay, California, gets the call a woman has been murdered. The boy is at a pay phone by the entrance to the freeway. His dirt bike lies ten feet away, along the shoulder where he's dropped it. The wind weaves sand through the still-spinning tire spokes. He has to cup his hand over his ear to hear the officer's questions above the passing trucks. He relates a series of horrifying images, and after he hangs up he sits in the dirt and cries.

Two Sheriff's Department patrol cars speed out Route 138, Palmdale Boulevard, and then take the hard turn onto Route 15 heading northeast. They drive without sirens through Barstow, passing the ghost mining town of Calico, all clapboard and tin just north of the freeway.

Two deputies in one car. A sergeant in the other. They ride in black silence. After all, this is the country of Charles Manson and The Process and Sunset Boulevard witchcraft. It is the country that spawned such phrases as "Thou shalt kill" and "Helter Skelter."

At the Calico Road exit they find the boy by his dirt bike. He is a wispy excuse for twelve, and he holds the sergeant tightly as he is led to the patrol car. He guides them north, pointing the way up through Paradise Springs Road.

The wind grows worse, blowing its poisonous alkali chlorides and carbonates down from Inyo County and China

Lake. Moving up through the Mojave Desert they pass the Calico Early Man Site, where scattered on the shores of ancient, dry Coyote Lake are the oldest known remains of our ancestors in North America. Here a solitary core of studied diggers found rudimentary tools of stone and arrows, fossilized fletchings, and puzzle parts of clay jugs. The crude trappings of commerce, the crude trappings of war.

The patrol cars move off the main road and onto a broken trail that traverses a forgotten playa set between the Calico Mountains and the Paradise Range. Their vehicles rock and heave over the sifting climb of slow dunes.

The boy's hand comes up and points again. His legs arch onto the seat in an almost fetal position. Ahead, the sergeant, one John Lee Bacon, makes out the antiquated silver-hulled trailer where the woman lives, shining dully through the dust. They pull up and stop, and as the three sheriffs step out of the vehicles they unsnap the guards on their pistols.

The blowing sand is like cut glass against their skin. The trailer stands before them, defined by a garden of bottle art mortared into cement stalagmites, rusting chassis, old chairs, and pitted road sign warnings within a labyrinth of cholla and creosote and yerba santa plants that the woman has grown for their powers of healing and poison.

Sergeant Bacon is twenty-four years old, but his ax-thin face already shows the early signs of dissipation. He orders one of the sheriffs to track his way around the trailer; the other will follow as a back-up.

The little they know of the woman has come from the boy, who occasionally rode his dirt bike across the playa to charm her out of a soda, and what they've picked up over their radios. She is called Hannah by those who know her. She has no last name. No driver's license. She has lived there as long as anyone remembers. Her skin is honey-colored black. Her hair is white and hangs in bush locks almost to her waist. She is known to walk barefoot for miles singing out loud, unafraid of snakes, cleaning the desert floor of debris. Some say she is mad, others are more pitying and call her harmless and eccentric. Occasionally she would be seen in the churches of the surrounding towns drinking beer from the bottle and laughing at the locals.

As they approach the screen door they hear the nickering of mobiles hung somewhere in the distance. Off-key brass and stone notes in a twilight chorus. John Lee can feel the sweat creeping out between his thumb and the hammer of his pistol.

They enter cautiously. The windows and air vents in the ceiling have been left open and the sand swirls around the frayed furnishings and unwashed dishes. The wind curls the edges of snapshots, taped to the walls, of passersby who once wandered across the barren plat and were caught by the woman's camera. A confusion of faces going back generations. Faces spotted up between wind-furled clippings from magazines and cookbooks, between pages of poetry and bits of humor. The wind tears at the backs of some of the clippings and they float away. But it is the stench that overwhelms the sheriffs.

"Sergeant?"

John Lee glances at the deputy, who points to the floor. John Lee walks over to him and kneels down. He sees an arterial line of blood, dried the color of cheap wine and flecked with sand, running the length of the trailer toward a sheet hung across the bedroom doorway. The sheet lifts and turns like an apparition, then falls away. Through the sand both men can see the sheet had been hand-painted with a heraldic lily and a rose.

John Lee stands and starts for the bedroom. The deputy follows. They step carefully past the tracings of blood that have pooled out where the floor wasn't level.

They turn the sheet back. The small grotto of a bedroom is filled with shells and fossil stones. The air is poisoned with flies and their noses begin to burn from the vile odor of rotting flesh. Then they see her, lying on her side at the foot of the bed.

One moment taints John Lee's dreams forever. He will see it all in fragments over and over again. The gas-bloated frame. The skin where it has burst apart and the open lesions rank with white maggots leeching pink-brown muscle. The bullet wound to the side of the skull that leaves shards of bone with blood and brain jelly trailing up the wall like the spanning wings of a bird. The eyes driven from their sockets by the concussion of the shot. The knife wounds across the back and chest that leave bloody chevrons on the woolly white seaman's sweater. The skin sluiced in bizarre patterns that border on ritual. And in a wrinkled turn of her coarse garment, a single pearl.

It will all become an indelible part of his subconscious.

All that night Homicide and Forensics units hunt for evidence, but the sand had beaten them to it, papering over whatever tracks and prints might have existed.

There is one slim lead. A son named Cyrus. Hannah had taken care of a child she'd found abandoned on Fort Dixon Road. He was a tall boy with large hands and brooding yellow-green eyes, and as he got older he carried himself like some solitary acolyte. Twice he'd been sent to juvenile hall in Los Angeles for possession of narcotics and assault. But this just dead-ends. The boy had run off three years before, when he was seventeen, and had not been seen since.

By morning the newspapers get word and they rush the playa in their Jeeps and Travelalls. They're hungry for a story, and this one reeks of lurid headlines.

One reporter, while wandering the playa, discovers in a dry riverbed a few hundred yards from the trailer a totem of sorts. Granite and limestone boulders squared up block by block form what resembles a primitive furnace. Etched into the rock are prehistoric signs. A bird. A bull. A tree. Symbols of earth and air, fire and water. And in the center is a snake devouring itself. The sign of Ourabouris. The same sign that is discovered during the autopsy to have been tattooed on Hannah's shoulder. All this the news draws up in squalid detail. Hannah's death is christened "The Furnace Creek Cult Murder."

THE JUDGMENT

2

Case's screams tear at her very bones and wrack the hallway outside her small apartment in the rehab house. She crouches on the bathroom floor before the toilet. She is only twenty-nine, but the free fall back into her two-hundred-dollar-a-day habit has left her gaunt. Her skin is yellow, her arms marked with blue-black welts. Two days off the junk. The third is always the black hole. A pure moment of hell before the resurrection.

Her stomach heaves in spasm. A guttural sucking out of the air. The woman in the apartment next door, trembling from the horrid screams, calls down to Anne.

Anne rushes through the dark hovel of the living room toward a crease of light, where she sees Case clawing at the white floor tiles, digging her chewed fingernails into the grouting.

Anne sits and tries to cradle Case in her arms. Case's head jerks toward her in jarring lurches.

She was a small girl again. Not more than ten. A street runaway with small pointed breasts. She was naked and she was being carried by four of them like some vestal virgin. She was taken and forced inside the skinned torso of a dead cow. There was blood everywhere. She could feel the sweet sticky hourglass of the cow's ribs press up against her own. The weight of its breastbone forcing air out of her. She felt as if she was going to suffocate and she gagged.

She vomits before she can reach the toilet. Anne tries to press twenty milligrams of Robaxin into Case's hand for the spasm, but she knocks the pills away and they twirl across the bare tiles.

"I'm gonna fuckin' go at this straight up."

"What!"

"I'm gonna go at . . ."

"Why! Why suffer the withdrawal?"

Case rocks back and forth. "You're not gonna hear any of that 'It's not my fault' shit, or 'Nobody should blame me' or 'How can I help but be a heroin addict' and 'It's not so friggin' bad.' I want to suffer." She gasps. "Get it. Fuckin' A. I want to feel it all. I want to fuckin' bleed so I'll know . . ."

Anne stares at her, frightened. Case grabs hold of Anne's face, twisting her fingers through the woman's dreadlocks. "I want it to cut me to ribbons. Then I'll know."

Cyrus clawed one hand onto her vagina and the other around her ass and he dragged her from the bloody carcass. She hung in his arms. He smeared his hand in the blood that covered the floor. He wiped it across his mouth and tongue and then he kissed her and pressed his tongue far enough into her mouth to make her choke. She retched and he pulled back and held her by the hair and whispered, "You are born again."

Fuckin' death. Her stomach contracts at the very words. Helpless, she's thrown through a flash fire of thoughts. *You. are born again.* Vivid life moments, three frames in length. Gutter and Lena and Granny Boy. Flashbulb fast. Sinister and moving and tragic. Snippets out of some Jungian MTV nightmare. Every black-and-white blowjob and backlit truck-stop hump. Watching your tits mature in blue-ice light under the pawing sweat-filthed hands of businessmen and junked-out middle-class housewives. Just one great juke hole to the upside-down cross. *You are born again.* Grovelling at the spray-painted slogans of the Left-Handed Path. Serving his alleged only begotten son. Knifing drug dealers to cop their stashes in pitch-black parking lots on moonless nights. Robbing neon-framed gas station attendants for a few bucks or on a whim. Kicking some shopkeeper half to death 'cause Cyrus overheard him talking about his faith in Christ.

You are born again.

She grabs at the stanchions that support the sink. Two bars to a cage. Or the two pillars Samson pushed apart to cast down the temple. No fuckin' chance of that.

You are born again to the Left-Handed Path.

What she would do for a little juice right now. Just enough to . . .

You are born . . .

She forces herself to live through the final beating, when she broke from Cyrus. The boot-hard kicks that broke her sternum and fractured her skull and the taste of . . .

She begins to feel herself split apart.

"I will not break . . ."

She's living out a full dose of Mach One, and her teeth are clacking so hard they sound like the bones in some seer's cup right before the roll of prophecy. There's no sleep for junkies on the way down. None. Just reckless, restless nausea and diarrhea and cold sweats and fumbling speech.

"I will not break . . ."

Anne grabs a towel from the rack and wipes Case's cropped black hair, which sticks up in sweaty greased clumps. She wipes at the sweat pouring off the edge of her nose and chin.

The old rage puts on its wolf's-teeth mask. The tiled floor becomes the white stone slab waiting for her corpse. Case curls into a fetal position. Her drenched T-shirt clings to her back, and the cold from the tiles leaves her shivering.

Anne runs into the bedroom to get a blanket and covers her up.

"I will not break. I will not . . . I . . . will not . . . I will not. Fuck you, Cyrus. Fuck you. I will not break . . ."

She repeats the sentence over and over again. A delusional broken mantra she drives into the very essence of her being.

"I will not break. I . . . will not break. I will not . . ."

Saliva hangs in a string line from her lips to the floor. She hears a siren along Hollywood Boulevard swell up, shrill, then slowly slip away down past Western Avenue. She begins to cry. She cries from the center of her being. Cries for the little girl born to be left behind.

3

CHRISTMAS WEEK 1995

A small wooden windmill sits on top a mailbox near the entrance to a dirt driveway that crooks its way up a hill and onto a flat prow of stony ground and ends at a fifties-style ranch house. As the windmill's warped vanes creak, five figures emerge from the brush like a coven conjured out of the black earth.

They are a patchquilt of jeans and leathers. Bare-soled boots and chain-braided vests over scrubby T-shirts. One, a boy named Gutter, has a safety pin awled through his lower lip. Another, a girl named Lena, has her hair greased back and dyed up like a rainbow. Their faces and arms are tattooed with anarchistic designs. They have pistols and knives wedged into their belts and boots. As they fan into the darkness they are a vision of post-apocalyptic rock-and-roll revenants.

Cyrus stops them about fifty yards shy of the house and looks the grounds over. The bushes by the front door are tasseled with holiday lights and dance to the wind like illuminated ghosts. He looks back down at the road. Via Princessa

cuts a silent, pitch-dark path around the hills toward the freeway. He listens and waits, his senses taking everything
in quarter by quarter. The only sound is the windmill's
rusted spoke arcing round its unvarying center. He gives orders silently, using a spartan wave of the blue barrel of his
shotgun.

He sends Granny Boy and Wood across the driveway
to follow a ravine that backs up and around the house
toward the shed and corral where the girl keeps her horse.
Lena is sent along a row of cypress trees to the near side of
the house, which faces the Antelope Freeway. She is to
check out a set of glass patio doors that lead from the den to
the pool. Gutter is left behind in case some car comes along
Via Princessa and turns up into the driveway. He's only to
make for the house when Cyrus lets him know it's dyin'
time.

Gabi sits alone on the window seat listening to her CD
player and watching the headlights of the cars on the freeway flare by. She takes a kind of mindless pleasure imagining the lives tucked away behind those flooding headlights
that fill out the dark and then dissolve on toward Canyon
Country. At fourteen she is flush with the idea the whole
world has a date with something interesting—except her.
She is all will and dreams trapped inside a child's body.

The door to her bedroom is cracked open just enough so
she can hear the vague intonations of an argument between
her mother and stepfather.

She gets up and crosses the room and slips out into the
hallway. She peeks around the corner and sees the kitchen
squared up within and beyond the dark frame of the den. Her
mother steps into view. She is rubbing her right hand with
her left, then the left with her right. It is a gesture of her
mother's Gabi knows all too well, and it means she is about

ready to cry or lunge into an angry outburst. Occasionally she does both at the same time.

The den carries their words through to the hall like some huge woofer.

"Talk to me, Sam."

"About what?"

"Oh, Sam . . ."

"There's nothing."

Her stepfather's tone has that uncommunicative edge she's heard in a lot of their conversations lately.

Her mother passes out of view, and now the room is just a backdrop of white kitchen cabinets hung in space.

"Sam, don't you know when you talk like that you give yourself away."

"Sarah, I mean it. There's . . ."

"Don't do this," she says angrily. "I won't stand for a shut door to your emotions. I left Bob because of that."

To hear her father's name spoken that way, used as some sort of negative example, makes Gabi feel sick and angry. And lonely. That's the worst of it. To feel like you're the sum total of someone else's separation.

It hurts her to listen, so she goes back to her room and sullenly closes the door on them. Her dog has already found the warm spot on the window seat where she had been and is making himself comfortable. She slumps down next to him and curls her feet under his belly.

"Make with some room, Poncho."

He's part cocker and part question mark: the floppy ears and pooly eyes of one, and the scruff-box short hair and gangly long legs of the other. He had been her father's birthday present to her and a way of keeping them close.

She glances out the window to find herself there in the night, staring back miserably. The long slender face, the skin a burnished summer yellow pooling around deeply set eyes. The details of her features swim a bit in the glass, but their import is unmistakable. Each day she is evolving more and more into the image of her mother. And at this moment, as much as she loves her mother, she hates her for having such a profound effect on her very being.

She looks back across the room at the clock by her bed. It's closing in on 10:30.

She and her father have this little ritual every Tuesday and Thursday night when he's working the late shift. At 10:30, as he cruises past on the freeway, he slows down and throws on the overhead flashers of his sheriff's patrol car, and she responds by flipping her bedroom light on and off. It's their secret way of saying good night.

Through the tangled cross of manzanita trees at the edge of the slope, Cyrus watches the nigger sheep and his porcelain wife arguing in the kitchen. If they only knew the book of life was about to close on them.

Lena makes her way back from the house along the lip of the ridge, using the high grass as cover against the moonlight. She slips up behind Cyrus and leans against him.

The years of pills and junk have left her with a face that seems to hover between life and death. She points a hand toward the house. On the back of each finger is tattooed the date of a death she has had a hand in.

She whispers, "Besides the front and patio doors, there's one more. And that goes to the service entrance behind the kitchen, there, on the far wall. I couldn't find signs of no security system."

"Just the nigger and his brood in there?"

She nods. "I crawled right up to the house and that's all I saw. They got a dog though, but you could finish it with just a good set of teeth."

"Give me the hypodermic."

She takes a black needle case from her back pocket and

hands it to Cyrus. He opens it. One needle, two vials of clear liquid. More than enough to play. He closes the case and slips it into the pocket of his frayed deerskin coat.

"Alright. Let's go wish the sheep a Merry Christmas."

"Why are you so sexually unresponsive to me?"

Sam leans back against the stove, short an answer. Sarah turns and grabs a photo from a nest of snapshots held to the refrigerator door by a miniature magnetic blender. She crosses the room and holds the photo up so Sam can see it.

"Is this all we are now?"

He looks at the snapshot Gabi took of Maureen and John at the last family barbecue. A perfect mismatch of people sitting side by side at a picnic table. Maureen a little too drunk to care about the disrespect her husband, John Lee, shows her. Sam says nothing, but he can't believe that of all the photos she grabbed that particular one. It's almost as if she were psychic.

"I don't know what you mean, Sarah."

"I mean, are we like them? Has our marriage boiled down to that? Just a hideous fraud. Something we make up along the way to get what we want until we want something else. And if we don't get that or don't want it anymore, well . . . we just cast it aside and keep what we have until . . . the next little thing comes along. Are we down to trade and barter?"

He can feel a guilty headache coming on. "I don't know what you're fuckin' talking about," he says.

Sarah swings the kitchen door shut. "Don't use that kind of language with me. Not in this house."

He throws up his hands.

"Do you know what commitment is?"

"Jesus, Sarah . . ."

"It's not just an idea, or a part-time gig. It's a way of life." She throws the photo down on the kitchen table and gives him a hard look across folded arms. "Are you having an affair?"

She watches him carefully. His huff across to the refrigerator, passing within inches of her. The tug at the refrigerator door, the taking of a beer, the twisting off of the cap. All done with an uncomfortable boredom.

He goes to sit at the kitchen table when, outside, Gabi's horse starts to stalk the corral, whinnying. A high, shrill call.

Gabi sits watching the freeway when something forms a withery outline just past the lamplit tiles of the pool. She leans up against the glass, cupping her hands around her eyes to see better. The bush grass wrestles and bends. Maybe it's a coyote or a wild dog. Maybe even a deer. Sometimes deer make their way down from the hills of the Angeles National Forest, which backs up their property. What a hoot. Christmas week and a deer comes to visit. But then something steel-like and shiny seeps through a row of trees. It glistens once. Twice. Like a broken fragment of a star. And then it's gone.

She begins to feel a little anxious. It wouldn't be the first time someone wandered up the hill.

She goes out into the hall. The kitchen door is closed but she can hear her mother and stepfather still in the throes of it.

Poncho follows her toward the living room.

It is dark except for the twinkling lights of the Christmas tree, which cast starburst shadows onto the ceiling. She stands in the middle of the room looking from window to window. She is wearing a T-shirt and shorts and feels unusually cold. She glances at the patio doors. They are slightly open. Only inches, but enough to let the night air in. Her mother always keeps them closed. Maybe she and Sam went outside when they were talking and forgot to close them when they came back in.

Gabi is crossing the room to close the doors when something shapeshifts up behind her. She sees its alter-image lunge across the ceiling.

She manages one scream. Just one, before her voice is swallowed by a huge hand. Then everything happens at once. The kitchen door is flung open and hits the wall. Her mother shouts her name as Gabi is lifted off the ground, kicking. The tree is knocked over, taking a scythe line of glittering light spots with it. Gabi claws at the hand over her mouth as her head is pulled around. She is face-to-face with gaunt eyes above cheeks branded in ink with lightning bolts that drip blood. There is another scream and a shotgun blast discharges and the whole house seems to echo and shake and reek with acrid smoke.

Bob Hightower is cruising the Antelope Freeway and going through his Christmas list of disappointments. Another holiday alone, without Gabi, without Sarah. The sum total of his life; he's thirty-eight, with a hatful of bad memories, and clinging to a job that is his last lifeline to order.

Come Christmas morning he'll get up, shave, put on a suit, go to church, then be the odd man out at either Arthur's house or John and Maureen's. They'll have the appropriate turkey dinner and they'll pass out the perfunctory presents, say all the right things, and then he'll drive home after dark, sit alone in his living room, the living room without even a tree, and get drunk and cry.

He looks at himself in the rearview mirror and tries to calculate who he is. He searches for the man who once incubated a kind of starry optimism. The face is the same, only the hopes have changed. Diminishing returns.

He should never have allowed himself to fall under his ex-father-in-law's influence. No, "allowed himself" is not a fair accounting. Succumbed is closer to the truth. He succumbed to Arthur's plan of manipulating John Lee into slopping him down behind a desk. He succumbed to the job's safeties and proprieties and potential advances. All for Sarah's sake. So she wouldn't end up a sheriff's widow. Was it all for her sake, though? He stares into the mirror to try to find the part of him that didn't mind succumbing to the job's safeties and proprieties and political advances. But what does he have now? He's a seat warmer at headquarters. A late-night fill-in. And he doesn't even have Sarah.

At least he has his faith. The one rock in a weary land that's lately been short of miracles.

Just ahead, between the black shape of the hills, is Via Princessa. He slows down and turns on the overhead flashers. Runnels of red across the hood of the car. He looks up toward the gravelly reef where the house is.

Not a light shines. It sits muted and stark. Just an outline against the moon-swept canyon. Bleak as his own heart. He pulls over. Maybe they went out to dinner. Maybe she fell asleep.

How can such a little thing like the flipping on and off of a light leave him so discouraged when it doesn't happen? He sits there and waits. The inside of the cruiser swims with the phosphory blood red of the flashers.

John Lee Bacon waits perched on a parcel of scrub rock at the cusp of the Shadow Range. There's an ashtray's worth of butts in the sand around his boots and a flask of bourbon hunkered down in his back pocket. Half drunk against the cold, he watches everything around him without expression. He pulls the flask and has another drink, cursing in short nervous bouts.

Through the beveled tiers of the Shadow Mountains, the

rise and fall of headlights. He stands and approaches the road. An old white van looms into view, sidles down the incline, and stops yards away. The doors open. Cyrus climbs out, followed by three of the others. He steps across the headlights and approaches John Lee. His boot spurs clang against the lit ground. The dust is full and floats around him.

"Well, look what the desert bred up."

"Don't start with your shit," hawks John Lee. "Just tell me . . ."

"Your boy *crossed over*."

A moment of finality.

John Lee nods. Takes a wrinkled envelope from his back pocket and tosses it at Cyrus. "Book closed," he says.

"The book ain't ever closed."

John Lee stares at him apprehensively. "What do you mean?"

Cyrus doesn't offer an answer as he counts off the loose packet of bills inside the envelope.

John Lee eyes the others. Gutter squats down beside one of the headlights. Lena sits on the bumper beside him and smokes. Granny Boy, still jacked up on speed from before the kill, is pacing and talking to himself.

"What do you mean?" he asks again.

Granny Boy mocks him by repeating, "What do you mean? What do you mean?"

John Lee tries to stare him down but Granny Boy holds up a hand, stretching his torn-gloved fingers. "Don't look too hard, Captain. The smell of blood got me off and the night ain't over yet. I'm still up for a little finger work."

John Lee turns away, but not fast enough to allow the boy to think he's got him rattled. He glances at Cyrus. "Did the nigger suffer?"

"I did it just like you would, if you had the guts to do it yourself."

"You know, I think you were more personable when you were just a junkie."

Cyrus pushes his face up against John Lee's. "You mean when I was your fuckin' field hand with my butt up in the air, doin' that 'Yes, sir' and 'No, sir' shit? Those days are history."

Wood, who is still sitting behind the steering wheel, leans out the open van door. "Why don't you let me handshake the inside of that fuck's asshole?"

John Lee doesn't move, but from the corner of his eye he makes out Gutter unsheathing a blood-slaked hunting knife. He starts to shave it through the sand, cleaning it off. John Lee lets his hand slip up toward the revolver he's got tucked inside his coat.

"By the way, I did that little porcelain doll wife of his."

John Lee looks like Gutter's knife was staked in his back. "You're fuckin' with me, right?"

"She made a good run at it, but came up short," says Granny Boy.

John Lee looks from face to face. Each shucked out and darkening.

Cyrus steps up behind John Lee, his mouth right beside his ear. "Not only that, but I kept the pretty-pretty for myself."

John Lee panics. "Gabi?"

"I didn't get her name."

Granny Boy starts to sing: "Well, he's just an excitable boy. He took little Gabi to the Junior Prom. . . ."

John Lee's heart pounds. He rushes forward and around the van.

". . . he's just an excitable boy . . ."

John Lee yanks open the van doors. Gabi is lying there unconscious. She is bound and gagged and naked except for her shorts. Her T-shirt has been swathed around her head. He slams the doors shut, gulps air, stumbles backward.

"Why?!"

". . . After ten long years they let him out of the home . . . he's just an excitable boy . . ."

Cyrus and his pack have circled up around John Lee.

"Why? You'll destroy ev—"

"You always thought you were in control!"

". . . And he dug up her grave and built a cage with her bones . . . He's such an excitable boy . . ."

"But you were only in charge. Understand the difference?" Cyrus's teeth tear at his words. "Do you have the true vision of where it is at? Has it started to crack through that lie you've been living?"

". . . He's such an excitable boy!"

"It's Furnace Creek all over again, Captain."

When Cyrus sees John Lee's face start to flush out with a fearful symmetry he leans in closer and says, "You don't know how bad you fucked up, Captain."

"You can't believe for a—"

"What did you think was going on inside my head all those years I'd shuffle through that fieldwork for you, Captain?" Cyrus screams in John Lee's face. He puts on a mock shuffling slave voice. "Yes, sir, Captain. I'll sell that smack you copped in a bust. Yes, sir, I'll get you some little boy so you can make hump movies to pass around with your belt-buckle stud queer-cop buddies. Sure. Just for a little taste. A few droppings."

A monstrous whisper of voices around John Lee laugh at him, throw trash talk at him. Cyrus's pack get off watching the Captain get punked.

"I was biding my time, Captain. Avengement. Retribution. Retaliation. Vendetta. Those words shrivel up your dick a little. Did you forget how you worked me when I was desperate for a little vein taste? Remember how you'd make me stick my ass up in the sky and you and your cop buddies make me be the bitch?

"Why'd you think I kept tight with you all those years after I cleaned up? It was the Path, dicksleeve. I kept the focus. I knew one day you'd want something done I could savage you and fatboy with. Where all that money you scored back then could not fill the hole I would blow through your lives."

Cyrus holds up the money John Lee has given him. He tosses it into the sand.

Gutter walks over and spits on the money. Granny Boy unzips his leathers and lets his cock give that cash a good cooling.

"We left the cunt back there at the house all nice and bloody and wrapped for Christmas," says Cyrus. "And the pretty-pretty, I'm going to take her and fuck her and shoot her up and let the young wolves here invent games for her pussy. We are going to rape her and film it and . . . I might even send you and fatboy a copy of that."

Wood begins to scarf his hands against the van wall like he's hot to climb in and get this hellbound train rolling. John Lee turns away from the sight.

"What is it you want, then?" he says.

Cyrus says nothing.

In a frenzy of collapsing emotions John Lee screams out, "What do you want?"

Cyrus does a little riff on the rock-and-roll classic "We Want the World and We Want It . . ." He breathes out one last word: "Yeah . . . It's gonna be pretty watching you and fatboy come tumbling down on each other. Wait till he finds out. You ought to go home and slit your throat tonight.

"Maybe I'll send the pretty-pretty back one day in a baggie. Maybe I should mail her to the FBI in a dog-food tin with a little note tagged to her clit to talk to you about it. What do you think, Captain? Is the suicide road lookin' good? Or maybe we ought to cook you up right here?"

Cyrus watches John Lee's hand start to quiver as it eases toward the inside of his coat.

"Forget it, Captain. If we were gonna kill you, we'd a taken you down in the dark without so much as a whisper."

His hand just hangs where it is.

Cyrus comes forward. His hand slides up John Lee's thigh, over his cock, lingering a bit, then up inside his coat. He slips the revolver out of his belt. He clicks off the safety, slips out the cylinder, and lets the bullets fall one by one to the sand.

John Lee remains where he is. He stares into freakshow faces bent out of the dark.

All the bullets have fallen to the ground save one. This Cyrus catches in his hand and holds up between two fingers inches from John Lee's face. Cyrus takes the bullet, pops it in his mouth, and swallows it.

"I'm the belly of the beast now, Captain. So consider yourself swallowed."

5

The hand-painted sign by the side of the road says: FIRST CHURCH OF CHRIST AND CHRISTIAN COMMUNITY CENTER RECONSTRUCTION PROJECT. Beneath that in noble blue metallic script is the phrase *Christians are on the move in Clay!*

A bulldozer lays waste to the old church while day laborers hose off a battered mastaba of slat, stucco, and collapsed spire to keep the dust down.

The church, a relic of pre-earthquake-proof simplicity, had been left by time an inconvenience on a barely usable acre of land. Short on parking, rec rooms, space for Christian counseling, Bible classes, and antisecular fund-raising, what else could religion do but suffer? To that end, a two-acre parcel of adjoining property and a trust fund of cash had been offered up in supplication by some sinner who, overcome with the best intentions death has to offer, saw re-building that church in his own name as a naked bribe at eternity.

Arthur Naci had been asked to oversee this project, and Clay's most formidable developer went about the task with Napoleonic efficiency. A moment of service in the long history of serving. He considers himself just another of Christ's foot soldiers living in the shadow of Los Angeles and trying to fight its impact with bulldozers, foundations, and crosses.

Arthur leans on the hood of his wagon, reaming a trio of engineers huddled up around him. Bob rolls up, stops, steps out of his pickup and waits. Arthur is stumping his fist down on the geologist's map spread out on the hood when he sees Bob. Cutting his attack short, he folds the map up and tosses it at the engineers, goes through a brisk warning, then waves them off like they were panhandlers.

He walks over to Bob, shaking his head. "You even got to watch your own, you know that? Sons of bitches. They're trying to cut the edge of the code book on the foundation without even telling me. We got a hundred straight feet of sand here and—ahhhhh! Watch your own, remember that."

"Yeah."

Arthur picks up something in Bob's tone. "What's wrong?"

"I'm not sure if it's anything, but I've been trying to call Gabi all morning. I'm supposed to take her to lunch today. Give her her presents. The phone's been busy all morning."

"Between Gabi and that daughter of mine, I'm not surprised."

"No, you don't understand. I checked. It seems to be out of order."

"Maybe it's off the hook. Maybe the dog knocked . . ."

"Arthur, Gabi knows we're having lunch. She should have called me by seven telling me where she wants to go and then again by nine after she changed her mind and then decided on someplace else. I know my daughter, and I'm a little . . . concerned."

Bob's tone is making Arthur nervous. "Did you call Sam?"

"I did."

"At work?"

"He's not there."

"Hmmmmm."

"Didn't come in to work today. Didn't call or anything."

Arthur stands there thoughtfully, with the gut-grinding belts of a bulldozer turning behind him. He looks at his watch. It's almost noon. He is trying to avoid the imperfect dramatics these situations arouse. Bob watches him as he glances across the lot to where six men are carrying the old church crucifix toward the back of a flatbed so it can be stored away until the new church is built. They are moving slowly through the dust left by the trundling wheels of the dump trucks.

"Well, what do you think should be done?"

Bob shrugs. "I'd go over there alone, but if it's nothing, well, you know how Sarah might get, me just showing up."

Arthur scowls at the way one predicament seems to pool-ball into another. "Divorce, shit. Let's get over there before my ulcer starts acting up."

They pull up in the driveway just past noon. The sun is December warm and then some. Around the house, trees pierce the pools of light. It is quiet to perfection.

"I don't think anyone's home," says Arthur.

Bob says nothing. But rounding a turn in the driveway he sees both Sarah's and Sam's cars in the carport. The cop in him starts to calculate possibilities. He lets Arthur get out of the car first, then reaches over and takes a semiautomatic from the glove compartment.

For a moment he feels utterly foolish. It's nothing, he tells himself. The father and the professional officer struggle with each other. Emotion and logic. One's success is the other's failure. He slips the gun into his belt and pulls his shirt out of his pants so it can't be seen in case he's wrong.

They reach the front door. Arthur rings the bell.

Nothing.

He rings again.

Nothing.

Bob notices the corral is empty. Where is Gabi's horse?

Arthur rings the doorbell again.

Nothing.

"Why isn't Poncho barking?"

Arthur steps into a bed of tulips and tries to look in the hallway window, but the screen obscures his view.

"Let's walk around the house," says Bob.

They pass the carport and now Arthur sees that both cars are there, and he becomes flat-out frightened. "You think they could have been overcome by fumes or something?"

Bob puts a hand on Arthur's shoulder to silence him. Then he points at the back door leading to the laundry room. It stands half open.

They climb the two concrete steps and stand in the crease of light that runs past the washing machine and dryer and on toward the kitchen.

Bob calls out, "Gabi? Sarah? Sam?"

Nothing.

Then Arthur tries. "Gabi? Sarah? It's Grandpops . . ."

Nothing. Just the silent face of white kitchen cabinets and the dark mouth of the doorway beyond.

Bob slips the semiautomatic from his belt. "You better wait here."

"Oh, Jesus, God. You don't think . . ."

"Take it easy," Bob whispers. "Okay? Okay?"

Arthur nods. He watches Bob walk through the kitchen, then on to the dining room. Bob steps past a chair that has been knocked over. Arthur hears himself praying. His hands tremble, and he feels sick to his stomach. He suddenly finds himself walking into the kitchen, even though he was told not to.

As Bob moves down the hall he begins to smell the faint afterburn of gunpowder. He comes to Gabi's bathroom. The door is closed. He presses it open with the barrel of his gun. As the room slowly fans into view he sees what looks like a dirty mop stuffed into the well of the toilet.

Wood grabbed the dog as it lunged at him. He grabbed it by the throat. It raked its claws at him as he stuffed it down into the well of the toilet and—

Before the sight registers in his brain, Bob hears a scarred cry. He runs down a length of hall and across the open living room with its fallen Christmas tree and straggle curls of blood leading out to the patio. He turns into another stretch of hall. He chases the cries, hitting photos along the wall, so they twist and fall with a shattering of glass. He finds Arthur collapsed on both knees in the doorway of the den, like some bull struck down, gagging up food and bile. Bob half steps over the gagging form and, passing through the doorway, comes flush up on Sam.

Death coldcocks Bob in his tracks. Sam is sitting against the wall naked. He has been trussed up with wire like a pig stalked and caught. He has been eviscerated, and what is left of his tongue bulges out of his mouth. It is held that way by a letter opener rammed clean through the flesh and used as a brace across the lips. Bob takes a first step forward, a first necessary step to separate himself from the horror that's swallowing him. His lungs feel like stone, and he hears Arthur saying something when he notices, pinned to Sam's chest and so covered with blood it is barely legible, what looks like some kind of playing card.

6

Case spends Christmas Eve like she spends most every other night since she got off junk, wandering Hollywood Boulevard. Junkies don't sleep too good, especially when they're working at being ex-junkies. The real world closes in with the dark, and that's when they have to face up to the boredom and madness of the straight life.

To burn away the nasties those feelings arouse, Case clicks off the miles between Western and La Brea. She scopes out runaways who work the phone booths and Dumpsters behind restaurants off Cherokee. She checks out cops scoring hookers for free head. She cruises the Chinese where marks with names like Mr. Plain Wrapper Iowa and Mrs. Remodeled Kitchen Kentucky get their pockets picked by faceless hands or hammered for a buck by some aggressive shoeless Rasta. She passes scruff-faced junkies of all creeds and colors and stations in life, all with the same knight errant eyes for a hit. It's a theme park of life addictions, disguised as civilization.

It's also where she gets to swallow a full dose of the boredom and the madness to see how it tastes going down. And if it can stay down. Can she actually become a loose part of it without having to leave needle marks in her arm to get by? Every block is a test. Every Hollywood Boulevard star she walks over is a little distance covered, though to what end she has yet to discover. She never talks to anyone who tries to hit on her, and she never looks in storefront windows as she is not ready to see what she looks like looking back. But tonight the street is just overlit space crowding her thoughts about that kidnapped girl in Clay as she debates with herself about whether she should write the authorities a letter.

Case sits in the dark alone at the small Formica table in the windowless kitchenette of her apartment in the recovery house. The thin beam of her flashlight scans the flaking paint along the ceiling scrollwork, then drifts down the grease-skinned wall above the stove. It arcs like a prison searchlight along the refrigerator, stopping at some article on self-reliance or some aphorism she wrote down that has the juice of a philosophical idea she can cling to and is held in place by cheap magnetic replicas of knights and maidens that she bought as a joke at Pic and Save.

Three times she's tried to beat the junk, and twice she's taken the fall. They say the third time's the charm. Kill the horse with this shot, baby, 'cause those veins can't do another ten years of hard time.

She leans forward with an unfiltered cigarette hanging out of her mouth and aims the light down at the table where black-and-white headlines form up through the darkness: CULT MURDER IN CLAY . . . HUSBAND AND WIFE BUTCHERED . . . DAUGHTER ABDUCTED . . . THE WORST MASSACRE SINCE MANSON, SAYS D.A. . . .

Newspapers are always so clinically lurid, she thinks. Pushing the envelope of socially acceptable slash and burn. Unaware and ultimately uninterested in the truth behind their bullshit teasers.

There is a knock at the door.

"It's open," says Case.

Anne walks in, but with the living room dark and the shades drawn, she can't see a thing. She just stands there and calls out, "Case?"

Case points the flashlight to guide her. Anne's shape filters past the furniture. She comes into the kitchen and looks around, then leans against the wall by the table.

"Why are you sitting here in the dark?"

"I was thinking."

"About what?"

Case lets the light fall across the headlines she'd been looking at.

"Oh, yeah. I read about that. But why are you sitting here like this?"

Case rests her head against the wall. "I breathe better in the dark. I don't know why. I just do. Maybe it's anxiety. Did I ever mention that to you?"

"No."

"Well, I've mentioned it now. And the flashlight, sometimes, it makes me feel like I have some control against the dark."

She takes a long hit off her cigarette. Her eyes come back to the headlines. She swings the light up the wall, then lets it slide along that chipped sky of a ceiling.

"The girl's so young," says Anne.

"Young." The word slips out of Case's mouth, dragging a full history of personal loss.

"Case?"

"Yeah."

"Do you think . . . the girl . . . Is she still alive?"

Case turns the light on her own face. Lets it fan up from under her neck, causing something unearthly to the jawline and eyes.

"She could be," Case says, "she could be. But if she is alive, Anne, if she is, what she is going through ain't like nothing those 'sheep' out in Clay could ever imagine. That family looks to me like it was taken down by what we call a 'war party.' Blood hunting for Scratch. Blood hunting, Anne, blood hunting. Helter Skelter and then some."

Case turns off the flashlight and sets it down on the table, and continues to smoke silently. She moves her head as if to say something more, but doesn't.

"Why don't you come downstairs. A couple of the girls and their kids are gonna celebrate Christmas Eve. One of them went to Ralph's and bought a couple of pounds of Christmas cookies. Come on, we'll listen to Christmas carols and get a sugar rush. It will be good for you."

Case rolls her cigarette between her thumb and forefinger. "When I was down in San Diego in 1992, that was the second time I tried to kick. And the director of the program, this chicana named Liz, well, there had been some ritual murders of these German shepherds. They were hung, then gutted, blood was drained . . ."

Case's voice tails off a bit, becomes darkly remote, as if the story itself were again living in moments of her own life.

"Well, Liz got the cops to talk to me about these crimes. At first the cops weren't too hip to the idea. After all, I was some tattooed junkie ex-cult-member freak. I saw how they looked at me. Enough said about that."

Case blows on the tip of her cigarette and the ash pulses red hot. "Well, I'd seen this shit before. Body parts and blood are used for potions, you know that? You drink the fuckin' shit. It's supposed to give you magical powers. I did all that. Can you believe it?"

"Case . . ."

"The cops didn't have any idea. This was Greek to them. It took me about one day to find where they were gettin' them dogs from. One day to figure it. I walked all the animal shelters. Walked 'em. Never said a word. Just went lookin' for dogs. But all the time I'm checkin' out the workers. I know what to look for."

She points to her own arms, which bear a line of tattoos from her shoulders down to her wrist. "People on the Left-Handed Path have the sign. You just have to know what to look for."

Anne watches Case. Her hand's beginning to tremble, so she has to put the cigarette down.

"I helped them some after that. Of course, I was always a freaked-out aberration. There ain't no pity for the pitiful. All's fair in love and war, right?"

Anne takes Case's hand in hers.

"I got a good look at everything I'd done back then, looking at them dogs, after I was off junk, finding one strung up from a tree, still alive, but dying, eyes all . . ."

Case's mouth is too dry to go on. But even in the dark, the whites of her eyes stand out, desperate and stark.

"Don't be alone. Come on downstairs."

"The third time's the charm."

"Come on. Don't sit here and hurt yourself."

Case presses her fingers against her temples. She hears somewhere within the cell of her life something like skin being cut open. She looks up at Anne. "I was thinking about writing the Sheriff's Department in Clay."

7

Newsrats squeeze onto the roofs of their minivans, working zoom lenses to clear the line of trees that edge the Bouquet Canyon Cemetery and lock onto the plat of hillside where Sarah and Sam are being laid to rest two days after Christmas.

Bob looks across the caskets toward that lineup of vans. It has taken only three days, about the length of time needed for your average crucifixion and resurrection, to destroy a handful of lives and rewrite them through the distilled words and images of the theater we call our free press.

The *Valley News* reported that John Lee Bacon, head of the Clay Sheriff's Department, believed that because of

Arthur Naci's wealth and the fact the murder was so well planned, it might have been a kidnapping, or at least a kidnapping gone wrong and covered up to look like a cult murder.

BETA, the black cable channel, suggested in an editorial that the murders may have been racially motivated, arguing first, that this was the Northern Valley, a last bastion of crusader mentality where "black was the color, and none was the number," and second, that only thirty miles to the west, in Simi Valley, a jury of decent white Christians had acquitted the officers who had beaten Rodney King. Third, it posed the idea that this could have been "blacklash" against a more Christian jury who, thirty miles to the south, had acquitted an American icon, O. J. Simpson, in the murder of his ex-wife.

The *L.A. Times* and the *National Enquirer* both chased down a similar lead. An alleged tip, a phone call from an unnamed source, suggested that the murder was an act of revenge against Bob Hightower. To this end, both papers had a hard look into his background. Was he a good cop who was paying the price for putting someone away? Or was he, like so many other cops, dirty enough when the opportunity arose and now he had been issued a silent warning for some transgression?

Photographers hid in the trees behind his property. He had to fight through a bulwark of cameras just to cross his driveway.

The tip turned out to be sadly wrong. Bob Hightower was a desk jockey. A decent "cardboard" cop. A nickel package fill-in. A late-night cruiser when someone was sick.

They even went so far as to suggest he was a "kept" man. That he had remained on the force for two reasons. First, his ex-father-in-law was best friends with John Lee Bacon, the head of the department. And second, John Lee Bacon's wife, Maureen, a prominent businesswoman and Arthur Naci's partner, was godmother to the missing girl.

It was all part of a national spectacle, a shared depradation of another's privacy, another's grief.

Bob looks over at Arthur as he begins the eulogy. Arthur's voice is hoarse. It comes up labored and slow, and he sounds like a man much older than fifty-three. He stands there grimly poised between John Lee and Maureen. John Lee with his hands folded and she with one hand gently touching Arthur's elbow. A triptych study in friendship and grief backlit by the sun so their faces are cast without form and their shadows stretch out over the two mahogany hulls that will ride into the earth.

Bob stares down at the open hole and begins to cry.

Following the funeral, family and friends congregate at Arthur's house. Dusk is working its way across the canyon, leaving the upscale tract homes of Paradise Hills in deepening shadow. Food is served, Maureen works the bar. A small group has gathered around John Lee to ask him about the case. He starts, of course, by telling them there are certain details, known only to the police and the FBI, that he cannot discuss. But as he fields their questions, it becomes more and more apparent that nothing substantial has broken in their favor. Not yet. But in time . . . He speaks with the kind of dedicated earnestness that inspires assurance, and which comes from a lifetime of honesty or years of successful lying.

Arthur is overtaken by nausea and lies down in the den. Bob brings him a pillow, draws the blinds, and shuts the drapes. Arthur takes Bob's hand. "We have to take care of each other now."

"I know, Arthur."

"We're all we have."

"Yes."

"We have to find her."

"We'll find her. Rest some."

"We will, won't we?"

"We will."

"I'm scared, son."

"I am, too."

"You don't think she's . . ."

"Don't talk about it. Please."

Bob drifts outside alone. He stares off into the contour of the hills where the homes are neatly arranged toward the horizon. Lights have begun to be turned on in kitchens and living rooms. They seem like distant fires upon some stony heath. Beyond that, he can make out the low drone of the freeway, trucks and cars racing on toward the Mojave, toward the colorless sage of the night deserts of Arizona and Nevada. The world seems suddenly endless and devoid of perspective. Beyond his grasp. A feeling surges over him of the earth's sheer power at sweeping away the memory of everything that was. Everything. And he is frightened.

He goes and sits by the pool. Across the slow movement of water the last strips of daylight are like running blood, and he is shocked back into remembering how he found Sarah floating . . .

"I brought you a drink," says Maureen.

He turns. His face is pale, his mouth bent back against his teeth in pain.

"How you holding up?"

"Not so good," he says.

He takes the glass of Scotch she's poured.

She pulls up a chair and sits beside him. "Is there anything I can do?"

"Set the clock back five years."

"If I could," she says sadly, "I'd go further back than that."

Bob nods halfheartedly. She glances at the living room where John Lee is holding court. "If they only knew what a shit he is to live with."

"Not tonight, Maureen."

"You're right. I'm sorry."

They sit there quietly. When she gets a chance she watches Bob. There is a handsomeness to him that goes unappreciated by most but that she has found quietly enticing.

Maureen sat on the edge of the bed in the half light of late afternoon. She'd been out in Lancaster looking for some property over by the fairgrounds when she found this out-of-the-way motel called the Ramona. It was one of those forties-style attached bungalows with portal windows and stucco facing, one block off the Sierra Highway from when the town was just an excuse for a gas station and a diner. Now all that could be said for its rooms was that everything was in its place and had been washed or at least Lysoled.

She took a hit off a joint. She wished she felt shame in these situations, not because the thorny business of one's conscience makes demands on our pleasure and inspires us to stop, but because shame was pleasure in itself. A little Christian shame made the act all the more exciting. The shower stopped. Moments later Sam came out of the bathroom. He was naked and he stood over her by the edge of the bed. She sat there, his legs pressed close against her shoulders.

"I have an idea," says Maureen.

Bob is drifting, but he looks up from his drink.

"I had a long talk with Arthur. And we both agree. I know this might not be the right time, but . . . we'd like to have you come to work with us."

He is too tired to be surprised by anything and barely acknowledges the offer.

"Think about it. Let's talk. You don't need to be . . ."

"A 'cardboard' cop. Isn't that what I'm called in the rags?"

"We didn't offer 'cause some tabloid has to lie up a headline. It's just—"

"The truth," Bob snaps back. "Yeah. You know it, too, Maureen. I let Arthur massage John Lee into dropping me behind a desk, and I've been dropping ever since."

"You have not."

"Oh, please. All that time and field training gone to waste 'cause I let . . . visions of departmental sugar plums dance through my head. I guess I believed I was worth more."

"Your concern was for Sarah."

"With a few pinches of selfishness sprinkled in for Bob Hightower." He pauses, shakes his head, as if hearing something he wishes now he'd acted upon years earlier. "After the divorce I should have asked—no, demanded, that John Lee put me back in the field. But I was dropping through despair to downright self-hate and didn't care to stop the fall.

"So I'm turning your offer down, Maureen. I'm gonna thank you, but turn you down. Unless, of course, I end up with no job at all. Then we'll see."

She leans over, and her hand rests delicately on his thigh. "Anytime. We just thought maybe the change would be good for you."

John Lee has gotten up and is standing by the patio windows watching Maureen and Bob talk. He notices her hand, and it isn't the first time he's seen those quiet little moves of friendship.

8

From Christmas to New Year's, through the Epiphany, and on to Valentine's Day, the dates are marked off Bob's calendar with quiet desperation as the Sheriff's Department and the FBI labor blindly forward. Leads, slim as they are, disappear quick as a spindle of dust on the desert floor.

John Lee feigns strength and quiet support, but his guts eat away at him during every meeting when the least fact that might lead to Cyrus shows its face.

Every morning Bob goes to church and prays. Every day at work he scours the mountains of paperwork for some new fact as yet uncovered. On the weekends he travels southern California, interviewing the state's most respected forensic experts and homicide detectives. His car becomes a vault of files, photographs, and notes. At night, in the kitchen of the house he once shared with Gabi and Sarah, beer bottles and cigarette butts pile up as he goes through every call, every fax, every letter sent to the department, no matter how ridiculous and absurd.

The world around him has become the bizarre geometry of the dedicated and the delinquent. Of paranoids and conspiracy theorists. Of computer freaks posting hot lines with purported clues and women writing their regrets while sending photographs of themselves and offers of marriage.

Web sites carry a litany of unofficial "Gabi" sightings, and Christians send faxes of support against the nation's amoral vileness they say this murder represents. Other letters blame the media or pornography or drugs. A sacrificial few offer themselves up if someone, anyone, will just come and get them, or at least pay their bus fare to L.A.

The whole of this floods the kitchen table, overflows card-

board boxes and filing cabinets. Paper stalagmites tower up
from the floor, obscuring notes and fragments of information stickpinned to the walls.

The room has become the cluttered and dishevelled landscape of everything Bob feels. A delirium out of which no
order can be created.

At midnight Bob walks alone behind the tract, drunk, his
boots chafing at the gravelly ridge. Branches of dead leaves
brush his face with the last of winter as he tries to slog his
way through the naked madness of it all.

By the middle of February Bob's search has brought him to
the dregs. He reads through letters sent from the hard-timer
in prison who overhears someone say . . . from the ex-
felon on the street who for a few bucks would . . . from
the pathetic creature in the mental institution who is certain
the killers are living down the hall and keeping his daughter
in a foot locker . . .

It's only then that he comes across Case's letter.

9

On the evening of February 27 there is a knock at Case's door.
An ex-nun who had been addicted to painkillers and now lives
by the elevator tells her she has a call on the pay phone.

Case leans against the wall listening to Bob introduce
himself. His voice is deep and gravelly, his questions direct
and precise. As Bob discusses the letter, Case watches a
teenage mother at the end of the hall, seated on the fire escape. She is a fragile thing with a small daughter buoyed in
her lap. They sit on the grating taking in the sky as it yields
itself up to the night in purple streaks.

Case is surprised that after all this time he's called. He asks a little more about her background, and when she's done there is silence. She figures he'll just hang up, but instead he asks if he can come down the following night to talk further and show her some files and photographs.

How desperate he must be to finally come to her. After Case hangs up, she watches the mother and child fade to dim outlines against the deepening black behind them. She stays by the wall thinking, thinking about the man and his child, until all that is left is a glow of light from a single bulb at the end of the hallway and a night the color of steel and the promise of rain.

It rains on the twenty-eighth. A rain taken to gusts and slashings. Bob drives down to L.A. after dark. The freeway is a ragged line of vehicles slip-streaming through a gap in the foothills toward a dim triangle of light.

The whole trip is an hour of silent running. Just him and a blue emptiness inside the car, which is streaked with the shadow-line of rain trailing down the windows. As the wispy mirage of the city spreads out before him, he begins to consider who this Case Hardin is, beyond what the police in San Diego have told him.

He takes the Hollywood Freeway to Gower, then Franklin west to Garfield. The 1700 block of Garfield runs between Franklin and Hollywood Boulevard. It's a potluck of low-end apartments, two-story stucco and terrace, and a few straggling homes from another era, the little class they once had flaking away. Some of the buildings have rental signs on them written in Armenian.

He finds the recovery house about five doors up from Hollywood Boulevard. An old brick three-story affair that looks like it has wheezed through the last twenty years.

Case sits in the darkened window seat of her tiny living room watching the street. She smokes, she is apprehensive.

She sees a car slow and cruise the buildings' numbers and thinks this might be him. The car does a U-turn into a driveway and finds a spot to park near a barred and boarded-up grocery.

She leans in close to the window. In the murky glass the reflection of her eyes and the burning tip of a nervous cigarette are all she sees until a man wearing a black oilskin raincoat with the hood pulled up clears the trees. He makes his way along the sidewalk, carrying a brown leather case. He turns quickly up the walkway, his boots kicking up sprays of water.

It must be him.

She grapples with the moment. "I am here . . . and now," she tells herself, stumping the cigarette out against the top of a Diet Coke. She repeats, "I am here . . . and now."

The lobby of the building has been turned into a reception and waiting area. A bivouac of cheap metal desks and fake leather couches, sagging from long-term use. A goateed security guard holds the fort from behind a desk. He looks up from a sitcom. Arms folded, leaning back in his chair, he has that air of "try me." "Yes, sir. How may we help you?" He puts some measure into the word "we."

"Case Hardin. I'm here to talk to her. I have an appointment."

"Name?"

"Officer . . ." He cuts himself off. "Mr. Bob Hightower."

Hearing the word "officer" draws a few looks from the female residents hunkered down on the sofas in the waiting area. They stare at Bob. He can see right away they assume the worst, and their alliance, like warborn partisans, is with one of their own.

A woman behind Bob says, "I'll take care of Mr. Hightower."

He turns. Anne steps out of her office, offers him her hand. "I'm Anne Dvore. Resident manager."

They shake. She motions with a wave of her hand. "I'll show you to the elevator."

They start down the long hallway with its worn-out runner of carpet. Both are quiet. Bob looks the place over, sneaking glances into any apartment with an open door. Anne uses the time to get a picture of the man.

"By the way," Anne says, "I just wanted to tell you how sorry I am about what happened to your ex-wife and daughter."

Bob nods stoically.

They reach the elevator. Anne presses the button. Bob stares back down the hall. One of the women from the waiting area is now by the desk and staring at him.

"Are all these women here for rehab?"

Anne picks up a tone in his voice that she's heard before, judgment disguised as curiosity.

"It also doubles as a shelter for battered women. That's why we have the guard up front."

"I was curious about that."

He switches the heavy leather case from one hand to the other, then opens and closes his free hand to get the blood back into it. "I assume being the resident manager you're some kind of therapist."

She smiles. "Some kind. Yes."

"Can I ask you a few questions about this woman?"

There's that tone again, drifting over "this woman."

"Why not ask her?"

"Listen, since the murder I'm confronted with all kinds of people offering me . . . hope. A lot of them turn out to be flakes. Flakes I can deal with. It's disappointing, but I can deal with it. I don't come at this with any legal authority. But there are a few people I've met, on the other hand . . ."

He doesn't know this woman's relationship with Case, so he's not sure quite how to get where he wants.

"A few," interjects Anne, picking up where he faltered,

"are untrustworthy. And potentially dangerous. And I assume you're carrying in that satchel files that might be sensitive."

"I couldn't have said it any better."

"You didn't say it at all."

His throat tightens a bit. "I don't want to get off to a bad start here."

"Then just approach it, before you judge it, with an open mind. I'm sure you talked to the police in San Diego about Case."

His eyebrows raise in halfhearted enthusiasm.

"She was in a cult for seventeen years. She is a heroin addict going through recovery. She is what she is."

"Is she trustworthy?"

"She's not a saint, but she's not a congressman either."

The elevator arrives. Anne pulls open the worn metal door. "Room 333. Turn right when you get out of the elevator, back up the hall, last door on the left by the street. And good luck, Mr. Hightower."

"She was in a cult for Christ sake," said John Lee. He *grabbed her file off his desk, the one that had been sent from San Diego, and waved it to punctuate his statement.* "Assault *with a knife. Six months for conspiracy to sell heroin. Do you think this person is trustworthy?"*

"I'm only going to ask her a few questions."

"You want to ask her questions. Fine. Bring her in."

"She's in rehab down in L.A."

"I'll pay for the fuckin' cab."

"People like her aren't comfortable comin' in here to talk. I want to try and . . ."

"No shit, they're not comfortable."

"She contacted us."

"And I'd like to know why. What does she want? Bring her in here. Sit her junkie ass across from both of us."

"We haven't gotten anywhere with this investigation. It's been six weeks, there's no telling what Gabi is going through out there. If she's alive at all."

The words fall with a dead thud. Both men face each other soberly.

"She was in a cult. She is an addict. But she's also an expert of sorts. For profiling alone, she'd be—"

"Bob. Time out. Okay. Time out."

Bob leaned back, quieted. He didn't want to, but he did.

"I let you take all those files and run down every lead no matter what. I let you because it has to be done, and I let you . . . you . . . because I know I wouldn't want it otherwise if I were in your spot.

"But this. This chick is a junkie who was in a cult. She could have her own agenda. Maybe she's had it with methadone, if she's on that program, and she's trying to figure out how to score. Maybe she thinks she could wheel and deal a little info from you that she could sell. Who knows what goes on in those junked-out heads. If you were an experienced investigator who'd handled a few of these before, that would be one thing. But you're a desk cowboy, okay?"

Bob sat there listening impassively as he was told in no uncertain terms that he was incompetent. At least that's how he heard it.

"You want to question her. You bring her in. She won't come in, forget it. Then give her name over to the FBI. You understand?"

"Yes, sir."

Bob steps out of the elevator and hesitates. He knows he's broken his word. But what is more troubling yet, he's not sure if he's done this wholly because of Gabi or because of a need to prove himself.

Is it pride? The air stinks with something burned on a stove. He can hear laughter, doors closing. More laughter, a wispy uprising of voices till they dust away.

It is pride. A door at the end of the hall opens and the light outlines a woman. At this distance she looks more like a girl, really. Wiry slim, with faded jeans and black boots and hair cropped like a Marine's.

She steps out into the hall. "Hightower? Mr. Hightower?" Her voice is like dry leaves brushing over wood.

"Yes."

He starts down the hall. A few long seconds and they are face-to-face.

"Case Hardin?"

"Yeah, that's right."

Case wears a sleeveless T-shirt, and Bob can see that her arms are covered with tattoos, a fever line of ink designs from wrists to shoulders.

"You want to come in?"

"Yes."

"Did you find this place okay?"

"Okay, yes."

She steps back clumsily over the threshold and he follows. She sidesteps to let him pass.

"We should go in the kitchen there, it's got a table, we could sit and talk."

He sets the leather satchel down on the couch so he can take off his oilskin raincoat. She stares at the satchel, assuming the horror of his life is there.

"I just wanted to tell you, up front, how sorry I am. I watched it all on TV and . . . I'm sorry. Your wife . . . ex-wife, she looked—"

He cuts her off clumsily: "Thanks."

"—nice . . ."

Thanks.

He finishes slipping off the oilskin. "Where can I hang it?"

"Drop it anywhere."

"It's wet."

"It's alright."

"Maybe we should . . ." He points toward the closet.

The whole process of going over there and getting a hanger and hanging it up, the whole ritual of it, is a little too much for her nerve endings.

"Drop it right there. I mean, you can see the place ain't the Ramada Inn."

She tries to smile. He takes the coat and neatly arranges it over the back of a chair by a wobbly wooden desk.

She glances at the satchel again, then at him. He is taller than she imagined from seeing him on the news.

He follows her into the kitchen silently, carrying the satchel under one arm and eyeing the shabby rooms.

"Sit down. You want some coffee? I need some."

"Yeah, that would be alright. I've been going at it since six this morning."

"I'd offer you a beer," she says, "but I'm on the wagon for the next forty or fifty fuckin' years."

Case takes a small packet of coffee and tears at the plastic wrapping with her teeth. She turns to him. "The coffee is shit. It's one of those mail samples."

"I'm not a connoisseur, so don't worry."

"If you smoke, go ahead. Use anything handy for an ashtray."

Bob smokes, watches her make the coffee. They don't talk. Her hands tremble. Her moves are jagged and taut at the same time, as if she were cranked up on speed yet bound by some invisible wire. There is something sadly benign about her face, with its broad forehead and jawline of bones that protrude like the thin spine under a bird's skin. Her eyes are dark, almost black, and they seem blacker against her white flesh.

They sit and talk. Bob opens his satchel and takes out a yellow legal pad. He begins by asking Case questions about her past and her life in a cult, about her time in San Diego, her falls back into drugs. He makes little sidesteps into her illegal activities, into her present state of mind. His eyes slide back and forth between Case and his notes. She sits there, answering each question. She smokes and coils her hands one around the other until she's a knot of venom over this interrogation.

"Can I ask you something?"

He looks up from his notes.

"You don't trust me, do you?"

"What do you mean?"

"I mean, you've grilled me with this Nazi kind of attitude and asked every fuckin' question except what size Tampax I use and do I like takin' it up the ass. Jesus bullshit Christ, what do you think I . . ."

Without any indication of being startled, Bob replaces the upturned pages of the notepad. Case sits back and presses one booted foot against the rim of the table.

"If I'd have asked you," says Bob, "to come out to Clay, to the Sheriff's Department, would you have come?"

She eyes him a long time, her jaw forming a bias across her cheeks. Her arms spread out across the back of the chair like the wings of a hawk getting ready for fight or flight. "I read you, Lieutenant," she says. "Or is it Sergeant? Or Squire? Or Boss Man? Or is it . . . Desk Boy?"

Angered, he slips the notepad into the leather case. He closes it, stands. He walks out of the room without a word or a look. She gives his back the finger.

At the front door, though, something comes over him and he stops. The rain gutters along the roof and down through rusty drains. A harsh rattling, comfortless sound. Case stares at him through the framework of the doorway. He's boxed in like some character on a strange, dark stage.

His voice is barely audible across the lightless room, but she can hear in it waves of sorrow through slow breaths. "I have lost a wife," he says. "I have lost a daughter. I do not know if she is dead or alive or how to find her or if I ever can.

I'm desperate and close to giving up. I am here. Maybe I did not approach you quite . . . Maybe you could help me a little?"

She leans forward and rests her elbows on the table and presses her thumbs into the wedges of flesh above her eyes.

"I'm a junkie," Case says, "and junkies tend to be short of patience and manners on the ride back to that other reality. I'm fighting with myself most of the trip, and I don't sleep, and I shake, and I hate most everything I see. I shouldn't have said what I did. I should have 'asshole' tattooed across my mouth."

She looks up and through the door. "Please. Come and sit down."

Bob drops a stack of manila folders on the table, then looks across at Case. "Do you consider yourself an expert on satanic cults?"

She can see that the top two folders are filled with photographs. "There are no experts. Only survivors."

He considers this. His fingers tap at the edges of the top folder. "Yes, I can see your point. Survivors."

Case notices a beaded Indian bracelet tautly wound around his left wrist. It seems out of place somehow. Too delicate, really. And yet . . .

"I believe this was a cult murder," he says, "not a front for a kidnapping or a failed kidnapping or a robbery or any of that crap you get in the paper or on 'Inside Edition.' I have photos here from that night. Do you think you could deal with looking at them and telling me what you think?"

She stares at the stack coldly. She lights a cigarette. There is something absolute and terrible to this, and she wishes more than ever she hadn't written. She is sick inside, but she won't let on. She reaches for the folders as if she were reaching into a fire for a perfectly flamed coal.

"I'll deal with it," she says.

"What I'm doing now," he says, "I have no authorization to do."

"Oh?"

"Do you understand my position?"

She considers this in light of her own human weaknesses. "Maybe you shouldn't, then."

She waits to see if he will take back the folders, but he just sits there, pulls a pack of cigarettes from his shirt pocket, and lights one. He sits there, breathing deeply and studying her. There is something steady and remorseless to his face.

She pulls the folders toward her. She opens the one on top. It is filled with family photos. With snapshots of Sarah and Sam, of Gabi riding bareback out the corral gate, of Poncho caught in the act with a steak bone on the kitchen steps. Case spreads the snapshots across the table. It is a simple collage of middle-class life with all the trimmings. In one of the snapshots she notices Gabi wearing a beaded Indian bracelet similar to Bob's.

"Can I ask you a few questions?" she says.

"Sure."

"Was Gabi into drugs?"

"Not at all."

"Not even a little bit?"

"Nooo."

"You sure?"

"I'm sure."

"She hang with a druggie crowd?"

"A druggie crowd . . . Noooo . . ."

"Any of her friends into satanic shit of any kind?"

"Look at those photos. Look." He pushes one toward Case, then another. "Does that look like the kind of girl who's into drugs or hangs out with that kind of crowd? Come on. I know my daughter. And this is a small, family-

oriented Christian community. We don't have much in the
way of deviant behav . . ."

He stops.

"It's alright," she says. "We all came from one of those
small family-oriented communities. Once. Even me."

She opens the next folder, and there the remains of that
night confront her.

*Sarah stumbled, or thought she stumbled. She didn't know
that spray from a shotgun blast had ruptured one of the veins
leading from her shoulder to her neck. The hallway was a
black tunnel, a wild menagerie of sounds.*

*She snatched at the air, trying to reach her daughter's
cries. There was smoke and another gravel of gunfire and
she thought she saw a boy with a shaved head and metal
spikes shaped like a cockscomb growing out of the center of
his skull leap over her with a banshee yell.*

*The glass wall of patio doors and the moon's eye and the
winking lights along the pool all seemed to swim and slur
together in one queer molten image that swallowed her, and
then another shot hit her full in the back after she had
cleared the doors.*

Case takes the photo of Sarah floating in the pool and
turns it facedown. She glances up at Bob. He is a wall of
silent rage.

He pushes himself up on his arms and turns away. He
stands by the counter and rests his hands on the ledge of
the sink. He stares at the chipped face of the wall, a faded
yellow.

Case begins the walk from photo to photo. The next ones
are of the dog shot and stuffed down into the toilet and spittles of blood along the tub and tiles. The ones after that are
of the horse lying dead in its stall, its eyes gouged out and
its genitals hacked off and its groin damp and dark and
shiny.

Case turns to the photo of what was once a man's face.

Cyrus kneeled into Sam. He curled his fingers through the wire that trussed him up like a pig. He rammed him back against the wall. Cyrus took him by the cock with one hand and with the other scored a letter opener along Sam's teeth. "You like to put your tongue where it don't belong and get that black dick of yours hard."

The metal blade of the opener pried apart the row of white molars. Cyrus whispered into Sam's ear, "You're crossing over tonight, Mr. Hard Cock. And it'll be a slow crossing over and triple-X all the way."

Case sits there lost within the eyes of a dead man. A heartless host of horribles comes warring up through her belly. Junkie witch revisits revenants. A silver blade for gutting, and blood token prizes. Screaming apostles bent and misshapen in moments of life burglary. All headlight bright to the memory.

The next photos show Sam lying on the autopsy table. He has been cleaned up for viewing, with his eyes fixed in the half-moon of sleep. The shots after that frame each wound, followed by a series that focus on his right arm, each one cropped up closer and closer till they've framed an area of veins in the forearm that look to be bruised from a syringe.

"Was Sam a drug addict?"

Bob turns. "No."

"This is a syringe mark."

"Is it?"

The way he asks her, she thinks he might already know the answer and is working her toward it.

"Syringe marks are a specialty of mine. Was he an addict?"

Bob doesn't answer.

She lays the photos aside. She is being handled and she now knows it. The next stack comes upon her like a thunderbolt. A dozen or so of Sam as he was left after death.

She begins to feel the acrid taste of bile in her throat. Even though she's seen the dead before. Even though she's been in on a kill, playing one of Cyrus's catch dogs. Even with all that, the formal brooding flatness of each shot can in no way neutralize the complete, unadulterated fury behind how he had been cut and branded and dissected.

Her fingers slowly push each photo aside. Then her vision blurs. The ashes from her cigarette fall to the floor in a nervous turn.

Bob notices a slight hitch to her expression. "What?" he says.

She shakes her head in an odd, confused gesture.

"What?" he says again, coming forward.

She looks up at him as he looks down at the photo of Sam's chest, where pinned to his heart with a stiletto and stained with blood is a playing card, or what at least looks at that distance like a playing card.

"Is there a close-up picture of that card?"

"Why?"

"Is there?"

She watched the knife pierce then halve the breastbone of that yuppie prick dentist with his white BMW and his white stucco house and his white golf shoes and white capped teeth. The blood drenched his shirt in frenetic sprays and each thrust opened a new wound and released a rush of arterial fluid out into the air with a short hiss and soon there were only a few clean untouched spots left on his golf shirt and she couldn't help but think, as bent as it was at the time, that those spots were shaped like white orchids attached to a red gown. And as the last of his breath seeped out the wounds, Cyrus held the card up and ran it past his dimming eyes.

"You haven't answered my question."

"You haven't answered mine."

"The Judgment . . ."

"What is that?" he asks.

"The twentieth enigma of the Tarot. The angel signaling . . ."

"Judgment . . ." Bob leans down, crowding Case between one hand gripping the back of her chair and the other crabbed over the photo.

"Why did you stop at that?"

Her eyes tug at the photo of Sam's arm.

Bob's voice takes on that cold cop casualness. "Why did you stop at that?" he repeats.

Cyrus lifted the hypodermic case from his pocket. He opened it with care and removed the syringe, playing out the moment for all its texture. Shots could be heard down the hall, then Poncho's rending yelp. Granny Boy had scrabbled up on all fours alongside Sam, who struggled against the wire that held him. Granny Boy held up Gabi's picture for him to see and spoke of the obscenities he would play out on the girl. Cyrus filled the syringe with clear liquid from a vial and Sam cried out in hoarse gulps. Cyrus held the needle up before Sam's eyes, and he let a little fluid squirt a taste of torture out its silvery pin.

"Ah, poor Prometheus, without even a rock to hide behind."

Case spiders through the autopsy photos till she finds the one of Sam's arm. "Was it a paralytic he was injected with?"

His face draws closer to hers.

"Was it?"

He grabs her by the arms. "You've been asking me some pretty odd questions here."

"Was it?"

"What do you know?"

She looks down wild-eyed at the cracked and speckled linoleum floor. He can feel her arms shivering.

"Go away," she says.

"That's not an answer."

"Go away."

"Please . . ."

"I can't . . . Right now. No . . ."

"What do you know?"

"I'm not sure."

"I could make you talk to me till you are sure."

She pulls free and shoves herself away from the table. As she stands some of the photos spill onto the floor. Bob steps over them and grabs her again.

"Nothing? Is that it? Nothing?"

She rips free of his arm and takes another step back.

"What do you know? Tell me! What are you hiding here?"

She stares at him.

"What are you covering up?"

"I need to think," she says. "So, just go!"

He takes a step forward and she howls an ugly, scarred call: "I told you! Get out! Let me just think awhile! Let me . . . let me alone to just think this out!"

THE RITE OF SEPARATION

10

Case sits on the edge of the roof's coping. A shrunken form in the rain with her hands curled up inside her shirt. She watches Bob's car turn over with a chugging line of muffler smoke against the cold night air and the headlights pooling out into the darkling street. They slow as they pass the front of the building. She leans back, using the dove-gray mist to cloak her as she stares down into the void of the windshield. That dark vexed face of his will haunt her now.

The rain moves in disordered streams across the black tar roof, down the rusting black drainpipes. The rain washes away nothing. It never did. The sump we all live in is too vast.

The Ferryman sat with a joint *in the claw fingers of his prosthetic arm. He watched indifferently as Cyrus kicked the living shit out of Case. He sat on a flea-infested corduroy couch under a canvas tarp awning that stretched out from the slat and sideboard five-room hutch he'd built around an old trailer.*

Case tried to stand, but Cyrus kicked her in the stomach. "You want to defy me? You want to defy me?"

Lena watched from the perimeter of the awning's shade and winced as Cyrus kicked Case again. She cried and tried to speak out but the wind blew up and swallowed her words as the tarp riffed like a noisy banner of war.

The Ferryman's dogs, the pack of them, howled and turned wind circles along the boundary of the fight.

Case was on her knees. But as Cyrus shouted at her, one wobbly hand rose up in defiance and gave him the finger.

He put his boot in her face. It hit flush on. A tooth cracked like a cheap cup and blood sprung from both nostrils.

Case fell backward.

"You want to try me again, bitch . . ."

She lay there dazed, her arms splayed at odd angles like those of a starfish.

"I got another boot here."

The dogs sniffed and snarled at her body as it crabbed at the sand, and when the smell of blood juked their senses they began to rise up on each other with bared teeth fighting for position.

Among the rubble of the yard, Gutter leaned against a doorless antique Wedgwood stove. He played the white shell like a steel-drum street-corner artist, singing, "Freedom's just another word for . . ."

Lena rushed over and took it to him with her nails and handfuls of flung dirt, and she spit and kicked as Gutter kept right on keepin' on, just another baby-faced killer out of Grimm's Fairy Tales.

The Ferryman sat there with the joint resting neatly between those silver metal parrot fingers as Cyrus grabbed Case by the back of her leather vest and dragged her over the bleached ground and over a landslide of bottles and a low pile of castaway boards. Lena rushed up behind them. She whimpered and pleaded her lover's cause, and with the dogs strung out behind her they were like a goddamn fuckin' parade on their way to an execution.

The Ferryman leaned to one side and balanced himself on his good leg so he could stand. His prosthetic leg hitched with each step as he made his way across the shade to a trunk that he kept along the wall of the house. He used it to store weapon parts. In the top drawer was a designer Bijan .38 taken as part of a settlement for a lost half-kilo of smack.

Lena kept following behind Cyrus till he'd had enough and turned on her. He was still holding Case off the ground with one hand gripped onto the back of her vest when he caught Lena in the hip with his boot and sent her squabbling like a turkey back into the dogs.

Then he stood Case up. He held her in place long enough for her head to clear. She tottered slightly. Her eyes began to focus up. She spit blood out of her mouth.

He shoved her. "You want to walk . . ."

Her chest flared and drained.

He shoved her again. "Walk! Go on!"

The dogs had caught up now and were close around her boots. They slopped at the damp dark where the blood had clotted in the sand.

The Ferryman fired three fast shots into the air and a series of echoes throated back across the flats.

Cyrus's eyes peeled off in the Ferryman's direction, but the shade from the canvas tarp left the African's face unreadable.

"The dogs were making me crazy," he said.

Cyrus regarded the moment without the least expression. The Ferryman did not move. He remained where he was, posing with the joint, then punctuated the moment with a leisurely toke.

Cyrus pulled Case toward him. The blood and sweat had caked dust down her face, and she looked like some aboriginal dried mud doll. "Choose your madness, girl," he said, "because the catch dogs are on you."

I I

It is the first warm night of the season to come. The moon is moving into a new quarter above the rim of the high desert. A shard of snow-white finery against a black sky.

In his front yard, the Ferryman sits on a low stool beside Lena with his prosthetic leg stretched out. He is hunched within the arc of a single halogen lamp, his eyes tending to the fine and dexterous needlework at hand as he adds a new date to the back of Lena's ring finger—12/21/95.

It isn't the first time he's recorded a date after a kill.

Lena sits in an easy chair with her head leaning back against the musty mess of tuck and roll. She is hammered on smack, and her eyes sag and bob.

Music drifts out across the wildland over speakers hung along the eaves of the hutch. Gutter is inside the trailer, sucked up to the boob tube with a crack pipe and reruns of "Star Trek." And Wood. He is totally raw. He's punked on speed and giving the Ferryman a hyped-up rundown of the murder, laying out the whole night like some bob-eyed, jittering Herodotus.

"You should have seen us . . . Cyrus took us into that yuppie Christian tank and we . . . we ate their food . . . we drank their blood wine . . . we raped their women . . . we . . . we . . ." He fires an imaginary pistol down into the toilet, where he can still see that fluffy little mutt fighting for its life. "One more headstone for the Path. Yeah . . . We brought the jungle to that house. Blood and hair, baby . . ." His eyes are on fire. He weaves the fingers on both hands together. "That's what we were like . . . See . . ." He clamps his hands together in some warped gesture of family and prayer. "It was bang-move-bang-move-bang-bang-bang-move . . . Total fuckin' unity, and Gutter singing as he's popping shells into the chamber, and Granny Boy leaps over this white-bread bitch and . . ."

From inside the parked van comes Gabi's crying, cutting short Wood's little rant. Not full crying, but a pathetic gibbering that rises a bit then falls away or is muffled.

Wood glances at the van. "They must be puttin' the magic to her."

The Ferryman pays no mind to the crying nor to Wood as he puts the last flourish on the dated finger. He leans down and licks the back of Lena's hand. "Done, girl."

Her eyelids flutter. She takes a look at her finger. Another bone of pride for a twisted sister. With a weak turn of her head she waves a job well done.

As the Ferryman puts his needle and ink to rest the music begins to fill Lena's head with smoke. Some woman singing the dark night of the soul.

"I miss Case," she says.

The Ferryman moves off into the darkness.

"I miss the way we used to sleep together in the back of that van. I miss the way we used to kiss each other's arms after we shot each other up." Lena seems to drift. "I was the turtle, she was the bird. That was the whole thing between us."

The Ferryman says nothing.

"I wonder where she is now? Probably in some methadone clinic, copping a plea till she can get herself a score." Lena's voice fails a bit. "If she's alive at all." Her eyes slip away. "I miss her. Do you miss her?"

"I miss no one."

Lena looks up at the moon. It is like the slightest touch of light coming from an opening door.

"I only flirt with the living," says the Ferryman.

"I hope she ain't with the sheep," whispers Lena.

The Ferryman hears the girl inside the van begin to cry again.

• • •

Come midnight, Cyrus walks the ragged ridgeline north of the Ferryman's. With his poncho flaring in the wind he moves through the shifting shades of black. He looks off into the well of a playa set between the Calico Mountains and the Paradise Range. The forgotten ground of his youth, where the old woman Hannah had tried to raise him in her image and likeness.

He makes his way down to the valley floor through a slippery rampart of rocks. It is a slow night crossing the flat, chipped ground, and he leaves barely a boot track. He slips down into a dry riverbed, and up the far side he comes upon those granite rocks humped skyward like the fin of a great whale appearing out of a sand sea.

The old life comes back. The day you kill and move on from. He lights a match and holds it to the rock. Those paintings Hannah did are still there. Earth and air, fire and water. And the snake devouring itself, Ourabouris, the green head fang-wide and swallowing its orange tail.

He can see Hannah's eyes there in the head of the snake. Pagan jewels of beauty and knowledge, she called them, as she tried to usher his thoughts along the proper path. The old bitch could drink, too. Hold her juice and talk. A preeminent bullshit artist if there was one.

He blows out the match. He reaches for and fingers the loose gravel between a layer of stones. He finds a small pellet of limestone from the great rock fin and he swallows it. The world will be inside his belly, eventually.

Cyrus moves further out into the playa. The remains of Hannah's trailer are still there. Odd bits of the cinder block and glass stalagmite garden wall.

Life has finally come full circle with this most recent expression of his will at Via Princessa. He lets the years circle around him like the dust blowing across the Calico Range and revisits the chapters of his life.

He can feel the heat of that day, even now, when as a boy he was orphaned, tossed from a car by his mother and her military hump of a boyfriend. Cyrus had already been black-listed from the lives around him. The base psychiatrist was describing him as a sociopath, a potential criminal, while his mother was in a bathroom shooting up smack between her toes and Sergeant Joey, the human wallet she played camp-follower to, was in the serviceman's bar swigging down Jack Daniel's by the troughful as he swaggered through the zip-perheads he'd killed during the Korean War.

Fuck 'em all. Cyrus knew back then that life was a self-perpetuating fantasy of frauds. And that the only real demons to fear are those disguised as decent human beings. John Lee and fatboy proved that.

He watches as the dust blows through the rotting sieve of that old Airstream. Hannah was another piece of work. The grandmother of time, spitting earthy wisdoms from that pussy of a mouth. He put up with all that for a little bread and water and what he could con or steal. He got fucked try-ing to help John Lee close that deal. Of course, time re-warded him. He turned a lot of dreams to vapors on Via Princessa. That will be his Sistine Chapel.

He makes himself relive the ghostly years before the Path to reinforce the template of his strength. From the pretty province of juvenile halls to the manchild back alleys of Smack Road. All that time he watched them build up their Paradise as he went from giving blowjobs to beatings to black-throat lacerations to when he began the fight to beat the junk that robbed him of his will.

It was there, in that trailer, in that time, fighting down the withdrawal, that he found the true architect of the modern world. Where he found the essence behind the Son of Sam and Helter Skelter and Joseph Goebbels and Uncle Sam and the Pope and the Ku Klux Klan and the capitalist system and the Silent Majority. Where he found the only son of man— and he wasn't some jerk-off named Jesus. He was the architect who allowed for the zero-sum game with all its depravities. Who found beauty in blood, a christening through ultimate chaos. Who understood it was better to reign in some perilous extreme than to serve a life sentence of propriety out of fear. Fear that nothing is at the end of the road unless we cop a plea after a lifetime of shortcuts.

On that inflamed desert sea of night winds, Cyrus and his aggro band of young wolves sit like native warriors who've come through another day of dyin', together. He praises them. He reminds them of their place as bandogs taking on a bullshit society. As carriers of the great plague message. Their atrocities so far, culminating in the Via Princessa massacre, are a history replete and unto itself. Something horrible and haunted. Something for the pathetics to puzzle out. But ultimately, something to be acknowledged and idealized.

Most of them have been partying on smack, or ecstasy laced with a little battery acid, and cocaine with tequila chasers. But these foot soldiers for the Left-Handed Path are high on their own killings. They relive the blooding fury in that hilltop house. Cyrus begins to reshape the events as a myth, with a hot filmmaker's sense of pace and ferocity. Coloring the crime as an act of ultimate contempt, ultimate nonconformity, ultimate sacrifice, ultimate freedom, ultimate joy . . . ultimate service. It is, he says, a fixed point of infamy in a heaven of faulted lights, and their names will one day be as important to their god as the saints are to Christ the pig.

They can see themselves in Cyrus. The night culminates with Wood's initiation into the inner circle of death coups, as this was his first real hunt. Each member of the tribe has a special insignia: Gutter has a safety pin awled through his nose, Lena the dates of kills tattooed on her fingers. Cyrus presents Wood with patches of red cloth. On these he will have painted in white the anarchist's *A*, the sign of their ultimate meaning. When Wood asks Cyrus where he'll wear the trademark, Cyrus tells him over the most important path of his existence—his lifeline.

12

For the next two days Bob tries to call Case. An endless series of phone voices tells him, "She's not here," "We can't find her," "No one answers when we knock." Even Anne cannot, or will not, help him.

Over dinner Bob explains to Arthur what's transpired. Arthur recoils at the thought that something like her might have knowledge about "his" Gabi that Bob can't get. The rest of the meal is passed in silence, with Arthur mostly staring at his food and refusing Bob's meager attempts at conversation.

Anne sits at her desk, afraid for Case's life. "It's one thing to offer a man advice, but to want to go out and attempt to find the girl . . ."

Case is standing at the window, barefoot, looking out through the curtains at a pool of street light.

"If you were stronger. More . . ."

"I don't think I'll ever be more . . . And I don't think the girl could wait till I'm strong enough."

"If he took her."

"He took her."

"You can't be sure."

Case turns, her eyes bleak with certainty.

"You can't be sure," warns Anne.

"I know the blood sign of my countrymen."

"What kind of talk is that?"

"Down and dirty, but true."

"You don't even know if she's alive."

The curtains shift slightly as if a touch of air brushed past them.

"I read the sign of my countrymen," Case says again.

"What are you talking about?"

"Oh, Jesus," says Case. "He showed me one of the police murder-scene photos. This Hightower, cop. The mother-fucker who was dead had this Tarot card pinned to his chest . . . the Judgment . . . the twentieth enigma of the Tarot . . . That is Cyrus's sign game. His signature. He's the bringer of death. The taker of the soul. It's like a mock on the card.

"It was him, Anne. And I'll tell you something else. This was punishment to the max. It was fuck you in the face."

Case looks over at the desk, where she has set down the picture of Gabi that Bob slipped under her door as a "sub-tle" reminder after he was thrown out. She walks over and fingers the snapshot. "Cyrus used to say that once all the bullshit is stripped away, all that's left is what there was to begin with."

Anne sees Case glance at her arms, where the pussed blister marks from the needle are now dark thumbprints of healing.

"Redemption has a lot of faces," says Anne. "You don't need to find it by . . ."

A fierce look comes across Case's face. "I don't want to hear that. Don't try and brainfuck me by turning this around and making it some sort of redemption thing. That's so much Sermon-on-the-Mount crap and no better than when Cyrus used to lay on us one of his rants about the Left-Handed Path. We only agreed with him 'cause we needed to have something up our arms. That idea you have in your head doesn't put anything up my arm."

"Why, then?"

Case leans down and across the desk. "Do you have any idea what is going to happen to that girl?"

Anne sits there trying, trying to imagine what for Case is just simple memory.

"It's me times seven. He'll take that pretty-pretty and load her up on junk, and pretty soon he'll have her on her knees in some crack house takin' it up the ass from some infected junkie. He'll take pictures of it. Maybe video it. He'll make her go down on him while he shows her the pictures. He'll fuck with her till the movie's done, and over the credits he'll hang her upside down naked, and he'll field-dress her by gutting her from clit to . . ."

The words collapse in Case's mouth. Anne is too unsettled to speak.

"You ask why," Case says. "Maybe I miss the fuckin' blood. Maybe it's time to get a little retribution. Maybe it's just time."

Anne sits back. She tries to look into her psychologist's bag of magic for a response, but this demands the kind of primal honesty the job description doesn't include.

"They'll never find her," Case whispers. "Never. I might. I might get close. There's always a way to get close, if you know how to grovel. Maybe then I get her back. If not, I may get close enough to force them to kill her quick. At least that."

13

Case can read the sign PARADISE HILLS as soon as she makes the turn off Soledad Canyon Road. Bronze letters stamped into the fake stone columns on both sides of the entrance to the tract are lit by blue lights.

Nice friggin' name, she thinks. A real selling point for some hungry family with a couple of kids.

She drives up through the identical streets looking for

Bob's address. Something about these gully and hillside developments, some morbid stamp they leave on the consciousness of the land, has always affected her badly. Case didn't call, and Bob isn't home when she gets there. She waits, sitting on the side runner of the truck, smoking. In time a young couple with a Lab walk past. So does an older woman with bluish puffed hair in a running suit. They pass silently, but they eye Case through their own brand of family values.

The first thing Bob sees when he comes around the corner is a truck in his driveway. Since the murder, anything different or suspicious and he's reaching over to the glove compartment for his pistol.

He pulls up slowly, angling his car so the headlights shine obliquely through the truck's rear windshield. He sits there waiting for something or someone to move. He scans the front of the house. He shuts off the engine, and now it's just him and the silence and a dusky trail of headlights. He can feel his heartbeat quicken.

A moment later he spots a hand snake around the headrest in the truck. A body wearing a rummagy buckskin coat pulls itself up into view. The head turns. Bob sees that it's Case. She has an unlit cigarette poised between her lips. She cups her hands over her eyes as she looks back into the headlights.

Bob feels a sudden twinge of anticipation. A sonar dot of hope kicking up a little in the pit of his stomach. But he doesn't move.

Case gets out of the truck and walks over to his driver's window. She leans in. "Hey," she says. Then she notices the pistol across his lap. "I hope you ain't gonna shoot me."

"I didn't recognize your truck. And ever since the murder . . ."

"Let's talk," she says.

Bob looks her over closely. For the first time, he notices within those wild black pupils an acute state of focus. He climbs out of the car, slips the pistol into his coat pocket. He sees across the street a kitchen curtain close.

"I guess you've been here awhile."

"Long enough for the natives to pass the word."

He starts up the driveway. "Come on inside, I'll make us some coffee."

"No, thanks."

He stops, turns. She stands there uncomfortably and points past the house. "Let's just walk."

They cross the road. Bob's house is on a dead end at the back of the development. On the downslide of the slope. The land beyond is part of Angeles National Forest. Just scrub hills, really.

"How long you live here?" Case asks.

"All through my marriage. Gabi was born here. My father-in-law developed this tract. He helped me out buying the place by carrying the paper."

They walk out into a large field where the curb ends. It overlooks the development. "After the divorce, Sarah didn't want to stay. And I guess I wasn't ready to leave."

Case can see all the way down to the entrance of the tract, where two pooling blue eyes of light stare back.

Bob stops. "Why did you come?"

Case looks for a match to light her cigarette. "This isn't easy for me, okay?"

He nods, finds a match in his pocket, lights it.

"Not fuckin' easy." She leans into the flame, inhales. "Not easy to look you in the eye and tell you what I come to tell you."

He starts to feel a little apprehensive. "Okay."

"From what I saw in those pictures, the way . . . that man . . . was tortured." She half turns away. "I believe I know who took your daughter."

Bob scuffs his boot at the sand.

Case continues. "If so, I believe . . . she's alive."

Bob takes a long breath. His mind is a river of questions, but he holds back. He comes up to Case. "What did you see in the pictures?"

"Come on. The fuckin' needle marks in his arm. He was either a junkie or he was stung by a paralytic. He was meant to suffer. And that card pinned to his chest. You wouldn't cop to it—"

"You were right about both."

Her nostrils flare.

"We're gonna have a real talk now," he says. "Right?"

"Yeah."

"Who do you think took Gabi?"

"Call them my family. Actually, blood tribe would be closer to the truth."

"How do you know it's them?"

"Let's just say Cyrus is consistent."

"Cyrus?"

"Yeah. He's the patriarch of the group. Lead wolf. Big Brother of the Holding Company. The Bad Angel. Mr. Psych Job. Whatever name you want to call it."

"What's his last name?"

"I have no idea."

"How do you know it's Cyrus?"

"How do I know? I told you . . ."

"You said he's consistent. What does that mean?"

"He's killed like that before."

Bob's eyes become small pitiless spots. "How do you know that?"

Case rubs at her mouth with the heel of her hand, but hangs back on an answer. Bob has an idea of what he is going to hear and knows that if he wants to buy a little hope he'll have to sell a little truth.

"Tonight," he says, "I'm just a father standing in a field, looking for his daughter and talking to . . . a stranger."

She understands. "I've been in on a kill," she says.

Bob rocks back and forth on his heels. It has become so quiet inside his head that he can hear the night lizards scurrying over the rocks.

"Why do you think she's alive?"

"He didn't go into that house by accident. Didn't kill them by accident. This was blood. This was revenge. Maybe Sam was in some deal and he scammed somebody close to Cyrus. Maybe Cyrus was paid to do him." She hesitates. "Maybe he was paid to do your ex-wife. But taking the girl. He did that to get back at somebody. Maybe this is about you?"

It's all a little too much. Each sentence is like a cigarette being burned into his skin.

"How many are there in the pack?" he asks.

"I don't know now. Maybe four. Maybe seven."

"You run with them long?"

"Since I was ten."

Ten, he thinks. What the fuck was she at ten?

"When was the last time you saw them?" he asks.

"Two years ago." Her face saddens a bit. "One of them . . . about a year ago."

He takes a cigarette and lights it. He inhales quickly. His jaw is flexing. She can see he's got a semi's worth of rage inside, and if he could barrel down on her he would. There has to be blame somewhere, right?

"Would you give me descriptions of them all?"

"I will, if that's what you want. But if you're gonna try and get to them using the cops out of L.A. County or even the FBI, forget it."

"Forget it?"

"You don't know this man. He is a follower of the Left-

Handed Path. The world of the devil. And as warped as it is, you can forget this shit about gettin' your hands on him. He'll go down like those religious freaks in Texas the FBI jumped a couple of years back. And he'll make sure of one thing; he'll kill your kid before they take him. You know what he used to do for kicks? He used to find out where the heads of SWAT teams lived, and he'd sneak into their houses at night, crawling right up to their beds. He'd do it just for practice. Manson used to do that. He's also got friends who are cops. Guys he sells drugs to. Guys who are into Satan. Freaks in flag blue. You want your kid back, you can't go that way. You got to take it on the road yourself. Without the Boy Scout uniform."

"Alright. Suppose I do. How do I find them?"

"Follow the fuckin' wind."

"I need more than that. If my daughter is alive, where do I start? How do I start, if I don't put out an APB?"

"We just did."

"What do you mean?"

"Get yourself five grand in cash. At least that much. We could be on the road awhile. We'll drive and get us some guns. Stuff that's not traceable. Call me when you got the money and you're ready."

He looks at her oddly, confused. She turns to walk back to the street and her truck.

"Hey, I don't understand," he says.

She keeps walking, says nothing.

"Hey, stop."

She stops.

"I don't understand."

"You and me. We're going on the road to try and get her back."

"You?"

"Yeah. Me. Unless you want to leave it to a bunch of drumheads who usually can't find their dick in their own underwear, or who are too corrupt or lazy to bother. You want that, say so. And it's done. You call it."

"How do you fit in?"

"This isn't tract-home America you're dealing with. This shit is cold. It's drugs and blood and cum, and it's fucked so bad you ain't got no idea. None. It's not like stopping on Hollywood Boulevard at some satanic bookstore and picking up a few goodies on the occult. This is where people get off by smothering just plain folk like your . . . ex-wife and her husband."

While he is thinking all this over, while he is judging and weighing, she adds, "And no offense, but you, you can't go alone. I mean, fuck. You just don't send sheep to hunt wolves."

14

"I don't know how long I'll be gone, but my leave of absence papers are on the dining-room table."

Arthur leans against the bathroom doorjamb as Bob fills his shaving grip with a few last things from the medicine chest.

"I wish you'd reconsider this," says Arthur.

Bob closes the medicine-chest door. He can see Arthur there behind him in the mirror, his face distraught. Bob's eyes shift back to himself. He has let his mustache grow to alter his appearance and not come across so clean. For a moment he studies his own face as if the mirror somehow had the power to remind him of who he was and to center him to that.

"This is reckless, son, and dangerous."

Bob slips past him and starts down the hall. "I'm sorry,

leaving John Lee to you. But he's not gonna be happy about what I've done. And I'm sure he'd try and stop me. He might order me, then what? He's gonna know I lied to him about going to see the girl. I figure I'll probably lose my job."

"I'll take care of that, John Lee won't . . ."

"Let it be, Arthur, please. I made my decision, I'll live with the consequences."

Bob crosses the living room. Arthur is a step behind.

Bob stops at his desk. "I'll call you every chance I get."

Arthur comes up beside him, looks out the window to where Case is leaning against the side panel of the pickup in the driveway. She is smoking, looking off to nowhere in particular. She wears sunglasses, torn black jeans, a sleeveless cut-off shirt. Arthur can see that not only are her arms tattooed, but her back and stomach are both decaled.

"If something happens to you . . ."

"I'll be alright."

"You sure?"

"I'm sure we can't go on like this."

"No, I guess not." He shakes his head in a miserable ruffle at the prospect of the things that lie ahead and repeats, "I guess not."

Bob opens the desk drawer. He takes out two manila envelopes and a money belt. He opens an envelope. It's flush with packages of bills, thirty-five hundred dollars' worth. He tears the wrapping off one package, breaks it down into small pads of bills, and works them into one cloth pocket of the money belt.

Arthur is still watching Case. She flicks her ashes into the back of the truck, then her sunglasses lock on Arthur a moment. "She's such a tramped-out excuse of a thing. I wouldn't trust going on the road with her."

"I don't entirely trust her myself."

"Then why . . ."

"We've been over that." Bob is growing angry. He's got a head full of bad nerves, and this conversation isn't helping.

And leaving Arthur like this—another little gutting he's got to live with.

"If Gabi's dead . . ."

"Don't talk like that, I won't hear it."

"If she is, we have to know. But if she's alive, and that woman thinks she is, and thinks she knows who took her, I want to get her back."

"And you put your faith in her?"

"I put my faith in God. Her, I'm traveling with."

"What's in it for her?"

Bob stops a moment and glances out the window. It is a question that has plagued him since he and Case walked that field behind the house.

"Did she ask you for money?"

"No."

"Well? Doesn't it worry you?"

Bob rips open the second manila envelope. It is also filled with thirty-five hundred in bills. "The truth will become known, won't it, Arthur?"

"Jesus, boy. How do you know she won't try and sell you out?"

"I don't."

"How do you know she won't rob you?"

"I don't."

"How do you know she won't . . ."

Bob cuts him off: "I don't." He makes an angry sound and goes back to loading the pockets of the money belt.

"I'm not sure what I'm getting into. I admit that. But I'm going. I'm going. I'm dying inside, do you understand, Arthur? I'm dying. A little bit every day I'm dying. My child is out there. She could be suffering, or . . ."

His voice breaks. He puts the money belt down. "Fuck it all. It's better I do it right and die all at one time trying to find her."

Bob just hangs there, like a marionette waiting for a pair of enthusiastic hands. Arthur takes the money belt and finishes putting the small pads of bills into the cloth pockets, letting Bob know he'll concede to his will.

"Don't talk about dying, okay? Don't. There won't be any more of that."

Bob nods. He moves to close the desk drawer and notices his and Sarah's wedding picture. It shocks him to see it now. It is still where Sarah tucked it in that drawer the night she told him she was leaving.

Her timeless smile. Everything he looked for in life was in that smile. Every time he looked at that portrait, he was certain she was the rock upon which his life would be built. But now. All that's left is an image printed on a piece of paper left in a drawer, along with an old checkbook and a few letters and some dried-out stamps. Yet he cannot bear to close the drawer.

Case is suffering her own bleak bout of apprehension when the front door opens. Arthur gives her the hard once-over as he and Bob come down the walkway. Bob has two carryalls and a canvas coat. He dumps them into the flatbed of the pickup. He looks across the back of the truck to Case, who waits quietly.

They have arrived at the moment when they must jump from the ledge of predictable routine and into the ocean of the unknown. And neither looks comfortable, nor ready.

"Alright?" he says.

She nods.

Bob walks back toward the passenger door where Arthur stands waiting for him. Arthur puts out his hands and the two men hug. It is a long and somber moment. Arthur starts to cry. He slaps Bob's shoulders tenderly, as if he were a baby he was patting to sleep.

Case moves along the side of the truck toward the driver's door, watching them all the while. She can feel the sun on the back of her neck and hear children on bikes down the street. Watching Arthur and Bob only aggravates her sense of isolation and loneliness. It is the kind of moment she could deal with only when she was loaded. As she opens the driver's-side door, Arthur calls out to her.

"Hold on," he says.

He comes around the truck. "I want you to know something. I don't trust you a rat's ass worth. I know what those veins suck up. Now if something happens to my boy out there . . . Your fault. His fault. Nobody's fault. I won't put it under an act-of-God clause. You won't be able to make any excuse that will save your ass with me. You understand?"

Case says nothing. She looks past Arthur's shoulder at Bob, who has been listening to the whole conversation. Silently he climbs into the passenger seat. She presses her tongue against her upper lip and tries to slide around Arthur's surly frame.

He slips in front of her again. "You understand?"

She looks away, takes off her sunglasses, and, turning back, presses them right into his sternum and forces him back a step. She comes around him quick and climbs up into the cab. She turns and leans back against the open door. She puts her sunglasses back on and eyes him levelly.

"I'm blown away," she says. "You know that? Just blown away. As a matter of fact, it's left me a little wet between my fuckin' legs."

I 5

Bob stares out the window, watching the descending blocks of tract homes slip by.

"You didn't say anything back there. I'd like to know what you think."

He turns to Case. "Forget it."

"Forget it?"

"You're trying to help, so I don't want to judge."

"Is that so?"

"That's so."

Silence follows. Bob notices a man in shorts spraying his roses with pesticide. A woman hauling bags of groceries from the back of a minivan while a crying kid drags along behind her. There's a dog sleeping in a driveway, his muscles flexing through some dreamy chase. Life's details going by in a stately slow motion. It's all slipping away. He can feel it.

She eyes him hard. "You don't want to answer, okay. But I'd like to know."

"Alright," he says. "Alright. I believe if you'd had enough strength of character none of what happened to you would have happened."

He tries not to sound derogatory, nor to appear as if this whole fuckin' stretch of conversation is just too distasteful. "You want the truth. You got it."

Case shifts a bit in her seat. There is a sardonic clip to her voice. "Yeah, but I'm not quite sure I wanted a lethal dose."

She had no idea what town it was. Just another "trick" stop somewhere in Texas. Texas: too much sun, too much dust, too much space. And always too many miles between places you could politely piss in.

She couldn't have been more than twelve at the time. Yet she had the drill down cold. Cyrus got a room in some shit motel. She took a shower, put on a little perfume, a little lip-stick. She opened the window, no matter how hot a day it was, to get out the stink of Lysol and fumigants. She'd heat a spoon, shoot up. And then she'd wait like a lady.

That's how it went down in the redneck border country where grease and beer and Jesus were specialties of the house. Everything there was as real as the cinder block it was built on.

She sat naked on the edge of the bed. The sheets were coarse, cheap. Through a crack in the door she saw money

change hands. A flush of daylight followed along with
sounds of the highway. A middle-aged trucker and his old
lady filled up the room.

A perfectly good species of white trash. Overweight some,
baggy jeans, flannel shirts. A little gristle around the eyes.
They gave Case a good looking over.

She could smell the body odor on them as she waited. She
reached over to an ashtray by the nightstand. Her fingers
fumbled for the cigarette beside the hypo and spoon. She
drew in deeply and blew smoke out her nose. Her arms already looked like the odometer on them had been run pretty
far. She tried a coquettish smile. She was mimicking the
women she'd seen on television when they come on just so.

"Half an hour," said Cyrus. "And I want to get her back
in pretty much the same shape I left her in."

The woman nodded and sat. The bed sagged like an old
set of lungs. Cyrus closed the door behind him. One good
shot of smack had Case drifting.

The woman said, "You got nice white skin, baby doll."

Her trucker boyfriend took his John Wayne Stetson,
creased the brim, and laid it neatly on a table. He began to
undo his belt. It had a huge gold eagle buckle that shined. It
made a loud click as it snapped open.

The woman slid her coarse red fingers up between Case's
legs, which came apart with a slight rustle of sheet.
"Mommy and Daddy always wanted to have a little girl of
their own."

Case gets a quick hit of herself in the rearview mirror. Her
skin is drawn and white. A penny-size five-pronged star
stands out on her left cheek. She wonders why in the hell
that incident in Texas came to mind. Why right now? You get
off junk, you start to try and track these things. Sometimes
it's just busywork, like some burned-out worker ant going
from nest to nest looking for queens. But sometimes . . .
sometimes you want to try to follow that mystery up through
the main vein and back to the source.

She wonders if it's because at this minute she feels like a hooker again, sitting beside some trick with his squat answers but willing to pay for trade. No judgments, of course.

Maybe it's that. But maybe it's the child. Maybe seeing herself in the deep past is envisioning the child in the foreseeable future. Maybe imagining it that way will keep her angry and hateful. And she can use that diseased hate to give her the zealot's strength she needs to cut the demon down to size.

Maybe it's that. She hopes it's that.

"You a good Christian fellow, Hightower?"

Bob reaches for a cigarette in his shirt pocket.

"Are you?"

He taps the edge of it on the dash, packing it down. "I guess."

"You guess? You don't know if you're a good Christian fellow?"

There's a tone to "good Christian fellow."

"What's the point?" he says.

"Well, Mr. Good Christian Fellow. You ought to thank that god of yours."

"Yeah?"

"Yeah. You see, if it wasn't for my lack of character, I wouldn't have been where I was. Experiencing what I did. Screwing up all the way. And so I wouldn't be able to be here now, trying to help you. How do you like it with that spin?"

He lights his cigarette. It's a question he doesn't have an answer for. An apology would be simple enough, but that's not in the cards.

THE RITE OF
TRANSITION

16

Case pushes the Dakota pickup out Route 138, Palmdale Boulevard, and then they take the hard turn on Route 15, heading northeast to Barstow.

"Where are we goin'?"

"The desert. To see the guy who's gonna dress us for the party. But you don't say anything about what we're doin'."

"No . . ."

"No. You leave that to me. You see, this guy, he knows Cyrus, too."

They drive up through Barstow in silence.

The Dakota is just body primer puttied over a shell of ripples and bumps, but Bob can hear the engine's been bored out and has plenty of muscle, and when Case drives her boot against the accelerator the chassis snaps forward like a buffed halfback.

"Nice truck."

"Yeah. I'd like to own one like it someday."

As Bob glances at Case, he can see she's grinning slightly.

"Don't tell me," he says.

"No, sir, Mr. Hightower, sir. It ain't hot, sir. A little warm maybe, but not hot."

At the Calico Road exit the ruins of the old mine form a wind wall along the hogback. A brown one-dimensional world pitted against the sun. She follows Paradise Springs Road. It's spotted with shacks and cinder-block pit stops for liquor. There are billboards and abandoned Dumpsters. The ground is marked by coyote prints and dirt-bike tracks. What is left of a neon sign is now just a metal rim framing a few chevrons of white plastic. It rises up on a pole, in a lot where only the cement-block foundation of someone's hard work is left to tell the tale.

"Ravens," she says.

Bob has been watching all that passes out the window. He turns, and she motions with her chin toward the Dumpsters.

A small communal roost sits in a crafty lineup along the rim of a Dumpster. In the dry haze of afternoon they look like black and purple shapes painted there, watching.

"I was reading a book about Indians," remarks Case. "In myths of a lot of tribes in the West, the raven created the world. He was interesting, that raven. 'Cause he was both creator and trickster. This trickster, he's sort of like God with an edge, or at least a sense of humor. Would do as he pleased. The book said the raven created mosquitoes 'cause man had it too easy. Fuckin' A. I wonder if he created Demerol to cut the edge off all them mosquito bites.

"I read a lot since I got off junk. It helps keep me . . . occupied. You know what I mean? Helps keep away the hot burns that go on inside my head. In this book it said at first the raven made man out of rock. But he was too durable. So, raven, he turned around and remade man out of dust. What a joker, huh?

"I'm not into that god-myth dance," she says. "But the dust part . . ."

He says nothing, just watches those bristly crows lined up along the Dumpster like a scale of notes and thinks to himself, We better be more durable than dust.

The Dakota moves like a sloop over the dunes. Its tires spin out clay pinwheels on what may miserably be called a road. Then, upon one wave of sand, gloating there in the sun like some ephemeral gatepost at the frontier, is the Ferryman's.

"Un-American Airlines, arriving on schedule," says Case.

Bob sits up in his seat to get a better look. Ahead, a dark tangle of slatboard and tin and cinder blocks stolen from a thousand piles of refuse along the road. A sort of Quonset castle around a shiny trailer. An alchemist's kingdom of scraps and draff.

As the Dakota circles the front yard, the Ferryman's dogs come lunging out from between shadows and behind shrubs of cholla and worn couches. They charge the pickup, barking and snarling at the tires. When it stops, they press the doors with their front paws, scraping the metal. They lean in toward the windows with wet, white teeth to make their point. Bob sits back, but Case leans right into them, snarling and laughing and calling each by name.

Bob hears a voice from behind the truck ordering the dogs down. He turns.

Out of the rippling shadow of the tarp awning, the Ferryman steps into the daylight. He's wearing a smock kaftan made of an old gray striped sheet and jean shorts and cowboy boots. They're white alligator skin, scarred from the brush. His skin has a glossy chocolate shine. As he comes hitching forward with his prosthetic arm and leg, and those dogs whirling around him, he's like some biomechanical entity.

"You just be cool now, okay?" she says to Bob.

"I'll play my part."

"Right."

Case comes high-stepping out of the pickup. "Ferryman."

"Girl."

He slips that claw and arm around her and slides the claw up along her ass. They kiss and his tongue takes a little turn inside her mouth. He steps back, looks at her arms.

"You kept up with the living, heh, girl?"

"Just call me Little Miss Sunshine."

"Ready for prime time?"

"Sign me up."

She eyes the place. "I see you redecorated."

"As long as there's people and garbage, I'm in business."

They flash on each other a little longer. Do a real surfacy rap about "the old days." Then the Ferryman checks out Bob, who has been pretty much a snapshot in the background.

"What do they call this?"

"They call this . . . Bob. His last name will be whatever is on his new ID."

"Hey, Bob Whatever."

Bob comes forward. "Hi." He puts out his hand to shake. The Ferryman has no interest in it.

"Did you get me some armor?" asks Case.

"I got a whole toy store for you to choose from."

"Same place?"

He nods.

Case heads for the old pine-wood trunk lumped up in the shadows against the side of the trailer.

"Shall I do his ID first?"

"Decal work first." She runs her fingers up her arm. "I want some shit with real bite, too. No street-shop shit."

Bob starts to get an idea what Case is talking about, and it's something she hadn't discussed with him. He watches the Ferryman slide into the recess under the awning. Bob comes closer and sees him maneuvering a bar on wheels toward an easy chair. The bar has been fitted out as a portable tattoo artist's studio pallet.

The Ferryman checks Bob out. "You got some nice WASP skin there, Bob Whatever. This ink is gonna kiss you good."

It's not something he'd counted on. He finds tattoos classless and unsightly. A sort of permanent defilement. Bob goes over to Case. She has the trunk open and is handling a number of semiautomatics and revolvers that are laid out on the top shelf.

"I need to talk to you."

"Sure."

"I thought we were coming here for guns."

She points down at the row of weapons. "What are those?"

He leads her a few steps off and speaks lower so the Ferryman won't hear. "But what's the point of this tattoo shit? I don't want to look like some—"

"That is the point."

He goes to speak; she cuts him off. "Hear me now. Suppose come Sunday I went with you down to your nice little Paradise Hills Church. And I sit next to you looking just like I am now. You think I might get a few stares? You think most minds wouldn't be made up space-shuttle fast about me? You think I got zero survival rate in that social club of theirs? Well, you're walking into a different church now. And it's just as bigoted as yours. Only they won't kill with looks. And you don't look like you'd be with me. Now, the Ferryman ain't gonna turn you into a walking art show. But you got to show."

Bob breathes a long dry sigh. He watches the Ferryman set up shop.

"Why didn't you tell me this before, on the way out here?"

" 'Cause I didn't want to have this discussion more than once."

"Well, I don't like surprises."

"Then don't be surprised by anything."

"Don't fuck with me this way."

He turns and walks away. She kneels down and starts to check out the weapons. The bum's rush hits her full force. A real gut gashing. The whole fucking nine yards of heart plunder. She can imagine the juice going up her arm, she can feel its warmth. She can smell the heat coming off the needle and the backs of her arms going limp with cherry bumps.

She holds herself together by holding the trunk, by staring at the weapons, by conjuring the blood they'll spend. The fucking anxiety comes out of nowhere. Out of nowhere . . . shit!

Just breathe. Don't negative-think the whole thing with this Bob Whatever goin' south into Crapperville. Just breathe.

17

John Lee passes the morning with a number of other prominent law enforcement officers from the northern and western valley towns. They are together at a news conference in a show of force to back up Chief Randy Adams of Simi Valley.

The previous week at a city council meeting, Chief Adams had asked for tighter restrictions on handguns sold in Simi Valley. He'd asked that the applicants pass mental exams, get fingerprinted, and buy a million dollars in life insurance. The NRA, which was represented by its own show of force, booed and catcalled rudely at such anti-American ideas. After all, this is the nation of *The Deerslayer*, Darwinism, and Disney's *Davy Crockett*.

All this had started because a Simi Valley councilwoman named Sandi Webb, a pro-gun zealot, had been lobbying for the city to make it easier for residents to arm themselves.

The whole series of incidents had become a public relations nightmare for the quiet little bedroom community. It didn't help matters that Ms. Webb was known to travel to Los Angeles armed with a gun and that in Washington she had politely flipped off Senator Feinstein at a discussion over the assault weapons ban.

John Lee's speech is his usual taciturn, slim-volumed lecture. The stubborn party line on gun control and stiffer legal sentencing that falls from the lips of every U.S. chief of police and head of a sheriff's department. Afterward, reporters

draw John Lee into a question-and-answer party about the
Via Princessa murders.

The reporters beat him up pretty good, looking for some
fresh quote for the six o'clock news, but all they end up with
is a lot of slippery jargon. Before leaving to drive home,
John Lee goes into the bathroom and, seeing he's alone,
pukes. He may be able to hold the truth down, but for his
belly it's a tougher slide.

John Lee is slugging down his second Greyhound when
Arthur shows up at his house.

"Talking about the power of positive thinking," John Lee
says. "I was getting ready to call you. I felt like gettin'
loaded. You want a drink?"

"No, thanks."

John Lee is sloppily making toward the living room.
"Don't say no. Please."

John Lee always did get stiff easy. It wasn't a point of
pride with him, but . . .

"Come on. Just one. There's nothing worse than ruining
your liver alone."

"Well, when you put that kind of spin on it, who could
say no."

As Arthur follows John Lee to the bar at the far end of the
living room, he looks up one hallway toward the bedrooms
and then down a short hall to the kitchen. "Maureen here?"

"Maureen, no, thank God. It's the maid's night out. Bad
joke, I know."

John Lee slips around the bar and puts his hands out like
the homey shape of death embracing its next corpse. "What
may I serve you, sir?"

Arthur holds up his hand, spreading the thumb and index
finger about two inches apart.

"An admirable distance of a choice, sir."

John Lee pours three hard jiggers of Scotch into a glass
and then adds a single cube of ice. "Let her sail."

The two glasses touch and sound off one clean note.

"Here's to friendship," says John Lee.

"Friendship."

"It's all we have, you know." Then, as if he were burned down with disappointment, adds, "Really."

"Yeah," says Arthur. He sips his Scotch, then almost as an afterthought, he says, "And family."

"Family." John Lee's mouth sneers into the womb of the glass. "Now, are we talking the Brady Bunch family or the Manson family?"

He laughs, his fingers fumble gathering up his drink.

"Jesus, when you're loaded."

"Who's loaded?" John Lee looks down at his hands. "'Cause my hands are stumbling over to my drink? I'm suffering from an early case of Parkinson's, is all."

"John Lee, for . . ."

"I am."

Arthur just shakes his head. The whole reason he came over is getting sidetracked by the ridiculous. But he knows he's got to drop the truth on him. He reaches inside his coat pocket and takes out the envelope Bob gave him. He slides it across the bar.

"You need to read this."

John Lee puts his cocktail down. "What is it? My Dear John letter. You breaking up with me after all these years?"

"Just read it."

Arthur waits, watches John Lee have at it. He does a little mental accounting while he waits.

You have two men. They've pretty much walked their world together. Cut the same years. Bled in rituals. Laughed through their disgraces. Toughed out more than enough downers. Shared crimes, inconsequential and otherwise. Survived all that fast-food social bullshit of the seventies and eighties. But he agonizes over whether, if he met John Lee cold, sat down in a bar with him and had a few drinks, just like now, would they have anything in common? Would there be anything of character to moor their boats to? Probably not. John Lee has slipped away since . . .

"You didn't stop him!"

"I couldn't," says Arthur.

"Couldn't, or didn't?"

"Couldn't."

"I don't believe it."

"I tried. What do you think, I'd let him just go off—"

"Shut the fuck up a minute," shouts John Lee. He stands there seething. He flashes on bits of the letter: "She was in a cult . . . believes she has information . . . a feeling Gabi is alive . . ." He checks to see if the girl is named in the letter. She isn't.

"What's the girl's name?" asks John Lee.

"I don't know."

"What did she look like?"

"She was a junkie."

"What did she look like?"

"Medium height. Thin. Large eyes, short hair. Clean her up she wouldn't be half ba—"

"Well, this is fuckin' brilliant!" John Lee is dead cold sober. His mind is working through the faces he's seen run with Cyrus, quick as fingers working the beads of an abacus. It's not the girl he saw with him the night of the murder. He's sure of that.

He takes a long drink of his cocktail. Long enough so it eats at the horror that's setting in.

Arthur sees how bad John Lee looks, and he's worried now he didn't stop Bob.

"Just fuckin' brilliant."

"I couldn't tie him down."

"You could have called me right then."

"I thought about it, but if there was one chance in a million of getting Gabi back . . . I mean, we haven't had one break in this thing and . . ."

"Jesus, Arthur. How stupid could you be letting something like this happen? She could end up cutting his throat when he's asleep and dumping him in a hole somewhere, and he won't be found till some idiot hiker stumbles over a skull and . . ."

"Alright, goddamn it. Enough. I fucked up."

18

The Ferryman has pretty much outlined the great myth he planned to ink. Scarified on Bob's biceps is a video camera humanized to resemble the deformed Quasimodo. From its lens eye, drooping down over the broken lamplight jaw, comes blossoming smoke that shapes up Bob's shoulder and across part of his chest like a wing, or a shroud. Its black-lined span has talons on seven bony peaks.

Throughout the wing, or shroud, are hideous faces. Above the hunched bell ringer are two tattered flags. The motto on the first is ONE LOVE and on the second, HELTER SKELTER.

"It'll all be in hues of black," the Ferryman tells Bob. "You got the perfect skin for black."

Bob sits there, not moving, not joining in conversation.

"It'll be like the Flashman meets Fra Angelico. You ever read any of the Flashman books?"

"No."

"No. Too bad. You don't know what I'm talking about, then. But they have real style. Now about Fra Angelico. You ever see any of his paintings or see a book of his paintings?"

"No."

"No. Well, shit. We just ain't got nothing in common to talk about today."

There is a glint of mockery in the Ferryman's eyes. As he

goes to put needle to the flesh, he can see Bob's arms tense up. He leans over and with his claw takes a joint from an ashtray made of rattlesnake skulls.

"Great tattoo art does not come from bullshit stencils like you see in those dick shop windows," he says. "You can pre-conceive on paper, of course, but in the end the real master-piece quality shit, like I'm doin' right here, is drawn. It's all hand and eye coordination . . . Like a pilot. Plus vision. You have to have the vision."

He relights the joint and gives his lungs a good harsh dragon's worth. He offers the joint to Bob. But Bob isn't having.

"It's got to fit the skin," says the Ferryman, continuing. "It's modeled to the flesh, and so it becomes the flesh as the flesh becomes it. And it is the only true art that breathes. And like all true art, it dies when you die. That's how it is circumscribed, since there are limits to the flesh and limits to the art. It's like a marriage, babe. Which is a black art unto itself. Know what I mean?"

On that, the Ferryman gets a rise out of Bob. A sharp gri-mace out toward the gray hills. Bundles of muscles already taut along his biceps torque up through the trapezius.

The Ferryman uses his electric needle as a pointer. "You got a lot of anger in you, Bob Whatever. You don't relax, the body art can't reach its full potential. You understand?"

Not exactly something Bob wants to hear as Case walks by with two handguns pressed down into her belt and a shot-gun free-floating in one hand.

She glances at Bob. "He hasn't bullshit you to death, has he?"

"He's working on it."

"You find what you need, girl?"

"I'm narrowing down my choices."

The dogs have taken to following her. She lays the hand-guns and the shotgun on a picnic table.

"I'll pick out the backup weapons later." She glances at the house. "I got to use the head. Mind if I go inside?"

The Ferryman has leaned back into Bob's shoulder. He nods.

She lets the screen door slap closed behind her. Once inside, she watches the Ferryman and Bob. She crosses the room. It's a shabby, lightless hole of a place. There are crates of doodads on the floor and tables. There's an old hutch in the corner, something straight out of fifties suburbia, that looks like it bounced out of a Bekins storage truck doing about fifty.

She looks over at the hutch to see if the scrapbooks the Ferryman keeps of every tattoo he's ever inked are still there.

They are, cornered by sunlight, in a pile next to an empty rusting birdcage. Case looks out the window to make sure the Ferryman is still working on Bob's shoulder. She leans out of the way so she can't be spotted as she takes the top book off the pile and begins to search.

She bites her lip as her fingers go at it. Page after page of snapshots runs by: Poor-looking chickies with spiders painted near their clits or dragon devils climbing over the hump of their blowhole. A Hawaiian with the portrait of a pit bull named Dylan carrying a woman's bloody dress between his teeth muscled across a forearm. A bald biker with Sitting Bull tattooed on his thigh. A couple of gringo kids in a lineup, shirtless, with entities that resemble a neo hip-hop version of the Alien creature across their chests. A punker with a red octopus across his back.

But what she's looking for is a no-show. She takes the next book. Pages of skin surf jobs, but nothing more. She sneaks a look out the window. The Ferryman is still having at Bob. She's been in here awhile now. She grabs the third book. Nothing.

The Ferryman isn't one to buy smoke, and she knows it. He's out there counting the clock. What the fuck. She's gonna confront him anyway. But she'd rather have the facts to back up the cash she's gonna try and tempt him with.

Halfway through the fourth scrapbook she nails it. And it doesn't go down nice. There is a loose snapshot of Lena in a small pile of photos that haven't yet been glued in place. She's sitting in the easy chair smacked out of her mind, with a stoned, sloppy slur of a look, her hand held up for the camera like she was showing off an engagement ring.

It's all right there. Signed, dated, all but notarized on the back of her ring finger: 12/21/95.

Being right is nothing but grief, and grief itself has become a perversity. Chance oblivion. Chance it, girl. It's all part of the dark creative we call life. There is nothing about being right that death can't fix.

She sits, a block of window light burning right before her eyes. Everything smells of must and desert. Minutes clock past, and she keeps staring into that blanched space. Her mind is filled with a thousand excuses to be dishonest, but all they really do is make her cry.

Case comes walking out into the sunlight like nobody's business. She is carrying a small plate of food.

"I robbed your refrigerator."

"We were wondering what took you so long."

As she walks past she tries to pick up something in the Ferryman's tone, a shift in his manner possibly, that might mean he's suspicious. But he's just a needle at hard work on his vision. An artisan preparing a prince for a coronation, or a cadaver for Potter's Field.

She notices the Ferryman has the Book of Changes out, and Bob is stuck there rattling the three I Ching coins in one hand. She offers Bob a taste from her plate, but he's just a bundle of impatience sipping on a beer, and he turns her down.

"Give me another toss there, Bob Whatever," says the Ferryman.

Bob tosses the coins as Case goes over to the picnic table where she left the guns. The dogs glide along beside her, following the smell of food. "You're making that poor motherfucker toss the coins," she says.

The Ferryman has Bob repeat the toss till he has the proper configuration of lines and half-lines for the correct hexagram or sign, which he then begins to artfully paint onto Bob's skin above each taloned edge of the wing, or shroud.

When the Ferryman doesn't answer she hits him with, "Fortune-telling bullshit."

"Shut the fuck up, girl. I'm doing nothing. He throws the coins. He decides the fate. I only report the facts."

"Fortune-telling bullshit."

"You told me to do a good job here and—"

"I know. How much longer?"

He takes another hit off his joint. She can see he's totally ripped. And when he's like that he could go on forever, or till he runs out of flesh.

"Shut the fuck up, girl," he says again, mouthing silently the words.

She sits on the edge of the table and wraps some bread around a piece of sorry-looking spiced chicken. She tries to get a little food down, watching that stoned fuck go about his business. She gets a flash. In her pocket she can feel the snapshot of Lena she stole clip against her skin as the dogs grab at the space around her till they are one beastly shape with half a dozen heads snarfing up the crumbs that fall across her jeans.

Bob watches Case put the plate down and begin a final quality-control check of the weapons. She takes the revolver first. He's got a pretty good eye for guns and can see the pistol she's holding might be a Ruger, a 100 maybe, with some kind of modified grip that looks to be partly chipped.

A revolver's beauty, beyond its durability, is its simplicity of operation. It looks clean enough as she puts the wheelgun through its paces. He watches the cylinder turn, the trigger and hammer click-clock in a smooth crisp motion.

But it's her hand and fingers that he notices most. She goes about her chore with a grace and ease that is disturbing in its beauty. Her face is not taut, her muscles do not stretch. She is like a moment from some cooled-out Zen school.

Case lays the revolver down and takes up a smaller automatic. Maybe a Smith and Wesson, or a Firestar. It could be a Walther .380. Whatever it is, she's no fool. She has picked two always guns.

She takes a magazine pouch from her pocket, slides an extra magazine into it, then hitches it to her belt. She takes the automatic and goes through the reloading process. He watches her every move checking the weapon's performance: palm down on the floor plate, index finger extended down the mag pouch, thumb circled around the body, goddamn her—her hand comes up quick, the index finger offhand and even with the top bullet in the mag, the gun turned in the shooting hand to let the thumb depress the mag release—god-fuckin'-damn, she's going through your basic government-issue speed reload, and those ex-junkie's fingers have at it, and she's not watching the gun, either, she's doing it like a blind state trooper. Her hand flats the top of the slide and tugs it back, and she's ready to hot-load some ass.

There is a rawness to how she moves. Hand and weapon turn a series of mechanical moves into some poetic dance. She is sweating from the sun, sweating under her arms. Even the shiny metal of the gun has begun to look a little wet with her perspiration. And Bob's not immune to it. It's as if some door marked "forbidden" had opened just a breath and he saw something, felt something, before it closed again.

When she's done she lays the automatic beside the revolver. She takes another piece of chicken and sticks it between her teeth. She squats down and goes face-to-face with the mangiest scrap of dog in the pack and lets it snap the meat right out from between her teeth.

She stands and, taking a weapon in each hand, approaches Bob. She holds both weapons up. "Well, Bob Whatever, which one of these is you?"

He sees the automatic is actually a lightweight Colt .45. He glances at the revolver.

"That a Ruger?"

"Yeah."

"It'll do."

"How would I have guessed that would be your choice?"

The gun does a half loop between her fingers, and she hands it to him, grip first.

"I see they're both always guns," he says.

"If you can't hide them in your skivvies, they ain't worth dick."

She nudges up to the Ferryman. "How much longer this poor bastard got with the needle?"

The Ferryman is working the sixth talon up with a sign of the I Ching. "One more after this."

Case slips the automatic into her belt, reaches for the pack of cigarettes in Bob's shirt pocket. She lights the cigarette, heads over to the trunk where the guns are kept. "Fortune-telling bullshit," she says.

The Ferryman kicks back. "Bob Whatever rolls the coins. I don't ask. I don't answer. Time does that for me. For us all."

He leans forward as if to share a secret, but he says nothing. Using his claw as a roach clip, he rubs his nose across the upcurling smoke. His breath chugs through a healthy snort. Then he winks at Bob. "Last stop before the big dance. Right, Bob Whatever?"

"Just get this over with."

"Okay, Bob Whatever."

Case balances herself on the rim of the trunk, and sitting there rummages through boxes of ammunition till she finds

.45 shells. She starts loading her extra magazines. "Fortune-telling bullshit," she repeats.

"That's not what Jung said, girl. Nope. He knew that divining techniques were seen as foolish arcane games. But to him there was a sublime connection. As a matter of fact, he said they were based on the sound principles of synchronicity."

Case finishes finding a home for the bullets. "That's a lot of fuckin' cha-cha. You got too much smoke in your head."

The Ferryman eyes her coolly. "Let's look at this by way of example. Take you two. Just a couple of pilgrims driving down from Mallsville to pick up some groceries and be on your way. Who knows what you're looking for? Who knows what you've found? Who knows was this just a random stop?"

Case sees now he's fucking with her head just enough to let her and Bob know the game isn't happening without him knowing. Bob's had it. He sits forward.

"It's done."

"One more throw will tell it."

Case gets up. "Leave it."

"You won't be able to leave it undone. No way. You'll have to know." Bob pushes away the Ferryman's arm. The Ferryman twists around like some disordered aesthetic and wipes at the sky with his needle. "I have seen too many helicopters dance through spitfire and not fall. And others yet they fall . . . I always wondered what is the chance chance plays in any of it. There's no difference. There's always more helicopters. And more spitfire." He begins to riff Dylan: " 'And I just sit here, watchin' the river flow.' "

Case comes over and takes the needle from the Ferryman. They stare at each other. The wind ripples over the tarp awning, which lifts and bellies like a snake traversing soft ground.

Bob goes to get up. Case stops him. Then she straddles him and sits on his lap.

"What are you doing?" he says.

"One final touch."

She brings the electric needle up toward his face. He stops her cold, pushes her hands away.

"Not my face."

"Come on, daddy. You're gonna be in good company. All my lovers have one."

Bob sits alone in the cab of the Dakota daubing his cheek with a handkerchief bathed in alcohol. He looks into the rearview mirror. Beneath his left eye, about three quarters of an inch long, are the two wavy parallel lines Case put there. The symbol of the Nile, of the Egyptian god Hapi. The sign of Aquarius. Her month, her mark. With one slight vamp. The top line is black, the bottom line red.

She walks over and leans in the cab. "Time for money."

He reaches under the seat where he keeps his money belt hidden. He starts to peel out two thousand in bills.

"I need three."

"ID, two handguns, two shotguns, and a pair of backup handguns . . . two thousand. That was the deal."

"Still is." She leans forward, glances at the Ferryman. He is moving slowly with his dogs. A bottle of tequila hanging from his claw, his fancy Bijan pistol in his hand. The sun is arcing down behind him. Murderous red. The Ferryman has himself a shot of tequila, then begins to fire off into the distance. The dogs go wild on the concussion and begin to leap and squirrel and kick up dust.

"What a piece of work," says Bob. Then, eyeing Case, "Why the extra grand?"

"He knows."

Bob stiffens up in his seat. He starts forward. Case puts a hand against his chest.

"You take a walk. Let me deal with him, okay?"

"And if he doesn't deal?"

"We take his arm and leg. Then we start killing the dogs one at a time. He'll get the picture."

"Alright," says the Ferryman, "let's put all the friggin' chitchat into perspective. What are you doin' here with that sheep?"

Case stands beside the Ferryman looking out toward Furnace Creek. She can make out Bob walking the ruins of the old trailer where Cyrus was raised and then heading on toward the stone chimney. They are all half lost in the falling light. Just incidental pieces of some greater darkening headlands. She takes a roll of bills, twenty hundreds round, and holds them up. The Ferryman hoists his tequila bottle up under his arm and claws the money.

"Well, why you with that sheep? You're up to something. Syncro-fuckin'-nicity, Case. What were you looking for in the house?"

"See if this math works." She reaches into her pocket and takes out a folded-up newspaper article about the Via Princessa murder. She flips it open and holds it up against the wind for him to see. "One," she says. Then she reaches into her other pocket and takes out the snapshot of Lena and holds that up. "Plus one . . . equals Cyrus."

"Holy Christ, girl."

"Twelve . . . twenty-one . . . ninety-five. It's right there in your handiwork."

"Did you drop through the looking glass or what, Alice?"

"Right through. Bad news, too. They're humming the same bleak story at both ends of the rabbit hole. I need to find them."

The Ferryman works the money into his pocket, then gets his claw around Case's arm. "I don't give a shit what happens. Not to you. Not to Cyrus. Not to the world. But, you're just starting to get it together. Do you have a death wish? Screw the sheep. Cyrus, too. He's just another breed of sheep. I thought you saw through all that bullshit when you split from him. But this . . . They will leave your ass behind, girl."

Case reaches into her back pocket, takes out another roll of bills, one thousand round.

Bob has started up the hill toward them. It's time for the Ferryman to decide. He knows if he doesn't graciously take the money, things will get a lot less gracious.

He takes the money.

"Where is he?"

"Doin' rat patrol."

"And the girl? Was she with him?"

"She was alive two weeks ago. But it wasn't pretty. And the sheep, Bob Whatever. . . . Who is he in this?"

"Interested third party," she says.

"How interested?"

"Blood and bones, baby doll. It's all crossing-over time."

While the Ferryman considers what he's just heard, Bob makes the crest of the hill. He spots the Ferryman slip the cash into his pocket. A funny silence falls over Case and the Ferryman as Bob approaches.

"How we doin' here?"

"Just talking a little philosophy," says the Ferryman. He stares at Case. "I believe staying selfish is the key to survival." He turns to Bob. "What do you think, Bob Whatever?"

Case watches Bob to see how he'll handle himself.

"I think you don't give a shit what I think," says Bob. He looks at Case. "Business taken care of?"

"Taken care of."

The Ferryman turns and starts to walk out farther along the ridge.

"Well?" Bob asks.

"She was alive two weeks ago."

Bob's flesh tightens across his whole face.

"The game is on, Bob Whatever."

"Cyrus?"

"Cyrus."

He starts for the truck. She stops him. She points to the old trailer. "That's where he was raised. Cyrus."

Bob looks back out into the valley. Only a few last frills of scrubland run with light, the rest is part of yesterday.

"Did you ever hear of the Furnace Creek murder?" she asks.

The last they see of the Ferryman as they drive away, he is standing on a bald plate of rock at the precipice. He is naked now, swigging tequila and firing his pistol into the heart of the sky, his prosthetic arm and leg twitching madly with each shot. A strange seaman on the boat of the wind.

19

"What did the Ferryman mean, rat patrol?"

"It's a mock on some old TV show," Case says. "Cyrus goes on down to the border. The desert between Calexico and Yuma. Works as a middleman, picking up drugs brought across the line by wetback mules. Plays army while he's at it. Gets himself some high-tech equipment, night-vision goggles, the whole trip. Then, most of the boys, the carriers, after the delivery, he sends them to 'spic heaven,' as he calls it. Sometimes he kills 'em quick, but sometimes . . . he makes a kind of game out of it. Other times, some fool out there stumbles onto Cyrus. Some farmer or prospector or hunter. It's the slaughterhouse after that. Ground up, canned, and delivered."

"Is that where we're goin'? Calexico, Yuma?"

"Escondido first. Cyrus has places he shacks at when he's

working the desert. People he gets equipment from. If that's a bust, we'll try Bombay Beach out at the Salton Sea."

They do the hard drive south in the cool dark of the freeway desert. Anxious roadside light waves up through the front windshield, flashing the names of restaurants and service stations that burn out like matches in the rear window as they punch their way along Route 15.

They swing down through Victorville and Apple Valley and Cajon. A template of saloons and transmission shops and billboards parading Roy Rogers's museum and his stuffed pony, Trigger. A real tribute to chump-change identity.

"What did the Ferryman say about Gabi?"

"How do you mean?"

Bob half whispers, "You know what I mean."

"Nothing. Just that she was alive when they'd been there."

"That's all?"

Case's eyes remain fixed to the road. "That's all."

He suspects she's lying. Maybe he's even thankful for it. Maybe.

It takes another two hours between stops for gas and coffee to breach San Diego County. The steady drone of the road behind the Dakota's stereo lulls them, but all that changes when a road sign squares up for the Escondido exit.

Case turns off the radio. "Just a couple of miles now," she warns.

Bob slips the Ruger out of his belt and checks the wheel-gun's ammo. It's almost eleven. They cruise past weedy vacant lots and tracts of flat-faced homes. At the far end of El Norte Parkway is a trailer park sitting up in brush country. It's surrounded by a scratchy palisade of cypress and blue oak.

They park the truck in a field about a quarter mile away. They steal through the waist-high grass like tribesmen on a hunt. The moon runs silvery behind the clouds. The night is cool, but both are sweating as they make for the line of trees. Case is starting to feel her stomach seize up on her. She could vomit. She is afraid. It ain't up to wizards now, or shamans, or even therapists. No one to whisper, Here's how it goes down, bitch, if you want to do it right . . .

They wolf in low behind a knot of trunks. Thirty yards ahead there are a few streets' worth of trailers. They pick up the sound of a television going through a series of station changes and the smell of food being fried. Spots of light from the windows fall in patches on the gravel road and against cars parked in tight alongside the double-wides.

Case points. "Over there. That green double-wide with the porch up on cinder blocks. That's one of Cyrus's places."

Bob looks over to where she points. One light glows behind a brown curtain.

"You think the whole pack of them would bring her here?"

"Maybe," she says.

"He'd take that kind of chance?"

"There is no such thing as chance to him. You can only take a chance if you're afraid. If you're not, chance ain't nothing. He'd do it for that reason alone."

Bob wipes the sweat off his neck. "It's been a long time, right, since you were there."

"Yeah."

"The place could be someone else's by now."

"We'll find out pretty soon."

The rear door of the closest trailer opens. A ransacked-looking excuse of a housewife in a funky pink robe steps out into the dark carrying her garbage. Her German shepherd jumps into the light and scoots around her, his nose working the ground for a spot to piss.

Case and Bob slide down into the cask of the roots so as not to be seen. The dog seems to pick up their smell. He starts barking. His head turns in hard snaps. The woman calls him but he doesn't move, doesn't stop. The woman hangs there with a cigarette on the edge of her lips.

Bob can see she's got the kind of face that's been wrecked by decades of cocktails and bad attitude, and not one to go along gently. She keeps watching.

Case and Bob huddle there, hardly breathing now. Finally she calls the dog in, and her door closes and the yellow light of the room is swallowed up.

Case goes to sit up, but Bob stops her.

"Hold back a bit," he says. "She may be watching. She's the type. Believe me, I've been called in by enough like her to know."

Case nods and sits there.

They huddle up for maybe an hour, giving the old lady's eyes a chance to get bored. They talk and lay out the moves ahead. Case will play the Little Red Riding Hood part. Knock on the door and see if the Big Bad Wolf is there filing his teeth. If Cyrus is, and if she can clear the door by putting on a good junkie grovel, and if the girl is there or at least if she gets a sense the girl is there, she'll give Bob one sign. If not, she'll give him another. Bob will then move accordingly. But each move comes with the promise of blood.

If none of them are there, if there's just some coolie they got holding down the fort for room and board and a few toots, well, that's something else altogether. And Bob'll be given the sign to lay back.

Case is barely an imprint against the green cinder-block walls as she makes her way along the sundeck of the double-wide. She passes the window. A sliver of light seeps from the edges of the drawn curtain, whose ratty corners leave a thin, useless glimpse of the room beyond. There are no voices. Just music. Heavy-edged stuff on the slow side, thrumming from somewhere down a hallway. Case takes a breath, knocks on the door.

Bob watches from a twisted grotto of branches. No one

answers. Case looks back in his direction. There is a muscle-tightening pause as she knocks again.

Bob can feel the tension climbing up his neck. Jesus Christ, he's been here before. Back on Via Princessa. Waiting for an answer to a knock that didn't come.

He notices the old lady had made a return appearance and is now working the trailer windows. A church-owl of a face aiming right at the front door of the double-wide.

"Get your fuckin' face back inside, you . . ."

Case is still eyeing the dead silent fake-wood door. Enough with bullshit civility. She reaches for the doorknob. Everything from her stomach down through her ass turns to jelly.

Screw this up, girl, she thinks, and you'll end up some sewer cocktail making your way through the city's drain-pipes out to the sea. Just something some innocuous swimmer off the coast of Encinitas will get a face full of, in the quiet Sunday morning surf.

Bob sees the door open, and his eyes go back to that nervous speckled face inside her kitchen.

"Don't do it, Case," he whispers. He tries to wave to her. "Not with the bitch eyeballing you like that."

He stands and tries to get Case's attention. But in one cursed breath, she's in. In, and the old lady's heart-shaped face is staring at the green double-wide. She turns and glances at the telephone.

Bob feels the air whistle out of him. No, not this time. He does not need some "concerned citizen." Not this time.

He sees her take those first steps to the phone.

He curses silently. Don't touch that fuckin' phone . . . Don't . . .

She lifts the receiver.

He is shocked at the moment inside him. You can't have it both ways.

She begins to dial.

Maybe she'll have a heart attack right now. Nothing serious, just a little slammer to slow her down.

No such luck.

The living room is a vacant stand of furniture. Case did a couple of tours of duty in this place, and a few rancid memories come back. She leans against the dark where the wall is and listens. There is not a sound except that music coming from a back room.

She starts a slow course in that direction. Her hand down on the pistol hidden under her shirt in her jeans, following the lamplight, following the shadowy breakers beyond that.

She comes toward the music, toward a maze of short halls. She can feel the bass line from the speakers pound up through the floorboards. She's getting ready to put on her best shuck and jive for whoever might be home. Then, coming around a corner and into a bedroom that once was hers, she spots a naked piece of manhood lying on a red corduroy couch.

He's twenty, maybe twenty-five. Over six-foot-three. His body is covered with the hand art of some skin wizard. He's got coarse red hair and nipple rings, and the tip of his penis has been pierced. A diamond stud sparkles against pink skin. His eyes are closed.

No Cyrus, though. No Lena. None of the old rat pack. Just some new boy on the block. She notices a hash pipe and a needle on the carpet beside the couch, with all the necessary jewels around it for a good high.

She can't help but check the boy out. He's the type she used to do a lot of fifteen minutes with.

She looks around the room for some sign of the girl, though she's not quite sure what exactly that might be.

"Am I dead?"

She turns and looks at the boy, who is now lying there

with his eyelids half open. "I don't know," says Case. "Can you have a hard-on when you're dead?"

He moves a little. "If I was dead, you might be an angel. I would like to fuck an angel. But if I'm not dead . . ."

Case eyes him slyly, putting together the pieces of a play. "You'd fuck whatever's left, right? Let me give you a hint, alright? Leave the talking up to that cock of yours."

Bob is counting the clock. Five minutes went by twenty minutes ago. And what he gets for his worry is the slow crawl of a police cruiser turtling up the dirt access road toward the old bitch's trailer. He's got to start working on his options now. Got to either try getting Case out of there or let her go down and deal with it later.

The old lady isn't out the front door a heartbeat before she's harping away. She's got that nosy paranoid sense of dire urgency, something every cop fears but knows he better deal with if he doesn't want to face some charge of dereliction of duty.

By the time the cops start for the green double-wide, Bob is running back to the pickup, his arms caning at the high grass. He takes off his money belt and slips it under the front seat. He grabs a shotgun and shells and heads back toward the trailer park, toward that runny well of light.

He makes his way past the garbage cans behind the old lady's trailer, looking for a soft spot in the dark he can curl into. He gets a back-row seat nested behind some wild brush for the cops' slow approach on the green double-wide.

The loud knock cannot be mistaken for anything but what it is, and there has to be a voice coming back from inside because one of the policemen answers. Then everything is a collision of cross-purposes and bad timing.

Bob sees some jerk-off kid, a tall buck with red hair, come crashing out the back window with nothing on but black leathers, leaving a comet trail of broken glass behind him.

.

The old lady goes psycho right there in the middle of the street. This bony thing with a boom box for a mouth starts running as one of the cops rams the front door. His partner leaps the sundeck railing and kangaroos down the slippery side of a dirt garden. In the section of bedroom framed by the broken window, Bob sees Case scrambling to get her clothes on, scrambling to get her pistol. What the hell is she doing jackass naked?

It's all fugitive madness. He hears a cop yell "Halt!" and fire a warning shot into the air. The old lady goes down into the gravel like some pissant sinner at a tent meeting. The front door is hammered in by a blue shoulder. Every one of Bob's plans to get Gabi back is heading for the scrap heap.

It's dig-down time.

Bob gets ready to rewrite the party book. Give the boys in blue a little vamp on procedure. He'll show them a routine they ain't practiced. That much he knows for sure.

He brings the shotgun up and puts a fast shell burst into the front of the police cruiser. The radiator punctures like a main artery and a line of blue Freon sprays out twenty feet. Both cops come to a dead stop, trying to get a handle on what is going down. Thinking time is lost time, boys. There's another scream, and a dog starts howling. A baby begins to cry. Bob puts a second shot into the cruiser and the hood of the sedan is sent straight up, straight up like a blown jack-in-the-box lid spinning end over end.

For a moment Bob thinks he spots Case making a bust-out through a back door and rushing up into the darkness at the far end of the trailer park. He slips into the dark, back beyond the panic, out of view of the cops converging on the spot where the shiny black hood has slammed into the ground like the blade of an executioner's ax.

Bob is running now, full-tilt boogie for the pickup, knowing full well that if he's caught it's just a matter of where they send the remains.

He's behind the wheel now and spinning out through the

brush with his headlights off when he sees someone shape
up over a pile of fallen cypress limbs and stumble into the
darkness. He comes to a ground-grinding stop. The shotgun
door swings open. It's Case. She's got blood coming down
her cheek from a wound over one eye. She isn't even in when
she yells, "Fuckin' go!"

20

Gabi lies naked in the night sand, curled up and shining like
a lucent egg. The sand against her back comes howling up
the crooked wash eroded out of the hillside. The sand burns
her flesh in waves and slowly brings her to.

Helpless and mute, staring at the grim remainder of the
night sky, she tries to sit. The world around her is a bare ten
feet of wind-whipped yellow sand. Her aching left breast is
purple and swollen with nubbed red marks like sutures from
endless teeth bites. Her left arm aches where the needle was
shoved up into her veins. She is lazy and disoriented from
the heroin. She is exhausted from the nightmares. She is unsure what she dreamt and what she lived. She is alone in the
middle of some uncertain wilderness. Too confused to understand the fear that is coming up within her.

She remembers vague sentences, ellipsing feeble thoughts like
ether . . . Words in Spanish . . . Crossing into Mexico . . .
The one they call Cyrus endlessly talking . . . Crying . . .
Breaking glass . . . There were gunshots, weren't there?

Finally, like some newborn beast realizing it is alone and
without, she struggles to her feet. Wary and wobbling, she
cups her hands around her eyes against the wind. She cries
out to her father. Panicked and swaying, she moves, lost, but
some force leads her along. She follows the wind up through
the charred yellow rock.

Her eyes sting from the wind, but she fights to keep them open. She trips, slides down a stretch of stone. Rolls over, weeping. It's then she sees him. She struggles up on gameless legs. Looks for the will to lead her feet.

He is just an outline, really, a scarecrow figure above the rocks where the wind has thinned out. Beside some dark Jeep-like vehicle. It isn't Cyrus. It's not one of the others. It's not the van she was raped in.

She calls to him. He doesn't answer. She grabs at the rock with a child's fingers. Squeezing them like cleats against the stone, pulling herself up and shouting.

He seems to turn.

She blubbers out a few more cries, trying to get his attention, but the wind overwhelms her words. She sees him move, move just slightly. There is something like a nod. Something that tells her he has seen her.

To clear the promontory and reach him she has to crawl. She drags herself up the stone detritus like a crab, top turning as she slips back a foot for every few she makes forward. "Oh, God. Thank you. Please . . ." Her words slur. "Help me, please . . ."

A hand pulls her skyward so quick the breath is shaken from her lungs, and there before her the gaunt form of Cyrus holds the wind back as he leers down at her. The upper part of his face and skull are hidden behind some sort of mechanical headpiece with protruding telescopic eyes. It is the color of camouflage, and the lenses are cold black.

He waves a bony arm, playing the center-stage showman. He waves, but not at her. He waves at the outline she saw from below.

It is a man, or was. Years mark his brown face. He is naked. He has been lashed to a tall cactus. His body is covered with flay marks from knives and bottle glass. His mouth is swollen and turning black where his tongue is awled to the side of his mouth.

"How do you like my life sculpture, child?"

A flashstorm of images is unleashed inside her head, and she resees the moments she remembers hearing. The crying, Cyrus's endless talking, the burning needle up through her arm, the Mexican—it was him screaming through a whole world as it went black only to come back again in windswept color, and her curling into the sand to hide within its cool, dark membrane as that poor Mexican was cut again and again.

Gabi pukes onto the rock.

The Mexican tries to speak through his sewn mouth, asking for the death he had once hoped would never come.

Cyrus grabs Gabi's head and makes her look. The bile is stringing down her mouth, and her head wobbles like a prizefighter who has been hit beyond repair. "Take notice here, Dorothy," he says. "There's lessons to be learned on the Yellow Brick Road."

Wood and Granny Boy make their way up the back ass of the ridge where they have the van tucked away. Wood is carrying two five-gallon tins.

"There's a lesson, alright," Cyrus says. "There's a lesson." Squatting down he presses those telescopic eyes up against hers. "Some grub once said that every natural process is a version of a moral vision. You listenin'? That the whole plate of beings and things, actions and events, the whole fuckin' dig down, is one vast ectochrome flashed up and called eternity."

Wood crawls under the Mexican's Jeep and puts an ice pick to the gas tank and lets it bleed fuel into the empty tin.

Cyrus stares up at the Mexican through the infrared goggles. Above the Mexican's head are the bones of birds impaled on the cactus, driven onto a shore of spikes during the black winds.

"Well," adds Cyrus, "it ain't God with that camera eye. It ain't him. No, no, no. It's that bad boy down the block. And

he's doin' some finger-lickin' good portraits of his own."
Like a huge mantid lying in wait, Cyrus's arms come up. He
rests his elbows on his knees as if he were in prayer.

Wood slides the first tin filled with gas out from under the
Jeep and passes it to Granny Boy.

"Well, Vaquero," says Cyrus, "you had your fifteen minutes of glory trying to play Good Samaritan for this little
pretty-pretty here. I hope your God was watching, 'cause
you're crossing over."

Granny Boy begins to douse the Mexican down. When
he's half soaked and struggling with the little life he has left
against the wire that holds him, Wood crawls out from under
the Jeep and with the second tin finishes the job.

He tosses the tin aside and holds his hands up close so the
Mex can see. Across each palm a piece of red cloth has been
stitched, and painted on each, in white, the anarchist *A* with
the circle around it.

"You bet on J.C., Cisco, you bet on a *dead* horse."

Gabi lies there pitifully at the tips of Cyrus's boots, unable
to turn away.

The Mexican's eyes wander. His mouth twists with confused pleadings that only make the blood run more fiercely
from the wound.

Granny Boy begins to sing: "Cyrus said to Granny Boy,
'Kill me a son.' Granny said, 'Man, you must be puttin' me
on.' Cyrus said, 'No.' Granny said, 'What?' Cyrus said, 'You
can do anything you want, Granny, but the next time you see
me comin' you better run . . .' "

Cyrus stands and pulls out a lighter.

"Granny said, 'Where you want this killin' done?' Cyrus
said, 'Out on Highway 61.' "

In that one instant Gabi notices the poor human's feet
cudgeling the sand. The legs, glistening and damp, strain
against the inevitable. There is a spark in the wind, followed
by an eyelet of flame. Then Cyrus flings the lighter and a

pair of black eyes flash against a burst of pupil white as they are engulfed in flames.

21

Those first minutes clearing the trailer park are a blind frantic run. Case is looking into the visor mirror and wiping the blood from where glass cut her above the eye. Bob is deadpan and shifting hard.

"What the hell happened back there?"

"It was that woman," curses Bob.

"Why'd you start firing?"

Bob's got the pickup doing clean cruising speed as he swings off El Norte Highway and onto Broadway. He's running in the heart of a loose pack of traffic.

"Why'd you start firing, damn it?"

He gives the gearbox a hard lick and passes a low-rider.

"Jesus Christ," she says. "And I thought you were Mr. Safe-and-Sane."

He's about to put both barrels to her when a couple of squad cars bull-charge out of a Burger King parking lot half a block behind them. Bob downshifts, Case slinks around low in her seat. Bob's eyes are fixed on the rearview mirror.

"I don't know why you had to pull a stunt like that," she says.

"I wanted to get *your* ass out of there, is why."

The sirens kick in and a flashing whirlpool of red climbs up their ass. Inside the pickup it gets that cold autopsy-room chill as they clear the fast lane and slow.

They both watch the squad cars rush up on them and the flashers comet across the roof interior. They hang on the next moments like a couple of hard timers, but the taillights of the squad cars take a greyhound turn out onto Lincoln Boulevard.

Bob and Case get their first real breath in the last few minutes. There's one thing they're sure of, for the time being anyway. Their vehicle didn't get ID'ed at the trailer park.

Case now comes around in her seat for a little face-off with Bob. "I could have gotten my ass out of there," she yells.

"Oh, yeah?"

"Yeah."

He palm-humps the shift back into first.

She orders Bob, "Go down one more street, then go west on Dos Dios Highway."

He orders her back, "And cover the window with that visor before someone sees you wiping blood from your face and starts—"

She swings out the visor. "I could have gotten my ass out of there."

"It looks to me like your redheaded friend was using you as a saddle, so I don't know how the hell you'd have—"

"Fuck you," she screams.

"Do you know what would have happened if I didn't get you out of there?"

"What am I now, some candy-ass clairvoyant?"

"You'd a been busted."

"Ahhh."

"The old lady saw you goin' in. That's breaking and entering."

"I'd like to have seen them make that stick when they hit the bedroom."

Bob sneers under his breath, "Goddamn junkie."

Case turns on him, her mouth all pursed up like a viper's. "What did you say?"

At a Y intersection Bob hits the gas and peels out onto Dos Dios Highway.

"What did you say?"

The pickup is pressing now. Dos Dios Highway is just a black streak running into the foothills.

"You don't know what was goin' down in there!"

Bob turns to her. The blood, which she has wiped clean, has begun again to trickle out of the wound above her eyebrow.

"You're bleeding."

She wipes again at the blood. "You don't know."

"No shit. I'm watchin'. And I see the old bitch see you go in. I don't get a sign from you. Nothing. Nothing. I see her make a call. Still no sign. Nothing. Nothing.

"But I had a pretty good idea what would happen next. The police would put in a little appearance, and that old lady would have them inside that trailer no matter what. I didn't have many options. I didn't know if inside they'd come down on you. And when the police showed I didn't know if you'd be in the middle . . . I didn't know. I didn't know if I'd have to get you out. Go in as back-up . . . I didn't know. But once I saw . . . Red . . . come ass-kicking out the window and you . . ."

Bob is trembling like he is hot-wired with nose candy. He lurches for a cigarette on the dashboard, presses in the ashtray lighter.

"Jesus Christ," he says. "Do you think I wanted you to get busted?"

"I could have dealt with it."

"Well, thank you very much. I'll know better next time."

She leans back, closes her eyes. "Your confidence in me is inspiring. But remember, it was my ass on the firing line."

"Is that what they call it now? I must be out of touch. They used to call it something else."

For one second those death-camp eyes of hers open and she stares up at the worn fabric on the roof of the pickup. "You know, I believe we all have a kill clause in the contract of our lives. And I could say things to you right now, say things that would leave you groping to find out how bad I cut you up. I could. I could shave you and shear you."

Bob grabs the ashtray lighter and jams it against the cigarette hanging in his mouth. Once lit, he eyes Case. Gives her a ride with a look as if he were tempting her.

She leans her head around, watches him. Both of them look like they've been dusted with contempt.

"I could shave you and shear you, Bob Whatever, shave you and shear you before you could even swallow your pride."

"Get it on," he says.

She sits up.

"I don't hardly know you, Bob Whatever. But I think I got a pretty good touch on your m.o. And I bet I could list the reasons why your . . . late wife . . . left you."

Her eyes take on a centered kind of calculating look. "I'm right, ain't I, cow-trooper? Ain't I? The old lady gave you the road, didn't she? Got fed up stabling with Mr. Bob Whatever . . . found herself a buck she could talk to."

One side of Bob's body, the side where the heart resides, torques up. Torques up and his head is pulled to the left, as if the flesh on that side of the body had begun to warp.

Case makes a slight, decorous move with her mouth. As if she were begging the question: "Am I right, Bob Whatever?"

Along the curve ahead, a burst of approaching headlights. They get quiet and scared as they hear the heavy whine of an engine. Moments later a van passes close enough to blow warm air through the open windows.

Case and Bob are starting to reel a little from burnout. Not a thing more is said.

Farther on they pass Lake Hodges to the west. On the far side of the lake the single-bore searchlight of a chopper clears the teeth line of the hills. Silent as yet, because of its distance. They can make out its Cyclops-like turns, the light flushing out blue pockets of void along the brush roads that lead down to the lake.

"Is it a police chopper?" asks Case.

Bob slows the pickup to get a handle on its moves. The chopper starts to make low turns out across the lake. In the running moon of the searchlight, the surface of the lake, from the cut of the chopper blades, is a shimmering blue-black wave.

"It could be search and rescue," says Bob. "It's acting like it."

"If they sent out a chopper, would they have a description of the truck?"

"They could. But sending out a chopper is no indication."

The chopper makes a long sweep, the single eye turning away. Moving through a dark crease between the hills, the searchlight leaves what looks like flashes of lightning along the skin of the canyon walls.

"About ten miles further on," Case says, "near San Dieguito Lake, is a motel. Low end, but . . ."

"I hear ya," says Bob.

22

Jo and Joe's Motel is a twelve-room lineup fifty yards from the road and within walking distance of San Dieguito Lake. Wood and white stucco, with ample patches of stucco bark chafed from the walls and never replaced. The sign for the motel rests on a cinder-block pedestal beside a shantytown gas station and a fenced-in graveyard memorializing fifty years of automotive splendor. The sign itself is patriotic kitsch: against a white backboard the JO is done in relief and painted red and the JOE is done in relief and painted blue.

As they lug themselves out of the pickup, Case says, "It

has that homey bombed-out American feel to it, don't you think?"

But Bob isn't listening. He's looking back into the foothills where the horizon has begun to haze under the night damp.

"You want to push to Del Mar?" asks Case. "And get lost with all that freeway traffic."

He turns to her, considers what she's said. But the truth of it he keeps to himself. He doesn't want to do a mile more in that truck with her. Not tonight, anyway. Maybe not at all.

He showers in the dark. The hot water full on his face. He sits on the edge of the bed in the filthy little monastic room and stares at a wall whose shade of green, whatever it was when it was first painted, is now just putrid and pale.

He sits smoking, with one light on. A feeling of morbidity is setting in. A feeling utterly devoid of sympathy. He worries that he has done everything wrong from start to now. He travels back into the last few days, and like any good policeman at the site of a murder, takes notes. But these he takes on himself, on his character. Every detail, from the first lie to John Lee, to excusing himself from his job via Arthur, to his little diversionary tactic tonight with the shotgun.

He looks at himself in the mirror as he sometimes looks at strangers on the street. Unsure and uncertain as he might be of them, he was sure and certain of himself. Except now he is no longer himself. He is a naked man, with a good dose of burnout under his belt and a foul-looking tattoo draped across his shoulder. And that other mark on his cheek. And all in such short order.

Sitting there, honing in on his faults, he begins to realize that this is not the first time he's felt like this. His beliefs about himself, about the life he'd lived, about life as he thought it was, had all been rocked before.

There in the living room, while Gabi slept the sleep of the innocent and protected, Sarah had taken their wedding picture in its scalloped silver frame, opened the desk drawer, and laid it away.

He hadn't said a word as he watched, but he understood from the way she shifted her weight as she closed the drawer and took a slow, unpleasant breath. He had understood her look. Without one trace of apology. A look that had stillness and finality. The failure of the marriage, in that silence, had been squarely placed at his feet.

He has been shaken by tonight's events. The proper orbit of his beliefs has shifted, and he is frightened.

He reaches for his wallet on the dresser and takes Gabi's snapshot out from its place behind his new ID. The photo is all that is left of Bob Whatever's previous life. He looks into the heart of the picture, and it devastates him to know she is no longer sleeping the sleep of the innocent and the protected.

Bob and Sarah swim under a summer sky that hangs above the lake like a perfect painting on the open wind. At the far end of the lake, in a small cove, shore willows bow like ballerinas at the end of a great dance. Bob and Sarah are both naked, and they float like great, lazy angels on charmed clouds. Her belly is two months shy of giving up Gabi to the world, and it rises out of the water like a pink, lucent sun at the dawn of all their dreams. Bob places his ear against her belly and listens for his unnamed child. The skin is warm and taut, and Sarah runs her fingers across her husband's sandy hair and whispers, "Let's walk a ways."

They rise up out of the water, naked, and start through the woods. They walk hand in hand.

"Let's go see the house," she says.

Ahead is the cutline of the woods, and he can see the great earthmovers and trucks clearing the long rise of acreage that is becoming Paradise Hills. He suddenly is aware of the world around him.

"Come on," she says.

"But our clothes are back at the . . ."

"We don't need clothes." She smiles. There is safety in her voice, and he follows.

They walk up the long dusty road, past surveyors and engineers and the boys laying out the concrete slabs for the first homes. A great train of workmen, sweating and drinking coffee, double-checking their depths and distances with plumbs and rods.

Bob and Sarah walk in the full throw of sunlight, unnoticed, and the light reflects off the chrome stacks of the dump trucks and sparkles like welding fire as the great wheels trundle past them and slowly gouge up the footprints they leave behind.

As they walk together, Sarah is alive and happy and Bob is ashamed and embarrassed that the men will turn and see him. They will see him naked, and they would see his wife naked. In the face of her purity, he becomes all too conscious of human sin.

They reach a small sandy lot, squared off with rope, at the rear of the development. On a stake planted into the ground is a tag. On the tag Bob and Sarah Hightower is written in Arthur's hand.

They stand overlooking the dirt which is to become their home. She turns to him to speak. Her face has in it at that moment the legend of possibilities. It is lovely and warm and pink with youth. The life she bears shows in her eyes and skin, and her ethereal movements pull him into a sleep of wishfulness. Then in the cold dry dust of day she vomits blood.

He wakes to find the earth dark and the stink of the motel room all around him. He puts on a pair of jeans and, barefoot, walks out toward the road. He sits on the cinder-block

wall and smokes, the red JO above his head. He is still
wrapped up in the death sheet of the nightmare about Sarah.

He doesn't know how long he's been sitting there when he
hears the gravel reefing, and then Case comes up and sits beside him. She carries half of a six-pack in its plastic harness.

"Couldn't sleep?"

He doesn't answer.

"I don't ever sleep too good," she says. "Junkie dues, I
guess. Want a beer?"

He's reluctant to take one. She presses the can toward him
anyway in a kind of peace offering.

"Go on. I bought them off the manager of the place after
we checked in. He's an old pothead. We used to come out
here when we lived in Escondido to buy pot from him. But
he did a few turns in county, and now he's a good old boy.
Only grows a little weed for . . . medicinal purposes. He
didn't remember me too good but after a little cruise down
memory lane his brain cleared up. I don't figure you for a
smoker so . . ."

Bob sits there like a photograph, looking out at the road,
his eyes burning in his head. He could use a beer to wash
down that dream, only he doesn't want to go to her for it. But
in the long run it's do or do without, so he gives in.

Bob gets the first one loose from the harness and then
glances in Case's direction. She is sitting there with her legs
pulled up and her cigarette arm dangling like a question
mark off one knee.

"You want one?" he says.

"Oh-ho. Commandment number one: Junkies cannot do
junk. Commandment number two: Junkies cannot do booze.
From tequila on down to the beer chaser, all that's left for me
is the lime. Not even one of those friggin' chocolates with
the schnapps in 'em. I could eat a box of those. But it's all
history."

She sits back against the blue JOE. She kills the thought of a drink by counting stars. "I got an unnaturally consumptive personality," she adds.

Bob gets down half a dozen good swallows before he comes up for air.

"The walls of that dump are no thicker than a rubber," she says. "You can hear everything."

She notes he will not and does not look at her. Even as he took the beer, his eyes managed to avoid her. And now they're working the road. She bites her lip uncomfortably.

"I was sitting up in bed when I heard you come out. I was thinking. I was thinking, well"—she hesitates—"I was being a shit blaming you for what happened tonight."

Bob suddenly finds himself turning to look at Case.

"By the way," she says, "junkies are big on blame. I mean that's a real trip for us. Junkies have to blame somebody when something happens. Blame is big fuckin' business."

Her face takes on the cold detachment of a judge's. "You blame the failure of your relationships 'cause your daddy stuck his pee-pee in your mouth when you were five, or because instead of Mommy hugging you when you screwed up she took a pill and reamed your ass out. You blame the world 'cause you can't get a better gig than being the french-fry girl at a McDonald's. You blame strangers 'cause they don't know you're special or a star. You blame people you know for forgetting you're special or a star. You blame fate when you don't get what you want. And when you do, you blame fate for not getting you more." She holds up her cigarette like a pointer. "A junkie will even blame the cigarette for lighting up the person."

She rocks a bit. Her forehead wrinkles in the presence of the truth as she sees it. "Anyway, when I went into that trailer it was empty except for that big red stud stoned out of his mind in a back bedroom. He come to, and we got talking. He was pretty fucked-up, wanted some pussy. I gave him a little cha-cha about being one of Cyrus's coolies. You know, just another lost chickie coming back for a little smoke and a pillow and some home cookin'. I could come off like I knew Cyrus pretty good, which of course I do."

Bob is watching her intently now, and he sees a black cloud start to spread out from the center of her eyes and fill her whole face. It is like some disquieting eclipse. "It always amazes me," she says, "how much you can get out of someone if you're willing to put a lip-lock on their dick. It just goes to show you how little any of it means. I guess we're all junkies in one way or another."

Her voice is unbearably sad. "I fucked up back there. I didn't think it all through, otherwise I wouldn't have put myself . . . and you . . . in a position like that. Not with the girl out there and all, but . . . "

Her head comes around carefully, as if she is about to share a secret. "We didn't come away empty."

"What are you saying?"

"I'm saying . . . Red . . . made good with the tongue."

"Cyrus?"

"Oh, yeah . . . been there. A week ago. He is working the border. Most of the pack with him I know. One . . ." She stumbles on that word, on using a faceless description like "one" for Lena. She goes on, avoiding for now what she feels will inevitably be a confrontation. "Most I know."

Bob grabs her arm. "Was Gabi with them?"

"Fuck. How am I gonna get into a thing like that with him? Excuse me, Red, did Cyrus have this kidnap victim with him? A fourteen-year-old chick . . ."

Bob lets the arm slip away. "Yeah, you're right."

"This guy is just a house coolie. Keeps the furniture warm. You know. Passes messages."

"Of course, you're right, what am I thinking?"

"Well, don't finish thinking till I finish talking. 'Cause I know who Cyrus is working the border with."

"What?"

"I found out. His name is Errol Grey."

"How?"

"I seen this message machine with all these messages on it. So . . . I start copping Red's joint, get him nice and flushed. Then I . . . 'accidentally' kicked the machine on. And there ain't ever no man who is gonna stop getting his joint copped to turn off an answer machine. Well, Mr. Errol Grey . . . Mr. Slick-Ass, Carry-My-Stool-Specimen, I-Never-Say-Please-and-Never-Say-Thank-You Errol Grey was getting a little anxious. There was lots of 'Where are you, Babe?' and 'We need to talk, partner.' "

"You know where to find him?"

"Fuckin' A. Errol put a lot of shit up my arm," Case says caustically, "and I got your basic thermal package to zoom in on people like that."

Case sits there listening to Bob toss out questions that she's expected to answer, but all the while, each aggravated minute, she is pointed at one thought, one needling desire. She wants some slight acknowledgment for what she did. She knows what she did was chancy, even foolish. But still.

Bob is now star-wheeling on what comes after what comes next.

She begins to feel like one of those police informants. One of the necessary diseases of the times. She's seen those empty-eyed souls on the border of life, who for a few bucks lay it all down so the bossman can make a bust that never ends up sticking. A few bucks under the table in a filthy envelope and then the wave of an arm to excuse them—but before they're even up from the table, before they've even pocketed the Judas money, they can hear the soft conversation that precedes the hard snigger as Blue Boy gets his licks in.

Devalue the information you pay to get. Devalue that which brought it to you, and you don't have to ask yourself the hard question: How come you couldn't get it on your own?

She knows, of course, this is just the junkie in her trying to rat-bite the ex-junkie, trying to carve up her goodwill.

That a serving of Bob Whatever's shortcomings doesn't have to end up on her plate for swallowing. She could let the hate get her off and look for a main vein to take it out on. Just a little pinprick, as Pink Floyd once said, and it's sleepy time on Anxiety Row. But still . . .

So they sit there, like two ragged soldiers of the road, each locked into the puzzle of their lives.

23

Examining in a pocket mirror the deep fault lines that have grown up around the edges of her mouth and chin, Maureen remarks to herself in a resigned mood, "Ah well, maybe a steady diet of martinis and collagen is the answer."

She snaps the mirror shut and sits by the bar at the dogleg end of her living room. She is a small gathering of one. She reaches for the Bombay gin and the shaker with freshly manicured nails and goes to work on number three and four in the batting order.

She looks out the glass windows that form the west wall of the living room. Her eyes drift over the terraced rows of the Paradise Hills tract which give way to a sun that isn't yet pink. She quips, "I'll be down before you will today, Mr. Sun."

The phone rings. It's her business line. Fuck 'em. Instead, those nails work the built-in wall console searching for a soft spot on the dial where she can get her shot of sixties music. She gives the gin and ice a few good turns, then tests those babies to make very sure they are bone dry.

She stares at the bar a moment. It has always been a sore spot in the decor. Her taste leans toward white, with hints of gold leaf or little splashes of color—notably red. She believes in the Three Musketeers of style: decorator fabrics, decorator carpets, decorator prices. There is a decided air of the Florentine and the rococo to everything she bought and paid for.

She enjoys her bad taste. Takes pride in it. It draws attention to her, singles her out, which she thrives on. It qualifies her in the most certain way of all, that she can well afford to be thought badly of. It always reminds her of the most tested need of all—that she, with her money, is in actual control of her life.

But that bar is John Lee's pride and joy. It is chiseled from dark wood and rimmed with wrought iron. A hulking pseudo-antique with bar stools that have seats of cheap imitation black leather. Sometimes the black would rub off on a light skirt or pair of pants. Cut into the bar's face is a conquistador helmet copied from the painting of a conquistador that came with the set and hangs dramatically behind and above a line of liquor bottles Maureen has nicknamed Murderers' Row.

John Lee likes to say the bar gives him that old-world feeling. As if Coronado himself, or at the very least one of his prized lieutenants, had braced up, slapped down a handful of doubloons, and ordered a round for the boys. Then, after a couple of tall cool ones, they'd truck off into the Arizona desert for a few years' hard target practice on a nation of defenseless digger Indians.

By the time number three hits the deck she's got a good buzz on. She starts to mind-walk through the music, picking and choosing her memories as selectively as she would a dress for a first date, or a dance, or her wedding . . . An old Beach Boys tune . . . one of those girlie groups singing "Will You Love Me Tomorrow" . . . Percy Faith's "Theme from *A Summer Place*."

To her those songs represent a time of permanence. The time of the rock-ribbed world. Of simplicity squared. We were, she feels, a country that seemed to eat from the same plate, breathe the same air, look up into the same clear sky, and see the same God who looked down on us with His blessings, as we were the one people of His image.

Of course she knows this is all so much prepackaged memory. But she sits there anyway, a little drunk, a little teary-eyed, and she can't help her suffering as she stares down at a picture of Gabi and Sam and Sarah. She can't shake loose the feelings, and she won't put away the photo.

There is nowhere to place all that. It stands in opposition to all things. She knows how much a broken heart is worth on the open market; she's been trying to peddle one for years. But this does not alter her emotional view. That music, that music bleeds to the very heart of things. It gives her strength, even though she hates knowing that it enjoined them all in a cleverly cloaked fable: Illusion is at the center of all reality.

She's got number three pretty much worked over when John Lee's Caddy tires into the driveway. By the time he's coming through the door, she's got number three scored and number four poured.

John Lee tosses his keys down on a table in the foyer. He's carrying a small folded garbage bag that looks like it might have a couple of videos in it. Stopping in the hallway at the far end of dogleg, he reads the signs: wifey dear at the bar, glass tinkling like the tail of a rattler warning him not to get too close. After a perfunctory hello, he turns and heads toward his study.

Maureen has noticed the bag under his arm and smirks. She turns to watch the smog help kick up a brilliant sunset. John Lee comes back into the room, around the bar, and pours himself a healthy Scotch.

"I talked to Arthur today," says Maureen.

John Lee takes a drink, relaxes into a "so what" look.

"He says he hasn't heard from Bob in about a week."

"Bob is a fuckin' idiot."

Maureen's tongue starts to rim the inside of her mouth. "Really?"

"Really."

"As defined by whom?"

When she sits there like that, with her head cocked up and around and not moving, he is reminded of a deer that has been shot and stuffed.

"Is it true you offered Bob a situation managing the development?" he asks.

"Talk about old news."

"So it's true?"

"Yes. I felt that since . . . He needed a change, John. A healthy change. Arthur felt the same way, too."

"Don't consult me on this."

"Consult you?"

"The boy works for me. It was me that got him the gig over a lot of . . . Just de-ball me at every turn, right."

"Pass me the shaker and the gin, I have a feeling I'll need a few close friends inside me."

"Be your own fuckin' bartender."

"Okay."

She gets up, comes around the bar. They try to make as much space as they can for the other, as if any contact would lead to ultimate contamination.

"You know, John Lee, when I first met you, back in the Paleolithic era, I found you modestly charming and weak. But like the polish on a cheap pair of shoes, your modest charm has scuffed away to leave you as you really are.

"Now, to your weakness." Her tone drips with the malicious. "I didn't mind it so much when I was young. There was something docile and sweet about it. Of course, I didn't know any better, and in your uniform you surely gave out the wrong impression. Sometimes I actually believed you were sensitive. Imagine that . . . But your weakness by day brought out the mother in me, and at night, at night, it gave me ample opportunity to be on top."

"You're really putting it out there tonight."

"I'm shooting to bat three for four, baby."

There's just too much her, between her and her furniture and her music, so he goes over and shuts the radio off.

"I was listening to that."

"You better watch your mouth tonight, you piece of rank clit. I'm in no mood."

"I'd divorce you, John Lee, but I'd have to give up half the money I earned and then I wouldn't get the pleasure of grinding your guts into the ground a little at a time."

He shoots his drink down. That liquor wash he can feel right up into his pecs.

Maureen continues. "You don't know how many times we're at a social function, a party, a wedding, one of the many trivial pursuits we have to do together . . . You don't know how many . . . Oh, let's not forget church! Especially at church! Especially there! I'll just sit and wonder while they're giving out the communion wafer how many different ways there are you could possibly die of cancer."

John Lee's eyes have slipped toward the picture of Gabi and Sarah and Sam. Ultimately they lock onto Sam. It is like walking down the hallway of a terrible scream trailing to an end. A cocky smile no more, Sammy boy, he thinks. Even though repelled by the horror of it, by his complicity in it and the fear that it brought home, there is a blood-soaked spot in the white core of his being, a moral mischief knowing Mr. Cocky got it bad. John Lee gains a humiliating, morbid pleasure, imagining he could beam himself into the moment when the letter opener was picked through Sam's tongue and he could whisper in Sammy boy's ear, No more lickin' clit. Not with that mouth.

The blood rush goes right to John Lee's tongue. He shoves his glass hand in Maureen's direction. "Say what you want, but you're not gonna humiliate me anymore like you did with Sammy boy."

For an instant, she is caught off guard. There is a touch of irony to John Lee's presence, in the way he seems to knowingly relax within his own fury.

"You think I don't know about you using that managerial job crap to bait your humps. You think I don't know. A little pepper last year, a little salt this year. Bob ain't the next in line."

His tone becomes threatening. "Consider yourself lucky."

"What does that mean?"

"What does that mean?" he mocks.

"You heard me."

"Maureen, you could end up with your own personal Jack the Ripper slitting that sagging neck of yours!"

"Fuck you!"

He screams now, his voice cracking: "Don't fuckin' push it."

"Why don't you crawl back in your study and get yourself off?" she says nervously, but not willing to back down. "You know what I mean? At least I don't have to bring my humps home in a brown paper bag so I can watch little boys with their mouths—"

He goes for her. It is all an absurd blur. White knuckles tearing at a train of black hair. Her arm wheels across the bar, taking out shaker and ice. He goes to drag her from the bar. She evades his grip, tries to run, half stumbles, one high heel does a somersault away from a falling leg.

He's on her quick. His hands dig into her face. "Come on, smart-ass. Come on, humiliate me now! Come on."

One of his hands flies free, whipsaws back, and cracks her so hard in the face her jaw snaps and her teeth click hard.

A half turn and she sees herself in a wall mirror. Her face is the color of salt and spotted with blood. She tries to spit some of the blood from her mouth into his face but misses, and he hits her again.

She goes down and tries to crawl away, but he puts his knees against her spine. Gasping, she tries to hide her face. He hauls back an arm and aims at the bones in the side of her face with an open hand. His arm is moving scythewise and inside his head all he can think of is beating that face till

it looks like a piece of spoiled meat, when he flashes
on . . .

The gas-bloated frame that bore the woman, unrecogniz-
able. The skin where it had burst apart and the open lesions
rank with maggots leeching pink-brown muscle. The bullet
wound to the side of the skull that left shards of bone with
blood and brain jelly trailing up the wall like the spanning
wings of a bird.

It has become an indelible part of his subconscious. It
taints him and sears thoughts he has not yet had, poisoning
the well of innocence, if any such well ever existed within
him at all.

His arm stops. He stands. She lies there conscious but not
moving. Her mouth forms small bites of words. Her eye lifts
a bit and locks onto John Lee swaying there above her.

24

Come morning Bob and Case are racing through the asphalt
nervous system of the southland toward San Diego. The
shoreline has a splash of red tide in it, and small pockets of
smog are collecting over the last wetlands that face the freeway. It's only spring, so summer ought to be a double dose
of nasty this year.

They're both still pretty tight, watching for the blue boys.
Bob sips at a piggyback-size double coffee. "Tell me about
Cyrus."

Case sits there in the shotgun seat with her arm hanging
out the window like some spent trucker. "Chaos," she says.

She doesn't say a thing more. "That's it?" Bob asks.

"Isn't that enough?"

He starts to make a sound like a question but she cuts him

off. "I hear ya," she says. "You want to get into that *inner person* crap."

"I just want to try and get a handle on him, is all."

"Well, I'll give you a taste. I'll give it to you like he would, except for the little flourishes of psycho poetics he wraps it up in. Yeah . . ."

She lets her head lean against the door frame, lets the wind take a run at her.

"Yeah," Case says again, only this time with the cold-handed touch of someone fielding a proposition they aren't interested in.

"Our boy was a junkie. He was also a pimp and a shooter and a prostitute. He was a small-time field hand for the straight and narrow boys. Selling all their goods. Doing all that bow-down time.

"Well, somewhere in that book of his, I don't know which chapter and verse . . . You see, when he got hold of me I hadn't quite started to bleed yet and he was maybe twenty-six, twenty-seven. But somewhere before me he found the Left-Handed Path. That's what they call it. The Left-Handed Path.

"Whatever happened to him, I mean, however it really happens, as no one in their true mind ever knows, he put enough oven cleaner inside that brain of his and it was the end of the cloud master. Instant radicalization.

"He had the purpose after that. The focus. Zen boogie in shades of black. He saw the clear light. I know I'm mocking a bit, but . . ."

She takes a cigarette from her T-shirt pocket. She's two hours up and half a pack in.

"It got him off junk. I wasn't there, but I know some who were. The Ferryman . . . he saw it go down. Said Cyrus locked himself in that old trailer I pointed out to you. The one back at the Ferryman's. Over the other side of that hill."

Bob nods and for a stretch of moments notes a slick of red

tide reflected under the sun. He recalls all the blood in last night's dream.

"Locked himself in that trailer," says Case. "Like some Indian sweat lodge trip. They said he did it cold. And in one straight blow. In that grisly wrecked trailer. With summer dead on that metal roof. Nothing to perk him. Not methadone, not Robaxin. Nothing. Whatever was in that head of his had anchored him."

Bob grows anxious watching that red tide. He thinks about Sarah and what the dream could have meant.

"Thinking on it," says Case, "maybe I know what was in that head of his. Hatred. Hatred is the right strength oven cleaner to put in your brain and do the job."

"You talking about him, or you?"

Her head flicks to one side. "I don't know. I don't know where I start and he leaves off sometimes."

She sits back in the seat trying to feel the hard of it somewhere within her conscious self, trying for some pitiful small spot to ground her against the moving car as it winds through miles. Sitting there talking about Cyrus, the depth of the confrontation they're driving toward suddenly unfolds in front of her. She starts to get a little anxious and light-headed, and her voice is tremulous and angry in the same wave. "Cyrus, fuck. He is darkness at the break of noon, Bob Whatever." Her teeth look sharp against her pinched mouth. "He is the scream from a silent razor across your throat," she adds. "He wants to make insurrection happen. He believes in breeding corruption like people breed dogs. Defilement. Seeing families suffer. That's all the mojo in his head. Mankind has to go down. It's the burning wreck of a fuckin' bullshit middle-class *Titanic* and he is Captain Rhythm Stick putting it up their ass. That's why he is so dangerous. Death looks good to him. It's part of the prize. He's like those freaks who find Jesus."

Bob sneers at the insult of that comparison.

She counters, "If you're gonna try and put him into some capsule review of a psychotic, you're using your shirt collar as a dicksleeve."

He sneers again.

"As mad as you think he is, there's motive behind him. That's why I believe he didn't go into that house for nothing. Didn't take . . . your kid . . . for nothing. He's not a psychotic. You don't see it right. His religion, like all religion, is politics."

"Politics?"

"The politics of the what I want versus what you want."

"It isn't politics," he says. "It isn't religion. No fuckin' way. What it is, is plain old-fashioned butchery."

The great one-eyed hunchback camera painted on his shoulder starts to hulk up in the angry muscles that give the gearbox a hard kick. "And I want you to remember that's my . . . was my wife back there. And I don't want to hear comparisons about . . ."

Case gets aggravated. "You asked the question. I laid down an answer."

"Some answer. It sounds like you're trying to make a case for him."

"Good choice of words."

He doesn't catch the humor in her comment. Instead, he goes after her: "The way you talk is the disease of the times. You compare religion to that mojo. The world has become a secular comparison nightmare.

"Religion is not any of that. Not any of it. It is the unmoved truth that all principles spin out from. It is a moment of attainment. It is faith in being; it is being in faith.

"It all disgusts me so. There's only two real ways to handle this. What you can't clean up in the family, you clear up with a jury. What you can clear up in the family, you won't have to clean up with a jury. End of story."

She sits there like someone not interested in what the salesman is selling.

"If they did it right," he says, "the streets wouldn't be such scrap heaps of humanity with every kind of . . ."

Her look stops him. A look that is prowling his comments for the comment to come, waiting for his point, which is *her*.

"What you mean," she points out, "is an atheistic, ex-junkie, bisexual piece of scrap heap humanity like myself."

He watches road signs instead of answering.

"You're a real clit dryer, Bob Whatever, you know that?"

Bob whistles, shakes his head. "They got you pretty good, didn't they?"

"I wouldn't use the word 'pretty' and I wouldn't use the word 'good.'"

She kicks off her boots and brings her bare feet up. She rests them on the dashboard. She pulls her jeans up a bit to scratch her foot, and Bob can see tattooed around her ankle a kind of artful shackle.

"Your boy cleaned up his act, but he kept all his troops junkies, didn't he?"

"He sure did."

"Talk about the mojo. He worked your heads pretty good, didn't he? But I guess you can find a comparison for that, too. It's all religion, philosophy. Right?"

She knelt in the dust at the Ferryman's, collapsed under her own weight, twisted to one side like a broken squeeze box, tendrils of blood stretching out like liquid mercury from the corners of her mouth. Cyrus circled her, the ultimate ringmaster over the unfortunate creature. She was panting, groggy.

The weight of her head on her neck almost too much to hold, her weaving shadow made her dizzy, dizzier as small red gems broke free from the tendriled blood. Small red gems that hit the dust and jellied like a glass eye. She stared at the small bloodlets collecting dust and in each she saw a little girl. The one that was, the one that was to pass away. She could see herself curled up inside those small red um-

*brellas collecting dust. And she remembered the other little
girl curled up inside the carcass of a dead beast.*

How one life can be killed so many times is the question.
She looks out the window, scans the blue and silver glass
buildings that wink with sun, the harbor with its gray boats
built for saluting, the bridge over to Coronado with its sea-
side swells. It's just a blanket of picture-postcard existence
that seems literally thrown over the land. Just some great
human theme-park ride that has no bearing on her feelings.
She is like a tube of flesh inside a straightjacket skin.

"He didn't work our heads," she says. "I wish I could say
he did. It wasn't his charisma or chemistry, not his power or
power of prophecy. You could blame him like you blame
Hitler or Jim Jones or Rasputin or Charlie Manson for the
crimes of their coolies, but it'd be a fraud."

She leans around, all disheveled and tired and wearing a
long-sleeved shirt that her anxiety has sweated through,
leaving her armpits and back targeted by huge stains.

"The truth is worse. A hole looks into a hole and sees itself and looks full. I was, once upon a time, a junkie waiting
to happen. And I happened upon the right ringmaster, who
had a magic needle. And I bowed before the magic needle—
that was my devil—so when I got low enough I could make
a god out of it.

"The devil, which is only an idea, is an excuse for evil. A
philosophy, if you will. Just as God, the idea of God, is just
an excuse for good. They're the fuckin' needle, God and
Devil, and they're waiting for junkies like you and me to
happen."

He listens to this windfall with a kind of blasted-out certainty of at least one simple idea. "Words don't define what
faith allows," he says. He runs his hand through his hair and
turns his full attention back to the road. "I'll keep my faith,
you keep the rest."

"Remember something else," she adds. "From Simi Valley all the way out to that nice little three-bedroom commu-

nity of yours, you'd be surprised how many of God's children, who talk just like you, are smoking or snorting or shooting some chemist's handiwork the ringmaster brought them. You'd be surprised how many would be swapping sexual organs if they could."

The cop in Bob asks the question: "The ringmaster? You mean Cyrus?"

She nods. "He worked that valley of yours better than your councilmen."

"You know that?"

"Know it. Seen it. Done it."

25

They run east on 94 toward Baja and the border.

It's cigarettes and long throws of silence. Outside Jamul, Case takes over driving. At a rest stop, they pass each other around the hot running engine like two prizefighters between rounds. The towns east of Jamul have that eaten-up-by-poverty look, their main streets little more than boarded-up breakers trying to keep back the sand and sweep of Mexico.

Their plan is to check out Jacumba Airport, which is out beyond the Carizzo Gorge. Errol Grey keeps a small plane there when he flies down from Mojave to work the border. Somewhere along that pearl string of truck stops and bars, Errol Grey and Cyrus will have a date to talk about filling up their Christmas stockings.

Bob sits behind the dark of his closed eyes, evaluating the particulars of the dream and attending feelings of something forgotten, jump-cutting to the new information of Cyrus dealing in Antelope Valley and him breaking his habit in that old trailer by the Ferryman's. And what about that remark of

Case's right before the Ferryman wandered by, when she pointed to the trailer and told him that's where the Furnace Creek murder took place?

Was Cyrus in junior high or high school when the murder went down?

"What do you know about the Furnace Creek murder?"

It is the first thing said to Case in over an hour. She doesn't even look at Bob as she says, "Not much really. Only what Cyrus told me."

"What did he tell you?"

"He told me he murdered the 'nigger bitch.'"

Bob comes up in his seat, waits for her to continue, but she doesn't.

"That's it?"

"That's it."

"Nothing more?"

"If there was, it wasn't gonna be me that asked. I got one throat and I wasn't about to have it cut."

In the afternoon, Bob and Case eat at the Campo Food Station, which is within rifleshot of the entrance to the Campo and Manzanita Indian Reservations. No speculators dream here. It's just a pothole of cheap siding painted pink, with a single exhaust fan in the center of the ten-by-ten dining room that pulls out every conceivable stretch of living air but leaves behind the rank perfume of the disinfectant used to hose down the brick floor.

"You say he killed the old woman, then he went back all those years later to get off junk? He went back to the same place. Why? What was in his head?"

Case sips at a bowl of beef broth. Since she got off junk, that's about all her stomach can usually get down before dark.

"What difference? It won't tell you where he is now. And now is what matters."

Bob shifts away from her comment. He sits picking at his food and thinking. At the table behind them facing Case is a carload of maquiladoras chicking away in Spanish. Case listens and watches these borderland girls who are panning for the gold of room and board and a sleepwalker's wages in the fenced-off factories of the Zona Industrial. Even with their teased hair and faces powdered they look to be all of seventeen, full of long hopes and short budgets.

All except one. She seems older. Case notices that she has the crinkled look of a decade more of laydowns and she listens to her friends' high-pitched clutter as if she knows that plans are just a disappointment in the making.

The older one's eyes drift from face to face, only remotely pulled along by their conversation. A sort of night-eyed silence that seems to live quietly outside anything real. In that moment, Case sees Lena. Sees her sketched in faint moves the woman makes. The wild exhausted girl she had shared nights and needles with.

"I'm the turtle, Case, and you're the bird," Lena said. *"That's the way it is."*

One girl half whispers in Spanish to the older one about Case staring at her. The older one waves it off with the magic wand of the straw swirling around in her drink. They continue chirping in Spanish.

They all laugh and huddle up close, clucking away till there's barely enough room for sunlight between them.

"I went back to the house on Via Princessa," says Bob. "A month after the murders."

Case stops sipping at her broth. "What?"

"I went back. At night." He pushes his plate of chicken and beans away. He wipes a hand across his mustache. "Around the same time the murders were supposed to have taken place." He talks like one would in a confessional. "I walked the whole thing through my mind. What we know, anyway. I lived the whole of it."

"Why would you punish yourself by—"

"I'm making a point, okay?"

Case stops. The girls scrounge up enough among them to handle the bill. As they walk past, they slink a look at Case and then one at Bob. Case notices that at least two of them have the requisite gold crucifix hanging around their necks. Probably there like garlic, to keep the clap away.

"I sat there in the dark, crying," Bob says. "And after I stopped crying, I tried to draw out of those walls what I could about what went down and why. At least draw out of those walls what they knew, as if there were messages there I could pick up, like in a telepathic way. But I also went there for strength. To take it all in. All the pain. I'd draw in all that pain, and plan, and see through to the end of what went down and why and how and then what I would do if, no, when I got that fuckin' beast—"

He freezes up. He has overstepped his moment of honesty. He senses he sounds like a murderer in the act of becoming.

"Anyway. People go back to a place for a reason. Why'd Cyrus go back to that trailer?"

"Well . . . I was told he was raised there."

"In that trailer?"

"I don't know that exact one. Probably. I know he was raised there. On that spot. He walked it enough when we were out there. The woman who lived there raised him."

"The one that was murdered?"

"Yeah."

"I've got to remember when that was exactly. How old Cyrus was . . . If he was ever brought in and questioned. Go on."

"The woman that raised him. She found him on the road wandering around. His folks, or his stepfolks, they just trashed him one day by the side of the road."

"Why?"

"I don't know. The man was Army, the woman a cunt. Maybe they were both cunts. Maybe Cyrus was already

Cyrus. What difference does it make? He is, isn't he? Anyway, what little I know is because Le . . . I got it in bits and pieces over the few years I was with him."

"If I could tap into the office computer and start digging through those old records. There might be something . . ."

"Forget all that. We get hold of him you can dig all the records you want out of his heart."

Bob is turning a thought over in his mind and only half listening. "There is a moral government to all this. I know it."

"Moral government? Forget bullshit slogans."

Bob isn't listening now, he's intent on that thought. He continues: "Maybe the connection between one act of murder and the taking of Gabi is an exercise which I must deal with. Me. It's my job task. I mean. Two murders. Twenty-five years apart, fifty miles close. The same man at the center of two atrocities. Maybe it's random. There is no sure connection. But . . ."

"You're trying to sell yourself life insurance, right?" she asks. "That's what you're doin'. Make it all nice and orderly. You're puttin' the needle in your arm, boy. You're puttin' the needle in."

Bob stands and from his pocket pulls a few crumpled bills. He throws them toward her side of the table. "You'll eat your weight in dirt before you die, but you'll be no happier for it, and no better off. Stick to your own needles, okay?"

Outside, Bob is lighting a cigarette and staring at the coin-operated newspaper rack. He stands orphaned and pale in the dust of the roadside. She comes up behind him.

"About inside," she says. "I know where you're at." She looks up the highway. It is flat and empty. A thin paper of black color that swims with afternoon heat. Just something grooved out of the daylight to give an illusion of direction. "We all hunt Leviathan in our own way, Bob Whatever."

His eyes come around to take her in. She sees that he is crying. She looks at the paper rack, through the metal bars that brace the headlines.

TAPE OF MOTHER'S 911 CALL PLAYED
AS KLAAS MURDER TRIAL OPENS

COURTS: Prosecution suggests that defendant Richard Allen Davis stalked twelve-year-old girl before kidnapping her from her bedroom and strangling her.

He reaches into his pocket for some change.

"Don't read that."

She watches a pile of copper and silver flatten out across a sweating, tired hand.

"Don't put yourself in it."

He pulls up the scarred metal lid and takes out the paper.

The need to hurt oneself has almost universal resonance. It is the prophecy of the suicide bridge: where one jumps, others must follow. It is life's tribute to continuity.

As he begins to read, Case tears the paper out of his hand and pages sweep outward, cartwheeling across the lot.

By their rusted-out Toronado the maquiladoras are having cigarettes and checking their mascara. They take to the drama and watch silently.

"Why don't you just carry around the police photos you showed me that night? Why don't you, if you need this kind of fix? Why not?" She takes what's left of the paper and crumples it and tears it and chucks it to the wind. "I did my life sentence in that roach hotel where you came to meet me, blowing off smack, crawling through every room in my head, every room, every state, relived and reviled it all, right down to a bloody carcass, and I wasn't jacked, I tried to dig a hole in my bathroom floor till my fingertips ran with blood. That was my Via Princessa. I understand where you're at, but . . ."

She is shaking so hard her arms move like violent whips. "I have seen enough little girls suffer, okay! Okay! Enough suffering, man, enough."

Bob is, at this second, beyond the vocabulary of reason. Drained, he turns and walks toward the truck.

26

Jacumba Airport is about forty miles west of El Centro and just spit from that invisible part of the border where there is nothing on the El Norte side save an assortment of playas with eroded hillsides.

The airport looks as if it was put together with scraps of day labor. No tower; unattended; a two-thousand-foot runway made of cinder, chipped out of a short throw of field that joists up to a rocky stand of boulders heaped in the shape of hills.

The Dakota cruises the field as Case looks for Errol Grey's plane. There is not a face in sight, not a vehicle. Just a dozen or so two-seaters tarped or tied down.

"Looks mostly like weekenders or border rats," says Bob.

"Among other things," adds Case. "You see that plane there?" She points to a small red two-seater nicknamed Beansy. "Well, unless that's a clone it belongs to a sheriff out of Imperial Beach and his cousin. His cousin is a gynecologist. They were always crossing the border, doing charity work at clinics. Right . . . They were also a flying fuckin' pharmacy when they came back. Demerol, somas, European ludes. They kept me fucked up plenty with that drugstore. I even got my pussy checked, free of charge." Then, with some slight savagery to her tone: "Lucky me.

"But Errol now. He is clean. He flies in from the Mojave, gets organized, sets up his trades, flies back, carries nothing.

Has it hand delivered to home plate. Thank you and good-bye. Cyrus does all the mean machine shit down here. Then has some coolie do the carrying."

"Any of these Errol's plane?"

Her eyes move from plane to plane around the paling runway like the quick blinking cursor on a computer screen. She gets a skewed frown. "No. He had this drab-looking thing. But it was pretty nice inside. Had four seats."

"Of course, he could have sold that plane."

"Yeah," says Case. "I didn't think of that."

Bob gives the planes, the four that are partly tarped, a distant once-over. None of them is a drab four-seater.

They stop at the far end of the runway and look right into the pink and rose breach of the closing day. Bob starts to riffle through the debris that's accumulated along the dashboard, looking for his cigarettes.

"You finished yours an hour ago," says Case as she hands him one from her pack.

"Right. Thanks. When Errol Grey works the border, where does he go?"

"El Centro mostly. Yuma some . . ."

"You know where he stays?"

"Which hotel? No. I mean he moves around, I know that. El Centro is shit. But he owns a bar there. He owns lots of bars, that's his thing. Music. He's heavy into music. He hangs in his El Centro bar some."

"If he's not in Yuma."

"Right."

Bob puts his head back against the seat, begins a slow rub of the temples with thumb and index finger.

"Headache?"

"The sun fucks me up sometimes." He takes a puff off his cigarette. "We could stay here and wait, but if he's got a new plane and he's already here, we'll miss him if he meets up with Cyrus. If we go to El Centro and he flies in and goes straight to Yuma or somewhere else we'll miss him. Same thing if we go to Yuma."

"We're dancing, alright."

"We're gonna think this through a little more." His voice sounds beat, like the edge has been polished off it for the day. "A little more," he says.

He sits a long time with his head back and his eyes closed. His arm and face have scabs on them from the needlework. Brown, crusty fissures that are burning and sore as hell. He doesn't speak.

Case turns off the radio to make it quiet as possible. She sits watching the land ahead. It seems vague and unwilling in the off-light. After a long while a pickup on a distant road traverses the valley. It's just a small piece of silver at that distance, like a bullet moving above the hem of the earth and leaving a cat-claw of road dust in its wake.

"I want to thank you for today, Case. About the newspaper. I should not be reading stuff like that. It's not . . . None of us needs any more suffering than necessary, do we?"

It is the first time he has addressed her by name since they've been on the road. The first time she's been part of a sentence that is not fundamentally a condemnation. And it doesn't go unnoticed. She wants to thank him, but kindness escapes her suddenly in self-consciousness.

That burning fuckin' arm, and that burning fuckin' mark on his cheek. Bob opens his eyes and looks in the rearview mirror to see a face that's particularly hostile. A scrub and a shave would do wonders, but they're history now. Look the part. You're a junkie's old man, her hot cock, pimp, suck-up, whatever is called for.

He keeps staring at his face and his arm. The unfinished roll of the dice the only spot not scabbed in a large blot. Then the brain does a quick jump. It's like having your own personalized decal. Like having your own personalized license plate. Personalized foolishness like they have on boats, and . . .

"That plane of Errol Grey's," Bob says in a sudden rush. "It have nose art on it?"

Case turns. "What does that mean?"

He looks down the runway at a line of plain props, spots a two-seat light-blue Piper. Its metal nose is painted white and there are huge cherries painted deep, deep red in a wreath around the words THE CHERRY KING.

He points. "That's what I'm talking about."

A creeping possibility she considers. She keeps running her finger round and round in midair, trying to stir the brain.

"Yeah, it had some shit on it. But it wasn't on the engine like that. It was on the door. Does that count? It was on the door—it was small. Plaque size. It was like his initials done in a weird way. Or something with water, but . . . I was so fuckin' loaded . . ."

"People change a car, they don't always change a personalized plate. They change a boat, they don't always change the name. He may change a plane, but . . ."

She gets it. Gives him the thumbs-up. The Dakota begins a police crawl around the field, pulling up to plane after plane . . . Nothing. They reach two that are partly tarped, both with their doors covered.

"Check it out," says Bob.

Case climbs out of the truck.

Bob is watching the whole field on the outside chance someone shows. Case tries to pull back the first tarp, but it's tied down tight. Bob watches her as she reaches down into her boot and pulls out a stiletto. The blade comes up in a neat flashing line. One jerk of the hand and the tarp splits. She sneaks a look inside. Nothing. Doesn't even turn, just trucks off to the next plane, tapping the stiletto blade against her thigh. Bob cruises twenty feet behind her, keeps an eye on the perimeter.

Another quick slash. She lifts the ragged brown canvas with the blade.

She turns and lopes back to the Dakota. She leans in the driver's window.

"There's an old song lyric: 'If you ain't got good news, then don't bring any.' "

Bob looks a little grim before she smiles, stands back, and lets the point of the blade lead the way back toward the flapping canvas gill.

A small hand-painted sign reads FIREWATER, with the FIRE done like water and the WATER done like fire.

"I told you it was some chooch bullshit. Good thinkin', man."

"El Centro first?"

She snaps the blade back home. "El Centro."

27

El Centro is what the propagandists of the Imperial Valley call their big town. It even has signs billing it as the "largest city below sea level in the western hemisphere." Case remembers a time when Granny Boy spray-painted on the unblemished green of a sign: "The only problem is, it's below sea level but not water level." Then he added an exclamation point sitting atop a smiley face with vampire's teeth.

The town is an undramatic affair with streets raked out of the desert and innocuous squat-faced buildings.

Bob gets a handle on the place pretty quick as he and Case cruise the entrada of Heber Road. It's a workhorse town duking it out with poverty. An army of filthy jeans and work gloves sporting accents from Laguna Salada to Oklahoma, and folks netted up on stoops like cawing flocks of birds. These towns always have a shortage of lookers, male or female, most having fled for someplace where the minimum wage is not the maximum you can get away with.

It brings back drab recollections of his childhood in Keeler. A blot of a place in Inyo County where the imported toxins illegally dumped into dry Owens Lake mixed with the native salts and sulfates and created a dust-covered cocktail that choked you into drunkenness and disease. The town evaporated under this Rube Goldberg mushroom cloud till there were only a hundred inhabitants left. Bob had lived in a trailer with his father. A prodigy of divorce, as his father maliciously nicknamed him. The view from Bob's bedroom window was of the Great Western freight car his only neighbors called home. It had been abandoned there years ago, when the tracks no longer had a point of origin. His father was the lone security guard for the then defunct Cerro Gordo Mines. There was little to do there. Heat and loneliness came in an assortment of colors, and you had ample time to brood.

His father, though, liked the desert. It suited his hostile and imperfect nature. All this would have remained just so, except for the lung disease the winds brought that drove his father out to Simi Valley, where his peculiar talent for making sure gates were locked and things were in place got him a job as night security at Jefferson High. It was as students there that Bob and Sarah fell in love and began the circle of disaster his life had become.

Bob and Case find a spot for the Dakota over by Camp Salvation Park. From there they can practically eyeball the Pioneer Hotel, which is where Errol Grey owns a lounge that doubles as a nightclub.

They cross Heber and make their way up Fifth.

"When we get in there, lay back. Errol can be a dick or he can be okay. Depends. Just play bass, let me chat it up."

"Right."

The Pioneer is three stories of rooms decorated and re-decorated into a hybrid of styles. Early seventies meets late

Department of Water and Power with a half-assed border of red brick. It's even got enough fake wood trim for a landmark chemical fire.

Bob and Case enter the lobby. By the elevator a maid is blow-drying a hole in the wall that's been plastered over and is still wet. A parcel of transients is grouped around a television on which a sitcom with cartoon colors flashes mercilessly in the half light. They're a sordid bunch of hipsters, the types who'd backpack with twist-top wine bottles in their pockets.

Bob and Case hold by the door, taking everything in.

"If Cyrus is here," says Bob. "If we get close enough . . . he isn't walking away from us. Understand?"

"Got it."

"No matter where it goes down."

"Got it."

"Even right here in the fuckin' lobby."

"I got it."

The bar is around back and down a carpeted hallway past the bathrooms and pay phones. Halfway there, a band riffing through a practice session comes through loud and clear. Heavy metal with some Tex-Mex thrown in. Another turn takes them to a three-stair drop that leads to a pair of eyelid-curved swinging doors. One of the hall lights is out. They stop in the dark.

"Well . . ."

Case crosses her fingers.

They come on and clear the rim of the doors. Bob can feel the wheelgun under his shirt pressed against his stomach, which is turning clammy on him.

It's a stripped-down room. No windows. Black walls. A dance floor and tables squared up around a small stage, where the band practices. They're a rough-looking foursome.

Bob hears Case take a deep breath, almost like a sigh, or a warning. Her eyes tail toward the bar, guiding his look.

There are a few locals tucked away in one corner. But at the other end Bob sees a man's face turning toward them as if some instinctual chord-line from the music has pulled him to Bob and Case.

Case starts in his direction. Bob follows.

"Hello, Errol—I can't believe my luck, running into you."

Eyes behind a pair of nickel-sized tinted sunglasses take the moment in. Waves of liquid blue electric from the lights behind the bar fall across a face that remains expressionless.

"You're not giving me the bum rap, are you? That I-don't-exist shit."

Bob hears the perfect pitch of begging in Case's tone.

Errol reaches for a cigarette that has been quietly burning away. "The prodigal daughter returns."

Errol isn't more than thirty, and he's got skull-tight black hair except for a thin patch across the top that's longer and slicked back. Even sitting, Bob can tell that Errol's got at least six inches and forty pounds on him. Bob checks him out to see if he's carrying any metal, but those form-fitting black jeans and gray pullover don't leave much room for doubt. Errol rests his arms back on the bar, stretching out some, and from the look of those over-defined pecs it's a good sketch he's got a taste for steroids.

Errol takes a moment, notices Case's mark on Bob's cheek. "I see there's a new member of the family."

"Oh, yeah. Errol, this is Bob. Bob . . ."

"What are you doin' here, girl?" Errol demands.

Bob sits at a table instead of at the bar, five feet back of Errol, where he can play the mute shitkicker trailing his old lady and watch them both.

"We were driving in from Arizona," says Case, "and— Bob's got family there. And, well . . ." She squirrels down into the seat beside Errol, cutting off his line of sight to the band. "We stopped in Calexico for dinner and I remembered—I thought you had a bar here. I was here, right?

When you were dating that porno actress, and me and Cyrus and the others had come down from Brawley."

Bob watches but on the beat of that name, nothing. Errol boy has perfected the Armani pose. Bob wonders if he could hold that look with a boot up in his chin.

"Anyway, we were just tripping along, and I thought, why don't we come on up here. If you were here I could say hello and . . ."

Case starts to meander a bit, talking up trivia that could put comas out of business. She goes on, not even looking Errol in the eye, as if she were just making up a story to round out the emptiness. Bob notices her body language alter. An uneasy feeling starts to fill him up. She's either putting on some kind of perfect act he can't quite understand or she's breaking apart in the face of it.

Errol takes a look down at Case's arms covered up in the long-sleeved shirt. The band is starting to go into overdrive. Two guitars fight for dominance, point and counterpoint. One voice, hoarse, followed by a stanza of rough-and-tumble backups. Something about genocide and Utopia. It's black metal and it takes over the black room. Case steals a look at Bob.

He tries to nod supportively. Then he looks away. He notices on the wall by the bar a CHP poster with a bearded face and a pistol aiming right at you and the slogan IS TODAY THE DAY? printed in big white letters. It's the same poster he's seen at every CHP office in Antelope Valley.

It makes no fucking sense suddenly. That poster there. Them here. He's not sure if he should step in, drag this prick outside at gunpoint, and . . . Is it Case breaking up in the face of it, or is it him?

"Hot band," she says.

Errol nods.

"I could see them rockin' at the House of Blues. They yours?"

"I put a little money into them."

Through that cool electric blue of the lights Bob catches Case's eye working a spot of floor. "How's Cyrus doin'?" she asks. She barely mutters the name. Bob sits up a little in his seat.

Say something, you pumped-up bastard, he thinks.

Errol doesn't say a word. He takes Case by the arm and pulls her toward him like he might kiss her. Then in a slow, almost sexual way, he undoes the button on her shirtsleeve. She sees what is starting to happen, her eyes quickly flash at Bob, and then she tries, without being too obvious, to get loose of Errol's grip.

Bob isn't sure if he should get up and stop whatever it is, but there's something in her look for that one second, as if she has been caught in the act of lying, that causes him to hang back. In the next breath, in the moving burlesque of hand and shirt, a slice of arm is exposed to the ice-blue light. The skin is a bitter white, like the rind inside a rotting slice of lemon, and there he spots a series of festering needle marks up her forearm, tracing a helix of veins. Deep, deep purple, sufflated marks, like leeches who have dug in for the feeding.

Errol's lips work up a grin. "I'm happy to know you couldn't make it, Headcase."

Case pulls her sleeve down and buttons it back up. "Can I quote you?"

"We all have our little secrets don't we?"

Bob looks away, stares vacantly at the band. For the first time he notices their name on the white circle of drum skin, Santaria Salsa. They're crashing through a number like faith healers on speed for some weirded-out cause. Driving home every chorus with a scream. Them on one side of the room, and that IS TODAY THE DAY? poster on the other: madness. Nothing matches up. The uncontrollable wizardry of contrary predictions.

It's a fuckin' conceit that cast them as accomplices. An unfathomable con. When was the last time he saw her arms?

He remembers seeing them the first time he met her, and there weren't any needle marks then.

She can't look him in the eye. Not even a glance. He starts to walk out. Case grabs him.

"Let's go," he says.

"I need to . . ."

"We all have our little secrets," Errol says again.

"Let's just goddamn go."

"I can't go now. You have to understand . . ."

He pulls loose from her grasp.

28

The day of the '94 earthquake was our crucifixion. The day this church opens and holds its first service will be our resurrection.

This is what Reverend Greely had burned into a plaque. It was his war chant, so to speak. And he had judiciously placed it above Arthur's desk at the work site of the First Church of Christ and Christian Community Center Reconstruction project.

Arthur sits alone in the dark, below the sign marking the project site, looking out onto the grounds of the church. The architect's vision is becoming a building of purpose. Thanks in large part, he likes to believe, to his dedication.

Still no word from Bob. Nothing. Not one call.

Arthur stares at the sign as he stands. The bronze little more than a banded stain. He would easily trade this building for the here and now of his grandchild.

Before he leaves he stops at the granite baptismal pool, where a miniature stream and waterfall will empty into its polished stone channel.

It is here that converts and infants will be initiated into the body of Christ. He runs his fingers across the polished ledge of the font. He stares up at the moon through the steel beams that will reinforce the structure and hold the church steady against the rocking earth of the west Valley.

But none of this relieves him. He feels unusually small and threatened. That somehow the night will have its way with him.

Even here, where all things are born. Even here.

He drives home, pulls into the driveway. He sits almost half an hour without going in. His face has grown heavier since the murders. Another ring around the waist of years. He hopes someone will come, some friend, some concerned neighbor, someone who can sense his desperation from a distance. Force him to talk himself away from what he's feeling.

Arthur finds himself pulling out into the street. He finds himself driving to Maureen and John Lee's house without calling. He finds himself knocking on their door even though all the lights are out. He finds himself waiting in the silence long after he shouldn't. He finds himself picking idly at chips of white wood in the wall slats.

The door opens and he finds himself completely turned around. Maureen stands before him in a bathrobe and without makeup. In the touch of amber light Arthur notices two things: her bare feet and the face badly welted with blue-tailed veins.

"Maureen . . ."

She puts her fingers to her lips, looks out toward the street in case anyone is passing and can possibly see. He follows her into the dark hallway.

"What happened?"

"You have to ask that?"

"Where is he?"

"I don't know. In some emergency room, hopefully, beyond all reasonable help."

She crosses the living room. She goes over to the bar. A cup of moonlight fills the room as best it can. The last half of a drink is there waiting for her. She reaches for the Scotch bottle. "Have a drink. I'll make you one."

As she pours, she asks, "What brought you over?"

He's about to speak, but—to come to be consoled and instead walk into this . . . "Forget it," he says.

She pushes a glass of Scotch across the bar with just enough ice so he can hear it coming.

"Have you heard from Bob?"

"No."

She eases him back onto a bar stool. "Sit."

"I don't know what happened to him, Maureen."

"Bob is—"

"Not Bob. John Lee . . ."

"Nothing's happened to him. He's the same as he always was, only more so. Don't shake your head like that, Arthur. You know I'm right. We overlook things in life. We overlook the obvious because we are selfish for something else. I don't know if we pay more for our sins or our pleasures. But we seem to pay."

"You ought to divorce him."

"And give up half my business. *Our* business. The hell I will. I'll pay for his boots and his bread and his booze and his blue movies with little bo—"

"I don't want to hear this, okay!"

"You can't swallow that far, Arthur. He's not just the guy you drink with or shoot clay skeet with or have a pizza with and watch the Super Bowl."

She takes a drag on her cigarette and in an angry, frustrated, calculated moment she puts it out by stamping it into the wood bar. Arthur watches silently.

"Well, as long as I'm being so viciously honest . . . and you're here . . . I might as well confess something to you . . ."

He looks up.

"I've been wanting to. Needing to, really."

"What?"

"Just another failure of mine. Another shameful act. Did you ever wonder if death gets rid of all your memories?"

"Jesus, Maureen."

"The lost part of the tail wags the dog in my life. And living is the downside of death. You know that, don't you. How do you like that for a phrase? Maybe I'll have stationery printed up with 'Living is the . . .'"

"Maureen, I can't handle it when you talk this way!"

"I had an affair with Sam."

She says it so slow, so matter-of-fact, it sounds as if she were reciting the last detail off a shopping list to a child. Arthur doesn't quite piece the name and the man together. His thoughts seem to huddle around some hole.

"Sam. Sam who?"

"Our Sam. Sarah's Sam, for Christ sake. Sam!"

Arthur sits there mute.

"John Lee knew," she adds. "I have no idea how. Maybe he picked up a vibe. Maybe he followed me. That's how I got this . . . facial. Threatened to kill me if I ever did anything like that again."

He pushes his drink away. "How long was this going on?"

"Six months."

He closes his eyes. Swallows. Opens his eyes. "Did Sarah know?"

"I don't think so."

"How long did John Lee know?"

"I have no idea."

"He said nothing to me. Nothing."

Maureen goes over and sits on the couch, no longer able to look Arthur in the eye. He turns around to face her.

"Why Sarah's husband? Why my baby's husband?"

"I didn't do it because it was your baby's husband."

"Why him? With all the—"

"Humps available?"

"Oh, Maureen. Listen to how you talk about something as—"

"He was everything John Lee hated, alright. He was there. He was close. He was young. He was willing. He was able. And able to keep it in perspective. *And* he was everything John Lee hated. That was the chocolate icing on the cake."

Arthur gets up. He cannot grapple with this anymore tonight. Not anymore.

"Where are you going?"

"I don't know. Not home."

"You could stay here."

"I have to be alone."

"Arthur . . . Arthur . . ."

He stops at the steps in the foyer leading up to the door.

"I don't think John Lee wants to find out who killed Sarah and Sam," she says. "I don't think he does. I think down deep he's happy they got away with it. I think it's his way of getting back at me. Not that he doesn't want Gabi back, I know he does. But as for the other . . ."

29

Bob stalks the lobby, stands off to one side of that rat pack of losers around the television as they listen to pathetic sitcom punch lines. He hangs in there for all of two commercial breaks before he's had it and bolts.

He's out and down the four long cement steps of that worn hostelry when he hears a whistle and Case shouting, "Hey!"

He keeps walking. She catches up to him in the middle of the block.

"You're a fuckin' piece of work," he says, "you know that?"

"You bet your ass, Bob Whatever."

He stops, grabs her by the arm, rips the buttons loose and

pulls the sleeve up to see for himself, to see up close. "Clean and sober, huh?"

He throws her arm loose and she lets him. He turns and crosses the street, scooting between cars and almost getting sideswiped by a pumped-up Volkswagen, but she's right on him. "You fuckin' lied to me."

"You got that right."

"How long?"

"How long, what?" she asks, although she knows what he's asking.

"Was it the first day out you started shooting up?"

They hump up onto the sidewalk and shortcut the park in a diagonal through some low-hanging trees that rim its border. "Did you cop some of the money I gave you for the Ferryman and score yourself a couple of grams? When did you start?"

"When did I start keeping my shirtsleeves down?"

He pulls some branches aside, stares at her, keeps going.

"You didn't notice, did you? Friggin' eighty degrees in that shit-locker restaurant and I'm sitting there with my sleeves tucked down into my hands. You don't know shit about the junkie cover-ups. You're a desk boy at the door of the real world. And you're as easy to see through as a piece of cheesecloth! In that bar back there. Bang! You looked like a cow that just got the electric shock to the brain."

They start across on the grass, soft and wet under their feet. A few beer cans visible on the ground like fallen stars. A few pale shapes reside at the edge of the darkness. There for stolen moments or a place to sleep.

They cross the park in silence, and upon reaching the Dakota Bob jumps in and turns the engine over. Case's door is locked and he won't open it. Before he can pull out of the spot, she charges around and fights her way into the driver's window. Her hands clench around the keys.

"They call this fuckin' grand theft auto, babe."

He can feel her breathing into his neck. He lets go by ramming his elbow upward, the bone of it catching her in the jaw and slapping it hard enough to make her lip bleed. She comes around the Dakota. He flips off the headlights as she passes. She waits at the door. He unlocks it. Somewhere a few cars back he hears laughter. She opens the glove box and ransacks past all those accumulated papers to where a small leather kit is packed away.

She unzips the kit in three neat turns without looking his way. She holds up the open kit so a needle, assorted vials, and a small plastic bottle of Visine are center stage.

Bob watches all this with grim resolution.

She opens the needle, clearing the channel for a few squirts of Visine. Then she adds a little blue liquid from a vial. From another she twicks in a little orange ground powder. The potion immediately starts to fever and froth. White layers of foam float up through the glass trough of marked millimeters. She chambers the ass end of the needle back in place like a gunfighter and gives it a little squirt heavenward.

"Listen and learn, desk boy. Visine and a concentration of liquid cleansers from your local supermarket. Any cheap brand will do. The foam and the blue tint that looks like some old broad's hair is from Ajax. And that orange powder shit is Mother Nature's own ground-up ascorbic acid. Vitamin C."

She rolls her shirtsleeve up, holds her arm out. She injects the blue potion under her skin along the benchmark of a vein. It immediately welts, and within seconds there is a festering of grayish bubbles from the hole where the needle releases the flesh. The blood comes fast after that. Case grits in pain. A sound hissing through locked chalky-white teeth.

"It's a nothing concoction laid in just under the first layer of skin. Looks bad. Scabs up nice. You want to be a junkie, you got to look like a junkie.

"I learned this little gig from a real-estate broker in Long Beach. His boyfriend was a smack head, and when he couldn't score 'cause they were both dying for cash his lover would shoot this shit into his arm and check himself into a methadone clinic. Then he'd take the methadone and resell it on the street for smack for his boyfriend. Now that's the capitalist system when it's working on all cylinders."

She rolls the shirtsleeve back and tries to shake down the burning.

"Now, nobody but some airhead will believe I'm a shooter without checking me out like Errol did. And that's just for starters. Especially with an albatross like you hanging around my neck. Those fuckers might want to test me with a load. You understand? You understand!"

"So you can't just tell me all this right off . . ."

"No way."

"You don't trust me at all."

"I've seen you in action. Trust. Ahhhh . . . to do the right thing at the right time. You don't know the drill. Act like you're shocked, Bob Whatever, when somebody rolls up my sleeve, 'cause most of the guys like Errol will know the only reason I'm with a dicksleeve like you is money. Money. That's it."

Bob leans back in his seat. Case licks at the little bit of blood on her lip. Tenaciously keeps shaking her arm.

"Also, I knew. I knew you'd act the way you did. That in your head if you'd see this"—she raises her arm and presses it toward his face—"you'd think right away I was a liar. Just like you did! You'd play it perfect as a stooge. Who don't trust who? Who don't trust who!"

"So test my ass—"

"So mine don't get wasted. Right on."

She gets out of the car, leans against the hood, lights a cigarette.

Some street trooper with gang emblems passes with a pit bull in harness. The dog muscles low and tigerish and smells at Case's jeans while the trooper looks her over.

Case talks to the guy through the dog. "Nothing up there

for you, babe." The trooper hears her alright, but as he keeps on he gives her crotch the long look-see.

Bob comes out of the car, his shadow converging onto hers within the war circle of the lamplight. "Somebody throws you a lifeline," he says, "and you don't like the color of the rope so you throw it back."

She folds her arms, blows smoke out her nostrils in contempt at such rhetoric. "You're strictly the missionary position."

He starts again. "Don't you see me as guilty? No? Aren't I worth the benefit of the doubt? I should trust you but you shouldn't trust me?"

"You prove that about every ten minutes."

"For a person who believes in nothing, then at least all things must be equal in their nothingness. I must be as equal as you in some barren hole somewhere. Or is there some pecking order to your nothingness? What was that you said the night we talked about going. That night in the field behind my house. 'You don't send sheep to hunt wolves.' And I'm one of the sheep and you're one of the wolves."

"Strictly the missionary position."

"You lie to me so you can get me to react a certain way, then you hold me in contempt for it. Shit."

"The missionary position and not a trick more."

"Is that a slogan or just venom? You want to control other people's lives 'cause you can't control your own. And remember something else, the last time I looked there were more sheep than wolves."

"The last time you looked would be just that, the last time you looked."

"I'm looking at you. At you! Through the banality of your cheap whore tricks and lies."

She flicks her cigarette in his face. Without so much as a cue. Spits of red ash star across his nose and eye. His face muscles react sharply, his hand comes up quickly, trying to pad away the burning ember.

He jabs his finger at some ephemeral mark between her eyes. "I know why you're here," he whispers. "I know. And you've lied to me in the worst way of all."

She stands there waiting, facing off with him.

"I know." He comes forward, grabs her shirt, roughs her with a hard tug. " 'I'll help him get her back. Otherwise, if we get close enough, maybe Cyrus will kill her quick.' Right?"

Case's head bends back uncomfortably at hearing her private words come back to her this way.

"Didn't you tell that to the therapist back at the halfway house? What's her name? Before you left. You think we didn't talk? You think something like that would be left unspoken?"

Bob is all teeth and quiet tones, with a touch of guns behind the eyes.

It flushes them out of the amber streetlight. Puts them behind the crosshairs of a high beam like hunted doves. Bob and Case lock. They turn. A police cruiser has pulled up and taken dead aim at them.

That chilling cop stare on a bed of ice words: "Everything alright?"

The guns they're hiding feel like weights that could sink you down to the *Titanic*. They shuffle apart.

"Everything alright?"

"Yes, sir."

"Yes."

The light moves up, then down, stripping them. Cars slow. Drivers take the look. Bob and Case lean into each other.

"Move along now. And if we see any more of this 'foreplay' we'll do a little spot-checking. Understand?"

"Yes, sir."

"Yes."

The searchlight goes off.

They quietly gather themselves and get into the Dakota. Case hands Bob the keys. He sits a moment watching the cruiser take a right and start a long trek around the park.

"I did say that," she says.

He wipes at the burns on his face. "I brought it up to make my own point."

"If she had to go through what I . . ."

He hisses, "Don't speak of it. Don't. I can imagine it all."

She had been buried behind a bush under a piece of ply-wood. The police had been led to her grave as easily as one is led to a 7-Eleven. She was two months into serious ground time. A third-degree turn of postmortem special effects. Pa-thetic, deformed, swollen, rotted death. The body as it truly was, devoid of water, of life. A filthy corpuscle that once housed laughter and love and longings. No ice-cream sky. Now, just truth devoid of mystery. Bob could only think of Gabi as he looked down at the forensic pictures of Polly Klaas.

They had been circulated by brother officers up the state line. A tactical adrenaline reminder of who and what they were fighting. A hot line to ensure the right level of hate in a holy war.

Bob leans back against the truck door. "The child's face was full of wormholes. Madness. I had blood coming up from my throat I cried so hard."

She turns to face a man being smashed between what-ifs.

"I've seen on your face the kind of pain I felt. I've seen it in your eyes when you talk about Cyrus and what went down. And I've seen more than that in your eyes. And I won-der if my baby will have that look in her eyes when we find her. I came with you knowing that part of you may want her dead. You understand?"

Case feels her throat begin to close up on her, and she holds her upper lip in place by using the clamp of her lower teeth against it. She can taste the blood from where he rammed his elbow into her mouth. She rests her head on the dashboard.

"Oh, fuck . . . We're in the middle of some huge wound, Bob. Some huge wound and it feels like it's getting bigger and bigger."

He watches as the police car takes another slow right and begins running parallel to them on the far side of the park.

"If they're coming back this way, it won't be long."

"Errol told me Cyrus is supposed to be here by tomorrow. The latest, the day after. He's gonna arrange a little homecoming for me."

"After listening to him talk, why would he be willing to do that? Money?"

"No such fuckin' luck. He wants to see if I can grovel my way out of a good blooding."

3 0

Case and Bob set up camp in the Dakota about a block off the park. They sleep in the truck, taking shifts watching the hotel. They work the streets around the Pioneer, moving up and down the dark scrim of alleyways. A desert wind carries past the border stations the muggy dust of the factories in Gonzales Ortega. The day passes inconclusively; the night just passes.

Case wakes screaming and covered with sweat. She is alone in the pickup, pressed against the closed window. A small moon of foggy glass flares with each clipped breath.

Lena turned her flashlight on and up toward the stony roof of the cave. The branches of the acacia trees beyond the entrance dipped in the wind of a damp night.

"I wanted to bring you here," Lena said, "to share this with you."

Case let her flashlight beam follow Lena's along the smoky rock to a painted red sun circled by black, then white. It was done with brushes made from animals' tails.

"That's supposed to be the time of the sun's eclipse," Lena said. "It was painted by some Chumash shaman. Eclipses were important events in their lives."

The stone kept them side by side, huddled up like children of the running streams who bore out their gifts on the rock a thousand years back. Further up, on the painted rim of the universe, Lena pointed out a turtle and a bird borne together. Simple etchings done in red and black.

"Beautiful," said Case.

"I see them as us."

"How do you figure?"

"You're the bird," Lena whispered. "You have the ability to fly. To overcome. And me, well . . . I can only hide inside my shell."

With the ancient ways and rights about them, it was a sad lingering moment that brought Case's hand to Lena's.

"I may not be as strong as you think," said Case.

Lena kisses her. "But I'm weaker than you know."

The dust of centuries hung in the floating cast of a moment's light.

The second day passes in the slow waste of waiting. The third is no better. It's all noose-making time, but around whose neck? Bob goes out and buys two cellular phones from a chooch shop that specializes in low-end tech equipment. The place is run by an Iranian woman who still keeps a picture of the Shah above the cash register. He signs up for some hatchet-priced service plan, then loads and locks in a couple of numbers so he and Case can stay in constant touch when they're separated. They stay out of the Pioneer as much as possible, since Errol is growing short-tempered that Cyrus hasn't shown. Case finds something that resembles a hotel room in a second-story walk-up with windows facing an alley that looks up toward the Pioneer. The place reeks of fumigation.

Day four is like death. Case and Bob hang in the park by a rock with a plaque on it that marks this as the site of Camp Salvation. Some bald old Russian Jew with skin the color of pus recites for them the history of this forgotten square. How poor travelers coming off the parched eskers of the Yuma desert collapsed here. They had wrestled the waterless waste to a standstill only to find themselves without supplies, and without water, in some uninhabited wilderness. Unable to go on, they lit fires and they prayed. They prayed and they stoked fires. Two days later, trappers and Digger Indians came down from Mount Signal to discover the meaning behind those fires.

The old man points to the only piece of rock within view climbing off the plat of gravel desert floor. "That's Mount Signal," he says. "The border goes right through it."

The night of the fourth day is spent in a Chinese restaurant. One of the two surviving shops in a ten-slot strip mall. The food is dirt cheap. The music, phony white-bread country. Most of the dinner crowd is border Latin. A couple of truckers reminisce about Baton Rouge in a constant slapping together of beer bottles. Migrants all off that selfsame windblown esker of the interstate.

Case is moody, spends half of dinner sleeking chopsticks

through a dead salad with shrimp. As if on cue, she pushes her food aside and begins to tell him of her life since that day Cyrus stole her off the street. She spares nothing. She makes no excuses. She asks for no sympathy. She spells out each disaster and desire in disturbing detail. She is like some witness in the court of the dead, guiding the prosecutor through the black land of plenty.

She tells him in fierce detail about the dentist in Orange County, with his white golf shoes and white golf pants, whom Cyrus took down in a blood coup. How she had been working the windows as his watchman. The cold eyes of warning. She explains how the facts of that dentist's murder matched up with those in the pictures he'd shown her of the Via Princessa murders, from the paralytic injected into the victim to the twentieth enigma of the Tarot tagged on his chest. She remembers the town, but not the man's name.

As they walk the street after dinner, Case spins out the story of her life with Lena. From the first time they made love in the back of a filthy van to the bleak bloodletting of being beaten half to death and left unconscious to perish in an irrigation ditch.

To the east, above the Cargo Muchacho Mountains, flumes of lightning stretch across a brandy-colored sky. Case shows Bob the picture she stole from the Ferryman's album. Explains how Lena dates kills on her hand. Points out the ink art on a finger—12/21/95. She points out another date, two dates back on Lena's hand. The date that the dentist crossed over.

It begins to rain. They run under the Romanesque archway of a boarded-up Italian restaurant. They smoke and watch the street as the rain gutters fill and the vigas flood.

She tells him about Gutter and Granny Boy. She fills him in on their family histories, crimes she knows they've committed, places they frequent. She leaves out nothing she was a party to with any of them. In the act of trying to bare herself, she is also trying as best she can to build a case on which the others could be caught and taken down by him alone should something happen to her.

He listens and understands. And when she finishes, neither speaks.

She leans against one of the plaster columns that brace the entranceway. Bob eyes her quietly. She is not wearing a long-sleeved shirt, and as the passing headlights rush into the well of the entranceway they flare against that path up the white of her arms.

It is a muggy and deplorable night, even with the rain, that allows Case's shirt to play like the damp veil of some vestal sculpture. She begins to take on a strange elemental quality. Like the distant blue luminescence of the desert floor before the moon is full.

Case turns to him. Embarrassed, his eyes flit away, then come back. She points out the searchlights of the border guards on Mount Signal. They are swarming the rocky atoll like catch dogs. Some poor illegal is probably using the rain to try to make the run.

Bob leans against the other plaster column. And there together they watch the hunt along the mountain. An image in absolutes. Like guards on the face of some great shield at the entrance to eternity. And in the distance the searchlights climb and converge till eventually they are just the remains of heavenly stars caught in the sweep of the stone. Then they are gone.

Bob leaves Case in the alley behind their hotel room. In the doorway beneath the fire escape she thanks him for listening and not casting judgments.

Because of the rain he heads back to the bar at the Pioneer to wait and see if anyone shows up to do their little mating dance with Errol. The band that was practicing drives it home to a packed house. Either the rain or the music, or both, has gathered them all up tonight. It's a real touch of urban voodoo. Rednecks and factory hands and chickies with their skirts hiked up. There's your basic tabletop drunks and hotheaded rockers. But Errol Grey is nowhere to be found in that choked hole. Bob scans the room again, going from face to face, knowing that somewhere out there is the right freak with the right history.

He kills two beers with tequila chasers. He keeps flashing on Case leaning against that column. He looks in the mirror behind the bar. Five days without shaving, sleeveless shirt wet and dirty, his mustache drooping over his lip. He keeps staring at himself. It is just then, as he is walking among the not-quite-yets of his mind, that he hears a voice say, "Nice fuckin' artwork."

Bob turns to face a kid who's not more than twenty and looks like he was processed out of some angry white rebel tribe. Studded collar. A heavy dose of battered leathers and silver highlighted by an earlobe that has been cut away, leaving just a ring of flesh into which a silver-dollar-sized candle has been wedged and lit.

"Talk about a gothic ride on paint fumes," the kid says. His fingers dance over Bob's shoulder tattoo. Bob plays it all laid back. The kid keeps checking out the artwork and sucking away on a Corona. They do a few turns around a couple of sentences. Nothing spectacular.

Then Bob notices something in the freak's palms. At first it looks like he's holding a piece of red cloth in each hand. But when the kid puts his beer down to mooch a butt, Bob notices that the red cloth has been stitched in place, and painted on it is a white *A* with a circle around it.

Gutter comes sliding through a pack of beer hounds and up to Wood, and they go screw to screw with a head butt as if Bob didn't even exist.

"Come on, slash hunkie," Gutter says.

Wood nods, turns to Bob. "We got waste to live off of. See ya, dude."

Bob nods, watches Wood turn and put his head right into

the other kid's back and drive him through the crowd. "Put it in overdrive, Gutter!"

31

Case is in the shower when the cellular she left on the sink starts to ring. Bob's voice is like a bone blade cutting through the bad connection. "They're here!"

"What!"

"Gutter—that was one of the names you said, right?"

Down the back steps she slips the semiautomatic into her jeans. Starts to run into the face of a slick drizzle.

Bob does a slow cruise from the bar, following after Gutter and Wood. He picks up on the rat pack around the television. Something is drawing their attention away from the box, and they are whispering among themselves and eyeing the check-in counter.

Bob eases into the turn, sees Gutter working the house phone and Wood holding up the dead space beside him, the candle in his ear flickering away.

Case does a fast about-face in the Dakota, bringing the truck up on the chance they boogie. From Seventh she hard-turns through a red light down Heber. She tries reaching for the cattle prod she keeps tucked away under the seat.

Bob plays Johnny Low Key as he passes Wood and flips him a nod. Gutter is mind-pacing as he listens to the phone ring. Bob cruises the check-in desk, trying to eavesdrop. He rummages through a small wicker basket where the management keeps matchbooks. He lights a cigarette and scans their faces.

The phone is finally answered. Gutter comes on like a real prick. "What were you doin', taking a world-class shit or what? Who is this . . . ! It's a couple of crustys stinkin' up the lobby till you get your ass down here."

Case would run the next light but that dynamic duo who creep the park slide through the intersection in their police cruiser. They give her their best Batman glare on the turn, inching along till the light turns green. Just a quaint reminder of who is who and who is not.

Gutter and Wood are locked in a private conversation, which Bob is trying to circle in on. Wood's head cranes around Gutter's shoulder. "What's to it, man?"

Bob points upstairs. "Waiting for the old lady."

Gutter turns. His eyes scrag Bob. They've got that hooker's abstract boredom until they land at the spot on Bob's cheek where Case did her little Michelangelo. Bob picks up on a moment in Gutter's eyes as he stares at the tattoo. A kind of shift hit like he's seen on jail-cell cowboys when that first little kiss of Dex cooz's the system.

The elevator door shutters open. Errol Grey skims across the lobby, wearing a black oilskin raincoat and those same nickel-sized sunglasses.

Where the fuck is Case?

Case charges the lobby, moving with a boneless grace. Overhead the one-two punch: lightning, thunder. Case sees herself in the wavery glass of the sliding doors. Pale as a shiv of moon.

Inside, the lobby is empty except for those transients

slopped around the television. The cellular is strapped to her wrist. She flips it open, speed-dials Bob's number.

"Where the"—static on the line like poppers—"are you?"

"In the lobby."

"What took you so . . ."

". . . I brought the goddamn car!"

One of the transients turns and puts a yellow nicotine-stained finger to his lips and shhhh's her. She turns on him with acid dripping off her teeth. "Shut the fuck up, zombie . . . Bob, where are you?"

Waves of rain. Drumrolls sweeping in northerly gestures. Bob is walking south on Meadows trying to talk into the cellular. He squints against the coal-black night, struggling along behind the suggestion of three men a block ahead.

Benind the wheel of the Dakota, Case speeds onto Meadows. Head twisted to one side almost obscenely so she can hold the cellular. She can barely hear Bob through the static. Kick out the fear, girl, she tells herself. We're closing in! Kick it out! . . . Fuck. You might as well be jacking off under the sword of Damocles. She almost blows right past Bob as he tries to flag her down.

"What was with that doorstop in the lobby?" Gutter asks. "With the fuckin' decal work?"

Wood shrugs. "What do you mean?"

"That piece on his face. It didn't look weird to you?"

"Weird how?"

"It's the same fuckin' mark Lena has on her face."

Wood stares at him oddly.

"You better keep your head out of paper bags, prince.

That's Lena's old girlfriend's mark. She ran with us before going sheep."

"If this is a history lesson, you're tiring me out."

"It's just gothic to see it on some doorstop's face in the middle of Shitville a couple of years later."

Errol is having to work double time to keep up with his rank bookends. "It ain't gothic. She's here."

Gutter turns. "Who?"

"Headcase."

Gutter stops. "This is bullshit, right. 'Cause it's too fuckin'—"

"But it's true. Case is here. That was her old man you blew off in the lobby."

"Gutter is Cyrus's personal ass towel," says Case. "His number one coolie."

"Well, he checked me out pretty good. Spotted this mark, and I could see something in his face click and—"

"I hope I didn't fuck up," Case says.

The Dakota is doing a careful crawl, slipping and sliding from open parking spot to alleyway.

Bob leans into the darkness of the dashboard. "They stopped! See! Pull over . . ."

"You mean to tell me," Gutter demands, "that freak show back there is her old man?"

"She told me he's been her Visa card for the last year."

"And she does her little magic act all of a sudden. Cinderella knocking at Cyrus's door. Right . . . Her showing up like this is too fuckin' gothic."

"She's pretty junked out. She wants to come home. Do I give a fuck."

Gutter begins to pace. Wood tries to huddle up inside his

motorcycle coat. The rain is blowing into pools across the sidewalk.

Errol gets testy. "I don't want to stand out here in the middle of a fuckin' river while you try to put a couple of coherent thoughts together, alright? As for me, I figure Cyrus would love to blood the little bitch."

"Yeah, but maybe we should make sure she don't want to blood him any."

Through the sweep of the wipers, Case and Bob watch the three outlines haze into a small talking bundle, then clamber across the street and under the awning of a weathered liquor store. Gutter goes to a pay phone hooked up to the wall by the door.

Case hits the steering wheel. "Rat shit."

"Is he calling Cyrus?"

She nods. Her cigarette tip flares in the dark. "Fuckin' black magic," she says.

After a few minutes of phone time Gutter hangs up. He walks over to Wood and Errol. Errol slumps his hands down into his pockets and appears to ask Gutter something.

Gutter answers with a freaky pirouette of his hand for the others to follow.

The pickup pulls out into the dimness past a parked Volvo that's rotten with rust. Bob and Case follow the three men, who walk one block and then turn south on Route 111.

There is a roll of fear and confusion inside the pickup. A tin-sided garden of agony cruising in second gear. Ahead, the mist only half obscures the border station that turns Route 111 into Adolpho Lopez on the El Norte side.

"We're fucked if they cross into Mexico," says Case.

"We're fucked, but do we cross?"

32

Whatever confidence they share in their plan turns to wax facing the border. They pull over. For a minute they lose Gutter and the others in a throw of darkened one-story buildings.

"Whatever we do, we do it now . . ."

"Gettin' across, maybe," she says. "But if we're stopped on that side for jack shit, or if coming back we're stopped . . . how do we explain these?" She pulls up her shirt to show off the semiautomatic tucked in her jeans. Then she reaches for the cattle prod lying on the front seat. "Or this . . . On that side the only way anybody is gonna be looking at us is down."

He weighs each possibility, and each is grimmer than the last.

"Get out," he says. "You follow them on foot so they don't disappear on us. I'll drive across." She doesn't move right away so he shoves her at the door. "Go on . . ."

She jumps out. He tosses her the balled-up canvas coat he has stashed behind the seat. "Go on!"

Down toward the mist with her arms spread out like wings, trying to get that coat on at a dead run.

Bob drives into a lit stretch of road behind two trucks waiting to pass through the guard station. Under a battery of overhanging roadside halogens the mist is orange and almost foul in appearance. He opens the window, lights a cigarette, looks over nervously to where the foot traffic is moving along a caged-in walkway spanned by concrete arches. He tries to pick Case out against the rain.

Case can see the pickup forty yards out through the chain-links. She moves along under the concrete arches. Gutter and the others have already passed through the guard station and continued on to where the caged-in walkway turns and goes down a flight of stairs to the El Norte side.

The rain has made the INS boys uninterested and slow. Case feels herself pressing anxiously against the woman and small child ahead of her. They turn and stare at her impoliteness. When it's her turn she goes through without so much as a bump. She looks back and sees that Bob is still a truck away. She runs down the walk, takes the turn, and half jumps the steps. She has reached the bottom of the walkway when someone steps out from beside a concrete pillar.

"Hey there, Sheep."

She comes to a hard stop and wheels away. Her voice misses a beat. "Gutter . . ."

He leans back against the pillar, raises his boot to the stone. A few people hurry past, first one way and then the other.

"You're gettin' a little aggro, aren't you, Headcase?"

She works the coolie trade, hunching up her shoulders.

"Why you following us, Sheep?"

"I asked Errol to talk to Cyrus about me coming—"

He cuts her off cold. "But you just couldn't kick. You had to start playing Zorro. You and that doorstop of yours. I saw him in the lobby. I know the shit Headcase would try. I remember the child before she was dead to the world."

He makes a fist, holds it up for her to see. She recognizes the tattoo of a beer bottle with the fifteenth mystery of the Tarot as a label. The vessel of unwanted evils. Gutter's own personalized decal.

Bob clears the border station. The passing is short and sterile. The low-rent INS guards: one half asleep and the other couldn't be bothered. Bob cruises Adolpho Lopez. He drives slow, led by the metronome of the wipers. The tires splay apart the images of shop windows cast onto the waters of a running street.

At Uxmal he pulls over. He speed-dials Case's number. It rings in a series of quick clicks. He scans the square ahead.

He recognizes the names of national chains: Payless, Leeds. Shop windows glare with American goods for sale. With slogans conning you in English or in Spanish. It is more like America than America, he thinks. And the phone, it just keeps fuckin' ringing.

33

Bob backtracks to where the caged stairwell empties out into Mexico. He parks close by, walks the area like a soldier facing off against some alien perimeter before the fight to come. In one hand he holds the cattle prod close to his hip in the folds of his slicker; in the other the wheelgun stands ready in a pocket.

The street is empty save for a few stragglers going about the night. An occasional car or truck sprays rain onto the sidewalks. He dials again, gets thrown back in his face a flat-line of unanswered clicks.

He looks up the street where the mist seems to come up off the cement like coal gas. He spots a lone figure moving out toward him from the far sidewalk.

Bob starts up the street. The isolated figure shapes up in the light-pool from a pawnshop window. Bob sees it's Wood. He stays to his side of the street, but gets close enough so he and Wood are just two empty lanes apart.

"Headcase wanted me to tell you she's going a little night-skying with us."

"I don't understand."

"Night-skying—witches' mountain shit. The making of the dead."

"Where is she?"

"Over the hill and through the woods to Grammy's house . . ."

Bob begins to cross the street.

"It's best not to cross." Wood holds up his hand, making like a marionette. "Go on back to Appalachia or whatever white-trash penal colony you escaped from. And things will be cool. You shouldn't a been following us. It doesn't look good on your résumé."

Bob keeps coming. Wood angles a few steps back. An alley begins to open up behind him like the cave for Ali Baba.

"If she's blowing me off I want to hear it from her."

"Sorry, no prerecorded messages . . ."

Bob keeps coming. A cab runs the road, raising a wave of street rain against him. Wood steps back and, like an actor at the end of showtime, takes a bow. The mist flues out the alley and fills the night around him. A black and silver sprite, Wood traffic-cops up his hands and with the red padding in the palms wet and dull and the white circled anarchist's *A* wet and shiny, he screams out, "Judgment!"

He is gone as fast as Bob can charge forward. The alley is a dead blind, and Bob stops. He listens for a bootfall or a voice but there is only the steel dirge of the storm along the rooftops and gutter tins. One or two window lights from above and down the alley do nothing to improve the view.

Bob readies the cattle prod and pistol for the walk forward.

His feet hardly lift as he starts into the alley. The water runs over the ankle of his boots. His breath runnels through his nose like sandpaper. He flashes on that CHP poster by the bar, with the face hidden behind a gun. IS TODAY THE DAY? He draws up the pictures of Sam and Sarah and even those of little Polly Klaas. The unwilling dead breathe fire into the willing and alive.

"If anything happens to her," he shouts, "I swear to you, I swear, do you hear me . . ."

A moment later one of those window eyes blinks in a blind's move.

"Go fuckin' back . . ."

He is shocked to hear Case's voice.

"Case?"

"Go on back, Bob . . ."

He can't tell if her voice is coming from street level or higher up. There is a hollow ring to it as it waves from one wall to the other.

"Where are you?"

"Just go back! It's alright . . ."

At the end of the alley, sixty feet back, is a ten-foot-high brick wall with barbed wire curled across the top and held in place by metal rods.

"Just let me see you."

He listens hard but she doesn't answer. Within moments, somewhere beyond that brick wall a car engine turns over.

"Case . . ."

Something hisses near a Dumpster beside him.

He jerks around. There's a rush of boot metal, and a pinwheel of sparks comes flying at his face. He tries to block it with the cattle prod.

He watches the next seconds in half frames. Something red and dynamite-shaped ricochets off his wrist. He jumps back, chased by a tearing jolt that sends burning white-hot rays up his arm and across his eyes. He smells the slicker as it starts to singe. Blinded, he fires a shot off without the slightest hint of an aim. He stumbles over a rut into the mist and lands with his back against a prop of rotting boards. He stops breathing, clenches his teeth. He torques out for the fight he can't see but knows will come. A woman, somewhere high up, has begun to yell in Spanish. A figure leaps over Bob flashbulb fast, cutting the mist in half. Bob hacks at it with the cattle prod, which hits a piece of metal railing and sends out a fireline of sparks. The red flare lies guttering through the haze beside Bob, lighting the ground around him. He pulls himself closer within the folds of his coat, scrabbling sideways to become a harder target. The figure leaps out through the mist again, and he rakes the air with the cattle prod but misses. The figure counters with a knife.

His breath rushes out of him. He feels a lit match across his chest. The figure shouts coarsely, "Couped!" It then rushes out the open end of the alley.

He sits there for minutes with the gun aimed in case the figure returns. His hand comes up to his chest, feels where his slicker and shirt have been sluiced. He struggles to his feet, his eyes begin a half turn around the alley. That woman is now watching from a window. She is pointing down at Bob and talking to someone else in the room. Bob's legs are a little wavy, but he hurries away.

Walking back to the Dakota, with his hand inside his coat and pressed to his chest, he can feel the blood coming down his fingers. He climbs in behind the steering wheel and pulls the door shut. For a moment he rests his head on the wheel, but thinks better of it.

He pulls away, working the wheel and shift with one arm, driving the car badly for blocks till he finds a small empty lot and parks alongside a couple of Dumpsters.

He turns on the overhead light. He tries slow breathing. His hand comes out of the slicker so he can unbutton it. He sees his open palm has been imprinted with blood. Dark, with the skin behind it pale and waxen.

He flashes on Wood's hand with the insignia sewn there. Blood brothers now, hey fucker. He takes off his slicker so he can look at the wound in the rearview mirror. He grunts as he pulls the shirt up.

His eyes focus on the fifteen-inch-long beauty mark. Done with a fine hunting blade. He flexes the lips of the wound. Long, but not too deep. A dozen sutures will hold that kiss together.

He turns off the overhead light. He lets his head ease back onto the steering wheel. Just a few minutes' rest. A few minutes to gather his guts as best he can back in order.

Order. It used to have some position in his day-to-day existence. Now it's minute-to-minute, and even that is just a crowd of woes.

Fuck it. Weld that wound closed with fishing line and needle. And when that's done dig out the shotgun and a heart full of rounds, and then get a little aggro, as they say.

34

Cyrus sits at a table with a view of the road in what passes for a cantina. It is in the middle of Maquila Row. A mile-long encampment of low, mean-structured factories of cinder block and tin, asbestos and sheathing. Once just the desert of Baja California Norte, it now blooms with American-owned sweatshops and semis rigged out for points of profit across the border.

The rain has stopped. Cyrus turns toward Errol, who speaks in a low, controlled, but furious tone. "I don't appreciate waiting three days for you in El Centro. That's bullshit. You understand!"

Cyrus listens without interest, notices across the mud lot the van parked away from the trucks and battered vehicles lined up there. Lena is sitting behind the wheel as she's been told. But Granny Boy has gotten out and is drinking a beer. He motions to Cyrus that he's just talked to someone on the phone and then gives him the thumbs-up.

"Are you listening to me?"

Cyrus turns to Errol, his eyes like black ash. "I hear, but I don't necessarily listen."

"You can do all the shape-shifting you want for that crew of yours, okay. I don't give a rat's ass. I don't do charity work. I don't give to any church. And I can't be left sitting around waiting . . ."

Cyrus leans forward for a little playful confrontation.

"You want to know why I was late? We were doin' rat patrol. We had this little pretty-pretty with us. You know I like the taste before they even have hair on them."

"I don't want to hear this," says Errol.

"We were having her good when this spic came along. After I went through his wallet I saw he was some kind of mineral prospector and—"

"I don't want to hear this."

"Don't want to hear what? We have to keep our claws sharp, don't we? So I test myself. Unfortunately, I end up testing myself against amateurs."

Errol has had enough and gets up. He takes a map from his pocket and tosses it on the table. "Take a look. See if you have any questions."

There is no shortage of disgust in Cyrus's face as he watches Errol cross the huge room. The space is more fitting to a barn than a bar.

Errol orders another gin. The whiskey is lined up on wooden shelves. The bartender is Latin, from the far south. On the back of his hand is tattooed a pentagram. He looks at Cyrus to see if he, too, wants another drink. Cyrus nods. A couple of speakers are blaring out some homeboy Spanish version of "The Weight." Errol makes his way back through dozens of card tables and Salvation Army reject furniture, where factory dogs play cards and talk away their lives over beer.

Errol sits, passes Cyrus his drink. "You and I have a good business. I don't want to get into any Hunter Thompson bull-shit with you. Okay?"

Cyrus is thinking that Gutter and Wood ought to be rolling in with Headcase pretty soon. Then he'll put this yuppie swine through some real weed-crawling.

"We all keep our claws sharp," counters Cyrus. "So don't tell me you're not fuckin' with me, alright?"

"How am I fuckin' with you?"

"The dead one."

Errol gets a little nervous, as he doesn't understand. "You're talkin' cryptic."

"Headcase," says Cyrus. "Maybe you're fuckin' with me just a little for being a few days late by telling her you'd hook us up, huh?" Cyrus's movements are controlled and precise as he drinks his tequila, but there is fury around the bloody thunderbolts under his eyes.

"I thought maybe you'd want to bleed her a . . ." Errol stops. Sees this whole thing is a fuckup. That no matter what he says, it won't go. He has touched off something and in doing so crossed over into the demon's country. He tries to get the moment back by sliding the map across to Cyrus. "The pickup will be west of Algodones. Tomorrow night. Two mules . . ."

Cyrus has yet to take his eyes from Errol, and in his red shirt with cutoff sleeves and black jeans he is like some blood-stiffened hide.

Errol takes a long drink of gin. "We're gonna get into it, and over what? That cunt. It was just . . ."

Cyrus folds his hands and stares thoughtfully at the face across from him.

"Are we in business or are we out?" says Errol.

"You're a phony fuckin' mock . . ." The architecture of Cyrus's face takes on a churchman's solace. "I know who you are," he says.

Errol adjusts himself in his seat, anticipating the bizarreness to come. He's seen this drill before with others. Sometimes it's just malicious indulgence, but other times . . .

"Maybe you're right, Cyrus. I'm sure I'm as phony as the next. But all I can tell you, if it wasn't for the me's of the world, there'd be no you." Errol gets up, but Cyrus grabs him by the arm and forces him to hold his place.

"You got it the wrong way round. I created the likes of you. For my own pleasure. And when I've had enough, when I've watched you defile yourself enough, I will have you in my belly. And you are dangerously close now to turning this quiet spot into the sight of a nightmare."

Errol stands there, just haunch and flesh and now fear, but he tries to will himself through it.

Cyrus spots the beat-up white Cherokee they've picked up lumping over the rain-swelled potholes of the lot. He can see Case wedged in between Gutter and Wood as the Cherokee pulls around. Cyrus looks back at Errol, smiles. He lets him go. He stands. Sees Errol ease up a bit but knows he still isn't sure.

"I'll bet," Cyrus says, "that for one second, even a swine flu like you was praying to that fag from Jerusalem."

3 5

Gutter leans over so his head is right next to Case's. "You can feel him, can't you? The Wicked King is knockin' on coffins."

He says it to cut deep. She can see Cyrus staring out the window. Framed by the bar's overhead fluorescent light, his skin looks more yellow than she remembers. She eyes Gutter watching her and Wood beside her tapping out a beat on the steering wheel. The cold silence of street wolves on the watch. Catch dogs waiting for the whip or the finger roll to call them to the kill. Suddenly time has brought her back.

Cyrus motions Wood to drive around behind the bar. Case still has the gun, and she keeps Bob's canvas coat close around it. Wood spins the Cherokee through the lot until he comes up along the passenger side of the van and slows.

Case spots Lena in the driver's seat talking with Granny Boy, who is leaning against the driver's door. For a moment her and Lena's eyes lock. Lena slides around in the seat. Her hand, with a cigarette in it, tries to wave, but it is a poor, melancholy excuse of a move.

Case nods back.

Granny Boy comes over and leans in the window. He's got on a perfectly grooved speed-freak grin. "Come back to the goats, huh, lost sister?"

"I'm ready for the velvet collar, Granny Boy."

Before he can get it on, Gutter shoves Granny Boy's face back. "Come on, Cyrus wants us to pull around the bar."

Case notes the disquieting way Granny Boy quickly stops looking at her. The Cherokee swings around, rising and falling through potholes. The trim of the headlights makes a sweep that catches Granny Boy climbing through a cloth drape that hangs across the inside of the van.

Case picks out a pair of whitish legs lying on the green carpet spread across the van floor. Knees facing down, close together. She can't stretch her look too hard with Wood kicking out and the van backing up, its headlights going on right in her eyes.

That trigger of desperate survival that junkies have is struck. If Gabi was alive they'd have to keep her somewhere. But talk about fuckin' mayhem, keeping her in the back of a van as you trip the border.

Of course, it could be some doper chick they picked up on the road who's stoned out. But it could be Gabi, the legs looked young enough, still with the baby fat on them. They were close enough to be tied. Fuck . . . Her head wheels are starting to cook, even fry some.

Case does the junkie nose-play shit: sniffing, wiping. She starts with the edgy body ticks. She motions with her head toward the van, tries to bait them out. "I see Granny Boy has got himself a little sex kitten."

A denuded stare between Gutter and Wood. Punk rhetoric in posturing.

"From birthmarks to teeth marks to needle marks," says Wood as he winks at Gutter.

"I can smell that Tijuana perfume from here," says Gutter, sitting back now and watching Case even more closely.

Tijuana perfume. Their old crack about teenage pussy. Unless they scragged some other piece, it had to be her. Had to be . . .

Errol trails behind Cyrus as he cruises past the bartender. The bartender is a taller man with white hair who carries himself like a judge, or a felon held in high regard. He and Cyrus exchange a few words in Spanish, and the bartender reaches toward a key rack on the back wall. He tosses Cyrus a motel key. Cyrus leans over the bar and the men share private whisperings. The bartender nods diplomatically, then they both make fists and the backs of their hands meet, pentagram to pentagram.

Cyrus turns to Errol. "Party time."

The Cherokee pulls around the bar into a large open field of weeds, mud, and rusty artless shapes of metal. Electric lights are strung along cables from the back door of the bar to a chorus of Port-O-Sans broken into two groups, each with its own hand-painted sign—one of a naked man, the other of a naked woman. One last bullet-riddled Port-O-San sits off by itself at the edge of an incline, with its own hand-painted sign, of a man taking it up the ass.

The Cherokee pulls up and the van squares alongside it. Case does a read of the situation. She could probably do Gutter and Wood before they even caught on. Probably. Probably get to the van. Maybe it wouldn't be easy to kill Lena dead on. Maybe not even possible. And what about Granny Boy? It's the longest twenty feet in the world if you fuck up.

"I know why you're here," Bob whispered. "I know. And you lied to me in the worst way."

She stood there waiting, facing off with him in the magnificence all bad temper affords.

"I'm looking at you," he said. "Through the cheap banality of your lies." He roughed her shirt up. " 'I'll help get her back. Otherwise, if we get close enough, maybe Cyrus will kill her quick.' Right? Isn't that what you told . . ."

She has just a few seconds of luxury to look into the heart of her own debate. Cyrus steps out into the night. He stops just a few feet past the door from which strings of lightbulbs emanate out to the Port-O-Sans.

She is shoved out of the Cherokee. Other car doors open. Slam shut. A few words are spoken. But she is focused on one thing: Cyrus. He walks toward her through the mud.

She could kill him, at least. She could do that no matter what. Blow his whole cosmic empire to ass-dust with as many shots as she can get off.

But she doesn't. She is not sure if she is suddenly afraid for her own life or if he has some power over her. And what about the child? What would happen to her in the minutes after the fall?

As Cyrus comes up to her he puts his arms out in the way of all kindness. "As Son of Sam wrote so correctly,

> 'Hello from the gutters of the west
> Which are filled with dog manure
> Vomit, stale wine, urine, and blood.
> Hello from the sewers of our mind
> Which swallow up delicacies.'"

When he is just a few feet away she becomes deathly afraid for her own life, but she fights herself past it. Just a few good hours, minutes, and she might get close enough to the girl. She puts her hands out. "Can I come home . . . please? Can I co—"

He hits her square in the face. Blood shoots out the piping of both nostrils. She falls backward into the mud and lands square on her ass. She totters toward unconsciousness. Lena starts toward her crying, but Cyrus orders her back.

A few of the factory boys are talking by the jakes. They look at the bloody thing sitting there. Cyrus squats down beside Case. He can hear the factory boys talking up their manhood. He stares back at them and offers a few choice threats in Spanish, and Gutter puts an exclamation point to the whole business with a shotgun tapping the window frame of the open Cherokee door. They move off into the darkness silently.

Cyrus turns to Errol. He holds up the motel key and waves it. "You wanted a little blood."

36

"I saw Maureen the other night," Arthur says.

"I know," John Lee says.

"You do. She told you?"

"No, Arthur, her mouth stays closed only for me. But the moment you picked this shanty of a bar I knew something was wrong. I was hoping maybe you'd knocked somebody up, something interesting like that, but . . ."

The Bugle is a pit stop out on Sierra Highway. A place that's earned its reputation for afternoon drunks and for the recorded jazz version of taps they play at last call. The place is run by a proprietress with huge sagging breasts, index-finger-long painted-on eyebrows, and a pirate bandanna turbaned around her head to cover up a bald spot. The place even has a cooler of sorts for milk, butter, cheese, and cold cuts, which works as a cover to the state so drunks who live on food stamps have a watering hole where they can waste their lives away.

"You got to lay off Maureen, friend. I mean it."

John Lee's eyes narrow. "Do you really think there is such a thing as friendship? I don't mean like when you're kids. When you're kids you're just moments and friendship is those moments. But when the horse is out of the gate and you're racing through the adulthood of your life—the hard years, Arthur—do you think there's such a thing as friendship? Or are all friendships just excuses to get things you want? Need. Get things accomplished. Close deals."

Arthur looks out across the bar from the dark back table by the washroom where they sit. "I don't like where this is going."

"You don't like where we've been, do you, friend?"

"I don't."

John Lee leans forward. "Our friendship is the past. Lest we forget." He smiles. "But we have our good days, don't we? As for the old lady . . ."

"I know she had an affair with Sam."

This gives John Lee pause. "How do you know this?"

"Sarah told me."

"Sarah . . . not Maureen?"

"Sarah."

"You're lying."

"She told me a week before the murders."

"And you said nothing to me?"

"I didn't want to hurt you."

"But you're willing to hurt me now."

"I do not want you hurting your wife."

"What makes you think that's what we fought about, if she didn't tell you?"

"You will not hit her again."

"Or? Will you put me up for public scandal? Am I to be

thrown out of the temple with the money changers? The cunt
went right to you—"

"Do you want Gabi found?"

John Lee can hear himself shifting against the leather
booth.

Arthur continues. "Your wife was having an affair with
one of the victims of a homicide. It might seem to some that
you wouldn't be in a position to devote yourself cleanly to
solving that crime. Some might wonder, *if* those facts become part of the public record. I would be forced to wonder
myself."

"So we're not talking about Maureen anymore, are we?"

"I am talking about you."

"You don't give a shit about Maureen. This is just a come-
on to keep faith with your business partner and social stand-
ings."

"Find Gabi. I mean it. Find her."

"What the fuck do you think I'm doing?"

"I think you're beating your wife and watching your
videos and—"

"Have you heard from Bob and his junkie queen? How
they doin' out there on the road? What would some think of
that? Why didn't you stop them? Huh? And how much did
you subsidize them? Huh? You mind your fuckin' business
now . . ."

Arthur sits back. He rubs his palms against the wooden
tabletop. He sits there like a great boar caught in the brush
and unable to decide whether to charge or back off.

John Lee looks into the stark pattern of half-light the bar
affords, where wayfarers drink and ramble through the small
talk of their lives. How many, he wonders, carry the secret
of murder within them?

"Maybe you and I overreached ourselves, Arthur. Maybe
there's no difference between us and that collection over
there except for one clean shot."

He presses his jaw in the direction of the bar, where the

proprietress is belly-laughing at some private joke with a collection of garrulous barstoolers.

Arthur does a slow turn through John Lee's cryptic comments: We have the good ole days . . . Maybe we over-reached ourselves back then . . . The difference between us and them is one shot . . . Arthur eyes his "old friend." "Are you fuckin' with me? Threatening me? Warning me?"

John Lee stands quietly.

"Did you go after Sam? Did you hire someone to go after him? Do you know what happened at the house?"

John Lee does not ignore the questions, he just lets them dangle there in space. He drops down cash for the bill. As he goes to leave, Arthur heavily grabs him by the hand.

"Sarah's death," he whispers, frightened, "Gabi . . . It wouldn't have anything to do with—"

"Don't go there," John Lee warns, "unless you are prepared for the fuckin' outcome."

37

A small tracer is wedged up into the dashboard of the Dakota, knocking out its yellow heartbeat signal on a marked grid. The signal has been holding steady for the last ten minutes, making it at least humanly possible for Bob to track Case. Bob drives south on Benito Juarez to where Mexicali breaks away into a gallery of arroyos and stream-beds.

He'd sewn a bug into the canvas coat he'd thrown to Case. He had hidden the coat behind the Dakota's front seat on the chance Case fucked him over and split with the truck some-where on the road. Now it's his only lifeline to her.

The miles go by in slow black. He's alone there on the road but for a few rigs blistering past him up toward the border. Moving south through that trace of scraped-out turf, Bob passes great scaffolds of metal abandoned along the roadside. They loom large as girdered dinosaurs against a moon come back from the clouds, thanks to a gulf wind. Most of it is toxic waste; drums and columns, laths and welding joints.

Now and then Bob can see pathetics loading trucks and makeshift pickups with scrap to sell in the colonias. The wound across his chest rages and he rages back, feeling he is part of that ferric landscape. A part of its dire reckonings.

Cyrus has Gutter and Wood drag Case through the reeking mud and into the Cherokee. Errol tries to back off from the whole business, but Cyrus edges him toward the van with a look that is childlike and bemused and wholly without sincerity.

From the back door the bartender watches the two vehicles cross that sumpy prado toward a fake adobe horseshoe-shaped motel on the far road. He smokes a gnarled cigarillo and regrets missing the skelterish pricking that may go down in that room while he serves headless mules.

The motel used to be a whorehouse that catered to Anglos who preferred their stuff with a little color in it. Now it's a roach hole for factory workers stacked sixteen to a room. Except for the back two units. One is where the bartender lives; the other is a playpen of sorts that's seen a little blood in its time.

When they pull up by those grimly attired units and try to get Case out of the car, Gutter finds her gun. He hands it off to Cyrus without anyone else seeing. Cyrus holds the gun in both hands, staring at it as if it were a piece of petty foolishness. He slips it into his pocket.

They half-carry Case in, shunting her between the shoulders of Granny Boy and Wood. Lena follows, but again Cyrus cuts her off. "Whoa, Batgirl," he says to her. "You gotta baby-sit Robin."

"Fuck the little cunt. She's almost totally out."

"Then just think how equipped you are for the gig."

Case's eyes pinch to focus, and she opens her mouth to pull in as much air as possible. She finds herself looking down past the wooden chair she sits on, through her legs, to a shoddy burgundy shag rug.

Her eyes come up with a bleary blinking wideness. The room is lit by two lamps. Cyrus sits facing her with his arms and head propped on the back of a chair. Errol stands behind him by a few feet, near the bed.

"We all want to come home in the end, don't we?" says Cyrus.

Case nods, adjusts to the light, to consciousness. Feels some blood still dribbling down her nose and into her mouth. She looks over toward a bureau where Gutter is sitting, and beside him Granny Boy and Wood have a spoonful of arm juice heating up.

"How much is it worth?" says Cyrus.

She turns to him. The room stinks of cheap fragrances. She goes to speak but Cyrus stops her.

"You better know the right price," he warns.

He leans over and takes a few spittles of the blood that has trickled down around her lip onto his finger and puts it to his own lips and tastes.

"It's worth all I have," Case answers.

Cyrus takes her gun from inside his shirt and holds it up. "Good answer."

The adrenaline clears her head quick now. Cyrus looks back at Errol.

"You know what the real equalizers are? Suffering and death. Everything else is day care. Suffering and death, they lay it out fast when it comes to who you really are."

He looks back at Case. "How do I know I can trust you coming home? How do I know you're not trying to fuck with me some way?" He holds her gun near her face. "What was this all about? Maybe you wanted to punch a few holes in the Messenger, huh?"

She sits there without so much as moving.

"You come tripping over the border, I wonder . . ." Cyrus looks at Errol. "People have all kinds of games. You too, Errol. You like games. Don't you, chief?"

"I don't know what you mean."

"Mister Firewater. Mister fuckin' yuppie redskin phony who changed his name so nobody knows he's a piece of scum meat from the reservation. Wants to be Mister unqualified white bread."

"What does this have to do with anything? I'm half . . ."

"How do I know you and baby dearest here haven't gotten together and are planning a little court politics against me? You help her get back home. I go do the score, pick up your stuff. And then she does me. And maybe the others. Maybe she sets me up for a couple of your coolies? How do I know? How?"

Errol can feel a dampness clam across his chest. He looks around the room. It's already started to change shape, as Gutter has slipped off the bureau and found himself a nice quiet spot by the door.

Errol churns out the words. "I'm not gonna buy into this." He turns to Cyrus. "I never travel with protection. I don't carry weapons. I don't scam and I don't screw anybody. And if I was ever gonna get into something so radical, would I use Headcase? Fuck no."

Cyrus answers with bitterness. "It's time you wear the death mask." He hands Case the gun. "Do him, sister."

"What kind of slashwork is going down here?" shouts Errol.

Cyrus forces her fingers around the gun. "We need blood to preserve the youth of America. Go to it, sister."

She stares into her gun hand. It reeks of choices, all rotten. Errol is dropping into panic like a plane that's lost all its engines. He tries to wand off the whole room but his arm hits a lamp, sending it to the floor and causing a collision of shadows along the ceiling. Great black images of Wood holding up the needle and Granny Boy doing a lewd mantra to get it on and Gutter playing bouncer by the door with fingers hitched in his belt. It's a torched ensemble of swaying light and muted faces and music from some car radio ripping past the window.

She could do Errol without so much as a bump in her thoughts. She knows that. And she could put the gun under Cyrus's neck just as quick and take out a few pints of brain matter.

But she must have gotten too clear too fast. She kicks the hammer back. It's like dropping into some hypnotic recall. The gun cunt from Cafe Armageddon. The vengeful corpse from the Land of Gog. She knows Cyrus can read her, and that he knows she can read him.

Two witches they are, who have tightroped miles of mind warp together. The past and the present all turning into one split second of their lives. The rattler and its tail working in perfect unison but striking out for points unknown to the other. As she kicks the chamber and lets it snap back into place, her fingers tell her in shades of weights and measures how this deal is going down.

"Play Travis Bickle," Cyrus whispers. "Go on. Do your Robert De Niro mohawk shit, but remember how far the door is . . ."

He can't fuck with her, because she knows the game now. So she's gonna ride this whole scene out. A griffin on a great black and chrome Harley aiming the gun at Errol, who is nothing more than a cutout scrap against a lit ceiling coughing up gibberish and gagging like he was forced to do a little deep throat.

The room is filled with Cyrus's swill as he points to his heart and says, "That's where we carry the true country!" And in the instant she should fire she turns the gun around and without the least touch of emotion gets her mouth around the barrel and pulls the trigger.

38

Bob walks that blinking yellow cursor building by building. From factory to warehouse to open lot through a half mile square of Maquila Row, till he finds himself staring through a battered roadside hurricane fence at a cantina where the flashing cursor pulses intense and spotted, like the heartbeat of a child in the womb.

He goes back down the road and brings up the Dakota. Parked there at the back of the lot, he gives the place a procedural looking over while he takes some rope and ties a mooring hitch to the stock of his shotgun, then slips the loop of it over his neck and slides the weapon under his slicker. He does the same with the cattle prod.

He cruises the lot from car to car, searching for Case. He must give off the smell of the unwelcome guest. La migra after the coyote. Maybe some white-trash racist biker come south in a hunting party of one, hot for wetbacks. He sees it in the faces of the drunks he passes, in couples posing against the bare moon, in the crews of factory workers pigeoned up around a bottle of rum cut with cheap cola and sipped from paper cups. They speak in a low native tongue that he doesn't understand and now wishes he did.

"I don't see the point," Bob said. "It's our country. It's our language. They should be made to speak our language. Otherwise all bets are off . . ."

Sarah listened quietly, cleaned the dinner plates, then turned to him with a look of polite disagreement and in poorly accented Spanish thanked him for his political wisdoms.

Inside the bar, things serve up no better as he passes through a world of faces. From a handful of whites he gets the barest of acknowledgments. When he stops and asks them if they've seen a woman and three men, describing them and his concern, they have nothing for him.

From the bar he scans the room again. He manages to order a beer and a shot of tequila with pathetic hand signals. That fuckin' yellow light has to be dead on. He starts to come apart in a chain reaction of atavistic thoughts that end with Case having been done in and dropped nearby in some ditch.

His chest burns from the wound and the homespun stitches. He shoots down tequila and beer to fire the engines for another walking circle of hell.

He cruises the shitters, working the muddy stench of ground beneath those ridiculous carnival lights that sway with the wind. He looks out in all directions, at the fields stretching black and hopeless all the way to another road and a scattering of squat buildings.

A hallucination of self-blame for all the events that ever happened starts to tear away the little space he has left inside himself for clear thinking. It's a night for foot-soldiering this rain-sogged caldera, and every fuckin' inch of it he swears to himself he'll cover. He whispers, "You just stay alive . . ."

He's walking back toward the bar door when something catches his eye. A short fellow with a battered face and bare legs and flip-flops passes through a clump of men talking by the door. A drunken gnome carrying two six-packs up between a couple of Port-O-Sans and wearing a coat that looks close, too goddamn remarkably close, to the one he gave Case.

Beyond the lights, on a path that steeps to a moon-blue incline, Bob cuts the small drunken man off from his destination. His face is at once hostile and frightened till he sees inside the open slicker a pair of gray barrels moving up to greet him. Then he is only frightened.

He starts to speak in quick Spanish, stepping back, his shoes slip-slopping on the marshy gravel.

Bob looks the coat over, grabs it, feels for the tracer sewn into the lining. His thumb finds the small metal nub.

"The woman . . ." He tugs the coat. "The woman. Where is she?"

The little man shakes his head like a vendor saying no to a deal.

Bob yanks the coat harder. "Mujer . . . Mujer . . ." It's all the Spanish he knows, and that from bathroom doors. "Mujer!"

The man's little eyes skit away, and Bob rams the metal barrels against a set of milky teeth. "Mujer—" Bob's other arm jerks the coat again. "Where, where?"

A hand missing one finger points at a silvery piece of wreckage lying about fifty yards out in a run of weeds that gullies down toward a sump.

A wave of the barrel and Bob's got the man pacing off the ground in front of them. About twenty yards out, the silvery hull starts to detail into the chassis of a gas tanker that must have taken it pretty hard in a collision some time back and been left to rot away. The ass end has been shorn off, cutting through part of what looks to be a Shell logo. That heraldic signpost had the *S* chopped off clean, leaving just an expletive behind on a sundried yellow plate.

The little man stops and his hands move with an awkward nervousness toward a point beyond the high weeds where the ground gives way. "Mujer," he says.

A nasty raucous dialogue comes faintly from that direction. A covert whistling of dog howls just under the peel of a breeze.

"Mujer," the little man says again.

Bob holds the shotgun against the man's throat and motions with his jaw for him to go on.

They clear the weeds in a few clumsy steps, and Bob comes around the man and forces him to his knees. His empty face looks up to entreat for mercy, but all he gets is a barrel slapped into the wet marl.

Bob's eyes adjust to the darkness, where in a swill of ground beneath the rig about a dozen men prey on the white outline of a woman who is being held down and humped.

Case lies on a dark raft of mattress in a sea of trash. One or two of the men are naked. The others shamble around the body like apes, watching her beaten-down struggle.

In one gagging rush Bob charges them. He fires the shotgun into the air and the men go scattering or crawling for cover and others fall back into a pack like wolves. He fires again and the sky around him goes stark white from the flash. The one man who was on Case tries to crab away and get to his feet, but Bob kicks him hard in the face and his arms splay and he slides down into the damp morass of garbage.

Bob kneels down beside Case, holding the men away with his shotgun. She is dazed and wobbly as she tries to rise up on her elbows, and Bob can see they'd been juicing her, as there is still a hypo stuck up into her arm.

Some of the men have run off, but five or six lay out in a far circle shooting off sentences to each other in Spanish. Like beasts come for carrion, they're figuring how to make a show of it.

Bob gets one arm under Case's. "Can you stand?"

She tries to see through all the hitting and the heroin.

"You got to stand. I think they're gonna try to take us down."

"I thought I . . . was standing," comes her wavy answer.

"Come on!"

He guides her up, moving the shotgun in a slow arc at the hunched-down shoulders and faces stalking the weeds or curled up around clumps of refuse. They start the game with a chant of wild sounds and hoot calls and low aggressive kisses.

"You've got to be able to stand on your own now. Do you understand?"

Case can hear the words move through her mind but they are like a slow, slow drawl. She answers by letting go of his arm and holding on for dear life with her feet to a broken cloud of mattress.

The catcalls and hoots reach the pitch of an orgied rite. An incensed demand for manhood rebels at being held off from the meat by one fuckin' punk with a gun.

Bob tries to steer Case up through a rutted stretch of weeds. He's got a sense that if the men are gonna come they'll have to get it on before he and Case clear the rise and end up in sight of a cesspool of witnesses.

They start up through the reeking ground like a pair of battered prizefighters, but the men come on in a fanning web, grabbing up rocks and poleaxes of piping and broadswords of wood sheeting. It's street-dog time now, and they're shouting to each other in Spanish about how to do the takedown.

Case tries to warn Bob as best she can about what she hears, but the words come out muddy and lifeless.

"Tell them to go back," he shouts, "or I'll fire on them . . ."

She scores out the words in venomous Spanish up the steep side of the incline, naked and pale as a border of moonlight and reaching with her arms for something to grab onto.

The men come on in bent, bandy-legged charges and feints. Then one of them flings a rock and hits Bob in the side of the neck. The shock sends him reeling to the ground. Case tries to stop his fall but can't. And the men charge in.

But the ground that works against one works against them all, and they can't coordinate the surge. A fat grizzled thing, shirtless with a scarred belly, gets there first. He grabs hold of the shotgun. He and Bob start the struggle around the gray weapon and twist desperately, but Bob frees one arm and gets hold of the cattle prod and brings it up quick as the man tries to take the gun away. He shoves the prod up into the man's throat and hits the joystick. There's a short static zap, and the man's voice shrieks and he collapses into a seizure.

Case slips down and tries to help Bob pull the shotgun loose from the man's grip. They get it loose and he uses the barrel of the gun to stake himself up. Another man is in the middle of a charge with a six-foot draw of pipe, howling like a Mayan warrior, when he's met head-on by a shotgun blast.

He is catapulted sideways and down into a sewered run of mud, and when he hits the ground it sounds like a hard slap across the face of the earth.

The men freeze.

Bob can barely get his breath. He stares at the reddening bloom across the moon-shaped white shirt.

"Tell them . . . Tell them . . ." He half grabs his breath. "If it's blood they want . . . to come on . . ."

Case slogs through the words.

They begin a slow, deadly backtracking up toward the lights, moving behind the unwavering eyes of the shotgun as the men hold their ground, frozen where they stand like bone piles in a charnel house.

39

Case sits wrapped in Bob's slicker, her legs pulled up like a battered child's on the front seat of the Dakota, watching the night miles of the desert along the Canal Del Alamo issue up toward the border.

She's coming off the nod after being shot up. Her voice is husky with stalled emotions. "When we were in that room and he flashed up my gun, I thought, Here comes the evil hour before the . . ."

She makes a weak stab like working a dagger into someone's heart. Her eyes begin to swim and she rests her head against the frame of the open window.

"But when he started to mindfuck Errol, I thought I might have a shot. When he's doing his face-to-face rattlesnake-to-ego fuck with somebody, it's just a game. It's not for the kill. And then he hands me the gun, so I'm in the game now. I think, I'm back. In the family . . ."

She takes a long breath through her nostrils to try to clear her head. They ride toward a coal-blue sky that presses the cutout edge of the hills.

"Yeah," she says. "Yeah, fuck me is right," she whispers to herself. "He hands me the gun," she says. "I can feel it's empty, man. I can feel it. Even swimming through my head I can. That's how I am with all this, from all the years. I mean . . . *then* he looked at me."

Bob turns to watch her for a moment. Her face is a wooden carving of the face she usually wears.

"Then I knew . . . I knew he would do me in his own way. So I quit the game and put the gun in my mouth like I was saying, Let's get it on. And I pulled the trigger."

Her face leans around. It is the color of autopsy flesh.

"You better stop the car," she says. "I'm going into relapse mode with some old witches."

He pulls the car off into a stretch of desert blackness. In each direction the brooding silhouette of untouched and untamed landscape. She wanders from the truck, shivering and naked inside the slicker. She falls to her knees. She begins to retch.

Bob walks toward her slowly. "Can I help you?"

She fans him away with an arm. "It's not the juice. It's my head."

Her body leans forward till her hands touch the ground and clench the dirt and squeeze till dust spindles through her fingers and the ground slops up her vomit.

She leans back, sits on her calves. She looks up and tries to get a mouthful of air.

"I fucked up," she says. "I should have shot him outside that bar when I had the chance. We know he's got her. It has to be her. I should have put the screw to him."

Bob approaches her cautiously, squats down behind her. "Then what?"

"Then what? He and I would kiss oblivion, that's what."

She tries to sleep as he drives north. They pass the Mexicali airstrip, cool with the sun's coming pink across the pumice rock and still life of planes.

Through a dazed restlessness she asks, "Why? Why would Cyrus risk trekking back and forth across the border with her? He wants her alive for a reason."

His own body is so beaten and stiff, so burned down from the night before, so caught up in the replay of a murder, that he can hardly think through another thought. He can hardly hold on to the wheel except by a double-tight grip of both hands.

"The answer is close to home, Bob. It has to be. It's a

vendetta against one of yours. I've seen this. I'm sorry. But
it has to be."

He nods, but at this moment does not want to know.

A motel; a mew of five stucco shacks that face an asphalt
road. The falling perimeter of a corral in high weeds is the
only other mark on the landscape between here and the
border.

Bob waits in curtained darkness while Case showers. He
sits on the edge of the bed with his shirt off and her words
in his head: "close to home . . . a vendetta."

He tries to see the face of the man he killed, but all he can
see is the color of the skin and the scream.

Case stands in the shower watching the water spin down
through the drain with the mud and filth of the night before.
She stands in the steamy white room before a damp mirror
and clears a view. Her tattooed flesh begins to fill out the
mist like the strange symbols on the cave walls seen all those
years ago.

What would the dead flesh say if it were found somehow
preserved centuries from now? What would it be worth, the
story imprinted there? She notices the huge black-and-blues
where her thighs were wrenched apart, and the broken vessel on her arm that has lumped out like a tumor from where
the needle rammed its way home.

And on her arm, Ourabouris. The circular green and orange snake with its head devouring its tail. You lived to bleed
another day, huh? Maybe there is more meaning to that fact
than even she knows.

She lies in bed wearing only a T-shirt and stares at the ceiling. He sits on a chair by the window, where the daylight

narrows through the short fall between curtain and frame. Across the road, on the withered posts of a corral gate, he watches ravens collecting for the day.

He tries to remember the story she told him about ravens when he hears the strain of her laugh.

"What?" he asks.

"You put a tracer in my coat on the chance I'd run. I'm lucky you're such an untrusting son of a bitch."

"I'm sorry I didn't trust you."

Her mouth rucks, her eyes close. "I'm sorry I fucked up."

"You? How?"

"I should have killed him."

"It wouldn't get us where we need to go," he says.

She does not notice that he used the word "we."

She begins to drift some. "It's rat patrol tonight somewhere around Algodones."

"I guess we couldn't find him there."

"Not likely."

"After that he's up to Mojave, right?"

"Yeah . . . And I'm sure Errol will be putting pins into his prick thinking about that reunion."

"We should cross the border tonight and get it on up to Mojave. Get in Errol's ass."

"That ought to be a sweet crossing, especially if the humper you flattened has got some relative with the pigs hereabouts and they tagged us."

Bob puts his head back on the rim of the chair, and while sitting there in mid-quiet is caught by the sound of his own words. "Last night in the bar I was angry because no one was speaking English and I couldn't understand them. I knew, I believed anyway, some could speak but were fucking with me. I felt they were fuckin' with me. And when I got my drink, for some reason Sam came to mind."

"Sam?"

"The man my wife married."

"Oh, yes . . ."

"I thought she married him in part because he was black. To point out to me the differences between us. Thinking about that last night, in that bar, the way I felt then, says an awful lot, it seems to me, about who I really am. And I'm not sure who I am is the man I set out to be.

"You see, I've discovered during all this that in some way I truly believed I was better than everyone else. That I had inside me some sort of ethical superiority. That the universe was bound together by all I felt and believed in. That Bob Hightower knew what was right, and all remarks to the contrary were just that—contrary."

He pauses. "I don't know why I brought this up."

She lies there a long moment, watching the single arrow of daylight that points across the ceiling above the bed.

She taps the bed. "Come over here beside me and lie down and sleep. You need rest. You need to shut the brain down."

He does not move. She taps the bed again and slowly he rises and goes and lies beside her. They both seem to be staring at that single fixed arrow that marks the way from wall to wall. She glances at his suture marks, which rise and fall with his breathing.

"I'm sorry you had to kill a man. I'm sorry it was over me."

"It's funny what we tell ourselves without saying anything."

"Yes."

"I'm sorry you had to suffer last night," he says.

"My body they've had, the rest they can never find."

She feels him turn over and away from her. And then she hears him begin to cry. She knows he is crying because he thinks he has failed some higher order. She wants to tell him that the world works best without God, because the world is compromise, and impurity, and truth—yeah, even truth—and none of those are God. Not really.

But she doesn't.

4∅

Cyrus and his war pack wait on a long gray escarpment. Far to the northeast the lights of Algodones begin to wash up on the shore of the desert through the faltering tide of dusk.

They move about the jagged dogleg of volcanic turf, listening to music from the van's CD player and climbing on the fossilized nubs like the children of vacationers scrabbling for the best view.

Cyrus sits alone near the open back door of the van, watching.

When they have picked up Errol's score they will head out to Algodones. Among their legion is an INS agent who works a border station and will assist their crossing. His sister was a sergeant at the North Island Naval Base and is a practicing sorceress. They share a small ranch on the Salton Sea. A remote portrait of dusty light and clapboard, where from the kitchen you can watch chickens roost in the remains of a wheel-less Dodge Caravan.

Cyrus has been a welcome guest at their rituals, and there are those who swear that beneath the Detroit-stamped chicken coop lie the remains of wetbacks and hitchhikers who have lost their way to the prowlings of the damned.

Cyrus glances over at Gabi. She is far back inside the van. She is neither bound nor gagged. He walks over and sits on the rear bumper where he can see her better. She is now leper to the child she once was. Her eyes are well into the hollowing process.

He motions for her to come forward, which she does. She sits near him. He takes her arm. The mark of the needle has found its way along a trace of veins. The slow helix of his will. He takes her by the hair. He searches that mute face for a seed of defiance that might be holding out against him. He begins to test her. "I know what you're thinking. One day you'll be safe. The police will come. Or maybe your grandfather will come. That dear, dear man. Or maybe your father. I know that Uncle Tom wasn't your real daddy. Ohhhh . . . They'll be weeping for you. For a long time. Some will bleed to death from the tears. Stricken by evil, they will say. Right, pretty-pretty?"

Her eyes blink. She does not move.

"It wouldn't matter. It's too late anyways. Too late, child. Even if I were to send you back. *Which I might* . . ."

He waits on that note to see what his words draw out of the dead pale of her face.

Lena came crying back into the van. Kicking at the doors and walls, punching at the ceiling and cursing Cyrus. She sat in the corner like a petulant teenager, the corner opposite where Gabi lay. Gabi watched, hidden by a hand across her face, with drained eyes and the dull bilge of brain matter deadened needle by needle, as Lena rambled on. A grim trick child herself.

She listened as Lena swore she'd kill Cyrus if he hurt some woman. It must have been the one she saw when she was alone in the back of the van. The one behind the bar, knocked down into the mud and kicked. The one she saw through the bent eyelid in the metal frame below the hitch lock who fought against Cyrus as she was dragged from that motel room.

"It doesn't matter," Cyrus says. "Nothing you can do matters. Because even in the end, if they had you back, you would be poisoned. You'd be a whore junkie who's been had by the dirt of the world. They'd speak about you behind your back. The men you'd want would hate you because of where you'd been. And the men you wouldn't want would want you because of what you've been. And some will believe there is a little bit of Patty Hearst in your blood. You don't know what I'm talking about yet, but sometime you will. Because people look for evil everywhere. But those wouldn't be the only reasons . . ."

She tries to hide from the carnage he offers by staying fixed on a point in the sky where the day's heat collects into the great bleeding rose of the sun.

"If you got back alive. If! Someday you'd ask John Lee or your grandpops why did all this happen. Do you think they want that? Do you think they want to come all over you with the truth? In the end they'd rather have you dead. And in the end you, too, would rather be dead. For you will blame yourself for all that's happened. As absurd as it sounds, you will."

His fingers do a slow crawl through her hair like lizards on the kill.

"Do you hear me? Think of that while you dream. You're the price of their paradise. That's how *I* fucked *them*. And no one wants to look into the face of what they've been. And they would know every time they looked at you that I'm there waiting. I am a piece of your heart now. The largest piece."

She holds her eyes to a last dop of sun. The deep hypnotic she tries to visualize into the flashing light of her father's cruiser. That is him out there on the dying landscape, coming for her, whispering to her parables and promises. She will believe in childlike degrees that which she can still hold on to. But clarity dies away into nightfall in the tomb of that van when she has to face them, one by one.

She will pray through God to her father. And through her father to God. She will make them into one. And she will pray that the one called Lena cuts Cyrus's throat in his sleep. For that also she will pray.

Cyrus pushes her back into the van, where she swaddles up inside a blanket.

"It's time we got you the devil's tail," he says. He looks out toward the country from where the mules are supposed to come. "Yeah. Maybe tonight."

• • •

Up through black ravines comes a wind. Through the wind, Cyrus watches, his head turning like a huge slow battleship behind the night-vision goggles. Three small matchflames of heat begin to burn out of the sandy moonscape to the south.

"They made it across," he shouts.

He points. Lena kneels beside a battery-operated signal flasher. She lines up the flasher to Cyrus's long fingers and begins to flick the on/off switch in a slow progression.

The three candleflames of heat begin to fix on the blinking star of the flasher. Their progress is slow. They lift and fall among the stony dunes for an hour before they are within shouting distance.

Through the windswept grit, an old malabarista and his two ragged young charges from Delicias start the long climb up the escarpment. They are weighed down under the burden of their full knapsacks. Cyrus orders Gutter and Wood down through that crumbling trough of a pathway with flashlights to guide them.

Cyrus and the old man share a long embrace, their talk a vile mix of English and Spanish. They sit apart from the others and Cyrus lights the old man a joint while the three knapsacks are taken to the back of the Cherokee. There, Gutter begins the meticulous warranty of each carefully wrapped brick of heroin.

The old man takes in long draughts of smoke as Cyrus eyes the two young boys sitting off by themselves. Moon-faced youths. Flat and cheerless souls squatting there at the edge of the rock, quietly turning over a few silent phrases between them.

"Are these boys anything to you?"

The old man shakes his head no. "Why?"

"No reason."

The old man gasps in a deep hit. "I did promise them freedom. I was going to give them something from my share and help them on. Maybe going with them to San Isidro. I have an ex-wife in San Isidro that I would like to—"

Cyrus cuts him off: "Kick around some."

Both men laugh. The old man's eyes move at the spice of the thought.

"Just enough to make me hard," he says.

When the white powder has been proofed for the market-place and the short cash handed over to the old man, Cyrus takes him aside and passes him half a bag more.

"And what is this?"

Whispering, Cyrus says, "I want to make a trade." Then his eyes light over toward the two boys.

The old man speaks to the boys with the wisdom of a parent explaining how his good friend will take them to El Norte for the fine work they've done. That a job will be in the off-ing, this too for the fine work they've done. He is a virtual chapbook of compliments about Cyrus, about how he has helped others who helped him. He is contrite about having to go back alone. The boys listen, swimming with the heady hope their dreams are coming true.

All this holds until the old man recedes back into the darkness and the vehicles are loaded and ready. It is then Cyrus comes up to the two boys and lets them have a good look at a Colt banger.

"Take your clothes off, boys from Delicias," he says in Spanish.

They stand dazed in their confusion, then look back toward where they came as if the old man might return and explain all this away. Cyrus fires the gun into the air and the boys strip down quickly. Their faces are etched confusion. The others watch. Soon the boys are naked and herded up alongside the van.

Cyrus walks past them, first left to right, then right to left, like a master sergeant before his new recruits. He stops at the one on the left and takes hold of his cock.

"Your God must have wanted you to be a priest," he says.

Too scared to respond, the boy can only tremble. Cyrus goes to the next, gives his cock a hard looking over, then takes it up into his hand.

"That's a real devil's tail you got there."

The boy is aghast and refuses to make eye contact.

"A real devil's tail," Cyrus repeats with hidden pleasure, letting the weight of it flex across his palm.

Granny Boy comes forward and rapid-fire bangs on the shell of the van with his palms. The boys jump fearfully. He continues on in drumroll fashion. One of the boys starts to cry, and the rest of the pack back Granny Boy up with a cadence of drumrolls against the van's body.

Gabi lies there, listening through the echoing metal to a crying voice that couldn't be much older than her own.

Cyrus walks up to the boy on the left and says in Spanish, *"You're crossing over."*

The boy's face, which had been locked in blind confusion, slowly begins to see its way, believing this "crossing over" to be good news. But before his lips can clear the teeth in a smile, the Colt jumps in and one shot takes off the better part of his face.

He is thrown back against the van. One of his teeth chings against the frame, scoring it. A hole of blood out behind the ear spurts the white of the wall like a whale's spout.

The other boy collapses into the sand, begging for his life, groveling around Cyrus's feet.

41

When Case awakens, she is alone. She tries to stand, but the rapes have left her insides swollen and bruised. She forces herself to walk, to muscle through the pain. She remembers something she heard once in Junkieland: Defilement, like good intentions, is always with us.

Bob sits against the western wall of the motel on a chink of cement almost wide enough for his ass. He whittles at the ground between his outstretched legs with a hunting knife. Case steps out into the light. Bears a hand over her eyes.

"What time is it?"

"Three o'clock or so."

She lights a cigarette. He continues to core at the ground.

"Have you slept?" she asks.

He continues to dig with the robotic dedication usually assigned to the mad or the lost.

She squats down and with a calm cradling voice asks, "Don't you think you should?"

"You're right, you know." He runs some dirt off the blade with two fingers. "The reason is close to home. Whatever the reason is. I had this dream days ago. About my . . . about Sarah and I and . . . Well, the short of it is we were walking up through Paradise Hills to our house. The house my father-in-law built for us. We were naked. She was pregnant. There were men there, workers, watching. Then for some reason she vomited blood."

He presses the knife back into the ground. A deep thrust that turns out diamonds of salt-and-pepper rock and pewtery dust.

"It's all just fragments. You know. Memories, dreams. They strobe at you. I wanted to call my father-in-law to tell him we're alive. But I also . . . had a thought I wanted to ask him about. He wasn't at his house or the office. But Maureen was there."

"Who is Maureen?"

"She's his partner, best friend. She's known us all—Sarah, Gabi, us all—since . . . well, forever, I guess. She's one of the few honest people I know.

"She had money from her family and when they went into business, Arthur and her, he was a contractor and they bought up land. Mostly probate stuff. When I was dating Sarah . . . we were in high school then. I remember they bought up the land of someone who'd been murdered. Out of probate.

"I remember 'cause Maureen was drinking and arguing with John Lee about the bad karma of a thing like that. And Sarah and I were out by the pool thinking how utterly stupid adults were."

"The old lady out at Furnace Creek?"

"That's what I asked her."

"But her land is still there? Empty."

"Empty and useless as shit. But she had other land . . ."

"The old lady?"

"Yeah. Maureen remembers that discussion in the house about the property." Bob stops digging. His throat turns dusky. "Paradise Hills. The tract where I live. The place you came to. That was *her* land."

Case blows the smoke out of her lungs in one great huff. "No shit."

He looks out into the perfect isolation of the landscape. Well across the road the ground reaches far up into a long, terraced hillside of boulders and rabbit brush. If he could have trucks and workers and a creek pool to swim in, it could be that same hillside of his dream.

Case tries to put time and motive to the whole thing. "Cyrus was a junkie back then. So his brain was pretty fried. He could have thought himself wronged somehow. Especially him doing the cold throw on his habit in that trailer. That's heavy shit straight out of the *Twilight Zone*. When you put that extra sting to it—look out."

"But he told you *he* offed *her*."

"Right."

"And twenty-five years later came back . . . ?"

"Don't be surprised at that. Cyrus is the ultimate scalp hunter. I mean it. His pants—they have scalps on them. Braided hair held in by studs. Hair of people he's done ten years after they wronged him. Ten years. Some fuckin' cop that arrested him once, put him in truancy hall. He wrote his name down on a piece of paper. Kept it. Tracked the bastard. Found him in a little house somewhere near Disneyland. Retired. First time he went to off the guy, his life was such shit Cyrus decided to let him live and suffer. A couple of years later, he's tracking him still, the guy's daughter gets married. Has a kid. The old shit is now into the grandpa trip. Happy as hell. Bam! That's when Cyrus got him." She shakes her head. "He's a fuckin' black hole, man."

Bob sits stiffly, staring at the hole he's dug. He considers what Case has said, what he has survived so far, what he has discovered by talking with Maureen. He almost gasps, "Twenty-five years later . . ."

"Down and dirty," she answers. "You have entered Club Scream with this motherfucker."

He reaches for her cigarette, takes a long drag and holds the smoke in, as if trying to warm the hole around his heart.

"Have you only just thought about this? Only since you called Maureen?"

"No. When you first said you didn't believe it was a random act. And at the Ferryman's. When you talked about the

Furnace Creek murder. It was in my head after that. But I
lied it away."

He starts to dig again at the hole. She watches his strain-
ing fingers around the bone handle.

"Why don't you go in and take a bath and get some sleep?
We have to cross the border tonight. I'll get you food if you
want."

He continues grouting out the rock with a pathetic and
limitless anger.

42

Case delivers Bob into the unfused bajada of broken rocks
and boulders. From there he must walk four miles to cross
the border just south of the few blocks known as Midway
Well.

The plan is for her to drive back to the Mexicali-Calexico
crossing, make it through the INS station with the truck. He
will carry the weapons so there's no chance of them getting
busted. Then she'll turn east and wait for Bob at a tin-
sheathed diner of sorts that has a death grip on the Route 8
and 98 interchange.

He will start for El Norte and perform the ritual of the
coyote, the foreigner, the wetback, the desperate one, to
enter back into the land of his past.

Before he embarks on the long walk they sit in the truck
wrestling with nightfall and looking into the maze of skull-
colored rocks the headlights play to.

"The Hard Rock Cafe, huh."

He smokes, nods imperceptibly. "It's got to be done."

"Bring lawyers, guns, and money."

"Guns and money, anyway."

He looks at his watch. The mountains to the west have become black as checkers, with a few remaining bits of their red counterparts along the teeth line.

"Port of entry," she says.

"Port of entry," he says back.

As he gets out of the truck she adds, "I'll buy you breakfast on the other side."

"I got all the money."

"I got enough for breakfast."

He closes the door. "Wait up for me."

"Yeah."

He moves off into the embryonic yellow of the headlights. A slow march with shoulders cross-beamed by the shotgun. Without warning, she wishes she had touched him. His outline becomes a snowy blend of the high-backed dark, and she kicks on the high beams to buy a few last feet of him.

She sees him turn, using the shotgun as the pivot around which he comes. Fingers off the barrel rise into a good-bye.

Sweating through that chilly cape of night, Bob marches woodenly until he reaches a boned pier of rocks. There he kneels and looks out across a cratered valley for signs of the border patrol in their all-purpose vehicles.

He looks for the faint marks of dust their tires will spume up like distant whales on some smoky sea. Or the white searchlight fanning and stalking forward.

Once he is exposed in the flat country, he must watch for any sign of a patrol. The truce he has with himself disintegrates and he begins to see worlds where Arthur and John Lee and Maureen could spell out the cause of the driving death before him.

If that is so, if they were players in part to blame for Via Princessa . . . well, his mind begins to plan out atrocities. Horrific acts that would make even a Cyrus proud. Inside him a killing landscape unfolds, as alien to him as the landscape he trots through. Over that course of hard miles he is alive to its violent reality. It fuels him onward. The desk jockey they, and he, so thoroughly nourished is clearly dead.

Then the face of the terrain to the west turns for the worse. A white beam flashes upward, then descends. A great hole out of the blackness rises again.

He kneels down. The sand is turned up a mile off and coming. It's time to run, coyote. Time to run.

Case can feel drabs of poison from the night before running through her veins. The soft purple river of blood carrying the last stories of heroin from nerve ending to nerve ending.

She watches past the road hour after hour. Past the hulking shapes of headlights rushing by.

Eventually she crosses the road. Walks a long stretch of bedraggled sand watching for Bob in the remains of the night.

She does the battle of putting it all aside. She is sitting morosely alone on a stoop of rocks that lead to nowhere when suddenly a figure andirons out of the earth. A speck against a shield of light coming on and coming on. She stands and blinks like a bird but her eyes are weary. She starts forward out into the desert.

It's him. She can see now he is dragging with exhaustion. Filthy and sweat-stained.

Upon reaching her he says, "I did some running last night. I did some running."

"Border patrol?"

He looks back like a soldier who's cleared the wall, and nods.

She puts her arms around his shoulders and lets him rest there. She feels his heart pumping out through the muscles of his back and into her hands. "I owe you breakfast, Coyote."

43

She drives. He sleeps.

She puts some fire into that Dakota as she halfbacks up Route 5 through that great basin of worldly possessions, L.A. proper.

With all that's on her mind, the whole fucking drive up from the border is like a run through some parallel universe of car dealerships and warehouses and Holiday Inns and cemeteries and the arched yellow monster and billboards hovering electric above the sides of the freeway like dream-machine frigates. The full litany of franchised eyesores.

The hours are one long extended strip mall flanking the road, much the same way shill games and food stands flank a boardwalk. The endless rush of blasted color and flatness from Long Beach to a sky-exhausted LAX.

She floats the radio dial. Comes upon some college station down near Mar Vista in the fifth hour of a Dylan retrospective. The DJ is trying his best to drop his voice that extra octave of approval as he leads into the soundtrack for "Pat Garrett and Billy the Kid." He does a few riff minutes about Sam Peckinpah's take on Pat and Billy and his skew on that morality tale.

They are humping it out to Mojave. California City, more precisely. To a bar Errol owns called the House of Usher, where they're planning to make a snuff film out of his ass if he doesn't come across with his planned tête-à-tête with Cyrus.

All this going through her head with an underpinning of Dylan's rustic guitar and spurs tambourine. Bob is asleep with a little bit of sunlight falling across his chest where the smiley face of his knife wound peeks through. There's the war sound of the tires on hard cement. The pressing metal of

six lanes charging traffic with their word-picture faces.
Heaps of flesh all. Dispersing out through a waste of social
landslides with no idea, none, how much blood is on their
minds. It's a blasted allegory that only the third mind of a
William S. Burroughs could do justice to.

The House of Usher stands pat. It's a kick-ass chain-
shattering beer and whiskey bar. The place is shoulder-to-
shoulder people taking in a blue-plate chickie Warren Zevon
with a five-piece backup doing riff poison that would put a
nice dose of sweat up between your legs.

To Errol she's all mouth and nipples and a fist hammering
out chords at the smoky air around the mike. It's good to be
back on home turf. He's nursing a shot of tequila. Laughing
with friends, giving out the high five as he does the long
stroke down the bar. A word here, checking out the shape of
an ass there.

"Fuck Mexico," a voice he recognizes says.

He turns.

Case gives him one of those hotel-desk smiles, and all he
can kick back is some glassy stare like he's just felt something dead under the sheets.

Bob comes up behind him, puts a little chest into his back.
"Yeah, fuck Mexico," he whispers.

Errol turns again. Shifts his look between the two of them.
He fumbles through a greeting, a weak confounded patron-
age that she answers by taking the shot of tequila from his
hand.

She sniffs it. "I used to love tequila."

She passes it to Bob, who shoots it down.

"Check those headlines, babe," she says to Errol. "Junkie
queen back from the dead."

"Jesus Christ, I don't want to get into the middle of a psy-
chodrama between all of you."

"Maybe you don't understand. That shit back in the motel

room. It was a warning you should read. You're on the verge
of being dead or alive . . ."

It is written that America's most cherished landscapes are its
deserts. And the Mojave stands as America's quintessential
desert. Possibly for the fact that it sits between Los Angeles
and Las Vegas, two of the nation's most powerful demiurges.

Yes, it is also known, thanks to some *Los Angeles Times*
quip artist, as the Bermuda Triangle of California. Within
the borders of its spare geography, cemeteries of nameless
people have walked never to be seen or heard from again.

For their private talk Bob and Case escort Errol down into a
saline hollow far enough back of the House of Usher that the
music just hangs on the edge of the night air. They walk beneath a black sky held in place by a pinboard of stars.

"You know where Cyrus is. We want to meet him
head-on."

Errol plays with the collar of his burgundy silk shirt, kicks
at some burro grass. Case squats down and watches him.

"Hunted! Stalked! And slain!" she says.

Errol looks up.

"I know what's wheelin', you fool, fuckin' prick. 'Cause
you got some business thing goin' on you're alive and well.
Forget it. When Cyrus started with you in that motel room
he already had the vision. He may be putting the black evo-
cation on your ass right now. The Eliphas Levi. I'll bet
you're cooked between St. Mark's Eve and St. John's Eve."

"You're just trying to fill me with a lot of junkie devil shit
'cause you want to revenge your ass for—"

A revolver hammer clicks.

Errol's head cocks about.

Bob's hands are folded across his waist, in one the revolver stands ready.

"Don't go ragging on her with that 'junkie shit,' " Bob warns. "Don't. We have business to attend here."

Errol puts his hands up. "Sure. Any way you want to sell it is fine with me."

Case scoops up a few rocks. Errol's whole body language is the ten-inch-cock stare. She knows he's trying to square out the con on how to serve his own ass while keeping himself alive. She tosses the rocks one by one into the sleeve of a stream a few feet away that's being helped along by a runoff of sewage. Arrow weeds grow out of the mealy wet soil, mixing in raggy lines with the burro grass and giving the hollow an opposing natural geometry.

"I don't know how to make it right for you, okay," he says. "I know what Cyrus did was shit, leaving you to . . . But it wasn't me. Not me. In that room, man, who had the gun on who? Who fucked with who?" His fingers point from her to himself, then again from her to himself. "It's all asylum shit that went on down there."

"We have to know where he is," Bob says.

"I don't know."

Case tosses another rock hard into the stream. "This is all talk sickness."

"I'm waiting for him to contact me."

"We need to know where he is," Bob repeats.

"He said nothing to—"

"When he needs a place to stash or chill out up here he hit on you. I've been there, man. I made the calls to you, remember? What do you have, synapse damage all of a sudden?"

From inside the bar the singer's voice, distant and distilled out of some thundering dream and in the pull of a refrain: "It's just a kiss away . . . Kiss away . . . Kiss away."

"I told you, Case," says Errol. "I don't know. But . . . why fight him over . . . I mean, it happened. Okay. But you're alive. Is it worth it?"

The hint in his voice. The callous judgment of what she is

versus the price of what she's worth is all she needs to hear. Bob knows her well enough from the way she's rocking back and forth on her boots and the turn her eyes take, getting black angry, that she's gonna blow.

"You're fuckin' with the black rider, Mister Yuppie Boy."

Bob can see her hand moving toward her boot. He takes a step forward.

"We ain't making another pass at this," she says.

"I told you I—"

She is up and across the stream, lunging at him with a hand shawled in darkness. Bob moves to stop her. Grabs hold of her in mid-flight. Errol snaps back as her hand makes its bird-quick move.

That half second saves his life. The steel tip of her stiletto just misses his jugular but takes a trowel line of inches out of his cheek. He collapses into the sand with his hands pressed to the side of his face. His blood strains through tight fingers while Case tries to break free of Bob and finish business.

"I'm coming up out of your dreams if you don't tell us," she screams. "I swear. I'll play witch and disciple across your throat while you fuckin' sleep."

Bob stumbles to his knees, trying to hold back her rabid thrashings. Errol crawls away from her kicking boots, leaving a red scrapbook for the sand to leech.

"He's up in the Bristol Mountains," Errol cries. "At a ranger's house. First road east of Bagdad Way that goes north into the mountains off the National Trail."

Errol gets himself up and lurches away. A clumsy footrace to safety.

Once he's gone, Bob lets Case go. She comes around with her knife.

"You should have let me kill him."

"No."

"We're gonna have to kill him anyway. He'll screw us."

"Let it go, for now."

"He has to. His mind is already there. The body will follow."

"I couldn't, alright?"

"You couldn't?"

"No."

"Because of the other night? For doing that piece of—"

"That's right!"

Her knife shanks the air. Once, twice, again. Carving up
thoughts. "Errol enjoyed the other night, you hip. That night
you don't want to remember. He enjoyed watchin' me get
dragged out and needled. I know that dick-hard look!" Her
voice quivers. "We're gonna have to kill him anyway. He's
gonna turn. It's prepackaged and ordered. And you should
have let me cross that bastard over."

44

"Arthur, I talked with Bob."

"When, Maureen?"

"He couldn't talk long."

"Where . . . how is he?"

"Mexico."

"He's in Mexico."

"Yes."

"How is he? Is everything . . ."

"He sounded pretty tired."

"Why didn't he call me?"

"He tried, but . . ."

"He's alright?"

"I guess so. He sounded pretty stressed."

"Gabi . . . Anything about . . ."

"He didn't want to get too deep into it."

"Too deep, what does that m—"

"He was stressed out. Said he didn't have a lot of time. That he had to—"

"I miss his goddamn call, I don't understand."

"He said he'd call you in the next day or so."

"At least he's alive. Thank God."

"Arthur."

"I was beginning to—"

"Arthur, listen to me."

"What?"

"He was asking me some pretty strange questions."

"What do you mean?"

". . . They were very odd."

John Lee can watch his house from the dirt road that rises up into the national forest across from the Paradise Hills tract, a thin line of cypress trees affording him all the cover he needs.

He listens to Maureen and Arthur's conversation through a headset. The small black computerized surveillance kit is laid out neatly on the front seat as if it is in a showroom display.

He has bugged the phones at the house for years as a means of keeping track of Maureen's infidelities, or of any other quiet plans he would not be privy to, from their divorce through to his destruction.

"What did he ask you?"

"He asked me how we bought this tract."

"How we bought it?"

"I told him we got it in probate."

"In probate, that's right."

John Lee can hear the subtle rise in Arthur's voice.

"We got it in probate because . . ."

"Probate, yes . . ."

"Some woman had died, right?"

"Died, yes."

"I mean. She'd been murdered. Isn't that right?"

A long silence through the headset. A gaping pause that begins to swallow them both.

A gunshot turned against the night air . . .

Arthur had walked down to that strange battered chimney which seemed to have been built by some timeless sect. He stood in the powder-black hours, staring at the old symbols painted into the stone. Foolish and childlike abstractions, he thought. The stuff of the lazy and the minstrel. Foremost in his mind he was trying to plot a new way to convince the old woman to sell the land.

She had listened as she drank a beer with her bare feet up on the trailer's kitchen table. Her toes rubbed together, one against the other. They were black as flint chips and she rubbed them as if she were trying to spark up a fire.

All his and John Lee's convincing could do nothing. And that junkie kid she raised, he could do no better. It was the process, she said, not proceeds, that interested her.

A gunshot changed all that.

He rushed back to the trailer. A fire in a rusting barrel burned with refuse and through the smoke he saw Cyrus on his hands and knees. Blood ran from his nose and mouth. John Lee hulked over him.

"You stupid fuckin' junkie," John Lee screamed, then laced the boy's ribs and back with hard boot kicks.

The black smoke was a great tumbling spire that Arthur rushed through as he yelled, "John Lee, what happened?"

"The fuck shot her! She's in the bedroom."

Arthur jumped the mortared wall of bottle art and crossed the garden.

The trailer was dark except for one slant of moonlight that fell across the sheet-draped doorway to the old woman's bedroom. There was no wind, so the sheet was still. The heraldic lily and rose seemed to float against a white amorphous heaven. He pushed it aside.

He looked down.

She lay there on the floor. Her eyes were open but seemed to have lost their color. It was a bloody mucilage where the bullet had taken out a piece of neck and the lower part of her ear.

He stared a long time. This eavesdropping on death left him numb.

Then there was the frail movement of a finger. Like the motion of some dark caterpillar across hard ground. It began a slow scratching march. A failing point. He noticed her chest rise a bit and sink. Rise again and sink. Barely enough to be seen through the heavy cloth of her sweater. The milky white of her eyes seemed to clear and for a moment they found the shore of Arthur's eyes holding in the darkness.

"I'm frightened, Arthur."

"Don't be."

"I don't know why Bob's asking such things."

"It's alright."

"Is it? It scared me. His tone . . . it scared me."

"It'll be alright."

Another pause filled with the confusion of breathing and silence. The perfect riff of the coming hardcore future.

"I wish we were together."

"Maureen . . ."

"I do. You and I should have married."

"Maureen, please."

"You loved me."

"It's a long time now."

"You loved me."

"But I was married."

"But we should have been. We would have been better off. And you know it. There wouldn't be any John Lee . . ."

"You can't blame him for it all."

"Why not?"

45

East of Ludlow the old National Trail Highway, the original Route 66, follows its historical path through the Mojave. As Bob and Case head east, the truth of that road comes upon them. The remains of roadside diners and failed motels mark the yellow-brown landscape. The disintegrating shells of small homesteads and huge billboards are memorials to a post–World War II America. The town of Bagdad is just a sign. Amboy, a sign that a town of twenty is for sale. This architectural cemetery is all that's left of those who settled there and rolled the dice that Route 66 would last forever.

Bob and Case find the road Errol talked about. It turns up into a trace of volcanic cones. Dark, hulking shapes whose centers have been culled out for cinders.

The approach is a miles-long climb. The ground is odd ridges and fissures. The road, a thin bend of the dangerous and vulnerable. Bob walks ahead of the Dakota, far enough to see through every cut or fall.

An hour later they are far into the Bristol Mountains. The white saline flats to the east are matched in the west by the "terrible desert" that John Steinbeck once wrote about. A dry salt hell where the mountains shimmer like ebony crows.

Bob searches every wash, every dun-toned crevasse that fans out from the road, until, at the end of a caldera, he spots the crumbling frame of a two-story ranch house.

He waves Case up. They hide the truck in a spooned-out cutoff. She takes one of the backup handguns from beneath the front seat. They move among the naked rocks to where they can watch unnoticed.

"You think she could be in there?"

Case shrugs gravely.

"Look at the windows down beneath the porch. That could be a basement. They could have chained her down there. I say we make our house call now if we're gonna do it at all."

"Truth or dare," she says. "Let's turn up the dial."

They slide down a scarred hillside and crawl toward the house from the rear. They squeeze between crumbling posts held in place by wires. A few scrub oaks guard a well they slip past. They check each window. Each door. The silence is interrupted only by wind-stung branches.

A photographer's floodlight was thrown on. A black pentagram within a red circle painted on a concrete floor came to life. Another floodlight formed the axis of a stage. Cyrus and his troupe moved about in strips of darkness.

Bob and Case approach the house. They follow their shadows up the creaking wood planks of the porch steps. Their halting images pass a window. They look beyond the curtain into the lightless room. Case touches Bob's arm and his head comes up. Her gun barrel points to the next window over, which is open just a crack.

Cyrus knelt beside the kidnapped Mexican boy. He was naked, his hands and feet bound. A shivering adolescent until the needle shone transfixed in the light of Lena's hand. He then turned into a shouting mongrel, fighting against death.

Like burglars, they move through a room filled with crates. They stop and listen through the milky light-washed silence, and only the breathing hull of the house's chest answers back with a creak and a groan.

The boy's thighs wrenched and stiffened. Cyrus held his devil's tail and squeezed it hard. The child winced like a calf and Lena pushed his scrotum up. The needle pricked the flesh and pressed in fast just beneath the sack. The boy's world fell through screams and a rush of burning heat, and

Gabi was dragged mouth-bound from a scrap of blackened basement into the light.

Case looks up the dark wood stairwell, enclosed so it's no wider than a catwalk.

"You go find the basement," she whispers. "I'll go up."

He nods. "Keep watch out those windows. We'll go back out quick if they come."

They separate. Bob feels his way down a shadowy hall for the basement door. By the pantry he can hear Case start up the creaking stairs toward the second floor. Walking past the glare of the dining-room windows, he looks outside. He notices a wooden shed near the remains of a garage. The doors are open, and an odd pool of water has accumulated inside and out.

Two more floodlights snapped on. Now the four corners of that basement world were lit around the moment when Gabi lay in waiting with the pentagram beneath her.

Light through yellow shades. The spice of perfume, musk incense, and pot attack her nose with the tincture of the satanic rituals she had been borne under with Cyrus. Her fingers nervously flit across the hammer of her gun as she senses what she will find somewhere within these walls. The hush is broken by a rusted hinge on the floor below.

Figures in ski masks moved like prankster effigies, herding in the boy as he crawled about the room on all fours trying to get away. He wailed at the drug-cornered chaos.

Bob approaches the shed. There is an angry buzzing from within. He gets close enough to see flies in the threads of light that have come through the lattice walls. Flies swarming the dead air like an army of locusts. Flies on the walls in staked columns across the thin reefs of wood like living tumors. Their green bodies some mossy cline grown over dark-brown rotting timbers.

Cyrus cut the tape away from Gabi's mouth. She gagged but did not speak.

"*It's time to taste the devil's tail,*" he said.

Looking for Bob, Case finds the basement door. She steps down into the well of stairs, her hand reaching through the pitch-black for a light that doesn't work. She calls to him, gets only the cradling wood of the stairs' frame under her weight. Her face pinches nervously at the phosphorous bitters of gunsmoke and the damp of the earth below ground.

In his psychotropic delirium the boy is dragged over and tossed onto Gabi. Dazed, he tries to crab away. He is grabbed by the hair and pulled back. The black-gray head of a video camera zooms for each second of face. Behind the swimming phosphorous light and dark the picture-planet basement swims with shapes at converging angles shouting in English and Spanish, "Do it! Give her the fuckin' devil's tail, boy. Give it to her or . . . you will die!"

Bob's stomach sours from the odor of spoiled meat. Dried, rank in the air like some shank of flesh hook-hung in a desert market. He looks down at a foamy scum spinning about the hose nozzle that snakes into that pooling well. There is a half-used bag of lime by the shed wall and a shovel lies in the sand beside it.

Behind the teardrop flame of her lighter, Case scans the basement within the compass of four silver floodlights and the pentagram painted onto the concrete floor between them. Imprinted on the wall, her flickering shadow stares back at her between two inverted crosses cut from wood planks and nailed to the wall with cleats. She stands there, heartsick and shaky. She knows what's gone down. She's been an honored guest at these death rites.

Outside, Bob probes at the black muck with a shovel. Inside, Case notices the lighter flame buckle with a sudden turn of wind. She stands, sensing someone's presence.

She moves cautiously toward the stairs. Her eyes crane at corners the light can't find. With the smell of earth heavy in her nostrils and the gun held tight against her hip, she follows that poor flame up the stairway.

Something hard pushes against the shovel, and Bob lifts.

Brown muddy water slides off the shovel's tongue until the outline of an arm comes clean. It is dark-skinned and three fingers have been ritually amputated.

He recoils and the arm drops. He stands there facing one thought: His baby could be in that grisly sump. He starts shoveling at the water frantically, calling Gabi's name.

Case slips through the basement door and waits. She listens. She starts toward the dining room and sees reflected in the pantry glass the face of a man lunging from a dark alcove.

Before Case can get her gun hand up she is grapple-hooked around the shoulders by a pair of beefy arms. Two fast shots from her gun splinter the floor. Bob drops the shovel into the watery scum and starts running toward the house.

The man rams Case into a breakfront. The shock numbs her back. Bob shoulders the front door and the lock plate tears apart. Again Case is rammed against the breakfront, as she struggles to get her gun hand loose. Glass shatters; her gun hits the floor and goes off.

She can't free herself. She can hear Bob down a far hallway. She tries to warn him but the man throws her across the dining room. She spills over a table and chairs, and her face hits the floor hard. She lies there stunned.

Bob stumble-charges into the living room, working his semiautomatic out from inside his shirt. The man grabs up Case's gun to meet this new threat. Bob turns but he doesn't see the man aim. Case tries to clear her head. As Bob starts for the dining room, he runs straight into a flash of gunfire that rips out slits of wood less than a foot from his face.

Bob body-slams right to the floor. Another shot burns out the air above his head. Bob scramble-crawls for cover. The man kicks away a fallen chair and sets himself to fire down on Bob.

In these few seconds Case shakes off her swimming vision and grabs her knife. The blade clears the boot and she comes up slashing at a few fine inches of neck.

One cut. Quick and clean. One clean, fast grunt. A jet of arterial blood spits into the still air. The man comes about. His mouth and jaw move frantically. His legs quiver. The great chest in a park ranger's shirt mottles with blood.

Bob is up. He rushes into the room. Case steps back and away from the man's shoulders. The man's gun hand lifts to fire, but the gun has fallen away.

Case steps forward once more. She aims at the soft folds of neck just above the breastbone, then says, "You're crossing over," and she drives the blade in till her knuckles scrape against his jaw.

"Are you alright?"

She has collapsed down onto her knees and stares into a face at death.

"Case, are you alright?"

"Alright . . . Yes . . . yes . . ."

"What happened?"

"I don't know."

He steps over the body. "Who is he?"

"I don't know. Probably the fuck that lives here."

He helps her up, reaches for the gun, hands it back to her.

"I found a body," he says.

Her face comes around to find his. She nods as if this is not something unexpected.

"In the shed. It's buried in the shed. With lime. Under the water there. I guess to help it start to decay and . . ."

She looks back toward the basement door. "Was it . . . ?"

"What?"

"Was it . . . ?"

He understands what she's asking by the way her eyes narrow down into a frightened honesty.

"No. The skin was too dark."

"Was it a boy or a girl?"

"I don't know. I . . ."

He sees her glance again at the door by the pantry that opens into an unlit stairwell.

"We better get out of here," she says. "Now."

She walks over to the dead man and pulls the knife out of his neck. There's a threading hiss. Along the edge of the blade are blood bubbles, which she wipes on her jeans.

The whole time Bob stares into the kingdom of that door. He stops Case as she passes and points toward his suspicions with the jut of his chin. "You know something, don't you?"

"Let's just go."

"That body is not two days dead. Something's gone down here. What was it? Have they killed Gabi?"

"I can't say for sure."

"Don't lie to me now. I need the truth. I can't . . ."

"The truth I don't know now."

"Have they killed her? Have they buried my child out there in that . . . slime heap?"

His cheeks are the coarse gray of blankets slid across the dead flesh of children from war to war.

"They might have," she says.

"What do you know?"

"Let's just go. Please. For your sake, now!"

He takes a step toward the door. She tries to stop him but that only tempts him on. He pulls free of her, and she has to chase him down the stairs.

In the dark he lights a match.

He scans the grubby basement fresco with its foul odors. "What is this?" he asks.

"It's a death rite."

"A what?"

"They bring children to this. Novitiates. Drug them hard. Force them to . . . rape each other. Or worse. And in the end they're killed. Not all, but . . . mostly all. Some are kept. Like me. The rest . . . their blood is taken for . . . a taste of the spirits roaming in the night, as they say."

He blows out the match, looks up at the ceiling, closes his eyes in despair.

"Bob. We better get out of here."

Bob opens his eyes. He begins to pace.

"Bob, you know how many freaks one of these death rites brings out? Twenty. Thirty. They could be planning on coming back for some major blowdown. You don't want to fight them in here."

"Will *he* be back?" Bob asks Case.

"Maybe."

"That shit he has to deliver to Errol, would he leave it here? Would he think it safe here?"

"I don't know."

"Before a delivery, did he ever stash it in a safe house like this?"

"Yeah. But I don't think we got days to scope this joint out and see if—"

"We got to make him come to us."

"What?"

"*Him* to *us*. He carried the plague to ours. It's time to take the plague to his."

His eyes flip upward toward the ceiling. "Upstairs? He'll know it's us. Or Errol will have copped to him it's us."

"Yeah. So . . ."

There is desolation in his voice. "In the Roman Colosseum, when the Christians were sent to face the lions, the lions didn't always attack. They didn't get the gig. What they were there to do. So the Christians sometimes attacked them. Forced them to quick-kill. To end it. That's what we're gonna do to him."

"How?" she says.

Devastation across the shapeless mortality of his features as Bob turns away. "We'll start with something he should understand . . . Fire."

46

Within an hour the first flurries of smoke are spotted along the nape of the horizon by a couple of National Chloride execs who are lunching on chili at Roy's Cafe in Amboy.

By dusk there are helicopters circling the black mushroom cloud the wind is dragging toward the ocean. It takes the fire engines over an hour to make the grade through the foothills. By then the house is a mural of flames that yaw and spit through its charred shell.

Errol sits quietly in his office at the bar, staring at his food. His stitched and bandaged face a swollen and slow-moving Vicodin haze.

Outside, the sounds of talk and music mean nothing. He is a well-dressed privateer staring at the thought of death in the scraps of an unfinished meal.

He pushes the plate aside, leaves without a word.

In the alley behind the bar he goes to unlock his car door. A flash of bad news comes between him and the lock. He looks up, too wasted to move.

"I hope you didn't cop to Cyrus," says Bob.

"Have you been out there?" Hesitating, Errol glances around. Sees Case waiting by the Dakota, which is parked across from the entrance to the alley. "Keep her away from me," he says.

"She's harmless . . . for now."

Errol is a physical statement of defeat, pretty much mooked out on downers and fear. "Have you been out there?" he asks.

"Yeah . . . But no Cyrus."

"Oh," Errol says. He tries to open the door but Bob blocks the move with his hand.

"What! What!"

Bob holds out a cellular phone, presses it into Errol's hand. "We need you to pass on some bad news."

The word passes quickly from one friend of Cyrus's to another, and by nightfall Cyrus and Gutter are parked along the shoulder of the National Trail Highway in a borrowed Bronco watching the coroner's wagon trek up through a posted roadblock of police cruisers toward the house.

Cyrus walks a line of news vans and reporters filing video blurbs under a battery of handheld floodlamps. He picks up the few sketchy details that have surfaced: The charred remains of one person found in the smoldering ruins. The remains of another found in a half-burned shed. There is a rumor that the second body had been decomposing for two days, but this the police will not verify.

He has a sense of what has moved against him, but he'll know for sure when Errol shows. He crosses the road, kills some time by walking among the watchers.

A dozen cars are staked out around the site. Those who bring a camera and basket lunch to the moment of black death.

Heading back to the Bronco, he overhears a young woman talking to a friend about the "Vampire Rapist" in Florida, who spent only ten years in jail for kidnapping a hitchhiker, raping her, and drinking more than half her blood over a twenty-two-hour period.

Three dim-faced angels listen from their car seats as mama questions her friend: "I don't understand how anyone can commit such a crime and get out after ten years. By what rationale? How is it possible? What reason could they have for ever letting anyone like that out of jail?"

Cyrus turns and with a quiet, familiar reverence answers, "Crowd control."

Cyrus sees Errol pull up. He waves to Gutter. The three converge on a strip of brush a short way up from the news vans.

Cyrus has the light to his back, notes the gauze bandage across Errol's cheek. "What do you know?"

Terrified, Errol answers, "Headcase."

Cyrus does not react. "How do you know?"

Errol has to lower his eyes against the light from the floodlamps the police are setting out to guide their vehicles up into that remote trail. "I saw her less than an hour ago."

"The fuckin' cunt's got nine lives," hisses Gutter.

"Go on," says Cyrus.

Another forensic truck passes. Errol shields his eyes to watch as it slows and turns into the police barricade. "What the shit went down up there? The news is saying . . ."

"Fuck all that, chief. Go on."

"She says she scored the stuff you brought across the border."

Gutter eyes Cyrus.

"She does?"

"Her and that guy she's traveling with. They said they scored it out of the house."

Cyrus looks back up that narrow hallway of a road.

"Did you stash it up there? Did you?"

Cyrus glances at Gutter. His teeth rub against his lip. "They're trying to bet the magic . . ."

Gutter nods.

"Did they get it?" asks Errol.

Cyrus turns toward him. A dark precision to his voice. "How did she know about this place?"

"Your own," Errol answers.

Cyrus studies Errol.

"That's what she said. She heard in Mexico. Remember, we talked in Mexico—"

Cyrus turns away, looks back at the watchers.

"Before she'd even showed, we—"

"Close the hole up, chief," says Gutter.

Errol quiets, then says, "She wants to meet you. She and the doorstop."

"Does she?"

"Yes."

"And how is this to be done?"

Errol reaches into his pocket. He takes out the cellular phone Bob has given him and holds out his hand. "All you got to do is hit C on the speed dial."

Cyrus looks down at the phone, then up at Errol's face. "What happened there?"

"Knife wound."

"You didn't try and cut your throat, did you?"

"It was Headcase. Payback for Mexico."

Cyrus looks at the phone, then at Errol, who waits uncomfortably behind an outstretched hand.

In a treacly tone Cyrus says, "There ain't no watchers, Errol." His eyebrows form Vs above his eyes as they rise up in a black hoodwinking smile. "Most think they can beat the blooding. Live it out from the sidelines. But it ain't so. From minstrel to fool." He adds, "No watchers."

47

"Do you think we can pull this off?"

Case looks down at the cellular phone as she snuffs out a cigarette. "If he left that stash in the house, it's belly-of-the-beast time. It's too much ego cash for anything but. Now, if

he's got it and knows this is all just so much douche, he may
fuck with our heads for a—"

"But we took it to him at the house. He has too—"

"I wasn't finished. He may fuck with our heads for a
while. But we burned one of his safe houses down. He won't
let it pass. It's dyin' time for us both."

They sit quietly for a minute, entombed in the last table of
a boxcar-style rib and beer joint. Each table is just a small
map of light from the booth lamps swimming down a long
dark aisle. From their post they can watch across the parking lot and past the railroad tracks to the street. It's the shit-
crank section of Hinkley, which is on the road between
Barstow and California City.

"I saw you in there," he says. "I saw . . ."

She looks over the top of the cup of coffee she is nursing
with both hands. Bob's eyes are hooded as he stares at the
battle line of shot glasses and empty beer bottles in front of
him. "You could take him with impunity. You took it right to
him like you would have Errol. It's a trait I'd like to be able
to pull up out of myself."

"I know why you're talking like this."

"You do?"

"You want to find that moment because you think she's
dead." She pauses. "Or she should be."

"Am I that obvious?" he asks.

"No. I'm just getting to know you, is all."

"I prayed she was alive every day. I did. But I've also
found myself starting to pray that she is dead and not suffering. At first it was just thoughts I pushed out of my head.
But . . . Now that she's probably dead I find no . . . I
still pray she's alive and I pray she's dead. I'm the ghost of
two men. Bob Hightower is . . . He's nothing. A waste
really. And Bob Whatever, he—"

"Isn't so bad," she says. "Even Bob Hightower doesn't de-
serve your sudden self-hatred."

He rests his elbows on the table, his hands come up, and

he hides his face under an awning of both palms. From across the lamplight she can hear him start to cry.

The waitress passes, looking from Bob to Case. Case shakes her head to just let it be, then points so the waitress will bring him another round.

"I used to believe that every action of the soul was meaningful," he says. "Maybe that is old-fashioned. But I did. I did in the face of evidence that might have been otherwise."

He looks up, wipes at the tears. "That's what we all want, isn't it? Where all things inhere with meaning. That we are more than just . . ."

He sees in her face empathy for him, the man. For the plight of Bob Hightower and Bob Whatever. But he also sees in her eyes that same elusive terrifying stillness as when she killed.

"You don't believe in any of that, do you?" he says.

"No, Coyote, I don't."

"How do you get through, then?"

She sets the coffee cup down, pushes it aside, rests her arms on the table. Her face is darkly moving and eloquent. "I do," she says, "what any good junkie does. I try to do the right, now, in the right-now."

"That's it?"

"That's hard enough."

"Nothing more?"

"You mean no moral imperative beyond that?"

"Yes."

"No, Coyote."

"Then why are you here? Why are you in this with me? Is it revenge? Retribution? Blood? Honor? 'Cause it ain't about the right-now. Not with what you've been through when you don't have to."

Case leans forward to take the pack of cigarettes from Bob's shirt pocket. The lamplight catches her hand as it brushes against his and stops a moment, then moves on.

"I don't have all the answers. Revenge. Maybe that's why

I'm here. Retribution. The same. But of course I know that is not entirely fair. I am responsible for my own exile."

She lights the cigarette, inhales with her head back. "But I don't judge why I'm here. I'm just here."

The waitress comes with Bob's shot and bottle of beer. Case reaches for the shot, runs her nose across the tequila, sniffing. "Fuck," she says, "I could get wet just smelling it." She slides it across to Bob, leans back in the booth, brings her legs up.

He holds up the tequila, toasts her, and shoots it down. She gives him a thumbs-up sign.

"See," she continues, "I believe everybody knows what life really is about. Only they are just not ready for what they would call 'bad news.' They fight against it with God and the devil and all that holographic New Age bullshit. Yeah, I believe everybody knows there is nothing. Everybody knows down in their guts. It's x number of years, then the ground and done, and it frightens them.

"I believe the human beast is desperate and saw fit to retro a god in its own image to conform to what it wants when it wants it. To what it needs when it needs it. To what it must have when it sees suit to have it. And worse yet, it was Michelangelo's vision. You know . . ."

She stretches out her arm in a mock imitation of the God of the Sistine Chapel ceiling reaching out for Adam. "The big man," she says. "Great White, as I like to call him. The shark of sharks."

She shakes her head. "Yeah. White. And a man. You want my opinion, that was the original bullshit sin. 'Cause it set a precedent. It said the godhead—perfection—was a male. Which the white culture turned into their own native son. So everyone and everything else was a step down. Women. Blacks. Indians. Animals. Gays.

"Shit. It's Genesis. Which is just so much muckraking bullshit. So much moral and philosophical gerrymandering.

It's Hitler's *Mein Kampf*, but a better mindfuck people can get into.

"Those who buy the faith ostracize those who don't. And countries are built on the back of that faith. Civilizations on the back of those countries. The fuckin' dollar bill, man— 'In God We Trust'—what a fuckin' wink."

She flicks her ashes hard, and they rim the ashtray before dropping in. She takes one of the empty shot glasses and separates it from the others, letting it stand alone at the edge of the table.

"Then an outsider comes along," she says. "And has a thought. Other outsiders buy into the idea. You know what it is. Cyrus. They create a devil in their own image and like-ness. Their patron saint. And the war starts. And why not? Why should the outsiders lie down and die at the feet of the bullshit holy? You and Cyrus . . ." She slaps her arm where the needle would go. "You need each other. Like junk. 'Cause neither side can see it all for what it is without their fix.

"Everyone needs a club. Club God and Club Scream. On the same block. With different bands. But the riffs are begged, borrowed, and bullshit. And the cover charge is too much, no matter what. You want the real truth, Coyote, go knocking on coffins."

She points her cigarette at him. "And you want the real reason why you're breaking apart? To believe in your God is to believe in him. Cyrus. To believe in him is to believe in the power of it all. And I don't just mean what he did. I mean the implications around what you feel like. Being the rat's ass in the Great White's eyes. To believe in that is to believe in the reason for things to be what they are, and since that reason is beyond your grasp, you pray for your baby's death. The end of suffering. The end of some failure in the Great White's eyes."

She holds up the cigarette, lets it burn some. "But whose suffering, Coyote, hers . . . or yours?"

He sits there, troubled by her remark. "I don't know," he says.

"Right."

"I don't. I swear it." He pauses. "But what about you? What you said to Anne, that at least if we get close enough she'd be dead. Cyrus would kill her."

"It would have made it easier for me. I wouldn't have to think too much. Dead means you don't have to."

She holds out her arm where it is still black-and-blue from the needle that was jammed into it. "And I wouldn't have to confront my old religion either."

"I can't let go of what I have always believed," he says. "No. 'Can't' is not the right word. I won't. I've been wrong on many things. And maybe this, too, about Gabi. Maybe wanting her dead is a cowardly act on my part. Maybe it's because I don't have enough faith and I need more.

"I know I don't want to see the world as you do. I don't want to believe in a world that way. Call it whatever you want. Stupidity. Denial. I won't. Just so much shoveled dirt. That is beyond *my* comprehension. It lacks everything we aspire to. There has to be some greater force offering up what it wills. I mean, even something like you writing me that letter could have—"

"Maybe it's no different than you keeping me from slashing Errol the Stool-Specimen-Carrier's throat so now we can exploit him. And when you bugged that coat. Good luck out of bad, is all. Maybe that's the term of terms. The *real* Great White. People see what they see when they want to see it.

"Of course, there is one loose cannon running around that could pass itself off as the real thing." She looks around, reaches under the table and into her shirt. Bob watches her arm fiddle a bit, then come up with a closed hand. She opens it clandestinely. In the palm is a Frontier cartridge—a good old gliding metal jacket with brass bullet for better, deeper penetration.

"Take a look. This is the ultimate life form, the highest art form. The great equalizer. It crosses all political, social, and religious lines. It has no ties. It plays no favorites. It cuts both ways. It is as simple and profound as any fuckin' parable the Bible could slop up through all that magisterial garbage. It carries history on its back. All life falls before it. All faith resides within that virgin brass casing. The virgin birth, baby.

"Yeah. It births new religions and bears down on old ones. There's god, Coyote. Grin and bear it." She slips it into his hand.

He sits a moment with the shell firmly tucked away in his palm. "Thanks for that Spartan treat of reality."

"Of course, the whole thing could be just that," she says, pointing out the window toward the remains of a cinderblock wall in the next lot that at one time had been part of the shell of some long two-story building. Graffitied there in gaudy blue letters it says: Y'ALL IS FANTASY ISLAND.

Gutter holds the diamondback down on the table. It's stretched out to its full seven-foot length. The mottled underbelly in marked contrast to the white pine. Its tongue flickers at the heat of Wood's face, staring at table level, watching in veiled light as Cyrus loads a hypodermic with speed.

Cyrus slides the needle in at mid-belly. A slight crackling where the steel fang breaks through. The snake tries to fight the cold metal, but Gutter holds fast.

Cyrus puts the needle down and takes the snake from Gutter. Holding it by the head, he starts to walk the room, whipping the snake at the air. Getting that speed to venom through its whole body.

48

Case sits alone with the cellular while Bob goes out to the truck to get another pack of cigarettes. She stares at the phone, trying to will it to ring.

As she watches Bob walk to the truck parked over by the brush-strewn field and battered cinder-block wall, she notices a white Cherokee in the middle of a slow crawl around the dirt lot. She tries to squint against the glass to see if it's the warboys, but the light from the table lamp obscures her view.

The Cherokee does that easy turn toward nothing particular, and she's had enough. She's not taking chances. She is up quick, tossing money from her pocket onto the table and grabbing the cellular. She rushes past the waitress, almost knocking a tray out of her hand.

"Well, excuse me, honey," comes the smoke-stained voice. Then the waitress turns to a couple sitting in the next booth and shakes her head. "Freaks," she huffs.

Case presses through the heavy leather doors and out into the parking lot. The Cherokee takes another turn and stops, leaving a ripple of dust. Through the few rows of parked cars she can see the far door open and slam shut. The Cherokee takes off again, leaving a sidewinder of dust that screens the dark figure moving off at a forty-five-degree angle from the white Jeep.

Her pace quickens. She sees the Cherokee and the black outline converging on the axis of the Dakota where Bob leans into the open driver's door trolling through their clothes on the front seat for cigarettes.

Case shouts his name and starts into a dead run, but he doesn't hear. Her only thought is, How? How could they have found them here and this fast?

The gravel cuts away under her boots. Under a single run of light from a tall lamp that guards the lot she makes out the lanky shape that has broken into a hard trot and begun to lash something that looks to be a whip.

"Wood!"

She knows she can't reach Bob in time so she pulls her backup gun and fires three fast shots of warning into the air and screams again, "Bob!"

Bob snaps around, and a series of erupted images blows down on him. A Pan-like figure waving what looks like a snake. A car's headlights sweeping past him amid gunshots. His body, the quick mechanics of desperation and survival. The wheelgun torn loose from inside his shirt. Firing at the black form charging him, but too late.

The diamondback is cowboy-slung around his neck, and the pitted head slaps across his face as he fires a shot. A voice grunts. Dark leathers tumble into gray gravel. Bob tries to grab at the living thing coiled around his throat. Case in the far corner of his vision fires at the Cherokee coming at him. A crash of blue-tinted glass, and it steers away defensively. Something tears into a piece of his neck. Nerve endings razor down into the fault line of muscles.

He stumbles. Tires are rolling out dust. He looks toward the figure in dark leathers crawling back into darkness. Fires through the burning haze of poison. Misses.

The Cherokee makes a wide sweep around the Dakota, but the ground is rutted and the Jeep dips hard left, sending the right wheels airborne. The Cherokee lunges into the grubby lot, turning over on its side, driving a deep trench through the brush.

Bob is howling like a wild beast as he tries to latch onto the snake's head. But that speed-junked thing is a length of crazed lunging and spitting with pitted fangs. He is bitten again in the throat. He can't get it loose so he presses the pistol against its leathery skin and fires. Skewered streams of meat and powder-smoke singe his face and shoulder.

He stumbles down again and Case grabs him. She pulls the cabled lump of dead matter from his throat. Sees the puncture wounds with their stringy line of blood. Bob's head turns from one spot of violence to the next. In the field where the dust from the crash has risen around the Cherokee, he sees Granny Boy climb out through the passenger door, jump down, and start across the field in a sprint.

Bleeding and poisoned, Bob comes up like a raging animal and takes off after Granny Boy. Case tries to stop him, knowing he's only making the poison travel faster through his system. He hurtles a fence-high wall of detritus.

She knows she can't catch him so she jumps into the Dakota and speeds out across the lot, weaving past a scattering of people who are running from the gunfire.

The field is gray and flat and Granny Boy is a target that can be followed at a dead run. He looks back over his shoulder to see a demonic shadow of pumping arms closing with each step. Closing and howling as if death itself made up that voice. Granny Boy angles for the safety of a stand of woods at the far corner of the field.

Case whips onto the road, the Dakota's springs getting punished as she clears the tracks.

It's a hundred yards of humping for Granny Boy over the caked sand, with heaps of weeds blooming up through leftover concrete-slab fittings and over great rafts of broken cement. A hundred yards of humping toward that stand of woods leaves Granny Boy and Bob almost done in. But Bob is still closing ground, and he wilds out his hunting knife from a hip sheath.

Case is racing along parallel to the open lot. The angle of trees the two are running toward means she has to take a hard left at Thomas Road to cut off Granny Boy in case he tries to clear the woods and cross the road.

She cuts her headlights and blows through a stop sign. The torqued-out engine burns down the black empty street. Down a strobe of trees where slits of moonlight slip through the flywheel clipped frames of Granny Boy and Bob, Granny Boy and Bob, Granny Boy and Bob. Then Granny Boy's gone.

She swerves the pickup off the road and sideswipes a tree, tearing up the runner. She grabs the shotgun from under the seat and jumps out. She starts to scan the road and picks out Granny Boy kicking his way through the brush.

Granny Boy swings into the street as she pumps a shell into the chamber. He is looking back over his shoulder at Bob. By the time Granny Boy sees Case straddling the white line and aiming the shotgun at him, it's a fuckin' go-down. No time to skip-jump the shot, though he tries to dip left quick. The blast takes out both his legs. From ankle to knees he's strafed, and his forward thrust over sundered limbs sends him onto the asphalt like a high stepper that's been trip-wired.

Before Granny Boy's hands can spider up a weapon, Bob and Case are on him, kicking and punching and tearing away the Luger he's got strapped inside his leather jacket.

With blood fingering down his neck from the fang wounds, Bob takes a fast look up and down the dark street. "Let's drag him into the woods," he says.

Granny Boy is writhing at the edge of consciousness, and his only fight left is in his mouth.

Just off the road. A triangle of deep roots rising twenty feet. Granny Boy is tossed onto his back against a tree. His leathers are torn, exposing the cracked and dimpled mass of his legs.

Bob can barely hold on himself, pressing on with the last his adrenaline can give. He pins his hunting knife up against Granny Boy's eyes.

"Where is he . . . Cyrus . . . Where is he?"

A gravel hiss comes out of the boy's throat.

Without so much as a thought and driven with the blind pitiless agencies of a rawboned wilderness soul, Bob digs the knife into Granny Boy's collarbone. Digs it deep.

The warboy fights back with teeth grinding against teeth like the metal rim of a speeding blown tire along cement.

"Where is he?"

Nothing. Bob stumbles over and collapses.

Case kneels over Bob, sees how bad off he is. His eyes have begun to flutter. She feels his pulse, which is way out of control. She comes around fast, stands over Granny Boy.

There is a lot of history in the mute minute of this passing. Catch dog and coolie. Coolie and catch dog.

"I got to know, Granny Boy, I got to know."

His few words spit out. "Come get me, cunt!"

She takes a short step forward. "The girl. Is she alive? Granny Boy, the girl! Use your mouth now. The girl!"

There is an instant of confusion in his face as to why she would ask such a question. But it's all the same. He eyes her like some dead thing and curses out one thought: "Sheep!"

She pumps a shell into the chamber and bears down point blank at his face from just feet away.

"You're crossing over," she whispers.

He stares into the steel gray moment of his execution and before the call of his nerves can react to the brain his world and face are taken out in a shredding sun of white.

49

Case hammers the pickup through the black setting of desert road those twenty-five miles from Hinkley to the Ferryman's.

Her hand rides the horn. She brakes to a tire-winding halt, and from the darkness the dogs come and go wild about the truck. The Ferryman hobbles through an open doorway. Case tries to keep the dogs back while she lifts Bob from the Dakota.

The Ferryman swipes a claw at the dog pack as he hobbles through. Bob collapses into the sand. The Ferryman sees Bob's blood-swamped shirt. He looks at Case. "What happened?"

"We took Granny Boy down. Shot up Wood."

"Why you here?"

She points. "Snake bite. In the neck. It's bad, and I couldn't take him to no hospital. Not right on top of a murder."

The Ferryman looks over this complete mess of existence. "I thought you'd joined the living," he says caustically.

"It's been thirty-six hours on the hellbound train, so don't fuckin' work me!"

In a cramped frame of a room just big enough for a bed, Case strips Bob down. As he lies there, the Ferryman looks over his wounds. The arrant swelling and blackness around the puncture marks speak for themselves.

"You got any numbness around the mouth?"

Suffering severe weakness and thirst, Bob manages a slender yes.

The Ferryman feels Bob's pulse through the good side of his neck. It's cranked up and erratic. He looks over at Case. "In the refrigerator, behind the beer on the bottom shelf, vials with yellow stickers on 'em. Should say antivenin. Bring me two vials to start. And in the closet, back where the dogs sleep. Upper shelf. Bags of saline solution. Bring one of those. I'll also need syringes and needles and tape. But I know you know where that shit is."

"Fuck you," she says to the Ferryman.

She takes hold of Bob's hand. "You'll be alright." Then she gets up, moves like quicksilver through the tangle of waiting dogs.

Once alone, the Ferryman takes hold of Bob's jawbone with his claw and studies him almost scientifically. "I'm gonna play medic tonight, Bob Whatever. Do a little memory time on the night river."

Bob drifts through the milky light. His eyes crawl across the ceiling to find the black, black face of that wizened mariner.

"We're both going down that night river, aren't we? Yeah. I'm gonna load you up with antivenin, 'cause all that runnin', Bob Whatever, all that catch-dogging, has given those nerve endings a big taste. Burned them up pretty good. You might go into shock on your own from the way your heart's workin'. Or that antivenin with all the horse protein in it. That could put you into anaphylactic shock. You could go belly-up."

Bob's eyes slew upward, leaving only the whites before they flit back.

"You hear me?"

"I'm very thirsty."

The Ferryman shakes his head. "You hear me?"

Bob's gullet jacks.

The Ferryman leans in closer. "She should have let me finish rolling the coins. We didn't finish, remember. The Book of Changes." He runs his claw along the artwork of Bob's shoulder from ONE LOVE to HELTER SKELTER. His tone is nasty and impish at the same time. "We might have known what to make of this. You might be dead already, and we're just wasting time."

Bob tries to put together a patchwork of dissenting breaths but can't.

Bob lies in the dark, being fed intravenously. Case sits beside him with a cloth, soothing his fevered skin. He tries to speak, but by now he is just a jumble of confused words.

She runs her hand up across his stomach and stops to feel his heart. She looks back at the door where the Ferryman stands working a beer. "His heartbeat's a mess."

"I expect he might go into shock, fucked up as he is."

She looks across his naked body. Its wreckage painful to her. She wants to make it clean again. Her hand slides down his stomach and stops at his pubic hair.

The Ferryman cannot see all this in the dark, but he knows. He can read the breathing and silence.

"Leave that sheep to the wolves, girl."

She turns on him violently. "What?"

"You heard. Let him cross. Or finish him yourself. He's bad luck all the way around."

"Listen to me, Ferryman. He is going to live. And if you fuck with him, I . . . I will tear off that claw and plastic leg and beat you to death with them. You hear?"

He says nothing and walks away. Somewhere down the hall he gives one slight hitch of laughter.

When it comes to get him, it comes with jerking random snaps. Shivering with fever, vomiting. The window to the night a moonlit hole. The sheet a hard skin of discomfort. Hot and wet from the saliva of his bones.

Case lies beside him. She is stripped down naked and presses herself against him tightly. She whispers over and over again, "You're going to be alright." She puts her mouth against his chest and breathes these words. The warmth carrying them to the flesh around his heart.

He sees into the black ceiling past the flickering silent film of himself and Case cradled in the shadows, where his mind backwashes down the stream of memory, pacing a lightless bathroom in his robe with Gabi when she was just a child and suffering the croup.

That steamed mossy darkness. The frailty of living pink in his arms, hoarse with phlegmed lungs. The arms around him are the arms around Gabi's back then, and his arms between the dreamy realities like roots from an expanding tree of consciousness. And every time he hears Case whisper

"You'll be alright," he hears himself as he stares down at his helpless cradled pup coughing out its life. "You'll be alright, Gabi. You'll be alright."

He can feel Case's arm around his neck pull him closer, and in a moment of clarity he sees the snake Ourabouris tattooed on her shoulder. He tries to touch it as he begs, "You have to get her home."

"Shhh."

"You have to promise . . ."

"Shhh."

"If she's alive . . ."

"Shhh."

"You take her. You hear me? *You*. You take her. You're the only one I trust . . . Promise me."

She puts this down to the fever and hesitates to answer.

"Case . . . Promise."

He thinks he hears the faint tide of her words in his ear. "I won't forget this. Yes . . . I promise."

The Ferryman sits on a dusty couch, his dogs around him. He smokes a joint and looks out through the front door into the darkness. He can hear Case in that cell of a room down the hall.

He's got himself a good M16-level stoneout and watches the sun rise. Remembers those medevac choppers coming out of the heavens down toward the rivers. And the cadre of corpses. White-bundled skiffs caught in the mud tide streaming from the mountains to the sea.

A flying detachment of garbage collectors is what we were, he thinks to himself. Ferrymen all. There to scoop up the dead with nets. He wonders how many of those dead youth have come back. Come back to their next life too soon. With their anger intact. To become killers on street corners and coolly hip gangstas and white-collar legal bloodsuckers getting their revenge for an untimely death.

Case walks into the room, draped in a ratty blue blanket. "Is he dead?"

Exhausted, she slides down the wall, sits on the floor. A couple of the dogs slope over and curl around her, sniffing.

"No."

She looks at the snake tattooed on her arm, thinks of him in there when he was staring at it.

"Remember the day you needled this baby?"

He looks at the tattoo she's pointing at. "Yeah. We were down by the chimney."

"That was the day I was thinking I'm gonna break. I'm gonna give Cyrus the blowoff. You know I didn't know what this snake meant. But a year later, in rehab, somebody showed me in a book. A picture. I didn't know it meant rebirth."

She looks back down the hall. "Bob was staring at it a long time and I kept telling him the story. I kept telling him over and over again."

She stares into the circle of that snake. "I kept saying to him, 'You're gonna live.' And I remembered when you were doing the snake on my arm, I was thinking, 'I'm gonna live. I'm gonna live. I'm gonna break from Cyrus, and live.'"

5 0

Through the bedroom window the stars play bridge lamps across the distant hum of the desert. He can barely move, but he can feel Case asleep in bed beside him. He can smell her hair, and the soft odor of the woman in the night stillness. He can feel the settling of his system, like a downed prizefighter coming to after the long sleep. Weak and murky, but somewhere there is a deep easement along the muscles.

He lies there and listens to the breathing. His. Hers. The

earth's. The breathing slow and uniform and without rancor or hatred or fear. All part of some great breathing ecosystem. Some eternally calm oneness.

He moans, turns. In sleep's short fall she feels him move, turn, and she comes up quick.

A relief of afternoon light through filthy blinds across his face. His skin is ghostly but for the black welding wound around four fang holes. His lips move like great slow slugs. His mouth is dry as crepe.

He barely gets out, "I see . . . I'm alive."

"It sure looks it, Coyote."

"I'm thirsty."

She rises up from under the sheets and gingerly steps over a couple of dogs that have taken to sleeping by the foot of the bed. Her naked form disappears into the gray hallway.

He listens to the sinkwater and a dog's feet plucking at the wood floor as it moves around the bed and rests its head on the sheet by his hand.

She sits carefully on the edge of the bed, shoos away the animal, and hands Bob the glass. She does not try to conceal her nakedness. He drinks the water slowly. He is so dry that each swallow makes him feel he is immersed in it. He looks up at Case sitting with a baldric of light from one shoulder to her opposite hip. There seems to be neither purity nor exhibition in her. She is, as ever, the raw statement that is herself.

Watching her, it takes him a while to realize that her hand is over his.

"I'm glad you made it, Coyote."

He looks over at her arm, at the snake tattooed on her shoulder. His other arm rises weakly, moving across the light like a minute hand, and one finger turns the length of the serpentine motif. A kind of sensual trace across the dreams of her talking to him there in the hard hours of suffering.

"Thanks," he says, "for being the voice I heard."

Her face seems to ebb and flow with a moment of relief and satisfaction, until they hear the cellular ring.

It cuts at the air with its staccato beeps. Their minds drain of everything but Cyrus. Bob nods to Case. She crosses through the dusty light to the bureau, where the phone lies.

She clicks on, puts the cellular to her ear, and listens. Bob watches the tightening around her eyes. Seconds later she clicks off.

"Was it him?"

"Yes."

"What did he say?"

"He said he hoped we enjoyed the little party."

She comes back, sits on the bed, reaches for a cigarette. She lights it and smokes intently.

"What else?"

She turns to him. "He says he knows what we're about."

Bob tries to sit, or at least begin to move some. "What do you think he means?"

"I don't know," she says. "But I know his tone. It had 'fuck you' all over it. Trying to get at Cyrus is like trying to spit away the sun."

"Does he want to meet?"

With a chilling quiet bleakness she says, "Oh yeah."

"When?"

She shrugs. "He's gonna scarf around the edge of our nerves, I'll tell you that."

Bob tries to move a little more, but his body's a no-show. "I need you to make a call."

"To who?"

"Arthur. I want him out here."

She's not crazy about the idea of having him at the Ferryman's. Or, for that matter, playing Little Miss Direction-Giver: "You keep driving through the desert till you reach that lovely little pile of human skulls, then you turn left and blah, blah, blah . . ."

Bob has to lie back down. He's starting to drift with weakness. "Make the call, will you?" His eyes close. "I need sleep."

When Bob's eyes flutter open hours later, he's looking up into the haggard features of his ex-father-in-law. Arthur's mouth is moist and puckers in disbelief as he stares starkly at what could only be the war-torn imposter of the boy he knew.

"Oh God, Jesus, Bobby, what's happened to—"

"I'm alright, Arthur. Just know I'm alright. Beat up, but—"

"Every day, every night. Do you know how I've been suffering, son?"

Arthur sits beside Bob as carefully as his hulking frame will allow. He takes Bob's hand gently in his own. "I'll get you home, boy."

"I'm staying right here."

"What do you—"

"We'll be going back out on the road when I'm well enough."

Arthur's eyes dip, then come around toward Case. She walks out of the room. Arthur looks back at Bob. "What are you talking, Bobby. Look at you—"

"I can't talk now. I need sleep, but later. You haven't told anyone you were coming here, have you?"

"No."

"Not anyone? Not Maureen or John Lee?"

"*That woman* said you didn't want me to tell anyone, so I didn't."

Arthur closes the door, storms up that vestibule of a hall after Case. They meet head-on in the bare light of the living room, where she turns on him.

"Goddamn you," he says. "My boy is lying there almost dead. I knew when I first saw you, you were a disaster."

"I can see I'm gonna be the brunt of another of your astute observations."

"Don't get smart with me, junkie."

"Why not? One of us has to be."

They circle that littered tabernacle with couch and table between them.

"Why didn't you take him to a hospital instead of this shithole?"

"We saved his life in this shithole."

"Saved it . . . You fuck!"

Through the door to the kitchen area Arthur sees the Ferryman click by and stop a moment. Arthur crosses the room. "You are nothing," he shouts at Case. "You are garbage."

"You know, I despised you before I even knew you," she says. "And I was right. 'Cause I knew you even before that. You'd had me before that. But you want to talk about blame, Grandpa, I'll bet you find you're carrying a busload of it up that ass of yours."

He can see in her face now that he's gutted her a bit. Found a weak spot in her crude underbelly. "But I'm still right about you, aren't I?" he says. "That's why you're willing to risk my boy's life in there. It's for your ass and nothing else."

They're running off at the mouth so fast that neither of them hears a wounded voice say, "Arthur, that's enough." And then more belligerently, "Arthur . . ."

They turn to find Bob scarecrowed against the wall, naked.

"Don't talk to her like that."

They both cross the room in a race to his side, but Bob gives way, his arms flapping out in an unjointed fashion as he tries to stop himself from hitting the floor. They close in around him to try to help him up. Arthur elbows himself between Case and Bob, but Bob presses him back.

"Don't. You got to understand. If it wasn't for Case, we wouldn't know who took Gabi."

His eyes become stark blue shreds. "You know who took her?"

Bob nods.

"His name is Cyrus," says Case.

Whatever else she says, it's just words Arthur doesn't hear. Nothing more than sounds. His whole existence becomes a cold leaking wound and the timbre of a woman's hand on the floor scratching out a few inches of wood to let him know she is alive.

51

Case finds herself in a shed storage room where, in a free-floating stack of drawers, the Ferryman keeps his private stash of heroin.

Looking down at the balloons of white bitter crystalline compound bundled neatly as gifts, she begins to feel the memory skin of it all. A black-and-bluesy cocktail in the key of H comes a-calling. The beautiful high-five sense of self-loathing that needs a little vein tonic to cut away the highs and lows, leaving you in the perfect flatness of its murky landscape.

She can see herself in the drawer: the heroin, the syringe, the sport trappings of the lifestyle. Heraldic in their callings. And each balloon a lung of breath to blissful forgetting. The white blind flatline to pain.

Blame. The fact that if she had done something during all those years—put a bullet in Cyrus's head, cut his throat when he was asleep, something to end him. If for one moment she had risen above her own squalor, her own greedy self-serving private immolation, this chain of events that exists would not. As such, so much bleeding butchery would not be. The fact that she got out alive and is clean and here now is nothing to her.

"Were you gonna steal some or buy some?"

Case turns, for a second relives the thief's shudder. She looks up at the Ferryman, who stands just beyond the off-hung shed door, marshaled in grainy daylight.

She tries to calm herself. "I was just performing a little ritual moment of slaughter, is all. The old tapes, Ferryman, the old tapes. They still do hard time inside this head of mine."

She puts the drawer back as carefully as one would a dowry box of horrors.

She goes and sits on a stack of old crates. It wobbles a bit. The Ferryman comes over and sits beside her. Case stares numbly at a walkway of light that crosses the dark dirt floor. There is a thick smell of workmanlike time in the shed. The aroma of dust mingling with that which is forgotten and stacked within its boards.

The Ferryman speaks in a seductive tone. "Stay selfish. That's the key to survival. Walk away from these sheep. Walk away. Believe me, they are never the ones that die soon enough."

She eyes him judiciously.

"I mean it, girl. You have no idea how black the myth inside them is. It's a fuckin' trip wire you're walking over, trying to fleece your way through that world. You're just playing out a myth dance. It's all bullshit. I know. I know."

"Do you know this man Cyrus?"

"Do I know him?"

"Yes," asks Bob. He repeats the question very slowly: "Do you know him?"

"No. I don't."

"Are you sure?"

Arthur sits in a high-backed chair beside the bedroom window and stares imperiously. "I don't."

Bob is sitting up in bed as best he can, resting against a stack of pillows. He points out the window. "Do you know what's over that hill there?"

"I don't."

"Furnace Creek," says Bob.

Feigning thought, Arthur turns, looks out the window. The ocean wind has traveled inland as it does this time of day and is taking its toll against the sand. Along the hillside are breakers of yellow-gray dust.

The whole fuckin' world is giving way, that's all that's in Arthur's mind at the moment. The whole fuckin' world.

Bob is watching his ex-father-in-law closely. "A woman was murdered there years ago."

Arthur turns. "Yes. This is what Maureen was telling me about your phone conversation. Yes."

"And you got her property in probate? Paradise Hills, that is."

"Yes, in probate. She had died. Had no heirs."

Bob points out the window again. "Cyrus lived there, with that old woman who was murdered. Did you ever try to buy the land from her?"

"Did we?" Arthur's face moves through thoughtful poses. "Not that I remember."

"There are two separate murders. Years apart. The only people connected to both of them are Cyrus, you, and Maureen."

"Yes, I guess so," says Arthur. Then he lays down the thread of a false afterthought: "And John Lee, of course."

"And John Lee. Yes."

The bedroom is bare sheathing. Just wood and tin. And with the wind whittling through its seams, the room is like an ancient caboose crossing a desert wasteland.

"What could have brought him back all these years?" Bob

asks. "Was it because he thinks something was stolen from him?"

Arthur folds his hands across his lap. Looks down into the hard roots of knuckle and bone. He is caught up in a single thought: Could John Lee have been stupid enough, or just plain vicious enough, because of Maureen and Sam's affair, to have brought the monster back into their lives? He looks up. Bob lies back against the pillows woodenly, his head turned at an odd angle, exposing the blackening edema that has begun to show itself in the folds of flesh around the neck wound.

Arthur cannot look at him for more than a moment, and so he looks out the window again, through a glaze of sand, toward a place whose past goes to the very heart of things.

"Arthur?"

He turns. "Yes."

"You haven't answered my question."

He tries to think through a scenario of lies that would add up to some acceptable truth.

52

It is past midnight when Arthur leaves. Case opens the door to Bob's room without so much as a tired creak. Bob is lying on the bed in the dark, with one arm resting across his forehead.

"Are you awake?" she whispers.

"I am."

She crosses the room barefoot and slow.

"Did you find out anything?" she asks.

"He told me he knows nothing more than what we know now. But I think he's lying."

She sits in the chair where Arthur sat. "What makes you feel so?"

Bob gets his feet down on the floor, stretches his arms out on the bed for support. He's light-headed but holds on.

"I don't have a reason," he says. "He didn't act different. Didn't seem different. I watched him, too, for anything that I could grab onto and say was different. But there wasn't. And I still feel he's lying."

He works to stand. Wobbles. Case is right there with an arm around him. His pale and naked skin warm as an open mouth.

"Where are you goin'?"

"I don't know. I just need to move, I guess."

She takes the gray blanket from his bed. It is badly worn. She drapes it around his shoulders like a poncho.

"It's me, Case. It's me. I see him as guilty of something, but I don't know what. Jesus, he's Gabi's grandfather. Maybe there's an illness in me now."

He steadies himself, using her face for bearings. She slips her arms up around his rib cage as support.

"I admire you, you know."

She is caught off guard by this statement, and he can feel her against him twist self-consciously.

"You at least test your demons," he says. "I didn't confront Arthur."

"I don't mean to test my demons," she offers, then spots him a little piece of smile. "I just shoot them a look every now and then. Make sure they haven't given me the slip."

In the silent reaches between his flesh and hers comes his hand edging out. The back of his fingers silk the side of her face. She does not pull away. His hand turns again with a thickish grace down the cotton-strap walkway of her shirt and along her back, where a peregrine idol of peacock colors rests above the thin perch of her milky shoulder blade.

Breathing and silence are all there is. The far reaches of

the universe. The moments that are separated only by the boatman's crossings of the night river.

"I could, you know," she whispers. "I could. And I would enjoy the shit out of it. Maybe even more than that. Maybe . . . But you know what's out there yet. You know."

He presses against her, a breath's worth. "I know sometimes around you I feel like a boy trespassing in a man's body."

She rests her face on the blanket shawled down his chest. She nests in enough to feel muscles keeled on bone. Somewhere, though, in the belly of that hutch, she can hear the Ferryman moving about. A hobbler's dirge going room to room. The very essence of the watchman. Putting down light after light. "I wonder," she whispers again, "how well am I, compared to you."

53

"Arthur, listen to me."

"What?"

"He was asking me some pretty strange questions."

"What do you mean?"

". . . They were very odd."

John Lee stands off to one side, watching Cyrus with a wicked impudence as he listens to the tape. He would not meet Cyrus anywhere but in a public spot during the day after all that had gone down. And it had to be far enough out of the reach of the eyes that knew him. So a Love's Restaurant parking lot in Victorville became the anointed location.

"He asked me how we bought this tract."

"How we bought it?"

"I told him we got it in probate."

"In probate, that's right."

Cyrus grins cynically at the rise in Arthur's voice.

"We got it in probate because . . ."

"Probate, yes . . ."

"Some woman had died, right?"

"Died, yes."

"I mean. She'd been murdered. Isn't that right?"

A long silence follows. Cyrus looks up at John Lee. They are wedged between their two vehicles. John Lee is growing intensely aware of the people crisscrossing the lot. The talking on the tape kicks back in.

"Yes."

"Why is Bob asking all these questions?"

"I don't . . ."

"And that woman with him. The addict . . . Who is . . ."

A pink piece of ass was lying on a square of once-plush red carpet. Her knees were up, legs grinning wide apart. On her thigh was tattooed a spiderwoman with vampire teeth and long black legs working a web up toward where her fingers formed a V that held apart the dark patch around her vagina.

Cyrus crawled on all fours around the edges of the rug. He was pretty well whacked on hallucinogens and soapers, and his cock was all humped out.

In one of Cyrus's tortoiselike stumblings, John Lee slipped over him, winding the 16mm Bolex camera. He squatted down so he could get in licking-close to film that filthy little mountain of love, as he called it. Cyrus tried to get away but a battery of boots rose up under his chest and forced him back like a small child. The men laughed and gave him an ugly time, calling him a drugged-out blowhole and warning him he better leave a few teeth marks on the bitch and he better make that cock of his go or he could end up with some black hose up his ass if the show wasn't four stars.

"Now tell me who's been swallowed," says John Lee.

Cyrus flips off the tape. Removes it from the cassette player with quick brash movements. Tosses it to John Lee.

"The junkie fingered you for Hightower. The guy that's running with her. The girl's father. She put the hose to you. Now, tell me, who's been swallowed. You or me?"

Cyrus turns to Gutter, who waits in the driver's seat of the car with arms folded. He speaks to John Lee through Gutter.

"The world is a pitiless example of the shortsighted." Then Cyrus comes around to face John Lee. "I blinded a boy once," he says. "When I was fourteen. Out in Chatsworth. In the hills off Santa Susanna Road. I'd seen him with friends. Hotshot. Whole-life-ahead-of-him crap. Nice looking. Wore clothes our mamas believed in. Didn't know what hit him."

Cyrus makes a sleek sound like an electric arrow moving through silent woods. "I called him months later. I told him I'd done it and why. I told him I owed him then. And he owed me his sightless future. And every day he should know the greater part of his existence belonged to me."

He flips his fingers down along the tufts of hair studded into the leg of his jeans. "The taking of is the nature of all things. The taking of scalps, the taking of flags, the taking of men, of ideas, of patents, of wives, of pride, of trivialities, of slogans, of land. Of souls. The taking of, Captain Blood-soaked and sodomized. Call it our self-portrait."

Then Cyrus shrieks out loud. A piercing femalish banshee. White-shirted businessmen working their gums with toothpicks and their trusty Janes gobbling up each other's gossip as they follow behind turn in the direction of the two cars. Over a hurdle of car hoods, Cyrus grins and waves.

John Lee slinks back into the passenger seat, trying to make himself invisible.

Cyrus turns to John Lee. One arm comes to rest on the open car door, the other on the hood. Cyrus eases himself down like he's about to share a private moment.

"Tell Arthur, when I get the chance I'll dig up his little darlin's skull and mail it back to him. Tell him, *or I will.*"

John Lee sits there, an imperiled look cauterized on his face.

"You thought you'd come out here and get aggro with me. Not happening. Paradise fuckin' lost, Captain. Signed, yours truly."

54

The next morning Bob wakes and there is an odd silence inside him. A kind of psychic refinement where one's sensory skills have sharpened and the very least quiet speaks volumes. The truck and cellular phone being gone are merely facts he already feels.

Wearing only jeans and a blanket draped around his shoulders, he crosses the open yard. The dogs approach from beyond the shed, with the Ferryman not far behind.

"Where is she?" Bob yells.

"She put on new plates and took the truck to get it painted on the chance you got tagged from that little fuckup in Hinkley."

"And then she's coming right back?"

"She didn't say."

"I'll bet Cyrus finally called and you're goddamn lying to me."

The Ferryman just stares at Bob. His dogs move across the open ground, sniffing at the droppings of rats and mice.

"Of course I am," says the Ferryman. "Lying is the cornerstone of life, so why shouldn't I practice it?"

• • •

Chairs oddly placed on a rise. A surreal image, as if the desert were waiting for dinner guests to arrive.

Bob climbs the hill, sits in a broken-backed chair, and looks out toward the bare browning-yellow painted flats stretching between the Paradise Range and the Calico Mountains. In the distance rise small shields of sunlight off the battered rotting hull of the old woman's trailer.

"Center of the world, man."

Bob turns.

The Ferryman walks toward him carrying two bottles of beer. "That's what Cyrus used to say. This was the center of the world." He offers Bob a beer.

The Ferryman half hitches around, sits in the other chair. Bob drinks. The sun has left slight sweat streaks down his reddening face and chest.

"You should have fuckin' stopped her," says Bob.

The Ferryman pays him no mind, just keeps talking. "Cyrus could have been right. When you think about it. The center of the world."

His claw begins a slow sweep of the country. Second-handing from spot to spot in a twelve-o'clock crawl clockwise.

"There you got Death Valley. And there in the Panamint Mountains the forty-niners discovered silver. It's also where Charles Manson made up his party favors for Helter Skelter. Over there is the Nevada Test Site. Frenchmen's Flat and Operation Buster Jangle. You know they dressed up pigs like humans before they nuked 'em. It was called fabric testing. Over there you got Vague-ass. Capital of the white-knuckled dice roller. And there you got the Early Man Site and there Route 66 goes right through the largest hazardous waste dump in North America. There, Joshua Tree, and there the Sea of Cortez; each with the oldest species known to man on this continent. And there is America's favorite self-help nightmare: *Little Armageddon.*

He turns to Bob. "Shit, I left out Disneyland." He takes a swig of beer. "And all of that within four hundred miles. What do you think, Bob Whatever? Was Cyrus right? Is this the center of it all?"

"I think you should have stopped her."

"You know what I think? Dante meets Philip K. Dick. That's what I think."

Bob finishes his beer in one long bottoms up. Tosses the bottle to the Ferryman. With only his claw available for the catch, he can't cut it.

"I don't want to hear any more of your crap," says Bob as he stands and starts away.

"Cyrus thought this was the center of the world. 'Cause this was his place. Where he got his head screwed in tight for whatever it's worth. And since he thinks his life is the center of the world, then this place . . . You can see the Aristotelian madness of it." He points a claw at Bob. "Just like you. Selfish implausibility."

"What do you mean by that?"

"Too much white-boy carnival shit. You're not here to tell me where the hot holes are and are not. You're not gonna give me that somewhere-over-the-rainbow shit and I'm gonna do your housework. You got the wrong nigger.

"You want her stopped. Fuck . . . This country used to be grasslands, man, eons ago. And out here they found the remains of the largest reptile ever on the continent. A fuckin' tortoise. You and that turtle got your share in common. You are fossils trying to fuck around in the next world. But not with me, Bob Whatever. Not with me. Your circus of horrors is so much shit as far as I'm concerned. You want her stopped, you shoulda been no sleeping turtle."

The Ferryman tries to lean over and pick up the bottle but Bob gets there first. Hands it to him. The Ferryman takes it in his claw, but Bob does not let go right away. His eyes are still a little rheumy and dour. He could make a push-comes-to-shove hardball kick-ass drive at this nappy game bird. But looking into that face is like looking into the heart of the desert itself, whose essence tests the very ideas of infinity or emptiness.

Bob lets go of the bottle and says nothing. Then he moves down that slippery grade as slowly as the grand tortoise he was mocked with.

55

Case waits as she's been told. She's got herself locked and loaded in a motel room about a mile from the House of Usher. She's supposed to wait for the call, nothing more. Errol Grey, against his will, has been forced to play middleman and let his bar be used as a neutral spot for the meeting. He isn't happy with his newfound position, and since the knifing he's hired himself a couple of ex-cops with a taste for expensive designer drugs to play bodyguard. They're a duo of thick wrists and bad attitudes, but they keep to themselves and they're astute enough not to try to hump every chickie in the bar.

When Case got the call, Cyrus came with a few simple demands. He almost crooned his conversation to her. They all meet. Her and Bob and him. They bring the little party stash they'd stolen. They hand it over. Cyrus will pay a small finder's fee. A kind of conciliatory gesture in lieu of having to track them down and turn them into bloated satchels. Then she and her "toy" can drive off into the moonlight. Which they better do, and quick, after it's all done.

It's a lurid honesty Case isn't buying. And Cyrus doesn't know he's only getting one out of the three he asked for. It should be quite a come-together. For Case the go-down is simple enough. She walks in alone. Demands the girl for the stuff. If she doesn't get the right answer, it's over. De facto, babe. By gun, by knife, or by a jugular torn open with teeth. Cyrus will never get up from the table.

If he shows.

The first night is a bust. So is the second. It gets so she doesn't sleep. She can feel the creepie-crawlies working against her. She sits up in bed all night with a pistol across her stomach, staring at the door as if he might be able to magic his body through.

The junkie squeeze, as she calls it. Days three and four her veins start to burn. As if someone were working out their route using strips of hot wire. She knows the pain isn't real, just the haunted hours' flights of fancy. She tries to hypnotize herself into calm using the motel sign's flash-fading *S* that sigmas against the pulled shades.

Then the cellular rings, and she is on.

She takes a corner table at the House of Usher. The place is packed enough so that she feels fairly safe, even with the assortment of bad vibes being thrown at her from Errol and his two drumheads.

But it isn't Cyrus that shows, it's Lena.

Case picks her out squeezing through the smoky gloom of the bar crowd. Lena spots Case. Works up a gray smile in the dark reaches of the dance floor. A relic of an arm moves through a distant hello.

Errol has seen Lena himself, goes over to his crew, gets them ready to make sure this is played clean.

As Lena approaches the table, Case takes in everything carefully. She keeps looking toward the door to see if Cyrus is gonna show. When he doesn't, she looks up into the nervous, thinly disguised sanctuary of her ex-lover's face.

"Where's Cyrus?"

Lena comes back tentatively with, "Not even a kiss hello?"

Case rises. They kiss. She sneaks another glimpse at the

door. Lena's eyes fix on her, trying to read what emotion she can out of Case. She holds on to her hand a long time.

"Sit down," says Case, as she slips her hand clear.

They sit. Lena looks tired and frightened. Frailer than in Mexico, but Case had only seen her then at a distance. The junkie years have done their double duty, and the skin on Lena's arms has receded from the veins so much they are like strands of rope left in the sand after the tide has pulled out.

"Where's Cyrus?"

"Where's your toy?"

Case passes over Lena's embittered tone. She waits silently, and Lena becomes self-conscious.

"I'm sorry about Mexico," says Lena.

"It's alright."

"I tried to stop him, but . . ."

"Forget it," Case says sadly.

Lena mumbles, "Okay." She fumbles through a small lacy shoulder purse for cigarettes.

Each moment is stark discomfort. Lena's tried to make herself attractive and feminine. She's wearing a silk shirt and just a touch of perfume. She can't find any matches so Case passes her lit cigarette over.

Before she even looks up from lighting her cigarette, Lena says, "I wish we could go back to that time in the Indian caves. You remember? I wish we could."

"I'd like to try for better times."

Lena nods, looks up, her face in anguish. "If you can find them I'll . . . I'll meet you there."

Case nods impassively. Lena looks for something in Case's face, in her demeanor, that doesn't drain her of hope.

"Where's Cyrus?"

Lena flicks at her cigarette with a thumb. The flesh around the battered nail has been badly chewed.

"Don't keep asking, Case."

"He's a no-show, right?"

"Right."

"Fuckin' voodoo man."

"I got to be able to tell him you and . . . the guy you're traveling with . . . are here and you're carrying the stuff."

Case leans back, looks over at Errol, who is watching intently from the bar.

"Was Errol hip to this?"

Lena rolls her head from side to side as if avoiding a blow. "Errol is a fuckin' corpse."

"You know how deep I am into this, don't you, honey?"

That single word: honey. Lena's head comes up with a brittle quickness. A mime of desperate hope to her eyes.

"Where is he, Lena?"

"What?"

"Cyrus, where is he?"

"You better bring your friend here, with the stuff, and I . . ."

"He sent you 'cause he figured I wouldn't, couldn't cut you in the process."

"I don't think he gives a shit."

"You won't tell me?"

She hides her face as if the world might hear anything her eyes say.

"Don't worry," says Case.

Lena's hand is shaky. The skin along her neck almost a see-through yellow where the veins pulse madly in their lackluster blue.

Case rests her hand on Lena's. "Lena, help me," she says.

Lena doesn't pull away, but doesn't answer.

"Lena?"

She shakes her head now. "I won't lie to him. I can't. But you better do something." She looks back over at Errol, then at Case. "You better. He won't show and let you try and sewer him. And he knows, Case. He knows."

Lena snuffs out her cigarette, rises to leave, and her hand pulls away.

"What does he know, Lena?"

Lena hesitates. The music is raw as a hammer on sheet metal.

"Tell me, please. Don't let me go down."

"It's me who'll go down. Case, be here tomorrow. Out front. At twelve. Show together. Please, Case. If you're gonna show at all."

"Lena . . ."

Lena bends over, kisses Case again. Soft and touching and full on the mouth, with that long fearful sense of finality that never really comes when you hope for it. "I loved you," she whispers. "I mean it's still raw. I love you, now. And always. Always. Don't meet him ever. Don't. Run! Just run!"

"Lena, please."

"And be careful about Errol," Lena whispers. "It was him who told Cyrus where you were when you got hit. He'd followed you, then he went to see Cyrus."

Lena starts through the crowd. Case stands and follows after her. On her way to the door, Errol cuts Case off. Lena is already halfway out into the street when she looks back to see Case circled up by that trio of buffed suits. They're starting to give her the rough moves. Questions on the hard press. Not quite shouting face-to-face, but getting there.

Lena starts back into the bar in a rare moment of confidence.

"Let her loose, Errol."

"What?" he says, turning.

"Let her loose."

"What happened here?"

"Let her loose. We've got things worked out. Let her loose. You already been scratched up pretty good."

Errol pulls his hands back and away. Case passes Lena, nods a thank you as she makes for the door.

Lena calls out, "Case, remember what I said."

56

Bob is brooding on that broken atoll of a couch in the moonlight, smoking, when two pixels of light appear on the desert floor. Gleaming sensors that bleed away. He stands and watches. Somewhere nearby a mobile makes its music out of bones and glass and clay. The smoky lights rise again, cyanotic against the tilted sand, casting strobes into the sky that level out to long widening spills.

Bob crosses the yard as the truck pulls to a hard stop. Dust rises off the back tires and over the hood and around Bob. The dogs come barking out of their hidden scratch-hole hovels as Case climbs out of the pickup dead tired. There is a look of shameful failure in her eyes. The dogs scramble around her, leaping and snapping, and she has all she can handle in clearing a path through them to get to Bob. He waits with his arms folded and a cigarette hanging out of his mouth.

"I guess I should expect all kinds of shit."

He takes the cigarette from his mouth. "Four days without a word. What do you expect?"

"Yeah." Her head bows a bit. "Stick it up my ass. What the fuck."

Bob is hurtling through that funhouse of emotions with the wicked twins of rage and relief that keep a person torn in two, so neither part of his personality can get a divine lick in. He flings the cigarette away.

"Just tell me. What were you trying to prove?"

"The call came, alright? I set up to meet them."

"Alone?"

"They didn't know. I was trying to con Cyrus into a little face-to-face."

"Fuck."

"But he no-showed instead." She walks away, downcast, sees the Ferryman in a scrawny frame of window brushed by the orange light from an exposed bulb.

The Ferryman stares at them with distant objectivity.

"Well, come on," she says. "Cut me up good. I admit I didn't even call."

"Were you just gonna kill him flat out?"

"Flat out, Coyote. Flat out."

"I should crack your skull for being so stupid. And vain." He starts past her, stops, motions with the slight toss of his head toward the Ferryman. "But your friend taught me something. I ain't the center of the world. Think about that yourself. You aren't either."

He walks over to the couch, scoops up the blanket, and wraps it around his shoulders. She wishes there'd been more screaming. At least something to fight against after her failure. Instead she's left with his receding figure walking off into the night beneath the silent blades of the wind turbine like some lost prodigal wandering the wreckage of his exile.

She lies on the bed, boots on. The beamed ceiling a black mirror of the floor below. She feels cruelly alone, hemmed in by a quadrangle of walls and crates and a bureau cliffed around the meager bed. A stifling proximity that seems to open up only when Bob silently enters and sits at the foot of the bed.

He stares grimly into a dusty corner where a spider's loom-strings reach from a water-stained and relic-stuffed cardboard box to the broken staff of an Air Force flag.

She stirs and crosses the bed. She sits beside and behind Bob and puts her arm around his neck. He watches the spider's slow assault up against the darkness.

"I wonder if he knows where he's going. If he actually accounts for something at the far end of the string."

"Tomorrow Lena will be waiting for us in front of Errol's bar. If we're gonna get it on, it's gotta be then."

"Was it hard seeing her?"

She sits there weighing out her words. "I don't know. I was trying so hard to co-opt her. To co-opt her feelings. I don't know."

"We got to be of one mind," he says, "if we're gonna go through this. You understand?"

"I've hardly ever been of one mind, even on my own."

In the morning Case sits against the open back of the pickup. It's all packed and ready to go. English blues chords blow from the Ferryman's speakers as Bob comes out of the house checking his revolver.

The day is showing signs of getting ugly hot. The Ferryman is off alone with his dogs, heavy into the music as he riffs cords on his invisible wind-driven guitar.

Bob eyes the Ferryman as Case hands him a beer. "For luck," she says.

Bob pops it open, toasts, then downs a couple of gulps.

"That's his fuckin' bon voyage for us," she says, nodding toward the Ferryman.

"A moment to be cherished," says Bob cynically.

The Ferryman swings his invisible Fender over his shoulder, strut-hitches his way over to the truck.

"It's been a ride, Ferryman," says Case.

He nods. Gives Bob a glimpse. "I'll probably see you both again. At least once." He winks. "At the wrap party, as they call it."

Then he folds his arms over his chest and closes his eyes, giving a good impression of a corpse.

A silent Sunday. The sun at high tide against the dead shore of the sidewalk where Lena waits leaning against the pink and black stucco wall of the House of Usher.

A child witch in colors gaudy. She rocks against the wall, waiting. Hoping Case never shows or shows quick.

A light-blue pickup turns into the empty street. Slows. Passes. She sees Case. Gets her first glimpse of Bob. A stutter stop of jealous, ugly thoughts. The pickup makes a hard U-turn and pulls up in front of her.

Lena looks down at her hands. They are trembling.

Case climbs out of the truck. Bob remains behind the wheel. Case works through a clumsy introduction. Two faces, each with her mark on their cheek, stare at the other with muted animus.

"You have the stuff with you?"

"In the back," says Bob.

Lena glances at the open truck bed with its locked toolchest area. Case surmises what's going through Lena's head and takes her chance.

"Cyrus want you to see it, too?"

Lena hesitates. "No. There's no need." She looks at Case, then at Bob. She looks back at Case uneasily. "You wouldn't be that fucked up," she says, "to show up and not have it. At least I hope not, Case." She waits. "No? Alright. Let's get it on."

"Where's Cyrus?" asks Bob.

Lena doesn't even throw him a look. Answers Case instead. "Drive. Take 14 South."

"To where?" asks Bob.

"Just fuckin' take 14 South." She motions for Case to get in first. "I'll sit by the window."

They swing south through Mojave. Three faces staring straight into a sun-washed windshield. The colors bled from the faces in the glass. Bob lights a cigarette, offers Lena one. The billowy black of her eyes reflected in the windshield looks away.

"You and I don't have to not get along," says Bob.

"We ain't gonna be around each other enough for one way or the other, sheep."

"Take it easy," says Case.

"Yeah, sure." Lena puts her head back, closes her eyes. Case steals a look at Bob. They both grab a little moment of reassurance.

"Where we going, Lena?"

"Just stay on 14 till we hit Palmdale."

Case looks out the rear window to see if they're being followed.

At Palmdale Lena has them truck east on 138. The wind blows through the open windows. The air is weary hot. They begin the slow curvy climb from the flats into the San Bernardino National Forest. A favorite hangout of skiers and corpses. The mood inside the truck is getting to be a testy wordless contest. The ground gets harder and scraps of pine trees begin their slow birth up into the foothills.

It's about Lena's feeding time, and they stop at a gas station at the Cajon Junction. They pull off into the grass at the end of the station's lot. Bob takes a walk and keeps watch on the chance they're jumped. Case stays close to Lena.

Inside the pickup Lena gets her black jeans off and a leg free. "Remember how we used to talk about buying some kind of coffee shop somewhere?"

"Sure. Real radical chic, right?" Case watches as Lena taps at the gray flesh of her thigh, skin-surfing for a vein. "Got us both through some pretty rough times," Case says. "It's still a good idea."

Lena is readying a spoon of smack. Stops. Looks to double-check on Bob being out of earshot. "Let's disappear," she says. "You and me. Fuck everyone."

Case's mouth fishes for words. Lena is caught up on the thread of an answer. She watches Case. Waits. Picks up the commencement of sorrow in the chilly downturn of Case's eyes. The Spartan move of a hand pulling back into the reaches of her shirt, across her heart. A throat taut without speaking.

Hackles of anger run up through Lena's gut. "You ain't gonna pull it off. It ain't just him and me and Gutter. He's got others. A hunting party. Case, don't you understand? He's got you by the throat. He's already through the cracks and he's hungry." Her eyes half crazed with amorphous dreams that won't shape true. "You and that fuckin' sheep!"

Lena kicks hard at the dashboard. Case plops down on the siderunner, wiped out. Beyond the station is a decline where the roofs of boxcars a mile long lug their way down through Cajon Canyon. The muted iron couplings of the AT&SF like the rack chains of slaves on the run.

"Forget it. Just keep on the road to Palm Springs," says Lena.

Case nods.

A long moment. Lena murmurs Case's name.

"Don't," Case answers.

Lena sags, heats the needle. A singe of bubbles against the scarred concave apron of silver. Case looks up. The scene sears at her consciousness. A crossed index of rapture and wretchedness that were her personal annihilation. She turns away.

Lena whispers, "It's gonna fuckin' get us all anyway."

57

Lena is doing the junkie nod as they hit east on 10. They have her bookended in the front seat. Her head leans back, her eyes are like two dirty pools of water on the hot cement after a storm.

Case looks down at Lena's hand, which rests partly across her own thigh, and sees where the lick of the Ferryman's needle has produced a date in the flesh: 12/21/95.

Bob drives. Case notes his mouth and jaw move as he scans the road through the rearview for any sign of trouble.

"Let's get on with it," he says to Case.

Between Banning and Beaumont, Lena starts her comeback from the junkie nod. Lena tries to slouch away from Bob as best she can. Inside the Dakota the air is stifling, like breathing in waste. Everybody's nerves are getting hacked up pretty good in the silence until Case just comes out with it: "Lena, we got to find Cyrus. We got to know. So we can get to him first."

Lena grimaces through a laugh. "You don't need to find him. He'll find you."

Case tries to work her a little but Bob just flat out hits it. "Let me tell you something, you little cunt. What kind of fuckin' needle do you think they'll put in your arm if I hand you over for what you did at Via Princessa?"

They both can feel Lena constrict and straighten up.

"Via Princessa . . . ," he says again, with an extraordinary quiet in his voice.

On that, Case takes Lena's hand, even before she speaks, so they all can see the date stamped against the flesh.

"We got to know, Lena."

In a moment of controlled panic, Lena stares into the glaring bow of the hood with the road peeling away under it. Her stomach curdles.

"Pull the fuckin' truck over," Lena demands.

Bob keeps driving.

"Pull the fuckin' truck over," she shouts. Then, to make her point, she grabs the wheel and pulls right. In one scream the Dakota swerves through the slow lane, where an RV's brakes burn against the asphalt. The Dakota skates past the full force of a horn and spins out on the gravel shoulder, racking the sand in long scrolls till it comes to a thud against a rocky abutment.

Lena manhandles her way out of the truck. There on the flats Bob and Case close in on her. In the distance are miles of naked mountains that track the freeway. Bald white and battered brown. A vast, incomprehensible keep where the silent bones of the ages watch forever.

Lena approaches them with the shoulder-tight stance of a stalker. "Hello from the gutter," she rails. "You want me sewered. Put on the show!"

She turns to Case, brokenhearted. "I told you. Begged you. But you been brain-fucked. *Cyrus knows.* He knows why you're here."

She turns to Bob. Puts the thumb to him at the end of an outstretched arm. Works it in hard short cuts like she's gouging out an abscess with a stiletto.

"And you too. *Daddyman.* Right? Right, *Daddyman!*"

Bob takes a cautious step toward her. "What?"

"Cyrus knows. He knows you're the girl's father. He knows you're trying to get her back."

Bob's throat clenches. He hangs on her words.

"And he knows you both ain't got shit from that house. He knows. He knows you're scamming him to get close. He knows. It's a fuckin' slaughterhouse. And you've showed your tails." She comes around on Case. "Why? Why!"

Lena starts kicking at the ground. Her shadow is cast against the rocks like some jittering marionette. "Fuck! Fuck!" She grabs at her hair, makes grubby small fists, hits herself in the chest, in the legs. She's a demon-tripped engine in self-slaughter.

"Is she alive?"

Lena turns to Bob.

"Is she alive? My little girl. Is she alive?"

With fiendish plainness Lena announces, "She ain't a little girl no more."

That's all it takes. The whole earth seems to evaporate in the moment Bob spends to chest-pound into Lena. He's got her by the throat. Case jumps him from behind, tries to pull him clear before he kills her.

His hands close on the muscles well up into her jaw, forcing them deep into the bone. The whizzing tires of cars pass and slow, watching this wild briar of boots and fists and violent spitting. But none stop.

Bob keeps screaming, "Is she alive?" Case keeps trying to get her arms around his chest to pull him back. Through a wreath of dust around her head, Lena manages to wrack out a dry shred of words: "She's . . . a . . . live . . ."

But even with that, Bob won't let her go. He keeps choking until Case can finally scream through his rage, "People are slowing. One might stop. Then what?"

When that thought settles in he lets her go.

Lena tries to crawl away, gagging.

Bob's chest contorts with each suck-in of air.

Case comes around him, follows behind Lena, who's reached a small lift of rockside and tries to sit herself up to breathe. Case goes to help her but Lena's arm flaps birdlike to force her away. She begins to cry. Case leans down.

Bob yells, "What the fuck are you doing with that little rat's ass?"

Lena is gasping and the crying only makes it worse. Case tries again to get her arms around Lena. Lena is too blown out to keep fighting.

"Lena. Listen to me, girl. Listen. You're telling us the truth, aren't you?"

"The girl's alive."

"Lena."

"She's alive."

Bob wipes the spit from his mouth. "She's probably lying just to save her rat's ass."

"Fuck you, sheep!"

"Lena. Cyrus . . . Where is he? Where is he?"

Lena cannot or will not answer that.

"If he knows we're scamming him then what's he gonna do to us? Where is he?"

"What a fuckin' joke you all are."

Bob squats down, opens his shirt enough so Lena can see the gun there. "Let's just drag her into the brush and—"

"Stop!" yells Case.

"Drag me? You don't get it, sheep. The evil is on you. And tight! Tight as a fuckin' butt plug. And if you aren't in Palm Springs by six when Cyrus calls . . ."

"If he knows we don't have the stuff, then what is going down?"

"I don't know."

Case eyes her doubtfully.

"He's the puppetmaster when it comes to this. And you know he wouldn't tell me. Me of all people. He knows I might cop it to you. That's why he sent me. He's fuckin' with your head."

"She's lying. She knows more."

Case thinks through the situation.

"I don't know why you're whoring for this sheep," says Lena.

"I'm not whoring for—"

"You don't have to explain anything to this dege—"

"The Wicker Man is gonna put the wolf teeth to you, sheep!"

"We don't need you. You could die here as easy as anywhere else!"

Lena jumps up. Throws out her arms in some crucifixion shock move. "Do me! Do your exorcism shit! Come on!! You're a fuckin' joke!"

She looks at both of them from behind wild eyes. "You think Cyrus hasn't got the lock on both of you?" She points at Case. "He knows it was you that brought the cops down on the house in Escondido. You two are both gonna get leashed and shot."

She gets a little closer to Bob. Works her arm around like a member of some carnival troupe trying to hawk her trade. Below the tattooed date of the Via Princessa murder, a hallucinatory mosaic of Cyrus's mark is motifed on her arm. She lets Bob get a good look.

Then she whispers in the most cruelly singsong voice, "He knows when you are sleeping. He . . ."

Case grabs her and flings her toward the truck before Bob loses it. "Get in the fuckin' truck! Get in!"

Bob wants to shoot the fire out of those eyes. "Let's kill her now."

"No," says Case.

He turns. His eyes are cut hard stone as he looks her over. "It isn't because she was one of your fuckin' groupies, is it?"

"Don't!" Case gets right in his face. "Don't try and cut me up like that!"

"She's a fuckin' murderer and—"

"We're all fuckin' murderers here. Or have you forgotten?"

Bob steps back. They keep on facing each other in the heat.

"I'm fuckin' asking you." Then Case says, "Let it just settle out."

Bob thinks a moment, tries to negotiate a current he can ride that idea through.

"Alright?" she pleads.

A barely discernible "Alright."

Lena stands there watching them. Even curled around a bad moment they seem more together than not. So Lena leans into the Dakota and gets a palm onto the horn and rides it. She gives them the full-throttle bitch and a few choice words to go with it in a little nasty exercise reminder of whose hatred drives whom where.

58

Maureen lies in bed ravaged by a headache. Bone-pulsing deep. Temple to throat. As if the blood were tied in pulpy knots and being pulled through her veins by rope.

Behind her closed eyes, white spots flash. From her dark air-cooled bedroom she hears the front doorbell ring. Immediately when the door opens an argument ensues. She recognizes Arthur's voice.

The front door slams shut, followed by hulking sounds moving hard across the thin tunnel of hallway, then farther off into the living room.

Something thuds. A hand against a wall maybe. She sits up in bed. Listens. Rises. She leans into the opening light of her bedroom door, and there's a soft flourish of silk from her pajamas.

From the living room a harsh mass of sounds. Two voices. The sounds are getting more vicious but remain ill defined, so she starts down the hallway.

It's a long turn, then another after that, through the one-story pseudo-hacienda. The soft carpet covers her approach and the words start to shape with clarity like the sound track of a film fading in at the start of a reel.

"Cyrus called me," says Arthur. "And said you hired him to go into the house."

"And you're going to believe that psychopathic—"

"Why would he lie?"

" 'Cause he's trying to get back at us for Furnace Creek, baby, by fuckin' with *your* head, by making *you* turn on *me*. He wants us to eat each other alive."

"Don't give me the shell game, John Lee, alright?"

Maureen makes the living room just as Arthur shoves John Lee, and his body twists back against his precious bar.

She rushes into the room. "What's goin' on here? Stop! Arthur!"

She manages to get herself wedged between the two men as John Lee is coming up from the clutter of bar stools he stumbled through. Arthur stands there flat-footed behind two huge fists.

John Lee slams a bar stool back down in place where it belongs. "Cyrus is fuckin' with your head."

"With my head? He said you were the one that hired him to kill Sam 'cause he was fuckin' Maureen. Now . . . How did he know that? How! You tell me!"

Maureen can suddenly hear a huge sucking sound coming up through her throat. The pain behind her eyes from the headache sears.

"If he's a liar, then how did he know?"

"I don't understand any of this," Maureen hears herself say. She stares at her husband. His look reeks of the grim and unrepentant. "Who is this Cyrus?"

A question neither man wants to answer.

Maureen asks again. "Who is this Cyrus?"

"Go ahead, breast beater," says John Lee. "Tell her our little secret."

Arthur starts for John Lee, but John Lee is ready and he flings a stool. Arthur stumbles but comes up looking for blood.

"Go on, Arthur," John Lee says again. "Tell your 'friend' here the truth about who Cyrus is. Tell her how we 'got the property in probate, right?' 'Right.' ' 'Cause some woman died, right?' 'Right.' 'She'd been murdered, right?' 'Right.' " There is a queer cadence to his words.

Arthur stiffens up.

Maureen again stares at her husband. "John Lee. My God. Did you—"

"It was 'we,' darlin'. Not me. We. *We* were there in the desert when the old nigger got it. Your partner here was doing the hard sell. Cyrus—the one we're talking about—put her down. He was the little manchild fuck she was raising. He put her down good 'cause she wouldn't make the deal. And *we* thought it would be best if *we* just wandered off and let things be."

"Is this true? Arthur?" Maureen asks. "Is it?"

John Lee eyes him cryptically. Arthur backs away from the truth. Nods.

Maureen turns away, disoriented.

"You want to blame me for bringing him back into this mess," says John Lee. "Well, you can't."

Dusk has fallen blue about the room. Any dim chances of peace slip away through long silent moments. Maureen drops down onto the couch. Her tiny hands are pressed into balls, her wrists pressed against her temples. She can feel the dire call of blood pounding away from vein to vein. She begins to cry at the complete failure of everything around her.

"Why, honey," John Lee jackals. "Don't take it so badly. We were only trying to put a little away for our golden jubilees."

Maureen screams out at him. A vicious, broken, ear-piercing shrill meant to silence his tongue for just one minute of the madness she's locked in.

Again John Lee turns to Arthur. Again tells him in no uncertain terms that he did not hire Cyrus to commit any crime. Again says he does not know how, when, or why Cyrus could have any information about Sam and Maureen's little trysts.

John Lee gets back in the stride of steadied arrogance. The cop's ability to shape-shift into order-and-control mode. To give off that righteous indignation when you are called down by civilians. He turns, reaches over the bar for a Scotch bottle and glass.

But Arthur hasn't copped to everything Cyrus told him, including the fact that the phone is tapped. And those queer

phrases with their feeling of déjà vu John Lee used seem to
fit somewhere suddenly. Arthur doesn't know how much
truth there is in any lie. He does not know how much lie
there is in any truth, since he has long since lost the ability
to scale it. But he does know . . .

"You tapped the phones here, didn't you?" says Arthur.

John Lee drops three ice cubes cleanly into a glass. "Did
Cyrus say that, too?"

Maureen's eyes rise up between the pillars of her balled
fists. "Our phones are tapped?"

"If they are, then that . . . maniac . . . tapped them."

"Horseshit," says Arthur.

"Don't try to get me with your tract-home mentality,
Arthur. I only live here. And remember, if Cyrus tapped this
phone then he knows your boy is out there after him."

"Our phones are tapped," Maureen replies.

"He's fuckin' smart. Think about it. You better get to Bob.
Get to him. Get him off the road. And not for his sake. You
don't want Cyrus caught. We'd make a pretty trio in the papers, wouldn't we?"

"Our phones—"

"Shut the fuck up, you cunt parrot."

John Lee pours the Scotch, shakes his head at his wife's
stupid repetitions. He knows now he's got the upper hand,
even with the facts out. He can see it on Arthur's face. That
he's turning Gabi into a side issue against the more personal
threat of his own survival. Then he decides to press. "Did
Cyrus even say anything about Gabi?"

Arthur shakes his head no. "I didn't get to ask him."

"I don't like to say this, Arthur. He's stuck it to us all here.
All. The girl is dead. I'll bet on it."

"Shut up!" yells Arthur. His face is blood-red. The lips
bluish and hard. He doesn't want to think it. To imagine it.
He wants it all to not exist.

While he takes a drink, John Lee repeats everything he's

said. Slowly hammering away at his points. Maureen looks up at him from the low angle of the couch. She is not looking at the man. Not really. At a shape, yes. A form, yes. A human indictment, possibly.

Then, into that little corner of the mind where we all go mad from time to time, she slips. The pain in her head is gone and only the sheer slight drum-touch of blood against the flesh of her inner ear remains, like a heart already cut from the body but still beating inside a thin shell of music-box wood.

She stands. John Lee is still having at Arthur, sticking each detail well up his ass. Maureen catches a glimpse of John Lee's shoulder holster just inside his coat.

She starts across the room. The next seconds unfold as slow as a Valium drip. John Lee turns, and when Maureen gets the full close-up of that salacious grin she's come to despise all these years, the laws of constraint go jungle.

If someone had been sitting in their car across the valley on that dead-end road in the national forest watching the house with binoculars as John Lee had done so many times before, they'd have seen the fight he put up. How he managed to get the gun from her hand before she cleared his coat.

They'd have seen the violent mess the three would become when Arthur jumped forward and began pulling at their arms. When the bar stool skidded out from beneath him as he was pressed back into the bar and the three fell. And the turning of their shadows like acrobats across the ceiling as they crawled the floor toward the gun: that, too, they would have seen.

They would not have seen the sentences of their fight from then on to the end. They would see the exclamation point of smoke rising from beyond the bar and the couch. And the stilling of shadows. And the smoke continuing on and up across the ceiling to where its lacy color gave way in dissolved seconds before being pulled by air vents into the forever.

They would see that, but nothing more.

59

Bob and Case hole up with Lena in a motel room in Cathedral City, which is about halfway between Palm Springs and Rancho Mirage. It's a U-shaped courtyard of well-appointed kitsch. Wagon-wheel motifs and fifties Gene Autry mirrors with steer horns where you can hang your hat, or your gun belt if you're a carrier. Across the street on the open sand is a billboard advertising the Oasis Water Park, and beyond that the stark black line of Edom Hill and Indio, where singular lights flash like starships trailing the horizon.

Bob sits in the open doorway, his back against the frame, watching all this as he waits for Cyrus's call. He smokes and keeps his arms folded across his chest so no one spots the gun he's got tucked away. He intends to make sure nothing goes down here in Quaintsville, where truckers and families cross the open courtyard.

Lena is sitting on one of the beds. She's had her second feeding and is coming off the nod. She has the television on, but mostly she steals glimpses of Bob while Case showers. Occasionally he spots her and stares back long and hard to make sure that if there's any little nasty ideas in her head, they remain little nasty ideas.

The room is pretty much lit just from the television when Case comes out of the bathroom with her hair wet and wearing only underwear and a T-shirt.

Lena watches Case squat down and take a cigarette from Bob. They speak quietly so Lena can't hear them.

Outside, a mama and papa bear and their three little waifs stroll the gravel lot. The kids all have some kind of fancy up-scale toy flashlight, and they're spraying the night air with long swaths of white. Bob watches this giggling trio march along behind their folks in that drunken cadence that children have.

Case goes over and sits on the edge of the bed by Lena's feet. She spends a few quiet, solicitous minutes there, but it only serves to make Lena wary.

Then, turning to her and speaking in the lowest whisper possible, Case says, "You know where Cyrus is."

Lena moves slightly and the pillows follow suit within the slippery sound of their cloth cases.

"You fuckin' know, Lena."

Lena shrugs. And tries her best to keep her emotions shut off.

"You gotta help us."

" 'Us,' 'us.' How beautifully fuckin' romantic."

"I mean—"

"I know what you—"

"I mean *us* all."

Hours pass until they are just three sets of haggard eyes and a television.

The cellular rings.

Bob jumps up from the doorway.

Case reaches for the phone on the table beside her chair.

Lena slides down onto the edge of the bed.

Case stands. And there, on the other side of the line, is her old master.

"Have you come home to be swallowed?" he says.

Case nods to Bob, looks one last time to Lena, then says to her, "I'm sorry."

Like some kind of harried creature, Lena stands. Sees Bob slowly closing the front door. Looks back at Case. Her eyes slowly backing away and away.

"Cyrus," Case says. "We know you're onto us."

"Shit!" cries Lena.

Case cups the phone to her ear. Steps away from Lena, who tries to make a grab at the cellular but is stopped cold by Bob.

"Be quiet," he says.

"Lena told us everything, man. Every fuckin' word."

Lena tries again for the phone and Bob grabs her arms and flings her toward the bed, where she falls.

"You're in this now," he says. "You!"

"We want the girl back. You hear me?"

"You fuckin' fools!" shouts Lena.

"Cyrus? Cyrus? We want the girl."

Bob grabs Lena before she can shout again. Gets his hands around her mouth. Lifts her from the ground.

"Cyrus! Cyrus!"

"Remember those wind turbines out on Energy Road?" he says. "Where you tried to kill yourself that time?"

"How could I ever forget one of the high spots in my life?"

"Bring the money there."

Confused, she asks, "What money?"

"Why do you think I had you come all the way out here?"

"You're the magician. You tell me."

"You're still nothing but a coolie. You know that?"

"Yeah. So?"

"I told Errol Grey the stuff would be delivered tonight," says Cyrus. "And to have the money ready. You don't have my stuff. I'm sorry to hear it. But you've played field hand enough to know. You get out to Energy Road by tomorrow at first light, and I mean first light. With the money."

"And what do we use to trade?"

"Your lives, I guess."

Case looks at Bob. A troubled moment.

"What?" Bob whispers.

Case waves for him to be quiet. She walks into the bathroom and closes the door. She huddles in the corner of the white room.

"I don't need the girl anymore anyway," says Cyrus. "You can have her back. She's been picked pretty clean. You remember how I am when I got a pretty-pretty with a little baby fat on her. I might even put some bus fare up her crack for the trip back home. How's that?"

"Cyrus . . ."

He hangs up.

Case remains huddled in the corner. Looks around the cell-white room, which smells of disinfectant. Her eyes wander the plastic shower curtain of see-through lilies. Talk about a statement of the mind. She stares down at the floor, remembering her time crawling the tiles as she got off junk.

She goes back into the room. Lena is sitting in a chair, her head just dangling from its scrawny neck staring at the floor as if some message were hidden in the foot-worn western images of the rug. Bob stands over her, gun drawn.

"What happened?" he asks.

"Errol Grey has got a place here in Rancho Mirage. He's waiting to make the trade. We bring Cyrus the money, he gives us the girl."

"Shit."

"I know."

"He wants us to kill Errol Grey and take the money."

"That's it."

"Shit! How do we even know Gabi is—"

"She's alive," growls Lena. "I told you, didn't I! But you don't—"

"Because you're a fuckin' liar."

Lena's head drops back down.

Bob looks at Case. "Well?"

Case thinks a moment. She goes to Lena's purse. Takes out her smack and junkie toys. She walks over to Lena. Kneels in front of her. Lena has been watching all this carefully without so much as a word.

"You killed me," says Lena. "Is that why you didn't let that sheep asshole do me? So *you* could. Fuck. Now I can't go back."

"I know."

"But I got nowhere to go now." Lena sits there with her jaw a shriveled accordion of skin. "You can't fight him."

"But we are."

Lena smirks at the idiocy of it. "Yeah. And look at you both."

"Shut your fuckin' mouth, girl," shouts Bob.

Case takes Lena's needle and hands it to her. Then the smack. She unbuckles Lena's belt, pulls it through the loops. She ties it around her own arm so the veins welt up.

"Hey," says Bob. "What are you doin'?"

"I'll handle this," says Case. "Heat a spoon, Lena. Shoot me up. Go on. I've been weak enough to want to do it myself plenty of times. Especially since our little party in Mexico. But we know about all that, don't we? Come on. Shoot me up!"

Lena sits back, skulking in the chair.

"We filled those veins with one act of degradation after another, didn't we? And I don't mean with just that. Right? Lots of head shit, too, right! Come on." Case's voice cracks. "Till the back is broken, then the heart. Till all that's left is the fuckin' field hand. Come on. Watch me die!"

It is impossible for Lena to tell whether this is just a vicious outburst or some outrageous veiled point being made.

"Come on!" Case screams. Then her voice is flush with sorrow. "There's only two things left you can be. Who I am now or who I'll be after you kiss me with the needle once and for all. Get it. Get it! I stole your life. Get it! I shut you down tonight. You understand what I'm saying here? You're now me in that irrigation ditch on the side of the road where Cyrus left me for dead."

Horror could not be drawn better than in the slack eyes

looking out from the weakly lit corner of the room where Lena sits.

"Where is he?" asks Case.

Not a breath now will go unnoticed.

Lena glances past Case's shoulder to where Bob silently guards the door.

"Where is he?"

Lena thinks to herself she can't make it on a hard run. Case's gun—where did she leave it?

"Lena?"

In her jeans across the room.

"Where . . . is . . . he?"

She's not sure she even has the courage for that.

"Don't you get it? You're just a street junkie now!" Case grabs her face. "Where is he?"

Lena looks down. She cannot go eye-to-eye with Case. "I don't have the courage to fly," she says. "I can only crawl."

Case has heard enough. She lets Lena's face slip from her grasp. She stands. Looks down at the dried-out body and soul hiding behind a painted skin. "Go on." She pulls Lena up and marches her toward the door. "Get out!"

"Wait a minute," says Bob.

"Let her go!" She follows behind Lena, puts an arm hard into the crease of Lena's back. "Get out."

Lena tries to twist around for her purse and junkie paraphernalia but Case won't have it. "No. You're going out naked. Into the wolves' teeth. Just like us."

Bob grabs Lena. "Hold on. Case . . . Let's cuff this fuckin' bitch up in here, split, and call the cops. Tell 'em what we have. I know people we can . . ."

Case presses her hand against Bob's. "Bob, please . . ."

He feels her voice so filled with defeat that he lets Lena go. Case opens the door. Lena is trembling as she looks back toward the lifeline of smack left behind. Case pushes her again, this time out the door.

"Case," cries Lena.

Case shoves her again. Lena crumples a bit. Boots haunting steps on gravel. Case shoves her past the truck and into the moonlight of the courtyard.

"Case . . ."

Case turns. Lena is left fumbling for a few pathetic moments to try to buy something back of her life.

Bob watches from the doorway. Lena runs back to Case. Takes her by the arm. They speak a few moments. The dark outline of the overhanging balcony makes it impossible for him to see their faces. When they're done, Case nods.

She walks back into the room. Looks at Lena one last time and closes the door.

"Well?"

"Nothing."

"What did she say? I saw you nodding at something."

Case slumps down on the bed. "Nothing that could help us now."

Arthur sits on the couch for hours staring at John Lee's body. He watches the tiny tricklets of blood fall in slow order on the wood flooring around the bar.

Maureen sits on the bathroom floor in the dark by the toilet. Her spirit has collapsed under the long charge of adrenaline. Her gun hand rests on the side of the porcelain bowl. Its coolness soothes her. She is covered with the dark brandy of John Lee's blood. She wants the robe off, the blood away. But it is too much to even move.

Emerging through the dark is Arthur. He slides down beside her.

"I don't think anyone heard the shot."

"I guess by now they'd have . . ."

"But you can never know."

"Would they believe it was . . ."

"With all that shit behind us?"

"Oh God, Arthur."

She looks away from him and to the spots of blood up and across her hand, then out and along her arm. Marks that trace the blastline from where she held the gun against his flesh and fired.

"You need to know something," Arthur says.

She is too weak to respond.

"It wasn't Cyrus who fuckin' killed that old lady in the desert. He'd shot her alright. 'Cause she wouldn't sell her property to us. John Lee had extorted the kid, even promised him a cut. He was a junkie, see, and John Lee fed him with smack from busts, but he went ballistic when she said no.

"We went into the trailer." His voice wheezes. "She was alive. Barely. John Lee—he put the finishing touches to her. Made it look like . . . seem like a cult . . ." He chokes on the word.

Maureen does not look at him. She does not want to know how much is a lie. She doesn't care. She knows the truth is soundly somewhere between what he has said and what really was slammed home with a bullet.

"What do we do?" she asks.

"We try to survive."

They wrap the body in a tarp. A shroud stained with lavender from when Maureen sponge-painted a kitchen wall. They carry John Lee through the darkened house. Past windows where the neighbors' houses twinkle in small framed presses of moonlight. Arthur at the chest, she at the legs. He walks backward with straddling steps toward the inside door of the garage. She follows hunched over like some miserably tired charwoman, breathing hard behind the train of a sagging corpse.

61

Bob and Case sit at a table in the motel room. They fill small plastic bags with sugar and flour. They bind them up in gray tape. The table is stacked with the gray bricks, two overnight bags' worth. The price of a score, or a takedown.

"Gettin' in will be easy," says Case. "They'll frisk us pretty hard. Of course, when Errol sees it's us he may pop a load. Gettin' fuckin' gun-crazy aggro on us. Or he might be cool. But either way, gettin' out with money after they see this shit will be no friggin' snack. Especially if we ain't packin'."

Bob sits there with his elbow resting on the table and the thumb of his upturned arm pressing against his teeth.

"They'll chill after they frisk us," she says. "But then what? I could slide my knife up my cunt but I'd have a fuck of a time gettin' it out."

Bob is staring hypnotically at the dead space on the table between them.

"I was makin' some black fuckin' humor here," she says.

His eyes deeply creased, he looks up without acknowledging what she said. "He's got ex-cops working for him, right?"

"Yeah," she says. "He did, anyway."

"Cops have a system for frisking. Systems have weaknesses. We have to create for that weakness."

. . .

The moon is already halfway around the dark seam of the night when they climb into the balmy foothills just south-west of Rancho Mirage. A long spindly road past the rare gated estate.

On the seat between them is the smaller of the two cases with their phony kilos. This one is shaped like a duffel with curved handles. Its bottom is made of a hard Masonite-like board. It sits on four silver nubs, and what Bob discovered was that there is just enough of a channelway along the un-derbelly to tape Case's semiautomatic to it and let the duffel still sit flat.

He double-checks the tape and the gun.

Case lets go of the steering wheel with one arm, shakes out the tension. "From here on up, there's no more houses," she says.

They start the last half-mile climb. Their headlights flood-ing the wild brush. At each rocky turnout a great sprinkling of lights crosses the desert floor. Jeweled buoys on a be-darkened sea.

"Pull over," he says.

She slows and sides the road in a soft gravelly whoosh.

He sits looking back.

"Are you alright?"

"He's made us his whores, hasn't he?"

"I don't get what you mean."

"What we're doing? We're the catch dogs tonight."

She sits back. Folds her arms across the chest of her buck-skin coat. Her violet eye shadow gives her the sleek dark look of a hawk on the come.

"I was looking back down there and flashed on the house on Via Princessa. It was up on a hill like this. But not so high. Gabi would watch the road at night. I'd drive by. Pull over. Run my flashers. That was my good night to her."

He leans his head forward. Rests it on the dashboard. "You got nothin' to say, huh?"

"Sure. You know what I think?" she says. "Somebody throws you a lifeline and you toss it away 'cause you don't like the color of the rope. I don't think what we're doing is anything more than—as Cyrus calls it—crowd control."

The house is concrete and glass. A fragile container designed as stark low contemporary. With long sliding-glass-door views of Coachella Valley.

They pull up. Shut off the headlights. In a picture window, Case spots the two well-lubed drumheads from the bar.

She takes the heavier satchel from the bed of the pickup. Bob takes the duffel with the gun taped underneath. This high up, the wind blows pretty hard and everything crackles.

As they start along the pestled walkway they can see the drumheads cross the living room toward the door.

The chrome-fronted door is behind a gated open-air portico. Case presses the buzzer. The gate automatically opens. She and Bob glance at each other.

"Time to get swallowed," she whispers.

They enter and the gate glides shut behind them. They stand in the locked-off alcove of ten-foot-high walls. A half-moon cup of cement where two pink floodlights flank the door and give the man-made stone its showroom look.

They wait. The dry air, the silence, their raggle-tag selves. And all in that pink designer light.

From behind them a polite voice requests, "Put the bags down, please. And put your hands up."

Bob and Case turn to find they're staring at the thoughtful presence of a .41-caliber Blackhawk.

They do as they are told. The drumhead at the gate calls to his partner. The door opens and he makes a gentlemanly approach behind the tight grip of his side arm.

The frisking begins. The two drumheads work clean and

fast. They even find Case's knife hidden down in the arch of her boot. One accidentally kicks the duffel bag and it grates along the walkway. Neither Bob nor Case even glances at the bag for fear of giving themselves away.

Then the drumheads go about the business of opening the bag and the duffel to make sure there are no little surprises. It all goes down clean and easy. They close the bag and duffel back up.

Case and Bob are made to wait at gunpoint while the one at the front door disappears inside the cool white-tiled foyer and calls to Errol. He comes back and with a mute crook of a finger ushers them in. Bob and Case turn and reach for their respective bags. The drumhead behind them has already got his hand on Case's bag, but he's a second late for the duffel.

"Let it go," says the drumhead.

Bob does not let go.

"You haven't paid for it yet, Slick," says Case.

He starts to back them off with his pistol. "How 'bout I pay for it right now?"

"Forget it, Case," warns Bob.

She looks over at him. His jaw tightens all the way down to his throatskin. "It's okay."

He slips a look downward. Her eyes follow. He passes the duffel to the drumhead. She watches his foreplay as he gives the bag a half turn so the gun taped underneath, which was at the rear end, is now at the front and, possibly, still within reach.

The drumhead at the doorway orders them in. Case starts their little march by cutting off any view he might have of the bag. Then, with one drumhead in front and the other swagging up the rear, they begin their procession Indian file into the house.

They clear the foyer, pass down an entranceway of mauve wallpaper with original Indian headdresses. Pass a black-rock waterfall from floor to ceiling with colored spots of subtle lighting. Pass into a sunken living room of gray leather and Indian objets d'art.

The whole walk Bob is making sure he is not an arm's length away from the gun. The whole while Case is watching, looking for something within reach to grab and use as a weapon. The whole while they're both waiting for the moment when they got to make a show of it before any chance is completely gone.

Case looks back at Bob. There ain't no mystery nor sentiment there.

The moment it may be completely out of reach comes on down and dirty as Errol rises from the soft gray comfort of his couch, turns, and sees it's Case and Bob.

It's a blowout. Bad news squared by ten. Errol is humping up those red clay steps from the living room with his bathrobe flowing outward, exposing long tanned muscled legs, yelling he'll kill them both. Then thanks to fuckin' God, thinks Bob, Errol slips.

In that perfectly human moment when the drumhead in front reaches out to keep his meal ticket from doing a nosedive into the fancy Italian tile, Bob jumps back and grabs the duffel. The other drumhead, in a moment of self-defense, lifts up the duffel and pushes it out to try to slow the charge. Bob's hands scramble across the bottom of the bag, his fingers like the manic legs of a millipede looking for the trigger.

He scores it.

Fires.

The shot blows through the man's pelvis and pings a tiny hole of dust into the far wall, with just a touch of blood. The duffel comes loose from his grasp and Bob wields it around, one hand on the gun, the other on the curved handle.

Case hears him yell, "Get out of the way!"

She slamdives to the floor.

The other drumhead is just looking up when a shot sends him toppling back, one arm waggling, one leg pitcher stiff, a head jerked weirdly down into the chin. He falls, his spine hitting flush on the couch, his skull on the coffee table. The glass shatters into shark-teeth fragments.

Bob comes around, tearing the gun loose from the duffel's underbelly. The guard behind him is lying on the floor, motionless.

Errol is splayed out on the tile, his robe spread open. He is exposed. Case stands, moves back. Errol does not move at all.

"Alright, alright." Errol shivers. "Alright." His hand starts pressing at the air. "Alright, take the money." His back sinking as if he can avoid the bullet that will come. "Take the money, take it . . ."

"Cross him over," says Case.

Bob looks at her with bald shock.

"Snuff him," she screams.

Errol pleads for his life. Bob steps forward and raises his gun. Errol, without realizing it, begins to urinate.

For a moment Bob stares at the puddle spreading out across the tiles and through the silky damask of the robe.

There is a puzzle at work and the pieces are being taken away one at a time until the empty slot, the implacable void, is forever in play.

LE MORT AND THE RITE OF INCORPORATION

62

The thin paper of color is coming back to the sky. Restless light. Case and Bob set out to the north. Driving hard with satchels of money against time. With the past to the east, the future to the west. With the radio spewing news as they wait for reports of the murder.

Through the reaches of a Christian Mojave are billboards framed in fieldstone built by born-agains that spread Bible wisdoms, black on white, against the pink of a coming sun: WITH KNOWLEDGE COMES PAIN . . . ACT AS IF YOU HAD FAITH AND FAITH WILL BE GIVEN TO YOU . . . HUMBLE YOURSELF AND I WILL HEAL THE LAND.

These pass along the highway. Still and sure and stately. Yet there is only one truth, and they, Case and Bob, are heading toward it. Like Ahab, like Lincoln, with a fierce bigotry of purpose.

She is watching the road in silence. Intent on the haunting pockets of blue that border the as yet empty highway.

"What are you thinking?" he asks.

Without turning to him, and laboring through her words, she says, "I'm thinking about Gabi. I'm thinking about me. What she's been through. What I've been through. I'm thinking about you. From where you've come to have all that sorrow. And what you'll be. I'm thinking about the hole in the center of my heart, which is the hole at the center of my universe, the universe, all our universes. I'm thinking about

Lena and Errol and . . . I'm thinking about him. And all those veins lost through all those years. And I'm thinking about those two sisters—meaning and madness. Coming out of the night sky like I seen in a painting. Those two sisters. Chasing some asshole rube down the road in his red robe."

She leans forward, rests her hands on her knees, listens to the last sounds of her own voice. "Am I making any sense at all? Do you have any idea what the fuck I'm ranting about?"

He remembers a day at a pit stop in the heat. With its sweet greasy food and their little dogfight over a newspaper story on the Polly Klaas murder. And those chirping over-perfumed maquiladoras. He remembers. "We all hunt Leviathan in our own way," he says.

Energy Road is a mile-long cut off Route 178 in the Salt Wells Valley. It's the hard country along the Inyo County border. The land of furnaced playas from China Lake on through to the Panamint Mountains and Death Valley.

It is first light as they haul down that long empty road. In the distance a terra-cotta frieze of silver wind turbines, hundreds of them, begins to stand out like an army of knights' spears rising futilely to the wind against the black and brown mountains beyond. They rise amid huge power lines. Cabled trestles moving on into the as yet unlit recess of the white country.

The dirt road ends among these giant, silent, turning blades. Bob and Case get out of the truck. Fifty yards ahead, standing among those steel monoliths, is Cyrus.

It is as if he were the lone watchman of this country. An almost unhuman guardsman coming through great red sheets of the sun rising behind him. There is a swept loneliness to the place, and the stillness of seeping sand. Case and Bob are each carrying a bag of money as they approach Cyrus.

They stop just feet away. The two men now face-to-face.

Bob begins to fill in the details of what he had imagined Cyrus to be. The lightning bolts beneath his cheeks crinkle. "Gettin' your eyeful?" asks Cyrus.

"Where's my daughter?"

"You'll get to take home your legacy."

Case squats down. Opens the bag to show him the money. "Where is she?" Case asks.

Cyrus does not even look at her. He walks past them both toward the truck. Bob and Case glance at each other.

Cyrus moves around the pickup, notices the extra cylinder in the back for gas. "How you set for gas?" He taps the tank, listens to the slight thud. "You're in good shape."

He then glances into the cab. He looks around and spots the cellular phone. He reaches in and grabs it. He holds it up for them to see, and in one swift motion smashes it to pieces against the Dakota's hood.

He comes back toward them, points to a thin patch of rubble that might pass as some kind of bare macadam that heads on into the hills. "Your legacy's over that hill. When you see her, drop the money and take her. Easy . . ."

He passes them both. He stops and turns to Bob. They are just a foot from each other. Silence, augmented by degrees of hatred.

"When you get home," says Cyrus, "ask Arthur and John Lee who killed the old witch. You ask. You ask who put the first bullet into her neck. You ask. You ask about her scratching at the floor, dyin'. You ask. You ask who did the final turkey carving of that beer-guzzling bitch. *After* she'd been shot again. You ask."

Cyrus has the slow, unbreakable stare of the reaper. "You ask John Lee who hired me. Hired me—to go up onto Via Princessa and do the nigger and his porcelain bitch. You ask."

With each statement Bob seems to draw up inside himself in horror.

"You ask Arthur if I didn't call him. You ask. Have some

fun. Ask John Lee who tapped his old lady's phone. You ask. I can't kill you better than you can all kill yourselves."

Case watches all this go down. It's a fuckin' dreamscape, and not a mile away from where she bellied enough downers to put any bad omen to sleep. There's war engines inside her chest plowing against her rib cage. Yet it's all so still and quiet. Especially the two of them. Never a voice raised. Like businessmen talking life insurance or real estate.

It's all coming out, she thinks. All the black-eyed poison he'll have to live with. Yet he stands there just listening. Stoic, sure, but not immune. Case can smell the rage seeping out of his pores with every blow.

"I can see now," Cyrus says, looking Bob over closely, "why you're still alive. You have some of me inside you."

Just enough of a bitter curve to snake-bite Bob Whatever. Just enough. But he doesn't cop to it. The skin around Bob's neck wound clips up with a hard swallow, like the chamber of an automatic.

"And there's something else, then you can be on your way." Cyrus flecks at the scalps studded down the seam of his jeans. "I have invaded you. I will always be the greater part of your existence. Yours and John Lee's and Arthur's. And your little piece of pink meat down the road. Every moment of your life from here on in will be determined by what I have carved out of you. I own your subconscious, I . . . own. Now get out," he says.

Bob holds a moment to let Cyrus know in some fashion that this outlandish nightmare doesn't end at the precise moment he says it does. Then he turns for the truck. Case follows.

"Not you," says Cyrus. "You wait."

Bob looks over at Case. She nods for him to go on. He warns Cyrus with one glance, then starts for the truck.

Cyrus steps up to Case. Her back seems to lean away as he gets within kissing inches of her face. "Whatever happens today. Whatever. You are crossing over. I have put a bounty on your head. The word's out on you to all the wolves. They're gonna come up out of the gutter for you. You'll never have a night's sleep again. That I know. The creepie-crawlies, sheep. They're on you now."

He waits a moment. Around him and Case, dark scythe marks pinwheel from the on-high blades cutting at the coming sun.

"And as you cross over," he says, "I'll flay the skin from your bones while you're alive. And I'll cut out your cunt and swallow it while you watch."

63

They climb the rubbled beltway into the brittle foothills as they were told. Cyrus watches them until they are just a morph of dust rising through slag-sided vents.

The pickup bolts and hitches wildly over potholes and cranky sinks. They climb through each meandering wave of slipshod talus until they reach a promontory where the road slides down to the basin. Staring at them is miles of nothingness.

"He's gonna ride us right into a black hole," says Bob.

"How much water we got?"

Bob looks behind the seat, counts two jugs of water. "Enough so we'll remember what it tastes like."

The descent is mean. An hour of rock-tearing nightmares. The muffler is grouted when the ground beneath them turns to sand. The transmission is shaken half loose from its bolts. The shocks sound like a twelve-story crack-up diving into cement. They pass a sign hand-painted onto the rockface: NO GAS OR SERVICES FOR MILES—ASSHOLE.

A little roadside humor for the wandering fool.

Case keeps looking back, as if Cyrus might come creeping right up their ass. But she knows better. This is gonna be the long ugly march. The slow fuck you to death.

Across the open flats the ground becomes a moonscape. An immutable playa. The pickup makes its slow trot northeast. A thin plume of warning dust follows in their tires' wake. The temperature gauges start to take a beating. For a moment they think they see something on the horizon. A shimmering white parabola. There, then gone. Could it be the back of a van moving obliquely through the disorienting waves of heat?

They stop to get their bearings. Wait. But whatever it was, the horizon has swallowed it.

"Why is he doing it like this? Taking us all the way out here? Is he gonna give Gabi back?"

Her voice cracks from the heat. "Rat patrol, Coyote. It's a kill game. And we're the game. Oh, yeah . . ." Her tongue sticks to the roof of her mouth. "He's gonna take us way out. And somewhere out there . . . somewhere . . . he's gonna dump Gabi back in our lap for the money. The money he got us to kill for. But, by then, we'll be too far for any help. And he'll put the wolves to us. It's a blooding, Coyote. Clean and simple as . . . a slit throat."

Noon.

Dirt spewing up from the turning tires and through the open windows has left grimy tracks across their faces. Ahead the ground turns again.

Huge druidic rock shapes begin to rise out of the well of

the earth. The gas gauge is getting lower while the temperature gauge is going higher. Through a composition of nature
where oddly shaped tufa towers spire up like tombstones and
battlements.

It is an endless straight line they make.

Case dampens a neckerchief and wipes Bob's face and the
back of his neck. She does the same for herself.

Then they settle back into grim silence.

Two hours later, they feel the quick heart-thumping of the
tires as they cross a bridge built a century ago of railroad ties
over a shallow ravine for wagons carrying salt out of the
desert.

The pinnacles flanking that burned playa were born of
tectonic fissures when the ground was a lake a hundred thousand years ago. Their sundial shadows cast toward afternoon. A frightening sense of hopelessness is setting in.

Case opens the satchel on the front seat. She takes out a
few small packets and stuffs them in the glove compartment.

"What are you doing?"

She is tired, speaks with a shrug, "I was thinking . . .
If they show, they ain't gonna be counting it. If they
show . . ."

"They'll show."

"Yeah. But we may need some money later. You may need
some. I don't think you got much to go back to."

They have now reached a point beyond those tufa monu-
ments where the ground is a washed sheet of dry salt. Flat
and ghoulish. Laid barren as if it were the hub of a nuclear
holocaust or that Devonian moment when the earth was catapulted out of mystery and all was flung aside. A bleached
apocalypse. The true face of the father and mother, of death.

Shining as a shield. The witches' brew, or the cauldron of God. The ultimate dissolution, or the reflection of the white light. Call it what you want, it exists beyond that.

The burnished blue hood of the Dakota is a fast-moving bow. An incandescent eye-shutting mirage charging over an ocean of salt. They bear down against the glare with creased faces. Wavering now like sailors in the ebb and flow of the pickup.

"Wait . . ."

Exhausted, Bob turns toward Case.

"There." She points out the windshield. "I saw something."

They stop the truck. Watch. In the deep distance stand the heat-dazed Paramints where Charlie and his Hole Patrol searched for a sea of gold in the belly of the rocks, and beyond that the stark valleys the Indians called Tomesha, "ground afire."

They are barely footnotes against a horizon that may have tricked them.

"Maybe my head's just fried," she says.

Bob offers her some water.

They are sitting there with the sun burning holes into the black sockets of their failing eyes when a penny spot comes again along the rim of the world. Arabic in its sheetwide rippling. A metallic warrior engulfed in white grime.

"Look. It's them," she says. "I know it."

Their exhaustion burns away as the white salient of a van forms from this specter of running sand. The sleek metal grill coming on at a clipped seventy.

Bob and Case get out of the truck.

About a mile off the van starts to make a sweeping turn. "This is it," warns Case.

She goes for the shotgun. Bob goes for the money satchels. A hundred yards out, the van starts showing its ass end, then begins a long slow backup toward the Dakota.

Fifty yards away it stops. The rear doors swing open, and

there's Gutter and a couple of warchildren Case hasn't seen before. They spread apart enough to press Gabi out into the light. She is blindfolded, her hands bound behind her back. They shove her out of the van. She lands hard on her face. When Bob sees his child, he is so overwhelmed he screams out her name. When she hears his voice her head comes up like some wild, frightened bird. He calls out again. She begins to cry back. A haunted weeping plea, edging forward in the sand.

One of the warchildren has butted up behind Gabi. He presses a small Luger against the back of her head while he choke-holds her hair.

The drama of the trade begins to play itself out. Gutter yells for Case and Bob to come on with the money. They start forward. Case keeps her shotgun dead on Gutter.

They're only ten yards from Gabi when Gutter yells, "Toss the money over!"

Gabi still yelps pitifully for her father.

Bob glances at Case. "I'm tossing the bags over."

She nods.

He tosses the satchels. They land with a low thud. Gutter shoots forward, kneels, gets those bags open quick. He doesn't pay the least attention to the shotgun zoned in on him. He does a cursory hand-check of the cash. More for volume and show than a close count. He slaps the bags closed. Stands with a black-hearted smile. He steps back coolly. "Get in the van, Stick," he yells.

The kid with the Luger has got a skinned-down head shaped like a toad. He's got what might be a pretty face, more girlish than not. He lets Gabi drop and slips back to the van, where he gives Case a couple of fingers brushing across his cock.

Bob runs forward. Kneels at his daughter's side. Starts pulling loose the blindfold.

Case still has the shotgun aimed at the black square of space beyond the open van doors. As the van starts to kick out and pull away Gutter shouts, "How you gonna get back home?"

He points beyond Case, to the south, as the van doors slam shut.

When Gabi sees her father for the first time, she is so disoriented, and he looks so different with the mustache and tattoo and the scar on his neck, that she starts to unravel. But when she hears his voice again, and feels his arms around her, sees those eyes crying she remembers all too well from a world she thought dead, she starts to break down. A huge coming apart, with hands scrambling madly across her father's back, his shoulders, up his arms, burying her head in his chest as if trying to feel every touch of him so she can know with certainty she is alive and free.

Case looks back from where they came, calls to Bob. He holds Gabi tightly, looks up sobbing, sees Case point the shotgun.

Miles back, amid those pinnacles above the desert floor, a flare has been set off. Welding spots of white shoot upward in a tinseled arc toward the baking sun.

Gabi starts to rock like a child blithering out one word: "Him . . ."

Case steps back toward Bob, and kneels beside the girl. Bob looks at Case. "Cyrus?"

"Got to be," she says.

64

They wait through the falling away of the sun. Beyond their grasp, the stone-backed foothills give up the day's heat like dying coals at a fire, their gray skin going cooler with the advance of the dark blue icing of night.

Bob has the hood up, is checking the wires and hoses and

bolts making sure that what needs to be locked and loaded for a hard run across the flats is dead on.

Gabi sits inside the Dakota, huddled up in one of her father's workshirts. The great rush of freedom has given way to stunning exhaustion. A mind-staring emptiness. Case sits beside Gabi. She's seen this all before, in a mural of junkie faces and rehab breakdowns whose systems are eighty-proof Thorazine.

The sun is great shocks of blown gold and orange coming through the clouded summer sky, and in a moment of half-clarity Gabi looks up at Case and whispers, "I know you."

Case looks down into that filthy ragdoll face. "Me?"

"I saw you in Mexico."

Case's face wans at the hideous connection.

"I was in the back of the van. The door was bent funny, and sometimes when I was alone I could look out. I saw when Cyrus hit you. And when they dragged you into that field. I saw them rape you . . ."

Case runs a finger up Gabi's arm. Along the small purple beetle-back dots left from the needle.

"I thought about you," says Gabi. She looks up as if her father might hear what she is about to say. Her eyes press over the top of the dashboard. "I don't want my father hurt."

It is a deplorable moment. The innocent and absurd reticence of the wounded.

"I thought about you. When they were doing it to me . . ."

Case can feel that curdling tremor throughout Gabi's body, knows it full well. The very sensory touch of it goes back down her own dungeon steps through heart-mind fragments.

"They used to talk about you. And I thought, If I could be like that, like someone they hated, feared, like someone, you know . . . And thought, I could live maybe. I could just zone in on that. So I would pretend. I would close my eyes and think . . ." She sees her father moving around the engine hood, stops on the chance he comes over. When he disappears again behind the blue hoodsheet, she goes on: "You know what I mean? Not that I didn't think about my father. But . . . later. Later. I don't know. I needed something else. And I was afraid . . . he'd hate me."

Gabi curls up inside the lean angle of Case's shoulder. Whole blind moments of creation pull at Case. She feels those trigger pains for this raw thing of childhood that's been devoured out. For a moment she feels a wish coming, but she knows better. And for a moment she hates herself for knowing better than to wish.

"I don't feel well," says Gabi. "My whole body hurts."

In dusk, Case and Bob stand at the back of the pickup and talk through the facts that beset them. And on top of it all they've got a kid who's gut-surfing through the first hits of withdrawal. Case sits on the tailgate, her hands bundled up inside the pockets of her buckskin coat. Bob paces, occasionally glancing through the rear window of the Dakota at Gabi. Her head lies back against the glass. The night wind has started up. The light is going fast, the mountains are already black.

"We go north," he says, pointing, "or east, we got nothing. Nothing. Just miles of Death Valley. We go south, maybe. There's the China Lake Weapon Center. But that's not shit for miles, and I've never been that way."

He stops, runs his boot along the sand, leaving a clean mark. "Going back the way we came is still the closest."

"Trona's that way."

"Yeah. We might eventually see some lights on the horizon. Make a run at 'em."

"We can't stay here."

"I know."

"Come dark, they'll swarm us."

He nods. "There's fire stations in the hills. We could try to make a run for them. There's people there."

"Yeah. But do you know exactly where they are?"

"No. But we could pick a direction. Get as far as we get. If they jump us, we blow the truck. That extra gas will kick up some huge flame."

He reaches into his canvas coat for a cigarette.

"Are you counting on the search and rescue helicopters?"

He lights the cigarette, shrugs a bit at the prospect. "Counting on them is a reach, but . . . If those rangers pick up on the flames they'll have the choppers out fast."

"If they pick up the flames."

"If," he says.

"Could they get here quick enough?"

"I don't know, Case, I just don't know."

"If they don't, we'd have lost the truck. We'd be on foot."

"They'd be on us anyway by then."

"Yeah, you're right about that, Coyote."

Things look pretty bad all the way around. He sits beside Case. They form a sullen, hope-lost pair. She leans back for a canteen lying in the bed of the truck. Earlier they'd poured the last water from both jugs into it. She shakes the canteen, uncorks it, takes a drink. She then offers him the canteen. As he takes it, he passes her the cigarette. Going through this simple ritual, they stare south toward an unspeakable creeping darkness. She passes him back the cigarette, he the canteen to her. She lays it stone-flat across her lap, runs her fingers along the smooth metal plate of its belly.

Case looks back into the truck cab. Gabi is now just the barest of shadows. Her head moves listlessly.

We are asked to do things that logic leaves us incapable of. Case goes through the checklist of her failings. Out there, out there in the country grafted from a thousand riddles and a thousand koans, where all things are completely exposed, she knows the Lord of Misrule is waiting. Filing his teeth. Getting ready to come at them twelve months out of the year, leading a host of warped goodies to take them down. Happy holidays from the dead, child. Dyin' time starts early tonight. And she knows they're only worth what they're worth dead.

"Why don't we pack the brush right here?" she says. "Leave me with enough gas. I'll start a fire. This will draw them. You take off with the truck."

Bob looks at her, knowing full well what that means. He looks back at Gabi. Her head jerks slightly. Inside him is a stinging bedlam. A nightmare that can't be slept through.

"I can do it," she says.

Bob's eyes are full of fatigue and pain as he climbs down from the tailgate and stands. Even against the roiling night, feelings he has for Case speak to her in the tenderness of his features. "We'll go home together," he says, "or we'll perish here together. Let's start back."

He heads for the driver's side of the truck and Case is up quick and stops him with the tug of an arm.

"Thank you," she says.

The careful turn of his head. "For what?"

"For considering me . . . that valuable."

65

They move hard across the desert floor. No headlights. Gabi sits like petrified wood between her father, who drives, and Case. She is already suffering from the night sweats, 'cause she's gone well beyond her required feeding. A shotgun is wedged between her leg and Case's, just inches from where she holds Case's hand.

Every hole and hard spot they hit drives them like rivets toward the roof before they come slamming down. Gabi winces a cry with every hit.

"It'll be alright, baby," hushes Bob.

Then the black night explodes with electric fire. A white burning lance missiles toward them.

Gabi screams and ducks down. Case braces herself against the dashboard. Bob armlocks the steering wheel.

The flare rams the windshield. Sends out a phosphorous rain of thistles, blinding them. The truck goes out of control. Bob sees Stick rushing out of the circlet of darkness, firing his Luger. He sees Gutter charging the front end. Bob cuts hard right but keeps going.

Gabi slides down on the floor, wailing. Bob hits the gas, trying to make a run out of it. The ground ahead is going by so fast it's impossible to react to the nooks and rises. The Dakota takes a beating but the shots are getting more distant. Suddenly the bridge of railroad ties rises up out of the darkness at a hard angle.

Bob tries to right the wheels and hit the brakes at the same time, but it's too little too late. The tires trundle across the flat ties at a forty-degree cut, and going that fast the Dakota can't make it. The tires on one side of the truck instantly spin air and the pickup does a nosedive straight into the ravine. It hits hard ten feet down, hangs a second assend up, then dips against the incline in a thudding powderbomb of sand.

Dazed and cut with broken glass, Case stumbles out of the truck. Bob has to kick at his jammed door till it gives way in a croaking sigh. He grabs his daughter out behind him. Case scrambles back for their weapons. The gas pedal has stuck to the floor and the engine whines away, the front tires burning holes in the briny ground.

They try to collect themselves in the darkness for the fight to come. They hunker at the edge of the ravine. Gabi lies on the ground in a fetal position. She has become just a gibbering thing. Case and Bob look out across the flats. It is silent and dark as a sacred island of the dead.

They look at each other, fighting for their breath, fighting to compose themselves. A fierce psychic energy moves between the two.

"Get Gabi out of the way. Find someplace to put her. Farther up the ravine. I'm gonna blow the truck!"

Case grabs Gabi against her will and shakes her hard. Bob runs up onto the trestled parapet and hears Case yelling, "Come on! Come on!" He kneels, looks between the thick lattice pylons, sees Case dragging Gabi along the ridge-backed ravine floor under the bridge, sees the bumping shocks finally rattle Gabi's legs into some kind of order.

He stands, pumps a shell into the shotgun's chamber. He waits till Case and Gabi are clear.

A short way down that warped and eroded channelway they come upon the remains of a drainage pipe almost tall enough for a man to walk through. Case tugs Gabi hard, stumbling into the twenty-foot-long cement corridor. She gets Gabi down on the ground.

Bob hears Case scream to him to blow the truck. He takes aim at the gas tank and fires.

There is a depth-charge blow skyward that rocks Bob back-assed from the bridge into the sand. It's followed in fast order by a raw burst of flames that geyser up and leap and lick at the thick trestle ties. The draft below the bridge sucks in the flames that shoot across its underbelly.

Case looks out through that cement portal to where the ground is a fever of flames and fast filling with hard black-gray smoke. She looks toward the other end of the drainage pipe. There's access from both sides.

She straddles Gabi, who sits backed against the curving wall. "I have to go back up on top."

Gabi's got the ice-cold shakes and grabs Case's coat so she can't leave.

"Listen to me. Listen to me," says Case.

Gabi snaps her head from side to side, not wanting to hear.

Case takes the pistol from her belt. Tries to force-feed it into Gabi's hand. "Listen," she screams. Then, lower, "Listen. We've done this before, Gabi. You and me. We've done this."

Gabi stares into that bare face. Spartan in its calculated wrath and enmity. A fierce sound rockpoint, holding fast as death itself.

"Hear me. Think of me now. Be me now. Take this gun . . . Take it. Look through the fuckin' back door of that van when they dragged me out into that field. It was me, you . . . Okay. When they dry-humped you. It was you, me, okay. Okay."

The fingers give a little and Case gets them spread enough to press the handle of the gun in. "We've done this before. Oh, yeah. When I shot Granny Boy down. It was me, you. When I put one blast right into that prick's face. It was *us*. We did it. You understand?"

Case's voice has the lulling cadence of the killer. The sharp cut-sounds of the knife doing its death-quick evisceration.

"We've done this before. We've broken into them just like they broke into you. You hear me. We've done this. And we're going to do it again. Now. You, me."

Gabi's hand trembles around the spherical brushing and Case sees she may not hold up even yet. But there's no more time.

"I got to go back up on top. If they come . . ."

Case slams back the hammer, and Gabi's eyes flinch. "You hold it close with both hands. You, me. And you, me . . . do them. You, me. You, me. Do them. Just pull the trigger. And keep pulling."

Case runs through the choking smoke, calling to Bob. A great wall of white fire rises from the burning truck, heavenbound on the night wind. She hears Bob yelling and turns to find him at the edge of the bridge where teardrops of fire tongue through gaps between the wood pylons.

They meet at the crest of the ravine upward from the molten wreckage. The flames streak a hundred feet straight up amid whorls of ground smoke.

"Where'd you put Gabi?"

"In the drainage pipe. She has my gun."

Bob nods. The sweat on his face is being speckled with charred ash. He and Case try to stare through the blackening air.

A sound jacks across the desert night. They look back across the ravine. Was it a human voice, or just the fire snapping apart the plastic dashboard?

"The fuck is out there gettin' off on this," Case whispers. She turns to Bob. There is a fury in her eyes. "He's out there with his dick gettin' hard thinkin' about—"

The air is broken by a host of screams. A ghost-charge of voices from black redoubts on both sides of the ravine. A clan of spiked-hair derelicts and chick bull-studs, clean-skinned nasty boys and black blood-kill disciples.

Bob and Case get low to the ground. Case drops her shotgun, peels off her buckskin coat. Bob scans the darkness for where the first hit will come. He turns to Case. She's taken out her knife and is cutting a long thin line down the inside of her right arm.

"What the fuck are you doing? Case!"

She starts down the left, leaving a dark red tracer bleeding out onto the white flesh. He grabs her arm. "Case! What are you doing?"

She looks up. She has made out of her face a death mask to the call of the horribles. "I'm gettin' a blood rush up for the crossing over!"

For a moment Bob's head rests against the barrel of his shotgun picketed up in the sand. He closes his eyes. He finds himself searching for his god, desperate for him, praying to that crucified Christ to see them through. He opens his eyes, and Case is staring at him hard, as if she's climbed into his head and plucked out that very thought. Her only possible response to such a useless idea is to slam home a shell in the shotgun's chamber.

As they face each other, that legion of horribles screams out the promise of a blooding. Insane frenzied pledges. Then, as the flames hurl themselves onto the sky, the world around them goes silent. In that lapse of seconds there is now only the night wind and the flames, the ash and the smoke-colored ground combed through with the coming cold.

Bob can feel the chill of the assault just waiting. The slow breathing of those fuckin' aggro vultures somewhere beyond the ring of light, ready to blind out their lives.

"It's just a kiss away, Coyote," Case murmurs. "Just a fuckin' kiss away."

The back of Bob's hand wipes the sweat away from his eyes.

A shot cuts up the night. And then another. And a next, in rapid succession. Far off at first. But closing in. They're out there in the dark and coming on fast. They're a dead run across the sand from a half dozen different angles.

Bob and Case spread out to defend both sides of the ravine, and in one chilling landslide of fear the fight begins. A streaking sprite leaps over the rim of the burning wreck, legs pulled high. A screaming blot that one blast from Bob's shotgun takes out in a sunburst.

The punk tumbles down the incline, and Case is on him fast, boots kicking sand a half beat behind the hitching leathered carcass. As he slams to a stop against a piece of piping, Case puts a shot into the head, nuking the flesh away from the eye sockets and nose to make sure that even if he's dead—he's dead.

In a circling warp of night outlines, Bob turns to meet head-on a screeching bull-stud. Black and young and ripped from steroids. Bob fires through the blinding smoke at the twisting image but misses, and the figure is gone behind a wall of turned ash.

Case ducks down low, the flames of the bridge clinging to

the bottom of her boots. She spots a shape of motley colors sweeping that pit of salt, and she fires and fires and fires again and a leg is blown apart.

A form hurtles past. A human shell fragment that disappears over the bridge, leaping into the ravine.

Bob spots something streak by. He moves quick to finish it. There is a savage desperation closing in. He leaps over a pipe casing toward the frail figure of a boy gathering himself up. He's not more than fourteen, and on any street corner he'd be a nothing you'd walk past, but put an oversized bullet slammer into his hand and scar his face with fiendish tributes to the Left-Handed Path, and you've got a satanic Capone hunting for his first coup.

The boy's god grants him his wish in the shape of Bob Whatever. But it's bad news. Bob fires first. The boy's ribs are blown into a blood lattice of crate shreds. He lands on his back. As Bob comes on, the black bull-stud races along the length of the ravine ledge, then sweeps past his field of vision. One kill at a time, Coyote. The boy gasps as the wind escapes from the sacs of a ruptured lung, and while blood fills his mouth, Bob comes in for the life close.

The ground around Case is spattered with gunfire. Tracers of white sand. She tries to get away by making for the smoke from the burning bridge struts. She fires at a girl sweeping the far upper end of the ravine, but misses. She fires again as the girl cuts across a breath of moonlight, but misses again.

The ash smoke burns her eyes. She keeps retreating. The sound of a shotgun streaks past her back. She comes around to see the half-decapitated form of the boy Bob has just sent into oblivion.

Case is gasping. Bob's shirt is drenched and stuck to his chest. It's covered with the boy's blood, as is his face. The adrenaline has them wired from hell to the far side of the universe.

"You alive?" she screams.

"I'm alive," Bob screams back.

The pack is closing in. Case and Bob know they'll never get to the top of the ravine now. Not until it's finished one way or the other. Each takes up a piece of ground at opposite ends of the bridge. Then it starts. Numberless shadows come through the flames like lighted spears. Split images. Howling. Broaching the Stygian darkness.

Case and Bob are among them now, in the gasping smoke and flame. They fire point-blank at one and all.

A high female cry. A shoulder blade wracked in a fall. Case with the taste of raw iron in her mouth. Skin covered in hemorrhage. Bob bleeding down his back. Ink outlines tottering across the flame-swept sand.

A huge trestle tie on the bridge yaws violently, its charred midsection snapping into gray ash, a downward-crashing nightmare spray of cobalt hot sparks.

It is madness now. The first fights are for blood and land, the final fights for myth.

Cyrus's head moves slow as a monk's at vespers behind his camouflaged infrared goggles. He watches the heat waves of human life, locked in a brutal hecatomb against that fiery wreckage of truck and bridge. Then beyond, in the far distance, he picks out of the pitch-black murk of the Panamints a hunter's moon racing a hundred feet above the desert floor, coming on fast, in a hard mean straightaway.

Along that grim perimeter Bob sees Gutter snake-crawl down the ravine floor toward the drainage pipe. Bob is a vision of gaudy desperate motions. His face just a mouth-hole shouting his daughter's name.

In the tunnel womb, choking from the smoke-foul air, Gabi waits for death. She begins to hear her father's scrambling voice when the carnal smoke around her parts to reveal a face just as shocked to see her as she is to be seen.

• • •

A great white halogen-eye wind rides above the desert floor.
It scoops out blocks of sand from the darkness. Clearing the
banks of the ravine, the chopper blows a firestorm of cinders
up that grouted trench and along the salt flats under its
whirling blades of salvation. And before Bob can wade
through the detritus of charred and burning collapsed timbers and reach that larvae of pipe pieces, he hears a shot and
a scream married in a scarce moment.

On the far side of the bridge, the sheet metal of the
Dakota begins to warp and melt, and the stench of plastic
poison swirls in the air. Case searches through that congress
of wasted life-forms like a vampire on yellows and crack to
find Cyrus. With knife and gun at the ready, bent, she scours
each corpse and shadow.

She hears the ratty echo of a voice on a loudspeaker trying to get through the tearing hum of the chopper blades and
she hears Bob yelling for Gabi, but she keeps to the ground
like a white huntress wolf, wounded and ready for blood.

66

By morning, a huge area around the bridge has been cordoned off. The cops are keeping the news rats on the ground
well beyond the scope of their zooms, so it's up to the local
station choppers to try and scoop each other for the most
salacious close-up.

Arthur's house has also been cordoned off. The streets leading up to his place through the Paradise Hills tract are a
maze of news trucks and lookie-loos who finagled their way

past the gateman and neighbors hosting neighbors in shocked front-yard coffee klatches. Newscasters get their hair coiffed or finesse their makeup so they can look their spiffiest for the lurid gloss they deliver through toilet-bowl-white teeth.

They are a barrage of one-liners highlighting what little they know of Gabi's rescue and Bob's story with Case. They offer a general description of Cyrus and provocative attempts to explain his seamless escape. Also, the first reports of John Lee's disappearance in the last two days have begun to surface.

Inside the house a mob of police officers from John Lee's department, along with tech experts and FBI agents and sketch artists, all try to profile the facts, tracing events from that night on Via Princessa to the fight in the desert months later.

Gabi is off in a back bedroom, sedated and under a doctor's care for malnutrition. After a cursory exam at the hospital she was released. It was decided her privacy could be better safeguarded at the house. Also, word of her forced addiction is being concealed from reporters as best it can.

Bob wanders out from his child's room and back to the dining area, where Case is going through a long interview. As he passes through the cluttered groups of personnel, he notices officers and agents alike staring at him with a kind of dark fascination. There is also something sober and brooding behind their looks.

In a side bedroom of pale orange and gray, Arthur and Maureen talk with two supervisors from the Sheriff's Department and a homicide detective for the Valley district. Maureen is going over how John Lee got a call the night before last. How it was "allegedly" a lead on Gabi's whereabouts. He'd left the house well past midnight. He had told Maureen only that it was a long drive into the desert and he wouldn't be back till late the next day. Arthur then takes over, as the troubled and bereaved friend, explaining that

Maureen called him. She was worried and so he came over. They made calls to everyone they knew to try to find him. They tried the hospitals. Then they called the authorities.

Bob listens and watches from the doorway. He interrupts the conversation, asking the officers if he can steal Maureen and Arthur for a few minutes. The officers give way politely, and the two follow Bob through the living room and down into the basement. At first it seems like nothing, but when Bob latches the door Maureen and Arthur share a moment of quiet hesitation.

Bob leads them through a playroom and around an ornate relic of a pool table stacked with boxes of family mementos from the Via Princessa house. He recognizes a handful of pewter-framed pictures of Gabi in an open box. He stops and spends some time quietly looking them over.

"Bob," says Arthur. "What is going on?"

Bob picks through the box, finds a sweater of Sarah's he'd bought her long before the divorce. A pair of her blue cowboy boots. Combs she wore in her hair. He hovers over these. His chin clefts. "They've already accumulated the mummy smell of dust and mold," he says. Then, looking up: "Haven't they?"

"Bob," says Maureen.

Bob says nothing more. He leads them farther on back through the house to a small television room that is used now for storage. It has a single standing lamp for light, which Bob turns on. The air-conditioning has been off so long the room is thick with leftover air.

When they are in that small room, Bob closes the door behind them. He leans against it.

"I'll have the truth now, Arthur."

Arthur gives him an I-don't-understand shoulder hitch. Maureen sits on the arm of a deep-cushioned easy chair.

"What did you do to John Lee, Arthur?"

Maureen folds her hands. "Bob. What kind of thing is that to . . ."

Bob stares her down. Cold-checks her in mid-sentence. Gives her body language a hard read. She's an illusion of controlled decorum shrink-wrapped around a frightened stiffness. "And you too, huh?" says Bob.

It's a small room, and in two steps Bob is standing over Maureen. She is eye to eye with his belt buckle. "I suppose you know it all, don't you?"

Maureen does not look up.

"Did Arthur tell you he and John Lee were there when the old lady got murdered? Did he tell you Cyrus was there? Did he?"

He turns to Arthur. "Did you tell her?" He turns back to Maureen. His voice rises. "How come you're not asking me what old lady, Maureen? How come?"

Arthur nervously tells him to shush.

"I know about the old woman," says Maureen.

Arthur's chest heaves. "Maureen."

"Ah, shit," she curses. "The whole world is led by a hand-ful of empty hats."

Bob turns to Arthur. "She knows you were there, but does she know you and John Lee may have helped kill the old lady?"

Both Arthur and Maureen's heads come about.

"I was part of no such thing."

"That's not what Cyrus said."

"We believe him, now, is that it?"

"He hasn't lied as much as some."

"Be careful where you're going with this," Arthur warns.

Bob turns on him, presses into that bulky frame. "Because of you, we have a little girl upstairs who has been . . ."

Maureen can see Bob is about ready to torch the old man down. She is up quick, squeezing between them. "Stop. Please, Bobby. They'll hear you upstairs. Please."

"We wouldn't want that, would we?" says Bob, then, to Arthur again, "She's paying for your 'being careful.' *Our*

Gabi. You watch yourself with me, Arthur, I mean it. I've tasted a lot of blood lately and I'm not sure I got a full stomach yet."

"Okay," says Arthur.

"Maureen, what happened to John Lee?"

"I think we should just go back upstairs and . . ."

Bob flips off the light. They are in the dark now. He grabs Maureen. Her face is a robber's mask with a scent of bath oil.

"Maybe it's easier in the dark."

"Please, Bobby. Let me go. Turn on the light and let me go."

"Come on. As long as we can't see faces."

"You're hurting me."

Arthur flips on the light. Maureen is trembling.

"Look at your arms, Maureen. Look at them shaking. You've already halfway told me. Come on. You're big on going 'all the way.' "

"Let her go, Bob."

"Fuck you," he says.

Maureen starts to turn ice-rock against the architecture of his anger. "He paid to have Sam killed," she says. "John Lee. *Did you know that?* He paid to have him killed, and it ended up getting Sarah killed and Gabi taken. That is where the fault lies as far as I'm concerned. And I'll tell you this, too. I only wish that whatever happened to John Lee had happened to him sooner. Like last November. How's that for an answer?"

"You're the art of the half-truth."

"Most of life is not the art of truth at all, Bobby," she says. "It's the trading of trivialities."

"Is it?"

"Sure," says Arthur, with a coy ugliness. "Sure. Just ask Errol Grey."

Bob comes about. His face is ashen, except for the rage on each cheek.

"You think it's over with Cyrus?" says Arthur.

"Jesus, I need a drink," says Maureen. "This is getting too fucked up."

She tries to leave the room but Arthur stops her.

"He called again," says Arthur. "Two hours ago. While you were in with Gabi. That's how fuckin' whacked Cyrus is. Called right on my line. Imagine me sitting in the living room with him giving me an earful. And he did. Told me all about Errol Grey. How you and the junkie went in to get his money. Took Grey down. Now am I supposed to believe that's the truth or a lie? Am I? You tell me."

"I guess it's as true as you and John Lee killing the old lady," says Bob.

"This is too much poison," says Maureen.

Arthur politely forces Maureen to sit. He takes a few deep breaths to gather himself. "No one is clean, son. No one. Now what you did, getting Gabi back, you should get a medal for. I fucked up in the past. John Lee and me. But we never touched the old lady. When we went into that trailer she was dead. Carved up dead. We walked away. We washed our hands of it. We let the punk go. That's the truth."

Bob sees Arthur's mouth shiver a bit. Then he watches him reach down for Maureen's hands, which are rustling across her dress. He holds them both in his.

"You're a fuckin' liar, Arthur. I can't put it all together. I probably never will be able to. But I know you and John Lee were involved in killing that old lady in the desert 'cause you couldn't get loose her property. And Cyrus was there. You fucked him over, didn't you? Just some junkie punk John Lee had under his thumb."

Bob turns to Maureen. "John Lee went after Sam 'cause you were fuckin' him. He brought Cyrus in for the blood-ings, but Cyrus wasn't some junkie punk and he turned John Lee over. He killed Sarah, and he took Gabi to get back at John Lee and Arthur."

He turns to Arthur. "How am I doing? Care to share any

little tidbits of truth with me? Am I close? You want to try and con me with a few tears about how wrong I am?" He looks from one to the other. "Ahhhh . . . No matter what you say, I know. I know where it counts. In my heart. You're fuckin' liars, both of you."

"We all lie. We all fail. We all cheat in some way. We all have ugly spots on our heart and soul. Alright. Maybe I should go upstairs and have myself put away. Maybe Maureen should. Maybe you should. Maybe Gabi should be parentless."

His voice is just short of being tear-framed anger. He continues. "You took us down here to lay blame. Isn't that right? Blame. Fault. To find the ultimate cause. Don't turn away from me. We know I'm right. Who are you to blame? Who? Blame is only for the ultimate judge. And there is only one—"

"Jesus," grinds Bob.

"There is only one."

Bob tries to turn away in disgust. Arthur grabs him by both arms.

"There is only one. And *he* will judge. Us all. I have tried and I will keep trying to make up for my disasters. I will do the best I can. I pray each day for right to be made of my deeds. I do. I am sure, too, that not everything you did out there on the road is without shame. I am sure there are at least a few ugly spots on your heart and soul. Failings that are crimes, crimes that are failings. The world's true beauty is its ultimate forgiveness. Yes. Its ultimate forgiveness. *Even* in the face of our ultimate crimes."

Bob pulls his arms loose.

"And remember this. If it all came out, if every sordid detail surfaces, who suffers most? Me? Maureen? You? No . . . The child suffers."

Stiffly, Bob walks past Arthur and opens the door.

"The child, Bob. Remember that. The child."

67

In the kitchen, Bob pours himself coffee. Lights a cigarette from the stove. He stands alone near the doorway, smoking. Maureen and Arthur pass. They get into a conversation with a couple of federal agents. It's quite a little sideshow—worried wife and best friend of missing departmental chief. Even down to a few well-timed tears.

They notice Bob giving them a look that's hard-line. They return his look with a few chalky stares no one picks up on.

Bob turns his attention to the dining area, where Case is walking through an intense interview. She sits with her back to him, and the rest of the table is a board meeting of corporate cops squared up around her. To watch them watching her as they work through a detailed write-up of events is a cloudless statement in the contradiction of conventions.

She is quick and precise and clean, down to every drop of blood. She speaks with broad, vulgar hand gestures, and she leans into her words like a wildcat working in on its prey. Even her rape in Mexico she describes with blunt savagery to this sorry tableau of white shirts, who listen with bland but shocked patience. To watch them is to wonder what is the real world and what is not. Which side of the table would you bet on for your survival? He is also certain they will never be able to run Cyrus down.

Bob listens as she explains away the last days: the motel rooms, Lena, the setup, having to bring money for the girl. It is a slow dirge to Palm Springs and Errol Grey.

Errol lay on the tile floor with his face buried in his hands. His hands on the cold floor wet with his own urine. Bob leaned down like some possessed vulture. This was no masquerade to Christian compassion as he placed the gun up behind Errol's ear. He could not pretend to be the bar-

*barian who saw evil as some distant malignant force to be
dealt with. He felt it rising up within his own blood from the
deep and seething reaches he once would have sworn his
faith and civilization protected him from. He heard himself
whisper above Errol's shrieks, "Just don't move. And I'll be
quick."*

*Outside, he used sand the color of moonlit German silver
to wipe the blood from his hands.*

As he stares into his coffee cup, Case turns toward him
before continuing. A few blank moments pass. Her look
turns empathic, then rebellious. She turns back to the officers at the table as if she were facing the bar of history. She
takes a moment, then begins with blood-chilling candor
to lie.

She describes a fight inside the house and Errol's final
moments. The only caustic piece of truth is the fact that
three men were left dead. Other than that, the whole frightening piece of bloodshed was caused by Errol's ill-timed and
dangerous irrationality.

A sundown sky is again the color of wounds, but the crowd
outside Arthur's house has yet to disperse. Reporters rush at
officers who alternately enter and leave the house. Bob
watches the madness through the curtain of the bedroom
where his sedated child sleeps.

There is a light knock at the door.

"Come in," Bob whispers.

Case enters, closing the door behind her softly. Dusk has
fallen, powder blue through the sheer curtains. The rest of
the room is dark. Case stops by the bed. Watches Gabi. Her
eyes drink in the mood of the room, trying to believe in the
comfort of that moment, but she knows that behind the
serene sleeping face are demons to be dealt with.

Case squeezes up beside Bob as he peeks out at the crowd
taking up the street. "Geeks," she says.

His head leans around. "About before. Thanks."

"Fuck the ass-hunkies, Coyote. Let them go back to their TV dream-life shit."

"I really need to talk to you," he says.

She looks back at Gabi, nods. "Me, too."

With darkness they steal away through the wooden gate in the stucco wall at the rear of Arthur's property. It opens out into a dense line of blue oaks that begin the Angeles National Forest. As they cross the summered black foothills, Bob explains to Case what went down in the basement between him and Arthur and Maureen.

It isn't long before Case and Bob have been drawn to that same open field where they talked the first night she drove out.

"What is it you want, Coyote?"

He thinks about the violent legacies of his life.

"You'd like to break them down, wouldn't you?" she says. "To burn them hard at the stake. Fuckin' phony sheep. Fatboy and that overly made-up matron. You'd like to ban their asses from ever being near Gabi."

He sees she's baiting him, giving him enough lead line to bite. He looks across the dark filaments of the canyons where the lights of homes twinkle. Yet he is caught in a world beyond any fantasy.

"Be careful. Cyrus wants you to become a war junkie. So don't get too much at home in the wasteland, Coyote. You got Gabi to think of."

"You read me pretty well."

"Only pretty well?"

"I would take them down," he says. "But what am I, compared to them?"

This is a thought she has gutted through more than once. "You?"

"Me," he says.

"Well, let me tell you. If there was something of a center out of that whole mess they bred, you'd be it, Coyote. You'd be it. You're the one who got beyond that world down there to get it on. You're the one who had courage enough to back up what you did, and enough after that too." Her head lilts to one side and her voice drifts. "And enough to see something valuable where there was probably nothing."

He knows what she means and takes her arm to tell her it isn't so.

"Don't you know? Don't you see? You're the real father now. And called to act." Her voice fades. "Fuck."

He senses a dark passion being played out in her mind that makes her look away. She looks to the south and then back along those steep inclines of the Paradise Hills tract toward the conflagration of lights around Arthur's house. Somewhere amid that Gordian phosphored knot, Gabi lies asleep.

Case's heart suddenly fills with grief. She is shocked to find she has that much capacity to feel, and then to bear it. It is a stark revelation, especially now, especially as she knows she will probably never see all this again.

She looks at Bob. "You got to go back down that hill. *You* got to go back home and face the fat prick and the hose-queen phony. And let's be real, the law doesn't equally administer the same attitude all the way around. I'm not saying to get into sleight of hand. But you ought to just let it all slide."

He stares at her in shock.

"Yeah. You heard me."

A soldier's venom up through the veins of his soul.

"I see what's in your eyes," she says. "I can feel it over here."

"And what do we tell Gabi?"

"Coyote, what the fuck could you tell her that she ain't well past in her own life? She's lived through the worst of the bottom feeders. But if you're asking me. No one hides the future. You can't. It's got a life of its own. It's like beatin' smack. It's always out there, watching. The Devil Doctor is always out there, watching and waiting. But that's the choice you alone will make."

"What do you mean 'you'? Where are you gonna be in all this? I thought . . ."

"I'm going," she says. "That's what I wanted to tell you. Tonight . . . I'm going."

He can feel the stone footings inside him give. "Going where?"

"Just going."

"But there's things we haven't talked about . . ."

"Those are better left unsaid."

She steps back but he stops her with a grip on her arm. He tries to read the storm in her face. The challenge behind the blue and windy darkness she turns slightly into. In that silence, the dark clots of emptiness he feels press up through the thorax and into the bony tube of his throat. Choking. But in her eyes he sees something else he recognizes. He knows, he understands now.

"You know where he is, don't you?"

There is something in her eyes now that reads like flares along the roadside at night.

"Lena told you. At the motel. That much anyway. When you two were talking outside. I knew then . . ."

Case doesn't answer.

"You know where he is. No, if she'd have told you that, we'd have gone right there and done it. Maybe where he's gonna be, right? Or might be? You know, don't you? You have an idea? Tell me that much."

They stand close together, like two lungs keeping one consciousness alive. She looks back up at him.

"It isn't done yet," she says.

She leans up and kisses him with such passion and desperation she'd be unable to tell the difference. Finally she leans back. "Even though I don't believe in any of your shit," she says, "I'd play Mary Magdalene for you just to get you

off. I would. I might even take a little blood. But I'd give
you as good, man. I would. Now do me a favor, Coyote. Let
me go."

He does not want to, but in the scarce silken weight of the
moment, he lets her go. She steps back into the darkness,
and she keeps backing away.

"Take care, okay?" he says.

She nods.

"You'll need money," he says. "I'll borrow what I can off
my house. I'll sell my fuckin' furniture. I'll wire it through
Western Union. To downtown L.A. Enough for as long as
you need."

He can hear the dry grass breaking under her boots.

"If you need anything, wire me back. Anything . . . I'll
be here. Case?"

She slips like liquid mercury into the rising arc of the
night hills to become a pitch-black shape that recedes into
the greater black. Then he hears, "Watch out for the sheep,
Coyote."

68

A raven sits atop a stop sign at the near end of Encantada
Cuesta Road with a piece of red carrion stringing down from
both sides of its beak.

At the other end of the road, about a quarter mile or so,
backed up to the shoreline of the Salton Sea, is a small, remote ranch with a chicken-coop roost in the remains of a
wheel-less Dodge Caravan.

This is where Lena told Case Cyrus might do some chill
time. It is a place Case knows he's been a welcome guest, as
she herself has. She also knows of more than one poor sot

who lost his way among the prowlings and ended up buried beneath all the feed and droppings inside that roost.

South of Encantada Cuesta, the streets run east and west out from the Salton Sea through long miles of inclining sand between the towns of Niland and Calipatria.

This part of the California landscape is known as harsh and repellent. It is where blistered and cracked itinerants at the turn of the century went when they could find nowhere else to save themselves.

Here, homes are the shoddiest cinder block with false wood balustrades, or they are great open lots where a mobile home has been plopped down and a small garden pasted in that you have to water the shit out of to get a bare surface green. It is a slum really, but spread over vast squares of gravel and sand, so it doesn't look like a slum from the hills beyond. A running joke has it that this is one of those places where even a bottle of beer goes flat just looking at it.

On the incline two blocks over from the clapboard mess of a ranch, Case finds a house that is partly burned and boarded up. It has a garage and a shed. These too are boarded up. The garage has a second-floor loft. The property is protected by a rusty hurricane fence. It's for sale, but no one ever comes looking.

Case sneaks in and sets herself up in the loft. She breaks away a few vertical boards and battens under the eaves so she can sit and use binoculars to watch the Encantada ranch over the roofs of the houses between.

Case spends each foul day, each frightful night, in that unholy hot alcove with its festering dust and dead air. Weeks of bad-ass summer pass at over a hundred and ten degrees. She has only a radio. It is as if she were pitting her will against Cyrus, waiting for him to show. If he will at all.

The ranch is owned by an INS agent named Bill Mooney and his sister Carol. He'd helped Cyrus cross the border from Mexico with Gabi. They'd met up later with the sister, who was a sorceress of sorts. Before they'd headed back up through the Mojave, Cyrus had let Carol and Bill have their fifteen minutes with the child when she was blown out on smack. A real carpet-feeding, it was. After that, before they all split, Lena had overheard Cyrus and Carol talk about his using the place for a little chill time.

Inside her wooden catacomb the aridity and stink of the algae from the Salton Sea choke her lungs. The reeking cob-webbed wood ready at any time for the dry burn. The unin-sulated gabled roof a devastating oven. No matter how much water Case drinks, she can hardly keep her body fluids even close to being right. Scurrying from that cribbed coffin to vomit under the overhang of the shed roof beside the garage has become a recurring theme.

Over half the summer and not once has she ever been spotted by anyone passing. She lives on the money Bob wired to L.A. She bought a beat-around pickup she keeps parked two miles away in a supermarket lot. Once a week she sneaks out at night to go to a motel and shower. She buries her stool like a cat in the small walkway between shed and garage. She hangs in space silently when kids maraud the property, as they sometimes do. She speaks to no one. She watches the pathetic comings and goings at the ranch. And every time a vehicle trundles down that dusty talused road, she goes into red alert. But each time it's nothing.

The summer becomes a black hole in her life. Lattice-lit days and skyless perishable nights. Sometimes she wakes to find the staring eyes of bats watching from broken joists and exposed rafters. Bedeviled creatures of black crepe cut hor-izontally with white lines of razored teeth and pink gums.

The radio drones on about that cauldron of insanity called the outside world: A jet downed off Long Island people claim was hit by a missile or a bomb. Possible life on Mars discovered. A new abortion pill, a new fight. The conviction of Polly Klaas's killer, and his mad insult to the world claim-

ing the child's last words to him were that she had been mo-
lested by her father. But nothing at all about Cyrus.

She suffers through devastating loneliness. Thinks often
of Bob and Gabi. Begins to replay conversations she and
Bob had, adding to and subtracting from half-frozen moments. She realizes the inarticulate desperation of such
folly. Feels life is sucking the marrow from her bones, turning her into something the wind could blow into potash.

Through blistering waves of heat Case watches airboat
crews ski the glassy cloth surface of the Salton Sea, scoop-
ing up pelicans killed by the toxic pesticides and selenium
that drain into this forty-five-mile-long sump. She watches
poor children swim out past a garbage-slurried shoreline. It
is one long continuous defilement of the laws of nature.

Peeking out a broken portal of boards, she watches the
final lunar eclipse of the millennium. She finds herself crying sometimes. Sounds she only allows from herself in the
night. She buries her face in a shirt that once belonged to
Bob, muffling her sobs so no living thing might hear. It is
like trying to outlive the heroin times.

Then, one night, in the perfect calm of Indian summer, a
battered and gray-primered minivan does a casual crawl
down Encantada Cuesta. The evening is dun-colored as the
minivan pulls around into the front yard. Only a short walk
separates the passenger door from the front porch, and Case
wiggles upward with her binoculars, pulling out extra slats,
ripping them away so she can clear the roofs enough to cover
that square shelf of steps leading up into the house.

There is little margin for error. Her breathing stops so as
not to shake the binoculars. For a half beat beneath the solitary lamp a figure hauntingly leans out of the shadows to
hug Carol Mooney . . .

Case can feel her blood make the rounds.

· · ·

Case plans against a skull-colored moon, pacing starlight from meridian to meridian. She sees Cyrus's face once, just once, a moving shape behind a window fan that turns silently against blades of brief light. Her plan is set, except for one detail: when. It should be during the week, when Bill Mooney is off at the border working his INS job. That will leave only Cyrus and Carol to kill. But give the leopard time to cool his spots and sleep the sleep of the dead. In the corner of her room she sits cross-legged, waiting for nightfall of the third day. She watches the sun set through a hole of broken boards. The single eye of a thousand years hypnotically centered on one instant of pure time. Then, when it's the witching hour, the atavistic urgency to begin the deadly crawl comes upon her. She looks down at the snake on her arm, Ourabouris. She remembers the day she had that arted in the desert, the day she began to plan her freedom, and she whispers to herself, to Bob, to Gabi, to her gun, "It's dyin' time."

Cyrus's eyes open into darkness. He listens intently. Somewhere a mobile's plaintive chanting of bones and glass and clay dance on a string of night air. The kick of an engine winds out on some distant road. A fragment of garbaged tide crests.

He rises, naked. His lean and hungry frame is white against dark corridors. Through the space of a bedroom door he sees Carol lying on her side, asleep.

He continues down the hall, stretching like a great cat. He enters the head. In the dark, his piss rings the water. An arcing stream that suddenly locks tight when a gun barrel lips his neck.

"Relax," Case whispers. She tantalizes his hair with the gun. "Relax. Finish up."

He lets go, finishes pissing.

"I'm gonna step back now," she says, "so step back with

me." He does as he is told. "Alright, I'm gonna turn, so you turn with me."

She gets him turned and headed up the hall. She sees his head drift slightly toward Carol's room. "Forget it," she says. She holds a knife up against the shadows. In her gloved hand he sees the pale silver blade discolored.

She forces him up the hall to the living room. She gets him down into a musty easy chair with a high-flanged back. She turns a table lamp on beside him. She stands away with her arm outstretched and the gun doing a hard line at the side of his head.

The light is dim and harsh. It is only their faces now, cast beyond the open space of the gun.

"Why all the fuckin' drama, girl? Why not just do me when I'm pissing?"

"Because," she says viciously, "I like to watch. You know that."

He eyes her like she is garbage. "We're in the heart of the true country. So come on, field hand. Send me home."

She leans in just enough so he can feel the metal press like a boot heel against his temple.

"You left a long bloody dance behind you."

He sits there staring at her like some contemptible deity carved from the white marrow of his victims.

"The Left-Handed Path awaits us *all*."

"Fuck you," she says.

"You're just a shadow I'll leave behind. A footnote to the cults to come."

The boned-down essence of their lives comes into play.

"Why don't you do me? Why? I know. You want to see if the cock's got feet of clay. Right? You got a field-hand mentality. The prince-must-fall shit. Not happening, coolie. Go back to your fuckin' junkie dreams, Headcase."

His eyes move on in the slow pursuit of her courage. "Say it. You want it. It's the new juice you need for your arms. Right? My weakness becomes something you can build on.

A little piece of power you chipped away. Like some New Age stone you hang around your neck to ward away evil spirits. Bullshit! It's a way for you to cop out on your blame. 'Cause remember, cunt, you helped put me here. You're a coolie. From your fuckin' head down to your clit. And if you expect me to go down, forget it. I'm not like those sheep whose whore you are. I don't pretend to be. I *am* my freedom. I wear it. Look into my face. Go on. See it for yourself."

Suddenly there is a maddening quiescence to him. A hoary, ageless wisdom.

"You have nothing," he says. "You are nothing. There is nothing inside you, girl. And you know that. You are trying to buy yourself back with one bullet. You are just a hole the world shits through."

She lines the muzzle to its mark.

"You're crossing over," she says. "And a part of me is going with you."

Within that cavernous heap of years all the blue and stale and vitriolic imprisonments of her own making and the liquid river from the hidden spring of her unconscious form one surge down through the sinew of an arm.

The thunderbolts on his cheeks spear. His face tightens. A howling masterpiece starts to draw inward, like a building breathing with fire before it goes. Where the steel and stone seem to collapse into the sucking whale of heat that devours it.

Hannah watched a flock of great birds against the sky. Silver outlines shaped like arrowheads making their way. She sat drinking beer, with her bare feet up. Roasting naked in the sunlight to mark her time.

She looked out past the dunes, where the ground whispered about every death that haunted it. Gossip of the slain, poking fun at the fast-moving cars they heard whizzing by with all their tales of what would be.

She knew the boy was full of trouble. That his personal

tragedy did not equal his degeneracy. That he resisted the line between explanation and excuse. No matter. She would let him absorb what he would.

She took a handful of sand. Looked it over. Then she laughed like a half-drunk raven.

Cyrus watched her. He despised her aphoristic meanderings. He despised them, but he didn't know why.

Case leans down and whispers into that salt lick of wet bones that once was Cyrus, "Ourabouris."

THE FOOL

69

For Bob, the passing summer is an absolute merge of disturbing episodes and despairing isolation. He must wade through his personal life, becoming the gristmill for five-minute blurbs and hard-copy snippets. He must watch Maureen and Arthur, via the news, work the tragedy with stoic sincerity and grace. There is a resurgence of interest in the Via Princessa murders. It is not only a showcase for photographers but for new editorials flowing back and forth, rag versus counterrag, claiming the ranch house as the ultimate symbol for the coming war between Christian good and pagan evil. And nothing less than the laws and morals of a nation hang in the balance.

All this becomes a trying absurdity as Bob sets about the act of restoring his daughter's life. They must get through marauding nightmares and the horrible internal assault of her waking hours. He is both father and mother now, and he must reassess his view of the world.

He takes Gabi to therapy. They spend hours trying to talk through the madness. He tries to concentrate on the wounded simplicities of life: love, tenderness, need, resonant human contact. He finds the ordained world of the predawn light the time he is most connected to life.

He watches the sun and wonders about Case. He tries to imagine where she is.

Sometimes the destruction of what they've been through overwhelms him, and he picks a spot to hide and just cry.

Sometimes Gabi finds him, and he is no longer father and mother but just a casualty in the deep pit of a black ordeal pouring out his grief to a womanchild.

Even Gabi talks about Case. She sometimes remarks to her father that there are things it would be easier to speak of with her. Things Case would understand better and know how to deal with.

There is carnage in his soul that he cannot pretend won't always be there. He feels it every time Maureen and Arthur stop by and he must rough his way through it. Or when he leaves his house to find someone grabbing a snapshot of his house or him or Gabi. When he stands naked in the bathroom and looks at the scar on his neck and chest, and the Ferryman's unfinished mural across his shoulder. He wonders now about the last throw of the coins he never took. What it might have said. And, finally, at the small mark on his cheek Case inked there.

He is asked to come back to work at the Sheriff's Department. But he is also reminded, in the politest manner, that facial tattoos are outside departmental regulations. He is requested to have it removed. He resigns instead.

He reads in an editorial a statement that he underlines and cuts out and places on the wall above his desk along with a collage of others that have preoccupied his thoughts since coming home: "Modern man is the singular entity that seems to shrink before anything that has any meaning."

He wonders on which side of this thought he falls. Has he failed by letting it all pass, by letting lies become part of the living truth? And then he sees these thoughts for what they are—blame.

It comes to him that this is no different than the night Gabi shuffled into his room, crying desperately, and asked him if what had happened up on Via Princessa had in some way been her fault. Had she acted more quickly when she thought she saw something in the hills, or had she not left the glass patio doors open (and she's not even sure she had), could this devastation have been avoided? As he listened to his child blame herself, it seemed as if the nightmare had caused the one who dreamed it.

Bob held her through the whimpering aftershocks of that trauma and tried to convince her that she was not to blame.

He walks alone with these thoughts on the night of the last lunar eclipse of the millennium. Walks the same field where he and Case talked, swigging from a pint bottle of tequila.

It has become a second home to him, this patch of scrub. He drinks and paces. Blame will not devour him. The truth will not devour him. The insane mechanics of the world will not devour him.

There are now bitter ironies everywhere. Arthur is rebaptized in the stone font of the church he has helped build, soon after its first Sunday mass. When John Lee's car is discovered in a wash up Dove Springs Canyon Road, the police find it yields no clues to his death or whereabouts. Maureen establishes an organization for the victimized children of crime. As the months pass, Arthur and Maureen's attitude toward Gabi becomes nervous and robotic, as if the sight of her brings home the sickening reality of who they are. Their visits soon become short and perfunctory.

The dark star attached to Bob may never go away, but he won't kick it off, either. Not after what he's paid for it. He wanders back and up the scrabbled hillside, looking into the black-green earth. The same faith that carried him out of that fuckin' tract with an ex-junkie to find his stolen daughter is the same faith that carried him back home and carries him now. It is just colored differently. He squats and holds a clump of damp earth in his hands.

One night, Bob's eyes open into darkness. There is knocking at the front door and he sees a Sheriff's Department car in the driveway. At first he is afraid to answer, afraid that it will be bad news about Case.

• • •

By dawn he is pulling through a police barricade at the near end of Encantada Cuesta. He drives down that road strangled with apprehensions. He pulls into the yard. The forensic boys are there, Homicide, too. No coroner's van, not yet.

He takes out his dated Sheriff's Department ID tag and shows it to the sergeant in charge. "I'm looking for Lieutenant Anderson," says Bob. "He called me last night about a murder and . . ."

Bob notices something register in the sergeant's eyes as he scans the ID. An intrigued reshaping of the eyebrows is followed by "You the guy from Antelope Valley, right? The guy who went after his daughter?"

"Yes."

"Shit . . . Good fuckin' shootin', man."

Lieutenant Anderson is tall, gaunt. He wears a brown suit. It's as plain as his plain pale face. He's not yet thirty, but he walks stoop-shouldered beside Bob as he leads him up the porch and into the house.

"It's a shame," says Lieutenant Anderson, "what happened to that captain in your department. Disappearing like that."

"Yes, it's a shame," says Bob.

"I'll bet it was the son of a bitch in here that got him."

"Yes," says Bob, as if a curse were falling about him. "You're probably right."

"The woman who owned this place was also killed. Knife across the throat. From the way she was lying in there, I doubt she ever knew what got her. Her brother is an INS agent. He was working last night, but he seems to have disappeared since we notified him of the murder."

The entrance to the house from the porch takes them through the kitchen. It's a run-down affair. Cracked blue tiles and patchy white wood.

"Well, anyway, we got this weird call," says the lieutenant, "from a woman who said to come on out to this address.

That there'd been a murder. Then she gave us your name and said you could identify the man as the one who kidnapped your daughter."

From the kitchen, through the dining room, Bob follows the lieutenant. There are double rows of potted plants along the walls and vines that grow up around the window frames. The place reeks of tobacco and incense, and in each corner stands a huge floor urn bizarrely designed and painted.

"The woman actually called from here. Can you believe it?"

Bob feels a prefiguration of knots inside his stomach as they pass along the edge of the dining-room wall to where the living room starts to open out and he can see a crew dusting for prints and doing up their photos.

He clears into the open room, lit by a triptych of window squares, and stops dead in his tracks.

The hunt is over.

Cyrus sits in the battered chair where Case shot him. Pinned to his chest is a card: the final enigma of the Tarot. The Fool. Cyrus's head is tilted to one side as if some invisible friend were leaning down and whispering to him a secret. His eyes, what is left of them, are open. The right side of his head is a blown-out street lamp. A mass of mucousy brain matter dries sickly gray, the blood a simple brown.

The stark reality is nothing Bob would expect of stark reality. It is quiet and simple. He steps closer. A box fan windmills somewhere behind him. He looks over what was once the man. There is nothing expressed in the eyes or the face. There is not that one moment of implied disintegration he wanted to see in the drama of his enemy.

"Is that the man?" asks Lieutenant Anderson.

Bob does not answer. He is living out a horrific pleasure in seeing the bastard cut down and grouted. A sheer merciless adrenaline rush of black, righteous poison at this fierce bloodletting. Yet Bob's face is as calm as the lieutenant's.

"Yes," says Bob. "This was the man."

"The woman. The one who called. Do you have any idea who she was?"

She'd done it, Bob thinks to himself. She committed the ultimate sacrifice. Offered herself up as murderess.

"Mr. Hightower. Do you know who the lady was?"

He still does not answer. He looks at the card pinned to Cyrus's chest. Remembers that night in Case's apartment when they first talked of the murder on Via Princessa. He tries to imagine how it all went down in this room. Those last moments.

"Mr. Hightower. The woman gave us your name and number. Do you have any idea why?"

"I don't know what's in people's minds," he says, without looking at the lieutenant. "Not after what I've seen."

"And you have no idea who the woman is?"

"An idea? No."

"The woman who helped you find your daughter . . ."

"Yes, what about her?"

"Do you think she could have been involved with this in any way?"

Bob takes a long moment. "She is long since gone, I'm afraid."

Lieutenant Anderson eyes him skeptically.

"And you have no idea who might have killed him?"

"Yes," says Bob. "I do. The woman even told *you*."

The lieutenant's long angular face pouches up. "I don't understand."

Bob sticks his jaw out toward the wall beyond the chair. "You've seen for yourself."

The lieutenant glances at the wall where the light from the windows reaches up in three perfectly formed blocks of empty space. Written there in Cyrus's blood, across the flaking white, the words GOD IS A BULLET.

"Are you screwing with me, Hightower?" asks the lieutenant.

Bob stares at the bloody aphorism on the wall. He thinks

back to the night in Hinkley when he and Case sat talking in that seedy, dark barbecue hole while in her hand she held a Hornaday bullet and gave him two minutes of hard philosophy on what held ultimate power in this, our heartfelt world.

The lieutenant asks again, "Are you screwing with me?"

Maybe she was right, Bob thinks. Maybe the world does work cleaner her way. Better. Maybe the world works her way period. Maybe God is only a bullet. Maybe the ultimate parable is carried inside a cartridge with a gliding metal jacket and grooved points.

Of course, she could be playing a bit of coyote herself. Making the murder look like a cult killing, so the keepers will hunt through that wretched wasteland of crude desert for some aberration, for some Cyrus in the making. Maybe she is clever enough to be covering her trail. Or maybe she's just leaving it all open to speculation. Maybe . . .

Bob turns and passes the lieutenant on his way out.

The lieutenant stops him. "Hightower . . . You gonna answer me?"

Bob has no answer for the lieutenant, and walks away.

THE CUP
AND THE SPEAR

7Ø

In central Arizona, along the Mogollon Rim, at a truck stop packed with the dinner crowd, Case sits alone having coffee. She stares out the window, past a great line of rigs and into a country of deep eskers raked by a burning sunset. Gorges chiseled by the primitive artifacts of time are now cast so red it seems the ground itself is bleeding. This is the country once called by Coronado *el despoblado*, "the howling wilderness."

Behind the milk of her headlights, pounding through the dark swerves of midnight, in the clutches of that massive silent heath, windows open to crank in the air, waiting for the perfect turn that never comes, she can hear Cyrus in the radio's voice: "He blew his mind out in a car . . ."

Nothing abides alone. Not evil, not good. Yet she can't seem to rise past her privations. Every phone tempts her, but she is afraid to make the call. So she tries to drive her need into the ground. The thorn short a lily, the lily short a thorn.

In October, there are fires from Malibu to the Ventura Hills. The ground burns again in an act of creation and change. Bob sits on his kitchen steps, the last Saturday of the month. He looks up into a full moon that drips white blood across the channel of the sky to its partnered earth.

He drinks tequila and smokes. The phone rings but he doesn't bother with it. He sets his teeth against the dark inside him. But the ringing doesn't stop.

Don't make it be like all the other times, he thinks. Some
reporter who wants a little quick one-liner. Or the crawling
night-freaks who want to talk murder or guns or Christian-
ity or the Left-Handed Path or . . .

He would have changed the phone number, but he is still
stumbling through the heart of tonight's and tomorrow's and
next week's and next year's wishes.

He moves with the cautious motion of a spider across the
kitchen toward the phone. There is a second of silence after
he answers, and he would swear he can hear the drone of the
highway in the emptiness of that moment.

The dry California winds that bred the fires burn up
through his nose as he takes a long deep breath. "Case?"

Seconds waste by.

"Hello, Coyote," she says.

In the winter Sam's and Sarah's graves are desecrated. The
headstone is spray-painted with the letter *C* pierced by a
lightning bolt. The same sign appears on the doors and walls
of the Via Princessa house, which still sits empty on the bluff
above the Antelope Freeway.

Some say it's the work of punk vandals. Others say it is a
cult warning.

A reporter calls Bob's house to snag a comment, but she
finds the number has been changed. She takes a quick drive
out to the place only to discover from the family now living
there that Bob and Gabi have moved and left no forwarding
address. She then contacts Arthur and Maureen, but neither
knows where Bob and Gabi have gone.

ACKNOWLEDGMENTS

This book is the sum total of many lives. With that in mind and heart, I would like to walk through a short list of thank yous for those who helped nurture, shape, and polish this manuscript, and also my being.

First, to Sonny Mehta, who stands firmly at the center of this experience. It was he who set this book on its course, and who gave freely of his experience, talent, and commitment. To Sarah McGrath, who worked more than her fair share of judicious editorial hours carrying this manuscript to completion. To the Knopf executives Patricia Johnson, Paul Bogaards, Paul Kozlowski, and Bill Loverd, for their sincere and dedicated stewardship. To Jenny Minton, for a helpful push in the right direction.

On a personal note: To Deirdre Stefanie and the late, great Brutarian . . . to Deaf Eddie . . . to G.G. and L.S. . . . to my friends who are still in hiding . . . to Felis Andrews-Pope . . . to the Ferryman, who guided me through many, many miles of uncharted American life, from those shape-shifting corners of the California desert to the forgotten camposantos of Mexico . . . and finally, to my friend and agent, David Hale Smith, who always does more than he says he will and does it with the utmost care for my work. An ethical work-horse and dedicated family man, he has my deepest respect and admiration. A special thanks goes to him and to Shelly Lewis and Seth Robertson, his associates at DHS Literary, Inc. I will always define my good fortune in meeting David as kismet times seven.